Acclaim for *Edmund White's*

The Married Man

"Written with characteristic brilliance and the particular flair for poetic detail that so distinguishes his books, Edmund White's new novel is arguably his best to date. . . . Marvelously life affirming. . . . Nobody since Proust has written so well of Paris and paid such scrupulous attention to visual detail. . . . In short, nothing less than brilliant."
—*The Times* (London)

"Hauntingly lyrical. . . . An enduring portrait of an erotically charged relationship suspended by the needs of illness, loyalty and commitment." —*The Seattle Times*

"[A] beautifully composed novel [that] offers the reader myriad enticements." —*The Washington Post Book World*

"White is a worthy heir of that earlier anatomist of the transatlantic relationship, Henry James—subtle, complex, unsparing and profound." —*Daily Telegraph* (London)

"A masterpiece. . . . Bittersweet, at times funny, but ultimately dark." —*The Baltimore Sun*

"One of the most powerful, candid, devastating and moving novels I've read in recent years. It is both beautifully written and unsparing in its honesty."—Joyce Carol Oates

Edmund White

The Married Man

Edmund White was born in Cincinnati in 1940. He has taught literature and creative writing at Yale, Johns Hopkins, New York University, and Columbia; was a full professor of English at Brown; and served as executive director of the New York Institute for the Humanities. In 1983 he received a Guggenheim Fellowship and the Award for Literature from the National Academy of Arts and Letters. In 1993 he was made a Chevalier de l'Ordre des Arts et des Lettres, and was awarded the National Book Critics Circle Award and the Lambda Literary Award for *Genet: A Biography*. He teaches at Princeton University and lives in New York City.

VINTAGE

INTERNATIONAL

Also by *Edmund White*

Fiction
The Farewell Symphony
Skinned Alive
The Beautiful Room Is Empty
The Darker Proof: Stories from a Crisis (with Adam Mars-Jones)
Caracole
A Boy's Own Story
Nocturnes for the King of Naples
Forgetting Elena

Nonfiction
Our Paris: Sketches from Memory (with Hubert Sorin)
The Burning Library
Genet: A Biography
The Joy of Gay Sex (with Dr. Charles Silverstein)
States of Desire: Travels in Gay America
Marcel Proust

The Married Man

The Married Man

Edmund White

Vintage International
Vintage Books
A Division of Random House, Inc.
New York

FIRST VINTAGE INTERNATIONAL EDITION, SEPTEMBER 2001

The Library of Congress has cataloged the Knopf edition as follows:
White, Edmund, [date]
The married man / Edmund White.
p. cm.
ISBN 0-375-40005-2
1. Americans—France—Paris—Fiction.
2. AIDS (Disease)—Patients—Fiction.
3. Gay men—Fiction. I. Title.
PS3573.H463 M37 2000
813'.54—dc21 99-053980

Vintage ISBN: 0-679-78144-7

Author photograph © Barbara Confino

www.vintagebooks.com

Printed in the United States of America
10 9 8 7 6 5 4 3 2 1

To
Matthias Brunner
and
Stephen Orgel

The Married Man

Chapter One

Austin was twenty years older than everyone else in the gym—
and the only American. It was a place for serious people who
wanted a quick workout—pairs of students from the nearby
branch of the Paris university system or solitary young businessmen
who trudged about with Walkmen plugged into their ears making a
dim, annoying racket. Not very many Frenchmen wanted to build
huge muscles, at least not very many straight guys.

This was by no means a gay gym. It was just a small workout room
that looked down through smudged glass panes onto a public pool
below. The pool was Olympic size and even through the glass still
reeked of hot chlorine. It had been built in the Belle Epoque and
recently restored. Austin thought there might be more action in the
pool and the shower rooms, but he didn't like swimming and he'd sort
of given up on cruising. He wasn't young enough and what he had to
offer—his accent, his charming if broken-down apartment, his interesting profession, his kindness—wasn't visible in a shower room.

For some time Austin had been looking occasionally at a particular
newcomer. They had already exchanged two smiles and many glances,
brilliant little flashes of curiosity in this unfriendly place where looks
never lingered and even those guys who stood watch over someone

lifting dangerously heavy weights never used the occasion as an excuse for striking up a conversation.

Now the younger man was struggling under a bar loaded with too much weight, nor had he secured the metal plates—he was about to let the whole thing go crashing to the floor. Austin came rushing up behind him, lifted the bar and put it safely back on the stand at the head of the board where the stranger was lying on his back. None of the other men seemed to have registered the near crisis; Austin could hear the Walkman of the guy next to them jittering away like cicadas in a tin can.

"Thank you!" the young man exclaimed in French as he stood up. He spoke in a deep, resonant voice, the sort of "voice from the balls" that so many Latin men cultivate. He scrutinized Austin intensely. Austin was highly flattered by the attention. He'd long admitted to himself that he was the sort of man who needed constant transfusions of interest and affection. If his phone didn't ring for a day or if he didn't have a dinner date lined up he was suicidal by dusk. If his date yawned he was ready to bolt from the restaurant or do a tap dance on the table. Now here was this young man who, if he wasn't exactly Austin's type, had become so by taking an interest in him.

"I could see that you were, perhaps, unfamiliar—"

"It's all completely new to me," the young man exclaimed. Austin noticed that his white shorts were cut high, which only emphasized the power of his legs, not in a sexual but rather in a boyish way. "Are you English?" he asked.

Austin had come to count on French people commenting on his accent. It not only provided them with a safe topic but he knew everyone under forty in France wanted to live somewhere in the English-speaking world, at least for a year or two.

"American." He anticipated the next question and said, "New York." Then the next and added, "Although I've been here eight years." Finally, he offered, "As you can hear, it's difficult to learn another language after forty." He wasn't fishing, he just wanted to lay to rest right away the question of his age. "Is this your first time here?" Austin asked.

"Yes. My wife comes here to swim. She's down there somewhere."

He waved toward the pool with a vague hand, although his glance remained fixed on Austin.

The young man asked Austin to show him how to do the exercise properly, but, though observing the demonstration politely, he scarcely took it seriously, as his bright eyes and slight smile suggested. He seemed too alive to the moment to pay any attention to it.

When asked, Austin said that he was a "cultural journalist" who was writing a book on French furniture of the eighteenth century.

The Frenchman happened to be in the small locker room dressing to leave at the same time as Austin. He turned modestly away when he pulled on his bikini underpants and revealed nothing but the expected hairy buttocks, full, even luscious. Austin was ordinarily alert to even the grubbiest sexual possibility. That's what he was always on the lookout for, but today he'd already picked up a hint of romance, as though this guy could be courted but not groped. They kept up their banter which, if overheard, would have sounded forced, schoolboyish, but it was melded and, somewhat, *liquefied* by the flow of their exchanged smiles, glances, nods.

When they were on the street the Frenchman said he had to rush back to work. He was an architect on the other side of Paris.

"I'd love to see you again," Austin said, knowing he had nothing to lose except his dignity, which he didn't care much about.

"Me, too."

"Here's my number."

"Oh, you Americans are always so well organized with your calling cards. If you give me another, I'll write my number on it for you."

"Your home number?" Austin asked, pressing his advantage.

"My work number," the man said with a big smile.

Austin was surprised by the slight stiffening of his own penis. For weeks he'd been nearly impotent even in expert arms, and here he was, excited by a stranger's mere presence and the hint of a date. He liked that they were both dressed in coats and ties on a strangely warm day early in April at the wrong end of the Boulevard Saint-Germain.

"Hey, what's your name anyway?"

"Julien."

"Really?" Austin said. "That's the name of the guy who just dropped me."

Julien smiled, Austin guessed, not at his misfortune but at the explicitness of his remark. Sometimes it's okay to be American, Austin thought; we have a reputation for being brazen we must live up to.

Chapter Two

Austin was a forty-nine-year-old writer who lived in a two-room apartment on one of the islands in the Seine. His island was the Île Saint-Louis and the apartment was a third-floor walk-up with three big windows that gave onto the back of a seventeenth-century church. Austin could lie in bed and look at the church's slate-covered roof, pitched sharply, and a huge volute of stone almost ten feet in circumference that had been carved to resemble a spiral closing in on itself and slightly squashed on the top. Since it was almost always raining, Austin thought of the volute as a giant snail that might someday inch forward on its big, sticky foot. Pigeons took shelter from the rain in the gutter just outside the window and cooed comfortably, their little red eyes glancing up at Austin matter-of-factly if he stood just inside the window or opened it like a pair of doors and leaned out on the guard rail. At such moments he would have lit a cigarette, if he still smoked.

Nearly everything on the island was as old as the church, since throughout the Renaissance it had stayed an empty field where the monks from Notre-Dame on the neighboring island once grazed their cows, or where occasionally gentlemen in lace and white stockings had fought duels in the high reeds. They could look across the Seine in one direction at the steeples of Saint-Gervais and the back of the ornate Town Hall or in the other at the walls and towers of several vast monasteries. Then, all at once, the monks had sold the empty island to three ambitious developers, who'd gone broke putting up aristocratic houses on the quais and tradesmen's shops and their living quarters on the inner streets. Austin's street, the rue Poulletier, was named after one of these three unfortunate entrepreneurs.

Americans always gravitated to the Île Saint-Louis, he now knew, though he'd moved there eight years ago guided, he supposed, by nothing but his national instinct. Perhaps because it was small and easily comprehended, Americans convinced themselves they'd master it first, then branch out to the intimidating city surrounding it. He liked its look of forgotten grandeur—just below, attached to the church, was a convent that seemed uninhabited. At least he'd never seen anyone going into or out of it and the dusty windows were never lit or opened. The back of the church, however, contained an almost hidden apartment, presumably for the sexton.

At night Austin liked to come from a noisy bar or an exciting, talkative dinner party on the mainland and cross the black, rapidly flowing Seine to his poetic island, always five degrees cooler than the rest of Paris. The island may have been cold and damp, but who could resist the Pont Marie, the most graceful bridge in Paris with its three arches, each a different shape? So many of the tall, narrow houses along the quais bore historical plaques boasting names he'd never heard of. One of the names, Playbault, made him smile since he'd decided to pronounce it "Playboy." Another plaque announced that Mme de Sévigné's *cousin*, no less, had once lived here!

Often as not, almost all the quayside windows were shuttered and curtained, but in late May in the first warmth of summer it was as though the usual rules had been suspended. The windows were thrown wide open, old chandeliers were lit and the searching floodlights of the passing *bâteaux-mouches* glared off a silk-striped wallpaper the color of wine lees or on the flattened-out faces of men and women in evening clothes looking down and smoking, three to a window.

Until midnight the *bâteaux-mouches* never ceased their invasive light-attacks or recorded commentary. If Austin strolled along the quai, cruising, at the eastern tip of the island below the small park, he'd hear in German, English, Spanish and French the unvarying description of the Rothschilds' house, the Hôtel Lambert, as "the finest private residence in all of Paris with its celebrated Hercules Salon." Or if at midnight he'd walk down the center of the island on the rue Saint-Louis-en-l'Île, he'd glimpse, at the very end of the straight street, the sudden diamond-white effulgence of a passing boat, its banked floodlights too low in the water to be seen but the brilliance welling up like the glow of a comet slowly trailing past. The tightly clustered house fronts and the black pavement would be illuminated in an unnatural way, as though suddenly, surprisingly, everything was being filmed.

Austin had rented his small apartment furnished and most of the furniture was junk: a spavined basket chair, a gray scrap of carpet that had taken on the color of mud, a side table that creaked as it revolved like a Lazy Susan to reveal the bookcases on three sides. But in the sitting room by the window there was a handsome nineteenth-century Louis-Philippe desk; he'd quickly piled it so high that he couldn't find a space on it where he could write. He'd never enjoyed being an official grown-up author who sits at a desk and clatters his way through page after page of crisp foolscap or scrolls his words down a screen. He preferred lying on his creaky, lumpy daybed under a dangling lamp with its pleated yellow paper shade burned brown here and there by an overheated bulb. He'd scribble a line or a paragraph on legal pads he had to bring back in quantity each time he made a trip to the States, since the only lined paper the French seemed capable of manufacturing was covered with tiny squares for some unfathomable, irritating reason. He wrote only when he had nothing better to do such as making a phone call, preparing dinner for eight, working through a strenuous session with his personal trainer (although Austin called him "my sports professor," since he was translating into English *professeur de sport* and had not yet even heard the recently coined American expression, "personal trainer"). Despite all the activity and the luncheons out and the late nights and the packages constantly arriving on his doorstep by Federal Express or Chronopost, he did manage to write dozens of articles for American or English home decoration

magazines. He had no routine, no system, little ambition. He was lethargic and took at least one nap during the day, usually two. He didn't
like writing, which made him anxious, especially when it was going
well, since he feared spoiling with the very next word whatever good
he might already have achieved.

In January and February, when it rained nearly every day, he
loved to stay indoors and read. His apartment, owned by the landlady,
who lived downstairs, had been her husband's study. The deceased
gentleman had been an epigraphist, a scholar of Latin and Greek
inscriptions, and in the entrance hall were two incised stone tablets
he'd brought back from field trips to North Africa. There was also a
shelf of scholarly books in the armoire behind hand-made curtains in
a very 1960s pattern of overlapping dark green eggs beginning to pull
apart on a field of lighter green. The landlady was a very tall, very old
Austrian woman who'd come to Paris in the 1920s as a weaver and
painter. Several of her collages from back then were hung here, their
elements coming unglued and curling from the heat. A brightly colored abstract tapestry, felt circles on burlap, was unfurled above his
bed, although two circles had fallen off. The appliances—space heater,
telephone cords, electric plugs—had all been jerry-built and kept
blinking on and off temperamentally. The shiny, acid-green kitchen
seemed scaled more for a doll's house than human habitation. In the
bathroom, painted the same green, a minuscule washing machine was
wedged in one corner but the dryer was just a rack above the tub that
could be lowered, loaded, then raised by a system of pulleys. Sometimes it dripped on him when he took a bath.

He was lazy, creaturely. He dozed, drank tea, listened around the
clock to a classical music station. He turned up the heat, staggered out
to the corner restaurant for a buttery, sauced hot lunch, hurried home
to receive the phone calls from New York that started coming in about
four o'clock his time. The rapid, heavy-breathing, menacing American
voices intimidated him with their humorlessness: Oops, they're playing for keeps, he thought. He knew that behind these voices were perfectly made-up, stylishly starved women, who were at their desks
twelve hours a day, firing friends and setting up "focus groups"
(another new phrase) to terrorize their staff. Fortunately he was one

of the few ready and always available English-speaking journalists sta tioned in Paris, someone who could be counted on to work up an instant interview of Eric Rohmer for *Vogue* or do a profile of Judith Krantz in her luxurious new apartment, and be sure to put the emphasis on her brilliant French and expensive Impressionist paintings.

His friends told him he looked ten years younger than his age but once, on the sex-chat phone line, he'd misrepresented himself as thirty-eight and the much younger man he'd lured all the way across Paris at two in the morning took one look at him, shook his head and said sorrowfully, as he left, "Why lie like that? You're a nice-looking guy and if I wanted someone fifty I'd go for you but—well, that's not what I wanted or expected." Austin felt thoroughly ashamed of his untruthful advertising—and learned a valuable lesson: you always look your age, down to the last minute, and friends who say otherwise are deceived or deceiving.

He'd lived for five years with Peter, a handsome New Englander in his twenties who'd moved to Paris with him, picked up a degree in the history of furniture at the Louvre, then returned to New York in order to get a job as an interior designer. That was three years ago. Peter had worked just a few months in Manhattan before falling ill with shingles and crippling bouts of diarrhea. Peter still insisted that he had ARC (AIDS-Related Condition), not full-blown AIDS, a distinction that even in 1989 sounded outdated and, well, pointless. But Peter clung to it; he wouldn't allow anyone to trundle him off toward an early grave.

Austin loved Peter but he knew they'd probably never live together again. They went on vacation together—to Venice, to Crete, to Zurich, to the Virgin Islands—and they spoke to each other on the phone two or three times a week, but Austin didn't want to go back to New York, not now, maybe never; he'd reinvented himself in Paris and liked his new self. New York was a graveyard, or rather it was swarming with new and ever renewable life, all these fiercely healthy yuppies dressed for success, but, unbeknown to them, living among recent ghosts, brushing through them—Austin's dead friends, old clone ghosts in disintegrating bomber jackets and ectoplasmic T-shirts, their flesh rotting away but the gray mustaches still growing.

And Peter didn't want to leave New York. He was still looking for

sophisticated African-American New Yorkers he fan-
eaking Black men from the Ivory Coast had done
when he lived in Paris. Too foreign. Too tribal. No, he
...ed a certain mix of preppiness and funkiness in his men—a
bow tie and a good job and glittery social manner joined to long, slow,
tender lovemaking. Peter wanted a man who sounded like a Harvard
WASP when he telephoned from the office but who, in bed, would
call him "Honey" or "Honky" in a melting Southern accent.

Austin felt bad because he'd always promised Peter he'd take care
of him if he ever came down with AIDS. Of course Peter still looked
healthy and most of the time felt good. And surely Peter wanted to go
on living alone for just a while more, since he was still hoping to find
the love of his life, and Austin's presence in the New York studio
apartment would only crowd him.

Once or twice in the days that followed his encounter with Julien
at the gym, Austin thought of him, but didn't want to call him.
Although a married man could be a sexy fantasy, the reality was just a
nuisance—broken dates, whispered phone calls and sudden hang-ups,
never a meeting in a public place, unexpected spasms of self-hatred,
never a whole night in bed. . . .

And then his confidence had been sapped by his last lover, also
named Julien, who'd bewitched him for the last three years until he'd
suddenly dropped him two months ago for a rich collector. "Little"
Julien, as he called him, since he was small in every way except in one
crucial detail, never made a false move. He was worldly and supremely
practical but not unkind. He was willing to sleep with much older men
in exchange for trips, clothes, dinners, all the small change of sex
between the generations. What he brought to the bargaining table
was his inestimable gift for imaginative, inexhaustible passion.

Austin had met Little Julien at a cocktail party given by his friend
Henry McVay, the seventy-year-old patrician leader of the American
expatriate colony. McVay, a Philadelphia millionaire collector who
lived surrounded by his Goyas and Cezannes and who'd been in Paris
since 1944, when he'd arrived as a soldier, gave an annual bash for
prominent couples and cute guys. Little Julien had been one of McVay's
boys, a twenty-four-year-old with a fox face, an intense stare and the

strange smell of an old well, as though his fillings had started to rust in an excess of saliva.

At the very beginning Little Julien had accepted Austin's invitations on three separate occasions, but Austin never dared so much as to kiss him good night or to invite him up for a drink. As he figured it, at his age he mustn't ever make the first move with a kid, since nine out of ten would regard sex with a middle-aged man as obscene, even criminal, and he, Austin, was incapable of picking out the talented tenth, the blessed exception, that nearly unique boy who admired experience and accomplishment more than an uncreased face and a tympanum-tight tummy. Nor could he spot that one guy in a hundred who was age-blind and didn't judge another man as a commodity. Of course it was Little Julien who finally jumped *him* after the third date. As Austin was politely bowing and turning to walk away, Little Julien grabbed him and said, "Don't overdo it" (*Tu exagères*), pulled him into his darkened apartment and was soon testing Austin's gag reflexes, whispering sternly, "All the way to the bottom" (*Au fond, au fond*).

Now all that was over, the big sunbursts of sex, Little Julien's fleeting shadows of ill humor, his dull certainty that he would marry a woman someday very soon, his perverse refusal to stay on with Austin at the end of a dinner party. Little Julien always left with the other guests and it was only during a trip together—to London, to Istanbul, to Damascus—that Austin could sleep with him night after night and drink deep at that inexhaustible well of sensuality. Little Julien never gave sex on schedule; once when Austin complained about his unpredictability, he pointed out with inarguable accuracy, "After four years we're still having sex, which is as exciting as the first time. What other couple could claim as much?" Immediately after the break-up, Austin had been happy to be rid of Little Julien, who had never conceded any warmth or tenderness beyond their initial, rather formal amiability. They were like gentlemen in a Sade novel, with impeccable manners and a bottomless taste for debauchery—fellow practitioners but not buddies, certainly not lovers.

Weirdly, when Little Julien explained why he was leaving he mentioned several things that Austin would never have foreseen. He said that Austin was "too visible" as a homosexual; he could never have felt comfortable associating himself with someone so public about his private life. Then he said Marius, his new lover, was able to fulfill his "affective needs," which Austin, he implied, had neglected. Austin was shocked, since he'd always thought it was Little Julien who was holding *him* at arm's length. Given the first sign of openness, Austin had long been prepared to rush in, eyes melting. Then Little Julien mentioned that he didn't want to "end up" with a foreigner; he was drawn to Marius because he was French. "If Corsican," Austin muttered sourly, which only made Little Julien flash a flattered smile: "I see you've been collecting information on him." Or maybe Little Julien wanted a man with some real money. If he was going to invest his youth, his venture capital, it should be in futures with a future.

Or maybe Little Julien was simply afraid of Austin because Austin was HIV-positive.

A week after the break-up Austin began to feel wounded, rejected, lovelorn. Then he suffered terribly, though he knew how stupid he was being. It was only his vanity that was injured, which he readily admitted. If he'd left Little Julien first, he wouldn't have thought about him twice.

And yet Little Julien was not only the maestro of sex but also a roaring fire of creativity, both artistic and social. He had a fast, funny way of talking, unpretentious, intelligent but not intellectual. He couldn't sit still long enough to read except on vacations, and even then to read was more an underlined item in a program of repose and self-improvement than anything he ever actually did. Austin liked Little Julien because he was his link with chic young Parisian life, the sudden eruption of drunken laughter heard behind a seventeenth-century portal or a multicolored flurry of many young cockatoos across the dim, windblown magnificence of the Place de l'Odéon. Paris was a city that could seem uniformly austere and melancholy unless you could penetrate the gray shutters and dolly in on the eight candle-lit faces flushed with wine around the table or hand the embossed invitation to the wigged footman which would grant you admission to the feathered and ribboned masked ball (how the French loved to dress up as Valmonts and Merteuils!).

Little Julien had been his—well, not his passport into this secret joy, since most of the invitations had been addressed to Austin as a journalist or furniture expert or as just an amusing foreigner, but rather his guest of honor for whom he'd organized dinners at home or with whom he'd "double dated" (since Little Julien would never have gone anywhere public without a woman as his shield). He and Little Julien and their dates were always wearing black tie and gowns, dropping in on a smoky loft party for the Green Negresses or some other punk group of white men. Everyone else was in jeans and settled in, but Austin and Little Julien were always in formal clothes and "going on." Little Julien, who'd been a lawyer's clerk, had taken a paid year's leave of absence to study furniture-making; it was one of those enlightened and unfathomable French perks that were bankrupting the state. He revealed a whimsical talent for designing tables that were amusing used right side up and hilarious when reversed, and for rethinking every element in a dining room from the zodiac ceiling to the star-studded dishes and shooting star napkins.

Now the invitations drifted like the last flakes of snow onto Austin's mantelpiece and he glanced at them only long enough to decline them. Weeks went by and he saw only a few friends, and then only one at a time for a movie or a quick bite at a neighborhood crêperie. His island seemed suddenly intolerably sad, shrouded in mists that floated up in the day-for-night wake of a nearly empty, winter *bâteau-mouche*. He crossed the Pont Marie with its empty statue niches looking down on the Seine, black and shiny as mined coal between tourist boats, more and more widely spaced as midnight and the winter solstice drew nearer.

Chapter Three

The phone rang.

"Hello, it's Julien. We met at the gym."

"Of course. How nice—"

"Did I awaken you?"

"*Awaken* me? At . . . uh . . . *eleven* in the morning? Of course not. I've been up for hours."

"I just saw your card in my wallet and I thought I'd see how you were doing. Did you ever go back to that gym?"

"Several times since then. And you?"

"I've had too much work."

"Would you like to come to dinner on Wednesday? A few friends are stopping by. Around nine? But you could come later if your work keeps you." He gave Julien the building code, the numbers that had to be punched in to gain admittance to the street door.

From the precision and care with which he took down all the information Austin knew he would come, which neither thrilled him nor left him indifferent. Julien sounded slightly more eager, even more schoolboyish than he had at the gym, perhaps because being the one who was taking the initiative placed him at a slight disadvantage.

Austin had invited six friends who were in their early thirties, including his "sports professor," Pierre-Yves, a mad young psychiatrist named Hubert, a hilarious actress called Antoinette, a friendly woman, Isabelle, who worked for the Musée d'Art Moderne de la Ville de Paris, a loud American acupuncturist named Gregg, and one of Austin's best friends, Joséphine, who wrote and illustrated children's books. This was a group Austin had cobbled together to keep Little Julien amused. The men were gay and the women straight and everyone loved to drink and joke and exchange stories and have a good time till one in the morning; if they'd been upper-class Parisians they would have left promptly at midnight, but these friends were too inexperienced socially to know of this invariable "rule."

Austin thought that if Big Julien, this new Julien, was still married and had never lived openly as a gay man, then he'd surely be less spooked by a dinner at which there were three attractive, stylishly dressed women. And everyone was close to Big Julien's age, which might make him forget that Austin was some two decades older.

For years now Austin had been inviting these young men and women to his apartment every week or two for the evening. Because they were not earning much and were living on snacks, he knew the women liked putting on their best dresses and heels and heavily painting their eyes and lips to head across the Pont Marie to the dim, fog-wrapped splendors of the Île Saint-Louis. The men could be very open about their sexuality *and* shockingly flirtatious with the girls—behavior that appeared inconsistent, even self-contradictory to American eyes but that Latins, with their love of seductiveness, deemed perfectly natural.

On the phone next day each of them could be a bit bizarre—Joséphine paranoid as usual, Antoinette prudish, even pig-headed, Pierre-Yves hypercritical, Gregg as irritable as someone critically sleep-deprived. But in a group, when they'd drunk lots of wine, they were convivial, outrageous, and above all *light*—light as only Parisians knew how to be. They argued only about politics. But otherwise no one preached on a pet subject as Americans were wont to do when they weren't chattering about house remodeling or global warming. If Austin held forth on a topic he'd just been researching there'd be a furious exchange of winks and giggles or they'd all tuck their hands under their arms and lower their heads as though waiting for it to go away. Pierre-Yves had once seen an American movie of the fifties replayed on television, in which teenage hoodlums bedeviled their instructor whenever he started lecturing them by saying, "Gee, thanks, Teach," and now he would call Austin "Teach," too, at the first ugly sign of New World didacticism.

Austin had put together this circle to please Little Julien but now he was hoping it would set Big Julien at ease and amuse him, too. Not that everyone liked his friends. "I don't know what to think, Austin, of your teen evening," one older man had said the day after a dinner. He was a writer and had wanted, apparently, to talk books and literary prizes and discuss his recent rather stylish conversion back to Catholicism. For a moment Austin had felt foolish for all the hundreds of hours he'd devoted to chopping mushrooms, pouring out good Bordeaux and rolling joints for this band of kids.

His rowdy French friends, he imagined, might be taken aback by the reality of Big Julien's marriage, for even though they discussed their own bisexuality at length and their conveniently hazy and remote plans to marry one day, they would surely be confused by an attractive young man who was actually living with a wife.

The bell rang. It was Julien with small yellow roses in his hand. "Sorry, I'm early," he said. "I came right from work."

"Not at all," Austin said. He leaned forward to peck him on both cheeks but Julien shook his hand. Julien even smiled with mild satire, as if to say that he, at least, was too *virile*, too "old France" (*vieille France*) to kiss any man other than his father and brother. Austin steered him in with a friendly hand just grazing his back, his face impassive, as though he hadn't registered the minute rejection. Strangely enough, Little Julien had also disliked all these pecks (*bises*) among men, which he'd seen as effeminate Parisian insincerity. When Austin came back from the kitchen with the flowers in a vase and a glass of wine for his guest, he saw Julien standing by the window looking out. "What do you think of my parish church?"

Julien turned eagerly and seemed almost disappointed by the

ironic smile on Austin's lips. It was obvious that as an architect he was impressed by the massive, twisting stone volute.

Austin said, "Not that I'm a Catholic. Are you?"

Julien said, "Atheist. I'm from a long line of atheists on both sides. I just admire the force of the roof." He took the wine and seated himself in the chair Austin indicated. Julien was wearing an unbecoming pear-green linen blazer, double-breasted, with gold buttons that were too heavy and tugged at the thin fabric. The color was all wrong for his complexion—he looked sallow, oily, tired.

"I'm an atheist, too," Austin said. "I hate it when people say they're agnostics, don't you? It's so weak-kneed." He almost added, "Especially gays, the pathetic nitwits, who've been tortured and insulted by every known religion," but he directed his thoughts away from that dangerous subject, which might seem glib to Julien and not evoke the same associations for him. Austin was already sure that Julien was an individualist, as opinionated as he was unpredictable, and that his beliefs must be pieced together carefully. Maybe he didn't even use the word *gay*. Maybe he didn't even *think* that word. Maybe he was one of those men, like Lohengrin, who loved you only so long as you didn't name them.

"I know nothing about religion," Julien said with that sort of sweet gravity men use when they admit to a shortcoming they don't take seriously.

He went off to wash his hands—and *face,* Austin noticed, since he came back with a nose and forehead visibly less oily. Not that Austin minded physical imperfections now. On the contrary, he found them reassuring, as though they were credits that offset the huge overdraft he had run up by allowing himself to get so old. When he'd been young and appealing, Austin had used someone's slightest fault as a reason to reject him, just to weed out the ranks of admirers. But even then his natural inclination had been to respond to anyone who liked him, and now that there were so few men who even looked at him as a sexual being he could respond to them all with equal enthusiasm. In fact, he'd been so afraid of dressing too young or touching up his hair, which was beginning to gray, that he always wore suits and had even exchanged his contact lenses for donnish glasses, thereby thickening the erotic distance between himself and other men. Maybe it was only those who dreamed of punishing Daddy or of finally becoming teacher's pet who were pulled toward him.

Big Julien, he could see, now that he had him once again before his eyes and could study him, was handsome if not exactly his type. But did he, Austin, even have a type now? He used to say that he fell in love with blonds but lusted after brunets. But in recent years he'd slept with so many different kinds of men, and sometimes, unexpectedly, kindled to their unfamiliar touch, that more and more often he'd look at the least likely man and think, Maybe him? Maybe he could make me feel good? For in sex he was now less interested in a trophyboy and more attracted to the man who might bring him pleasure. He wanted pleasure, not prestige.

While he ran around with drinks and canapés the other guests arrived. He was delighted to see how effortlessly Big Julien fitted into this group despite the difficulty of everyone else already knowing one another. Or rather Julien appeared almost indifferent to fitting in. He was kindly, polite, smiling but dignified, and he seemed older than the other guests, as though he were a soldier back from the front among kids too young to have fought—or in fact, what he was, a married man.

Unlike Americans, French guests all smoked, drank red wine, ate red meat and white rice, white bread and white sugar. They had almost no food dislikes except white wine or sweet things (such as cranberry sauce) served before the dessert course or fiery spices offered no matter when. Salsas and curries were not acceptable. Garlic could be a problem anywhere north of the Loire.

Austin served his guests a first course of smoked fish and salad in a mustard vinaigrette and a second of lamb shoulder stewed with onions, tomatoes and white beans. Then he passed around a big smelly platter of oozing cheeses, though privately he knew that chalky goat cheeses dusted in cinders were more "distinguished" than these runny Bries and Camemberts, and that skipping the cheese course altogether was still more aristocratic, but he also recognized that he had to fill his skinny young guests up. For dessert, like all Parisians, he bought bakery sweets, since no one in his own kitchen could rival the layered and unidentifiable *mousses* that the French admired (and Americans dismissed as "synthetic"). Then there were *petit fours* served with the coffee and chocolate-covered coffee beans and *truffes*, those dense, bitter balls of cold butter and cocoa, as if the table would be declared indecent were it left undressed even for an instant. Austin liked the formula he'd worked out here at home of formal food and dressy attire in a cozy, broken-down apartment at the chic-est address, an event attended by high-spirited kids with unleashed tongues, high aspirations and a dawning worry about whether, just now, that bowl was for washing the fruit or their fingers. Oh, he was all for making them talk freely and volubly but he didn't want them to forget that tonight, like all the other nights here, was some sort of occasion. Since he never led the conversation (he was running back and forth from the kitchen too often and besides his French wasn't agile and funny enough), he needed to impose his personality through what the French called "the arts of the table."

Despite the blur and hubbub of service, he noticed that Big Julien seemed irritated by Pierre-Yves's excessive self-assurance. During their hundreds of gym classes together, Austin had carefully studied Pierre-Yves, who seemed almost too predictably torn between his French father and Russian mother, between a Cartesian trust in method and reason and a Slavic impulse toward intense feeling and self-destruction. The result was that he was always smiling coolly, pityingly at his interlocutor's "errors in taste" (the French side), when he wasn't running out for debilitating revels on acid or submitting slavishly to a cruel Brazilian lover, who actually beat him.

Big Julien and Pierre-Yves had drifted into an argument about politics. Since Austin had been trapped into another noisy conversation with the very drunk (and always slightly mad) psychiatrist Hubert, who was insisting for some reason on talking about photography "as a form of contamination," he couldn't follow Julien's and Pierre-Yves's dispute. But he could tell it was heating up to an uncomfortable degree.

And then it was over. The kitchen sink was piled high with dirty dishes, everything smelled of cigarettes, the pillows on the daybed had been pummeled to half their normal plumpness and the round white tablecloth had been stained red in one place, as though Caesar had been stabbed through his toga just there. Big Julien, the married man, did nothing to help. He stood between the open French windows and looked out at the immense stone snail shell, the steeply pitched church roof beyond and the roiling clouds above ignited by the city lights. Although the day had been unseasonably warm, the night was cool. Austin worried that Julien might catch cold after the flushed excitement of all the talk and wine and heavy food, especially since he was wearing only his ugly green linen jacket and he looked pale. And it was a weekday; Julien would have to go to work early tomorrow: he'd said the whole office was *en charrette*, which was architect's lingo for a round-the-clock blitz.

"Did you like Joséphine?" Austin asked him, standing next to him in the cold window, listening to the clip-clop of high heels as a solitary, determined walker passed by on the street below. He could smell the dish detergent on his hands, an acidic, grease-cutting citron, and he worried that it might offend Julien.

"Charming," he said. "But those opinionated men—have you known them for long?"

"Years."

"And do you find them fascinating?"

"Well. They're *friends*. I don't stop to wonder whether a friend is 'fascinating' or not."

"No. Of course not. Childhood friends are exempt from all criticism."

"They're not exactly *childhood* friends—I came to France only eight years ago. Do you have lots of old friends?"

"Yes, but I never see them."

"Why not?"

"I prefer to think about them. My friends mean so much to me, but only in my thoughts, in my memory."

"What a poetic idea," Austin murmured dreamily with a soft smile, because he thought Julien might kiss him. At a less romantic moment Austin might have objected strenuously to such a chilly notion. He wondered if it wasn't just an affectation Julien had invented on the spot so that he himself could sound "fascinating," a quality he apparently rated highly.

But Julien didn't kiss him and a moment later he was gone, but not before Austin had lined him up for dinner two nights later. At the door Julien gave him a big, helpless smile and let his hand sketch out something indecisive, between a hug and a handshake, which ended up as a sort of clumsy pat on the arm—the only awkward gesture Austin had seen this terribly conscious man make.

Chapter Four

The next morning at ten Pierre-Yves, dressed in new jogging shoes and a blue nylon track suit and crisp white T-shirt, was at the door, playfully exasperated because Austin was barely awake and not yet in his gym clothes. Pierre-Yves beat his hands together rhythmically and called out, *"Vite, vite, vite."* He'd been an Olympic ice-skating coach and retained a vigorous manner, though with Austin he was obviously working with hopeless material. Their whole "routine" (vaudeville, not workout) consisted of Austin's irrepressible desire to gossip in mid-exercise, whereas Pierre-Yves, at least in his official capacity, demanded that his student finish all twenty repetitions before jabbering anymore. When Austin said, "So I see you're not bruised today," or "What on earth were you and my guest Julien fighting about last night?" Pierre-Yves raised a warning finger and pronounced the next number louder (*"Dix, onze, douze . . ."*). He'd assumed the role of outwardly stern, secretly amiable taskmaster. Austin spent so much of his workout on his pale blue rubber mat on the floor, looking up at Pierre-Yves, that he constantly had a perverse, child's-eye view of this man with the lean, muscled legs, the compact torso, the smooth, hairless arms, the powerful jaw and small, neat features. When he was younger, in the pre-AIDS days, he'd seldom hesitated to touch another man seductively, a big grin on his face, but now he'd trained himself to recognize that he was positive, that other men were more reticent sexually than he, and that even if they weren't it was hardly likely that he would be their first choice.

"Did you like my friend Julien?"

". . . *Dix*-neuf, *vingt*. He has very strong opinions, *non?*"

"He said the same thing about you." They both laughed.

After Austin's next series of push-ups, Pierre-Yves started nodding about something as though he'd reflected further. "He's certainly a nice-looking man. He's married?"

"Did he tell you that? He is married, but why did he mention it, I wonder. Perhaps he was trying to keep himself from being too attractive to you."

Pierre-Yves shook his head twice, as though he was baffled. "No. Not at all. In any event, he's not homosexual, is he?"

"I should *hope* so. Why else—"

"Un, *deux, trois* . . ."

At the next interval Pierre-Yves was talking about his plans to accompany three drag queens to a ball.

"Will *you* be in drag?" Austin asked. The whole subject bored him stupid.

"*Me?*" Pierre-Yves asked, shocked. "I'll be their escort. The man." He added in English, "It will be a funny evening," making the usual French mistake of imagining *funny* was the adjective form of *fun*.

Pierre-Yves seemed cautious about Julien, but then people *never* made the least effort to be fair and objective but always imposed their idiosyncratic reading on a friend's new lover; they didn't stop for a moment to wonder if he had qualities that would make the poor friend happy. They only judged the newcomer according to whether he was perceived as a threat or an ally. Although Austin thrived on confusion, he expected reasonableness and calm from other people, at least when they advised him at crucial moments in his life.

Later in the day Gregg had dropped in unexpectedly for a cup of tea. "Hon," Gregg said, "that new Julien of yours is a *doll*." Gregg liked to talk like a waitress in a forties film and he often said things such as, "Time to cool my aching dogs," or "Your mom"—meaning himself—

"is plumb wore out slinging hash," by which he meant he'd had a tiring day inserting slender disposable wands into clients' pressure points. But his camp way of talking didn't mean that he was effeminate or insincere.

Austin had first met Gregg eight years ago at the gym, when they'd both just arrived in Paris. Back then Gregg had recently left a Midwestern college, where he'd been a dance major, in order to come to Paris. He knew no one. Paris had been a scintillating childhood dream, but the reality was friendless and dull, at least at first. In repose his face was a devastatingly bleak portrait of loneliness, as though he'd been irreversibly disillusioned as a kid. When he was engaged in conversation, however, he lit up, illuminated by curiosity and warmth.

At least he was friendly and easy-going with Austin, who was older and unthreatening, and he never hesitated to quiz Austin about the most minor acquisitions in his apartment. Gregg noticed even a new book, and every day the mail brought four or five of them, almost all catalogues of antique auctions or furniture shows.

He was pretty and sensitive but he did everything to hide it, slouching around, skull shaved, fine-boned body bulked up by army fatigues, only the trousers, when he bent to tie the laces of his military shoes, stretching across his rounded butt and bulging thighs to reveal the body he took such pains disguising—*and* building up.

He was always dropping in with a new story of a sex adventure.

"Mother, I was in the Parc de Vincennes this morning and I saw this hot kid, a real pervert, you could tell by his hungry, pervy eyes that he had a hungry hole, we went up a deserted path, just the occasional jogger, and the kid starts playing down there and *tout d'un coup* don't you just know your daughter was *fisting* that sick pig right there in broad daylight!"

"Dirty?"

"Leave it to Mom for the practical questions. No, that little Jean-François must douche every morning *just in case. . . .*"

Although he was vulgar and sassy, Gregg had deep inner resources of grief. He once confessed as he was massaging Austin (for he was also an occasional masseur) that he'd never known his father. In the small Ohio town where he'd grown up he'd assumed his dad must have run off with another woman soon after his birth; that was the version his mother had always given him. But then one day his mother and he were driving to the supermarket when they saw on a park bench a small, graying vagrant asleep, his face puffy, the upper lip bruised a dark purple. "That's your father," Gregg's mother had said.

As Gregg talked, Austin was lying on his stomach, his face turned away from him. He expected Gregg's palm or hands to . . . well, to hesitate. Or stop. But no, the rhythm was exactly the same. And his face lowered into that ruminative murmur men use when they chamois the car or whistle something, the soft murmur of thought joined to a hands-on job.

Now Gregg was running into the kitchen—"I need some of that Château Chirac," he said, by which he meant Paris tap water—and then he came back and said, between gulps, "Honey, you know I never give you advice, but that new Julien is *husband-material.*" He said it with a powerful stress on the *hus* and the *ter,* just as though he were going to zorro the air with a finger-snapping Z. "Seriously, doll," and now he was no longer a black drag but the cozy waitress again, whispering a Kool-scented confidence as the toast in the toaster behind her started to burn, "if I were you, hon, I'd *grab* that one. Or else your daughter *will.*"

Despite the weather-vane changes of voice and role, Gregg was serious.

"What should I do?" Austin asked.

"Invite him away for a weekend to some luxurious hotel."

"I don't have a car."

"Take the train to a nice little town."

But it was too soon to invite Julien anywhere except to dinner. He convinced Henry McVay, his rich friend, to have both of them over with Lauren Bacall, who was in town.

"God," Henry said, "can't it be just us *boys,* Sweetie?"

"No, Henry. Julien's a married man. And besides, she's a famous woman."

"*Quelle barbe,*" Henry grumbled, using the French idiom for what he was always saying in English, "What a bore." "Not that I dislike Betty Bacall for an instant. She's pure heaven. And *very* amusing." He paused, having exhausted his store of Parisian adjectives. "It's just that at my age I really don't like formal evenings much anymore." By "formal" he meant "heterosexual."

And yet when Austin had met him six years earlier, it had been at a big cocktail party at which only half the men had been gay and there'd been as many women as men.

Austin had met half the people there before. The handsome, seventy-year-old McVay, a few sheets (even a mainsail) to the wind, had said in his penetrating voice, "This is outrageous! I've been here for forty-five years and you already know most of my friends. It's a scandal!" He rolled his eyes dramatically to heaven.

Austin laughed, knowing he'd just been complimented. McVay, who seldom liked new people unless they were very young and decorative, preferably preppie blonds, nevertheless took to Austin instantly and started inviting him out all the time. They had known many of the same people over the years; even though Austin was twenty years younger, Henry was convinced they belonged to the same milieu. After all, they'd both often visited Peggy Guggenheim in Venice and they'd both been mentioned, if in different volumes, in Ned Rorem's memoirs. Most important, they were both connoisseurs, even if Henry *owned* the paintings and chairs he admired and Austin merely wrote about them. But Henry would forget that Austin was poor, or if not poor then someone who lived virtually hand to mouth, and would lapse into complaints about his servant problems, something he was far too much a gentleman to do with someone he'd fully registered was less fortunate than he.

Soon they were best of friends. When Austin's book on eighteenth-century French ceramics was published in New York and London, Henry had written him a glowing letter. It was the only letter from a friend he'd received, though a few specialists had sent him notes pointing out questionable attributions.

Austin would never have risked offending McVay by saying so, but he thought of him as a father. Austin's own father had been a heavy-drinking Southerner, a man so reclusive that he'd go days without talking but who, when necessary for currying favor to earn his living, could put in an impeccable social performance. This old guy who farted loudly, gabbled like a chicken farmer and wandered around his big eighteenth-century Virginia house unshaved, drunk and belligerent, had had the knack of dressing up like a duke on a yachting excursion when he had to. He'd treated his clients to a dinner of salty ham and sweet potatoes with pecans, cooked in Bourbon, kept his own drinking in check and kissed the hands of the wives on parting. He'd even made his dilapidated house gleam so that the water-stained wood floors looked antique and the hump-backed bed seemed worthy of having welcomed George Washington, as the family legend maintained. His father had been too poor and too lazy to hunt but he'd still had good old hunting prints hanging on the tattersall wallpaper in the main hallway, the one that divided the house in symmetrical halves and led to a staircase with steps rising in the smallest possible gradations, wide enough for ball gowns—stretched tight over many crinolines—to descend. Austin's father had floated down into the family grave ten years ago on a cloud of Old Turkey, leaving behind nothing but debts.

As it turned out, Lauren Bacall had already left Paris but McVay invited Nina Helier, a perfume heiress who was so old "she no longer had an age," as the French say unkindly (*elle n'a plus d'âge*), though she was still in full possession of her beauty—well, if not her *original* beauty then a concocted latter-day version of that loveliness. She presented her immortal face to the viewer impassively as a goddess might—an idol, McVay's oldest friend, the Count Montpassier, called her. When, just at the moment she was passing over the frontier into old age, she'd confided to Montpassier, "I don't really like fags," he'd spat out, "*Dommage*, madame, they are your future." She wasn't stupid and she'd instantly taken his point. That was when she'd abandoned her vampishness and become a regular guy, although for men of McVay's generation she'd always be a Legend—more refined, more fascinating, certainly more mysterious than a mere actress like Bacall.

Julien was hypnotized by her, although intimidated, which Austin could deduce only from his way of looking at her as though she weren't sitting there next to him *live*.

"He's a *charming* young man," Henry whispered loudly when the others had gone up to the terrace for coffee and the view. But no matter how much Austin ventured disparaging remarks about Julien to indicate that no comment would be judged out of bounds, McVay wouldn't take the bait. He stuck with his kindly, formal generalities. He wouldn't dish. Was it because Henry in fact wasn't attracted to Julien, who was perhaps too swarthy or Gallic for him, and therefore he hadn't really focused on him? Or did Henry regard him as Austin's new husband and thus beyond reproach or even characterization? *"Charming,"* he repeated with emphasis. "A delightful young man. He's from Nancy, you say?"

Julien and Austin walked along the Seine at midnight and stood on the wooden, pedestrian bridge, the Pont des Arts, and looked upstream toward the Musée d'Orsay and downstream at the point of the Île de la Cité that split the river in half. It was so late that all the illuminated buildings around them began to sink into darkness except the distant splendors of the Town Hall, which the mayor kept lit an extra half hour every night, just to prove his importance.

They stood side by side and leaned in to each other. A long, low barge glided under the bridge. Moments later its wake lapped against the massive stone embankments where gay men were cruising one another.

"What did you think of Nina?" Austin asked, because he was reluctant to mention Henry, too much a force in his life to talk about lightly.

"She's exactly the sort of woman I admire," Julien said. "Silent. Superb. Entirely artificial."

"You like artifice?"

"If there's one thing I despise it's a healthy, tanned, big-toothed American girl. No, what I admire is a pale Parisian woman, frail, a hothouse flower, expertly painted."

"Is your wife like that?"

Julien shook his head sadly. "Not now. She's become grotesquely fat and vulgar. But when I met her in Ethiopia she was delicate, sickly. . . ."

"Ethiopia?"

"Yes, she grew up in a diplomatic family. She speaks five of their languages. I'll show you pictures of her."

"What were you doing there?"

"I was teaching architecture in Addis Ababa."

"When? Under Haile Selassie?"

Julien smiled at Austin's inability to grasp how young he was. "No, just two years ago. The emperor was long gone and even the Communists were already on their way out."

"Oh. Of course." Then, following his own train of thought about age, Austin said, "I imagine Nina Helier must have been very beautiful when she was young."

"She's still a beautiful woman!" At that Julien, indignant, relapsed into a complex silence as though he was physically uncomfortable— nursing a sore shoulder, say. Austin was conscious of this tense, melancholy man beside him as they looked down into a river as restless as Austin's own mind. He'd known enough older men and women to realize that life and love go on and on, but he also understood that this affair with Julien, if it ever materialized, could be the last one that was thoroughly . . . reciprocal. Most of the old gay men he knew who had lovers were rich or famous or both and Austin was neither. He felt his time was running out. "How long have you been married?"

"Oh, a while. Quite a while," Julien said.

Austin had already picked up that Julien didn't like to be held to exact dates or if given a chance would dilate each epoch in his life in order to give every one a mythic weight, though he would have had to be forty to accommodate all the years he assigned to himself. "Was she the first woman—" Austin started to ask, then he suddenly interrupted himself, embarrassed.

Julien laughed scornfully. "The first woman I slept with?" He turned his full, mocking glance on Austin and called him "my poor little one." "*Mon pauvre petit*, do you think I'm one of those fags who tried to reform by getting married? By finally getting it up for one sisterly woman?"

"No, of course not," Austin answered sheepishly in a small voice.

"You do! I can see that. When I was just sixteen I told all my classmates I was homosexual, to get that out of the way, and it really wasn't difficult to say or to live with. But I always liked women. My older brother is homosexual, and I joined him out of solidarity. He's been with the same man since he was nineteen, perfectly happy, so you can imagine I had no problem accepting the idea of being gay, but it wasn't black and white for me."

Austin felt he was out of his depth, facing an older culture than his own, one much harder to sum up. His own assumptions struck him as shoddy. He was sorry he'd revealed his West Village smugness; he had belonged to a New York gay world for twenty years and it had left him with too many ready answers. "No," Austin said, inspired, "I meant was she the first woman you'd ever considered marrying?"

"Oh. It was very odd, but it was a lightning bolt. We met in Addis at the French Embassy during a reception and the very next day we left in a Jeep together for a weekend in the bush. We were heading for one of the Negus's palaces, which is now a very shoddy hotel, half-dilapidated. But we hadn't been driving more than half an hour when we had a flat. There we were, on a dirt path at dusk, surrounded by ostriches, which are very dangerous animals with lethal spurs, taller than a man and much faster runners, but a worry only if they feel cornered. Christine was terribly frightened and I held her in my arms. We spent a whole night near the Jeep until the next morning when at last another car came past."

"So that was it?" Austin asked. "Love at first sight."

"Yes, we were engaged to be married almost immediately and I would have married her right then and there, only Christine wanted to wait, she knew a little Romanesque chapel in Provence. . . . She left two months after we met to go back to France. Then I fell in love with a *second* woman, an Englishwoman who was there teaching English in a village. Americans laugh when I say I learned my English in Ethiopia."

"Did she have a very posh accent?" Austin asked, because he didn't want to pose the obvious next question. They had begun to walk along the Quai de la Mégisserie, past the closed pet shops.

"*Bien sûr,*" Julien exclaimed. "I'm certain she was from a very grand family. She's so gentle—a bit older than I."

"Oh?"

"I'm hopeless about ages, but I think she was, well, anyway, too old to have children. She *had* two children with her, ten and eight."

In all his homosexual inexperience Austin rejoiced, calculating that the late forties must be past the age of childbearing for ladies; he exulted in this new proof of Julien's airy indifference to chronological niggling.

As they walked along, Austin took Julien's arm, which felt very thin. Julien was warm and kind, so different from the standoffish Little Julien. Austin acknowledged that he was more attracted to Little Julien, that he thought about him every night and still masturbated remembering him twice a day—the flat chest with a few long hairs straying down the center, the olive hue of his arms, worthy of a Spanish martyr, and his delicate pink ears, which were the color of unhealthy, off-season raspberries. He remembered the hot, bitter taste of his anus, like stale cucumbers, and the heft of his buttocks. He remembered crouching on the floor below Little Julien, who lay athwart the bed on his back, legs falling over the side. Austin would look down the length of Julien's twisting, foreshortened body, as it worked and worked its sure but devious way through pauses and accelerations toward a release that required every bit of concentration and that couldn't skip a single one of these intermediary stages. But Austin was determined to push these thoughts aside, and to prove it he tightened his grasp on Big Julien's arm. Here was a man, a married man, not corrupted by gay life, not standing around a smoky bar with a shaved head, an ear stud or cursory job and a cynical smile already leaching the freshness out of his face. Here was a good man coming to him without intimate tattoos, pierced nipples or other body modifications.

"Christine and I were wild about each other sexually," Julien was saying. "We still are now, even when we quarrel all the time; we're separated, in a month we'll be divorced, but we're still so turned on by each other—"

"—that you still sleep with her?" Austin asked.

"No, not at all," Julien said smoothly. "Of course not, my poor little one, *mon pauvre petit*. That's all over. The bitch."

Austin decided he wanted to be a better wife to Julien than Christine had been, more old-fashioned, more patient, since it was precisely Julien's masculinity—banked and dowsed though it might be—that was the fire at which Austin wanted to warm his hands.

Chapter Five

Joséphine, the children's book illustrator, came over for lunch the next day. Austin wanted to know what she, as a woman, thought of Big Julien, though he realized she wasn't very typically female. Was any woman? Would he have felt right about speaking for all men? Gay men?

Joséphine was from Tours, reputed to be the home of the best French accent, and she did speak her own language clearly and elegantly, with not too much slang and no elisions. She had the fully awakened, gently satiric response to the absurdities of her friends that was characteristic of someone from a big family, a family of talkers and observers rather than TV watchers. Her beauty was regal: her long neck lengthened still more by blond hair swept up and stabbed haphazardly at the top by a comb or gathered into a ponytail by a red rubber band; a pointy chin and hollow cheeks, crowned by prominent cheekbones; and full breasts that visibly strained at the breastbone like two puppies pulling on their leashes in slightly diverging directions. She had long legs and disproportionately small feet, the big toe aristocratically shorter than the others. She wasn't fussy at all or coy or full of feminine wiles.

He'd read somewhere that women imagined men want to feel

useful to women and that they delight in performing acts of gallantry; Joséphine was not laboring under any such misapprehension. She knew exactly how ungallant men could be. She was so beautiful and confident that all she needed to do was tug at her thick lustrous hair with a brush, wriggle into jeans or black pantyhose and a short skirt and pull on a tight T-shirt and she was ready to go out. Tired with bluish circles under her eyes, she was beautiful, just as flushed and glowing at the gym she was beautiful; she had nothing but varieties of beauty to offer. He'd seen her in a black silk dress at the Opera, borrowed pearls around her neck, and she'd been so cold and exquisite that, on a whim, he'd introduced her with gratifying, hand-kissing results, to a snobbish fag as "the Princess Radziwill." But she was just as extraordinary at the end of a long, tiring trip (they often traveled together); she'd be beautiful even during childbirth, he decided.

She was as naive as a Kansan in Paris. Irony sailed right over her head. She never got a joke and the least bit of teasing reduced her to tears rather than the usual sulky, annoyed amusement. No matter how much Austin exaggerated or, in a New York reflex, said the opposite of what he meant in exasperated italics, Joséphine, wide-eyed, would say, "*Vraiment?* Really?"

She and Gregg had been lovers for six troubled, hilarious months full of laughter and tears. Now it was one of their successful party pieces, their tumbled, contradictory accounts of all their feelings.

The routine, of course, hid the sharp pain Joséphine had suffered as well as Gregg's sadness at bidding so many scalding tears to such lovely ice-blue eyes, the eyes of one of his only friends, after all.

Now Austin talked across the restaurant table about Big Julien. "He's very *vieille France,* don't you think?"

"*Vieille . . . ?*"

"God, Joséphine, sometimes I have the feeling *I'm* the Frenchman and *you're* the American. You know, Old France, proper, stuffy, *comme il faut.*"

She blinked, confused, in the lamplight that shed its warmth over their table on this gray, rainy late April day. "He has nice manners," she said hopefully, afraid to venture more.

"Do you think he's gay?"

"What? *Isn't* he gay?" she asked, alarmed again. Until she'd moved to Paris, apparently she'd never met a single homosexual or even thought about the whole vexing subject of sexual variety. She'd dealt with impotence, premature ejaculation, violence, balding, infidelity, logorrhea, prostate problems, and all the other things men might contrive to irritate a woman, but she'd worked from the simple axiom that all these men more or less desired her.

"Well, he *says* he's bisexual," Austin insinuated with a pretended skepticism and a vocal raised eyebrow, although in truth he had no doubts at all about either side of Julien's sexuality; he simply wanted to provoke a spate of girl talk.

"You *have* been to bed with him, haven't you?" she asked, going with chat-deflecting directness to the sore heart of the matter.

"Not really."

"Now Austin . . ." she admonished, raising one translucent forefinger with its clear, small, unpolished nail. She was calling for a truth that was just as unvarnished. She pronounced his name as though it were Ostend, the Belgian port. Her habit of catching him out was something she'd picked up from Gregg, a tic that she'd learned was considered generally amusing.

"Well," he spluttered, "I think even he is puzzled, but I don't dare seduce him before I've explained to him about being seropositive. Or what would you say?" He was half-hoping for some superior French worldliness that would get him off the moral hook.

Joséphine acknowledged Austin's health status only during those rare times when he mentioned it. Then she'd frown and narrow her eyes as though she were staring into a sunset that had given her a very bad headache. "Yes, you must," she said in hushed tones, but he wasn't sure she wasn't copying other people's conventions of concern.

"Should we have sex first a few times and *then* should I mention it? Won't he drop me right away if I tell him first?" Austin knew that if a gay American was overhearing him he'd be horrified at Austin's ethical wobbling.

"Yes," Joséphine said, as she disappointed Austin by waving off the dessert menu and ordering an espresso for both of them, a mother's disabused glance over imaginary glasses to show she'd brook no whining objections to her spartan good sense from her greedy friend. "Maybe it would be best if you got him hooked (*accroché*) before you sprang on him any unpleasant news."

Austin was surprised to hear his possibly imminent death demoted to the status of the "unpleasant" (*désagréable*). In truth, he had no symptoms and even looked embarrassingly robust.

Austin and Peter, his American ex-lover, had been tested together in Paris in 1986, three years earlier, because their French doctor with the Greek name had insisted. People said that the doctor himself was infected with the virus. Peter, a genuine escapist, had objected to the whole process, arguing Austin would be thrown out of France if positive and sent home to the States in leg irons (Peter had already decided to move back). "And you won't be able to travel and practice your profession," Peter said with such energy and fussy precision that Austin suspected he must be repeating something he'd read in the paranoid gay press. "In Sweden, they're sending seropositives to a prison island." Neither Austin nor Peter was certain you said "seropositives" in English, which Peter in particular found annoying and disorienting in his capacity as a super patriot who'd never condescended to learn any French beyond the most approximate bar-room gabbling. "In Munich they test you at the border and to stay in India more than a month you must undergo a blood test."

"So those places would be eliminated in any event," Austin pointed out.

"Anyway, who wants to go to Munich, European capital of vulgarity and fascism, all those middle-aged men linking arms and wearing lederhosen? And India is too creepy-crawly for those-who-are-positive," he said, hoping he'd found a formula for their condition that was both graceful and good English.

Cut off from America, from the massive protests and the underground treatment newsletters, from the hours and hours of frightened midnight conversations with friends by phone and the organized safe-sex and massage sessions, far from the hysteria and the solace, Austin did not know what to think of this disease that had taken them by chance, as though he had awakened to find himself in a cave under the heavy paw of a lioness, who was licking him for the moment and breathing all over him with her gamy, carrion smell but who was capable of showing her claws and devouring him today . . . or tomorrow.

Even after Peter moved back to the States, he had a lingering resentment against Austin for having insisted they be tested.

And Austin, too, felt that he'd gained nothing by knowing, since the only available treatments didn't seem to work. He'd had a cheerfully defiant conviction that learning the truth is always liberating, but since moving to Europe he'd come to doubt his democratic frankness, his "transparence," as the French called it, as though it were no more interesting than a clear pane of glass. He'd learned not to blurt out whatever happened to be passing through his mind and, out of the same curbing of instinct, he'd started to shy away from bald declarations of facts, even when other people made them. If another American called out anything in a loud, unironic voice, he'd exchange amused but slightly alarmed glances with his French friends—can humankind bear so much candor? he seemed to be asking. Isn't there something inherently alarming about so much explicitness, even when the subject is safe?

The worst thing about knowing he was positive was that now he was under an obligation to tell his partners. Not that he informed the man he picked up in the park or the guy he lured over on the phone-chat line. Austin had an American friend in Paris, a well-known gay novelist, who'd come out as positive on TV and in the press, and now he was obliged to be honest with everyone, but Austin was a nobody. At least he'd never made any public statements. His friend the writer was apparently having trouble getting laid these days—so much for honesty.

No, truly the worst thing was studying one's body every morning in the shower for auguries. Even in that regard he envied all those hysterical gay guys back in New York or San Francisco who knew to become alarmed about the slightly raised, *wine*-colored blemish, not the flat, black mole or whatever, who could tell just when a cough became "persistent" enough to be worrying or whether a damp pillowcase and a wet head counted as "night sweats."

He both feared and embraced the French silence in the face of this disease (and of all other fatal maladies). Something superstitious in him whispered that if you didn't think about it, the virus would go away. From one month to the next he never heard the dreaded three letters (*VIH* in French rather than HIV, as if the French version of the disease itself were the reverse mirror image of the American, just as the French acronym *SIDA* was an anagram of AIDS). Americans sat up telling each other horror stories, but they were later astonished when their worst fantasies came true, as if they'd hoped to ward off evil by talking it into submission or by taking homeopathic doses of it. The French, however, feared summoning an evil genius by pronouncing its name. Neither system worked. When the lioness awakened and felt the first hunger pains, she would show her claws.

He knew in his heart that the French approach was especially unsuited to the epidemic. His friend Hervé last year had been so *ashamed* of falling ill that he'd slunk back home to his village in the Dordogne without calling a single friend. Only his ex-lover Gilles had stayed in touch, although Hervé's grandmother irrationally blamed Gilles for having given him AIDS. Each time Gilles called she'd say that Hervé was sleeping but would call back later. A month later, the next time Gilles phoned, Hervé had already been dead and buried for eleven days.

It was as if a few young men in the provinces managed to escape to Paris where they lived for a few seasons, where they clipped their heads, lifted some weights, danced on Ecstasy, tattooed one haunch with a butterfly and had sex with hundreds of other underemployed *types*—and then they were driven home to Sarlat by their somber families, all dressed in black as if out for their Easter duties, and they disappeared in a whispered diminuendo, the score marked *ppppp*. . . .

What didn't work out about this system was that no young bright kid coming up to Paris ever saw his predecessor, skinny and crippled, hobbling back down to the provinces. The best prevention, the most convincing proof of the necessity for safe sex, was ocular evidence, actually *seeing* KS blotches on skinny arms or watching rail-thin old men of twenty staggering into a restaurant on two canes, sharpened cheekbones about to rub through the parchment-thin skin, the eyes as bulbous as an insect's. But in Paris, magical city of elegance and romance, men with AIDS were no more visible than the retarded, the mad or the lame—they'd all been whisked off to some shuttered house in Aquitaine. The French were masters of silence, and as ACT-UP claimed, "Silence = Death."

Austin invited Big Julien away for the weekend. In his Michelin guide he'd found a luxury hotel only forty-five minutes by train outside Paris, not far from the royal château of Rambouillet. They didn't need to rent a car to get there; theoretically they should be able to find a taxi at the train station. Fatuous as it sounded, Austin was relieved to be going away, for once, with a capable adult male, one who regularly submitted construction plans to the mayor's office and traveled by train to other cities.

It was the beginning of May. They took an electrified double-decker commuter train that quickly left the historic city behind and rushed past planned communities in the suburbs, the ugly apartment blocks oriented to one another at rakish angles (to prove how humane the planner had been) rather than laid out in the usual stultifying cemetery grid. When Austin said something dismissive about the buildings and the orange and black supergraphics on an aubergine-colored wall in the station shelter, Julien said he knew the architect, an Albanian refugee famous for his sound engineering skills ("No division of labor in Tirana," Julien said matter-of-factly), and his remark put paid to Austin's facile sneering. Austin was happy to have this handsome man beside him, someone so eccentric in his views, his way of referring everything back to Ethiopia, his indifference to gay life and his ignorance of its tyrannies, his unlikely clothes; Austin thought maybe Julien didn't even notice a detail like age: their twenty-year age difference. For Austin was wired very peculiarly. He wasn't like some of his contemporaries who felt they could reduce the gap by doing three hundred sit-ups every day until their thickened waists and slack skin looked like melting chocolate bars, the hot flesh oozing over the lines between the tablets. He didn't want to dance all night on drugs, his steps an anthology of four decades of approximated wriggling. He didn't want to shed his dated slang, the words *groovy, mellow* or *get down, girl.*

He liked this intense, brooding married man with the unclassifiable preoccupations, which permitted Austin, by contrast, to appear relaxed and relatively normal, even of a normal age. As they rode side by side in the train they kept stealing glances at each other. They were virtually alone on a Saturday morning in this commuter train heading out of the city. The walls lining the tracks were like ramparts; if Austin looked up he could see the windowless sides of houses rising above. Austin's only other French lover, Little Julien, had never gone anywhere with him in France, perhaps out of fear of being recognized by friends in the company of a much older foreigner. But Big Julien was here with his dark blue eyes, black hair, neat, courtly gestures, his deep, deep voice thrumming and resonating in Austin's ear, his sudden, utterly fake booming laugh, so out of character that Austin assumed it must be a private homage to a friend or relative he'd emulated in the past. No, he wasn't interested in the general impression he was making, even if he was playing to Austin, the unique member of his audience. Julien was a loner, seriously alone now that he was getting divorced, alienated from his father, too, for some reason. Austin would look over at this man whose body he'd never held and imagine they were about to be married, as old-fashioned virgins were once married; he daydreamed his way into the mind of a nineteenth-century bride who looked at these pale male hands beside her, tufted with glossy black hair, and thought she'd know them the rest of her life, that he'd explore her body with them for fifty years.

They had to phone for a taxi from the suburban station and drive out beyond Versailles, but the hotel was worth the trip: a former abbey with its low stone-faced Gothic buildings looming up over an ornamental lake with swans. The chapel was roofless, the empty, glassless rose window nothing but brambles of vacant masonry, the colorful petals long since shed and swept up. Separating the grounds and the fields beyond was a partially destroyed wall, once perhaps the side of a cloister garden; at least it had empty windows and under them stone seats worn smooth and deep by centuries of monastic meditation. The man at the desk, who had registered them with impassive good manners, now added, as a well-judged hint at friendliness, "The death scene of Depardieu's *Cyrano* was shot out there by the ruined cloisters."

A moment later they were in their suite with its copper tub and its long antechamber leading to double doors and, beyond, the bedroom with its double bed and its flung-open gauze-covered high windows that floated like panels of bird-riddled silence, empty and twittering, twin paintings by an abstractionist who'd turned wryly metaphysical. They couldn't wait for the bellboy to leave them alone.

They'd gone so long without ever having had sex that Austin felt a certain stage fright, but for the next two days they were all over each other, above, below, behind, like two boys wrestling with hard-ons they don't know how to discharge. Half the hotel had been turned over to a giant wedding party and whenever they descended for another long meal with its succession of courses they were always isolated from the other diners with their flowered dresses, big hats and corsages, their decorous toasts and gentle teasing, their restless children in rumpled organdy or clipped-on bow ties and their game old grandparents. No, Austin and Julien were blissfully irrelevant to the machinery of a big country wedding and as they wandered the grounds, feeling formal and drained from their furious, tangled bouts of lovemaking, they were always gliding past uniformed waiters stacking rented chairs or testing the microphone in the ballroom by tapping on it and whispering numbers. The weather shifted unpredictably between moments of magnifying-glass heat and cold, cloud-propelling wind.

They sat at opposite ends of the big copper tub in daylight that was filtered through smoked glass. The bubble bath lost its suds to reveal their strong, intertwined legs and their body hair undulating like algae.

They'd lie in the hotel's white terry-cloth robes on the bed and Julien would talk about his divorce. "We were fine in Ethiopia—"

"Except you had that affair with the Englishwoman. How happy could you have been?"

"No, no, *mon pauvre petit,*" Julien said, smiling at Austin's touching gay naïveté. "I loved her, Sarah, the English know the names of all the birds and plants, we French are always astonished by their expertise. We went with her children in her old car to a wonderful lake crowded with pink flamingos. But that doesn't mean I ever hesitated in my feelings for Christine. . . . She's dying to meet you, by the way."

Austin could feel the blood flooding his face and neck. "Me? But—"

"She's very interested in old furniture," Julien said.

"I'm not exactly a *bergère Louis XV,* even if I am slightly tubby," Austin joked, his voice suddenly turning hoarse. He knew if he was back in America his friends would croak, "Drop him. Married men are poison. You'll see. He'll go running back to her after he's finished experimenting with you." But over here, in France, in these posthumous, post-diagnosis, foreign days, Austin no longer expected anything to work, certainly not to be ideal; he would share a man with a woman and even meet her if need be, though he was afraid of her anger. "What went wrong, then?" Austin asked.

"She's a bitch. In Ethiopia she was fine. But the moment we came back—starting with the wedding!" His eyes shifted from side to side, as though looking for the best escape route; then he sighted it and ran. "My grandmother was revolted. She didn't want me to do something so bourgeois as get married." Inspired, he laughed his laugh, a hollow tocsin of mirthless pleasure. "They wanted me to be gay—anything rather than marry that *petit-bourgeois* bitch and her stuffy, petty family. They were so disappointed I was marrying that they wept. My grandmother pulled up her skirts at the reception and danced like Marilyn over the subway grill and my brother's lover clapped and crouched and shouted, 'Go, Granny, show them your pussy!'" (*Allez, Mémé, montre ta moule!*)

Austin smiled painfully. He didn't see anything funny in the scene and wondered if it had ever happened. If it did, he thoroughly sympathized with Christine and her parents. "But how old is your grandmother?"

"Oh, not that old," Julien said with his usual vagueness. "Her legs were still good then and she cut a fine figure, although now she's gone to fat. It's all the fault of that lover of hers, a real vulgarian called Modeste."

"It's nice, I think, that your grandmother has a lover. In America people stop having sex at a surprisingly young age. Few of us can say the words, 'my grandmother's lover.'"

But Julien wasn't paying attention. He'd turned on his stomach and was laughing, repeating to himself, *"Allez, Mémé, montre ta moule!"* The ugly words and the self-amused booming laugh didn't really go with his body, with the fine swirls of hair on his boyishly full buttocks, nor did the laugh fit the small ears pinned back to his head as though he were standing still in a ferocious wind, nor with the delicate architecture of his shoulder blades, lightly dusted with black hair.

If Austin was always alert to Julien's mood, feared boring him and followed his conversational lead, Julien wallowed, oblivious, in his own worries and obsessions. He seemed to be sick with worry. His skin had broken out on his face, two red welts on his forehead and small pimples clustering around the follicles where his beard was growing in. His nose was always oily. Gregg, who had all sorts of fetishes, had said to Austin, "That Big Julien is so randy and young he even has acne, slurp, slurp." Gregg always pronounced the words for his sound effects, and said such things as "Sob" or "Drool."

"My mother committed suicide ten years ago," Julien was saying. "She and I loved each other—she was the great love of my life. That's why I don't speak to my father. I hate him. It was his fault. He'd married her young. He didn't like it that she was—" He hesitated, then revised his thoughts. "That she was a concert pianist. He made her give it up. She sacrificed everything for him. Her family gave him money to start his pharmaceutical company. They gave them their house. She killed herself in Belle-Île at the summer house her mother had bought her." He pounded the mattress and said into the pillow, "The thought—"

"What?"

Julien looked up, astonished, as if awakened. "The thought that *he* is living there now with that slut, his mistress—"

"His wife?"

"Yes, I suppose he married her. The thought . . ."

Austin felt it would turn out to be a very long story and he wasn't sure Julien would be a reliable narrator. This Latin man with his black hair, with his lean neck shaggy because he'd long been overdue at the barber, with his low unstoppable voice that sometimes seemed the inefficient, power-guzzling motor draining his body of all its fuel—oh, he wasn't an impartial, objective American, respectful of the truth and impressed by any fair challenge to his version of things, ready to chuckle at his own absurdities. Julien was never the butt of his own jokes. No, he was a passionate Latin male whose body seeped anguish and oil and whose voice hypnotized his mind into believing whatever it had proposed and was elaborating.

"My mother's death was such a powerful thing for me," he was saying; now he was sitting up and hugging a surprisingly shiny knee above leggings of hair—there was even hair on the knuckle of each of his toes. It occurred to Austin that Julien had rubbed his knee bare with worry, but he knew that couldn't have been the case. "I was the one who found her dead. It was during my final exams for my architecture diploma, so I guess I hadn't been paying much attention to her. I knew she was unhappy. She'd asked my father if it was all over between them. She'd said, 'Tell me. I'm still young, I can find someone else.' In fact she was just forty-three, and she looked so young that when I'd take her out dancing everyone would ask if she was my sister."

Austin thought he'd heard the same story all his life, about the young mother, a story that always seemed so odd to him. His own mother had died of ovarian cancer when he was still a teenager, but he'd never wanted to pass for her brother, nor did she dance. Of course she'd been nearly forty when he'd been born, a plump graying woman locked into another epoch by her elegant Tidewater accent and soft, unambitious ways, whereas Julien's parents had been in their twenties and his father even now was just five years older than Austin.

The story had reached a head and Austin hadn't been listening. He figured out that Julien's father had lied and pledged his renewed love to his wife, but in truth all he'd wanted was continued access to her money. "When she realized he'd left her for that other bitch, not moved out but was spending all his time with her—that's when and why she attempted suicide. She survived and I just dismissed her when she asked me if I thought she should see a psychiatrist. I laughed at her and told her to pull herself together."

"You were at an entirely different juncture in your life," Austin said. "You had to marshal all your forces to pass your exams, you couldn't afford to be swamped by feelings, hers or yours." He'd learned in other, earlier affairs with confused younger men that a few words, wise to the point of banality, uttered at the strategic moment, could become talismanic for years to come.

"I still feel so guilty. Of course she needed to see a shrink." The French said, *"un psy,"* pronouncing separately the *p* and the *s*, like the sound of a slashed balloon. "But my brother was far away, off in Nice with his lover, and my father was with his slut and I was in architecture school in Nantes. Mother drove all the way across the country from Nancy to Belle-Île, you have to take a ferry over—"

"Isn't that Sarah Bernhardt's island?"

"Yes." He moved so that his head was pillowed on Austin's stomach, almost as though he wanted to stop Austin's distracting questions. "My brother was the one who started to worry about her and he told me to drive over there—it's not that far from Nantes. Nobody had heard from her in three days." He got up and went to pee, then came back, walking slightly knock-kneed, as though he was concentrating on a failing inner voice. He climbed down onto the bed and lay with his back to Austin, knees slightly curled up toward his chest. Austin could see his vertebrae mounting his spine, one by one, like drops of water growing smaller and falling faster. "She was dead. She'd been dead for three days. There was a note. The police took it, they promised to give it back to me, but they never did. I must file an official complaint. I want that note back—it's mine. I found it. She wrote it to me." He propped himself up and drank a glass of water.

"How terrible for you," Austin said, bending down to touch him but then quickly drawing his hand back. They'd made love so often this weekend that Austin feared Julien wouldn't see a touch as a neutral, friendly gesture.

"She was dressed in a pretty silk dress, but she must have choked on her own vomit. Her face was blown up as though her features had been stretched over a soccer ball. The apartment stank. My brother flew up to Rennes and rented a car but missed the last ferry. When he got there the next morning, luckily for him the body had already been removed."

"Where did you sleep that night?"

"In a hotel. I would have stayed in the apartment but the police had cordoned it off. I was glad it was off-season. There was nobody else in the building."

Night had fallen as he talked and added its high seriousness to his words. The window was still open and they were cold and Austin slid behind him and held him. Then he pulled a sheet over them. He asked himself if Julien was glad to be laid out on this slab, sheeted and cold but alive and in another man's arms.

Later that night, after they'd showered and dressed and dined, all alone now that the wedding party had left, Julien said, "You know, when I was a kid I always had a best friend, one friend; you have so many friends but I'm not like that. You're always saying, 'So-and-so is one of my best friends.' I don't have series of best friends. Of course I know a lot of people, but I always wanted just one friend, who'd be loyal to me, and I'd tell him everything."

Austin must have waited for the obvious conclusion with such wide, yearning eyes that Julien finally laughed and said, "But, *Petit*, you look like a puppy."

"I'm sorry," Austin said, offended.

Julien just ran over his prickliness and squeezed Austin's right leg between both of his and said, "You're really such a *bout de chou*."

"A *bout?*"

Julien explained that "the end of the cabbage" was an affectionate nickname for a little kid.

"I'm hardly *little*," Austin objected sweetly, thrilled with his new name.

Chapter Six

During their first weekend together, they took a taxi and visited the gardens and forests around Rambouillet (the unim-
pressive château itself, which belonged to the President of the
Republic, was off limits). Austin remembered (because it had happened during *his* century) that Marie Antoinette had had built here
her *Laiterie*, a small classical temple in which she could drink milk—
the milk jars were kept cool in an inner sanctum under a flowing
fountain, dense with allegorical figures. He and Julien finally found it
and went in; even on a warm day it was ten degrees cooler. The queen
didn't live to see the *Laiterie*, which was finished not long before she
was guillotined, but if she had she would have discovered nearby the
Veuverie of her friend (enemies said, her lesbian lover), the Princesse
Lamballe, a small cottage in which the inner walls were decorated
with pictures composed of shells—a strangely irrelevant setting for the
princess to mourn in (*veuverie* meant "widowhood"). Austin knew a
bit about the history of the place. As an architect, Julien took a more
austere approach and analyzed the *Laiterie* formally, as though its merits were conceptual, not associational.

They left the hotel for Paris on Monday morning.

As they saw each other with greater and greater frequency, until they were getting together nearly every night, Austin realized that he had indeed become Julien's little sidekick, his one best friend, his confidant, not his father. Julien had no idea of deference—nor of reciprocity. He never cooked Austin dinner or even offered him a coffee, and certainly he never asked Austin a question about his family or past lovers. Was his discretion evidence of his incuriosity and egotism or did he hope to win with it an immunity from Austin's prying? Austin never saw his apartment, the one where he lived alone. He covered Austin with kisses and smiled with a solar warmth, just as though he were the sun setting down closer and closer and peering directly into his eyes. He'd whisper, *"Petit,"* and *"Mon bout de chou,"* or say, *"Comme tu es mignon!"* (How cute you are!), but Austin knew it wasn't his face or body that was being praised, just his presence, his docility. Austin understood that straight men, married men, were used to partners who listened or half-listened to their monologues. Anyway, Austin liked listening, which he could always pass off as a language lesson since the words were in French.

Because Gregg had been the one to suggest the trip to the abbey-hotel, Austin called him when they got back to Paris.

"Well, Mother, you went and got yourself a nice Mother's Day present, I see."

"What? Oh, Gregg . . . *Daughter!* I honestly forgot the day. It's only Mother's Day back in the States, isn't it? Gregg, it was a great suggestion. I never pick out guys who might actually like me."

"I hear you. Your daughter's no better when it comes to doing for herself. So how's the meat?"

"Average. Like mine."

"Like *mine!* Like mother, like daughter—a small clit family. But we know how to thrum that little thing, right, Mom? Did you top him or did Mother get to *serve*—I know she loves to serve."

"We had lots of sex, but of course it was safe, safe, safe. Tons of frottage, *touche-pipi,* soul-kissing. No fucky-fucky—actually it was terribly romantic."

"Do you think he's hooked enough to tell him you're positive?" Gregg asked.

This entirely cynical question opened a door inside Austin's mind.

He laughed and said, "Not yet. Maybe it's because I'm not really in love or because that beastly Little Julien dropped me so brutally, but I've never been shrewder. I'm determined to open up new sexual horizons for him—"

"Meaning?"

"His nipples are more sensitive than his wife's. He told me that. She used to play with his—"

"—perky little devils," Gregg added.

"They *do* just perk right up," Austin said. He knew Julien would be horrified if he could hear this tacky, heartless camp exchange. But he, Austin, was so insecure in an affair—so eager to please, so intense in his devotion, so quick to accept the first sign of boredom as an irrevocable rejection—that in sacrilegious chatter he could reassert, at least for a moment, his freedom. "But I want to discover his bottom for him. Not to mention the beauty of bondage."

"*Bondage!*" Gregg shouted with outraged amusement. "You old Stonewallers are such shameless hussies."

"Oh, like your generation is so pure. *Excuse* me. Hel-*lowwuh*. . . ." Austin was merrily imitating the new Mall Girl slang or his very dim idea of it, but it was a fashionable reference designed as an implicit rebuke to Gregg's dismissal of Austin's "generation."

"But won't he be horrified by *bondage?*" Gregg asked. "Not that I should question Mother's *millennium* of experience. . . ."

Strangely, through all this talk of meat, tits, ropes and sexual technique, Austin knew he was communicating to Gregg his timid happiness and his fear of losing Julien whenever he would discover Austin's HIV status. In America, of course, Austin thought bitterly, they would have met at a Positive Boutique or on an HIV cruise and that would have been that, the introduction equivalent to an admission.

Julien complained of his health at dinner the next night (a *blanquette de veau*, mushrooms, pearl onions, carrots and veal swimming in an egg yolk and cream sauce that had taken Austin all afternoon to elaborate). "I can't seem to make this acne go away—*Petit,* this fish is excellent! I've been hacking away all day with this terrible cough, that's why I can't stay over, I'd keep us both awake. I think I'm coming down with the flu."

Austin felt a cringing, a tightening around his heart, as though someone were inching him gently closer and closer to the airplane's open hatch. He got up and cleaned the dishes. He suggested Julien lie down while he made some herbal tea—did he like verbena? Alone in the kitchen he felt his heart pounding, exactly as if he'd been accused of treachery by an old friend. He took his time putting the pretty but mismatched tea things on an old tray with sides that were inlaid with mother-of-pearl.

Mentally he ran through all their sexual positions over the weekend but could find nothing unsafe. He hadn't let Julien suck him. They'd kissed, but was that dangerous? Julien had held their erect penises close together in his hand, but surely that wasn't "at risk" behavior, as the pamphlets called it. Or was it? Anyway, the disease took months or at least weeks to declare itself, didn't it?

Of course the unconscionable thing was that they were both involved in a deadly game Austin had already lost and that Julien didn't know he was playing.

Usually Austin could forget the virus but it kept ringing back like a bill collector on the phone, calling at all hours, insisting upon its claim.

"Why don't you stay home tomorrow? And I'm sorry about the rich dinner."

"But I love pike in a *beurre nantais.*"

Austin thought he should say it was veal, but that would destroy the illusion they both fostered that Julien, as a Frenchman, knew everything about food, wine and fashion. And because Austin felt guilty about his continuing silence on the subject of his HIV status he couldn't bring himself to irk Julien in any way. He was pleading with Julien to forgive a crime he'd not yet confessed. He'd heard of men who'd gone on a killing spree when they'd found out their lovers had infected them. If Julien was just a nice married man gambling with gay sex, shouldn't he know the stakes? The stakes that he'd already accepted, all unknowingly?

Austin made an appointment with his doctor for Julien. They went to see him together. The office was just across the street from the Buttes-Chaumont, that vast park for the working class that Napoléon III had benignly inserted into a former quarry. Now, of course, the

workshops and the little villages of workers' cottages on the streets
leading off the park housed up-and-coming artists and photographers—
Austin knew a gay *couturier* who'd filled his cottage with medieval
kitsch (shields, tapestries, suits of armor). Even so, the neighborhood
felt forgotten and Austin had no idea why Dr. Aristopoulos lived and
worked there. His *cabinet* was up three flights, a cheerless suite of dim
rooms, unmatched chairs, a student's lamp and a coffee table covered
with last year's magazines and more recent HIV brochures. Somewhere in the neighborhood, no doubt, Dr. Aristopoulos had found a
comically hostessy receptionist, a woman in her fifties who wore puffy
dresses and had dyed her hair an egg-yolk yellow and who walked
around in very high heels, bowing and welcoming the skeletally thin
AIDS patients as though to a Pensioners' Ball.

When Julien came out of his appointment he was red in the face
and almost cross-eyed with anger. As they were escorted to the door
by their bobbing, tripping, smiling hostess (*"À bientôt, messieurs!"* she
sang out in a fruity voice), Julien said nothing, but on the dark stairs,
smelling of the *concierge*'s salted cod dinner, he hissed, "But he's an
idiot!"

"But why?"

"He wanted me to have the test."

"The test?" Austin asked stupidly.

"The AIDS test."

"Why?"

"Because he's worried about my acne and my cough and that wart
I have on my penis."

"But that's absurd. Unless . . ."

"Yes, it's absurd!"

"Unless you had a lot of sex with men these last few years."

Julien didn't say anything. When they were outside he took Austin
by the elbow and steered him across the street and into the park. Two
Indian women in saris were pushing strollers in which solemn, brown-
faced babies were propped up like gingerbread men with big sultana
eyes. The mothers were conversing so loudly that they reminded
Austin how most Parisians whispered.

Had Julien not responded because he was irritated that Austin—

and probably Dr. Aristopoulos—had asked him direct questions about his sex life? Or did he think the test cast doubts on his honor?

"I have to tell you something," Austin blurted out. "I'm HIV positive. Don't worry that you might have—from me. . . ."

"No, no, of course not," Julien said as a polite reflex. "How long have you known?"

"Two years already. My counts are very good, surprisingly good." His voice wobbled and he was short of breath. "They don't seem to be going down. I hope you're not angry that I didn't tell you right away, but I could never seem to find the right moment." Hey, how about the moment just before we had sex? Julien might be thinking, or so Austin imagined. "I'm sure Dr. Aristopoulos wasn't asking you to have the test because of me."

"No, no, of course not," Julien said, his politeness now striking Austin as ominous. Would Austin ever see him again? All he had was his work number and Julien could instruct the receptionist to say he'd call him right back or that he was out of the office for a few days—no, for an "indefinite leave." That's what she would say. They ambled under a promontory surmounted by a Greek temple. On every side there were flowers and flowering bushes, perfectly assorted and groomed, many of them probably transferred for a few weeks only out of the city's greenhouses until they were replaced by still newer plantings in bloom.

Julien sprawled on the grass just beside a sign that forbade doing so. An old Vietnamese man walking past shook his finger at him, laughing. Austin stood just on the other side of the foot-high fence of metal hoops, then felt foolish and joined him and felt foolish.

"Please don't worry about Dr. Aristopoulos. He's positive himself; some people say he's ill, though he looks fine to me. He probably is overly cautious."

"I don't think he's competent. Why aren't you seeing a famous specialist?"

"Several of my friends with HIV see him—"

"You have *several* friends with AIDS?"

"They're all in good health for the moment," Austin said primly.

"I've never met—or even heard of—someone infected until now,

until you. It just seemed to me a media circus, just some new puritanical horror invented by the Americans." He thought about it for a
while.

"Are you worried about Christine? Have you gone on having sex
with her?"

"Christine?" He smiled a mild, studied, imperturbable smile that
Austin read as a signal that he had gone too far with his grubby American questions.

Austin changed tactics: "You know, don't worry about . . . if you
want to drop me . . . I should have been honest from the beginning."
He propped himself up on his elbows and wondered if the grass was
staining his seersucker jacket and the seat of his trousers. Julien was
wearing his liverish green linen sports coat. "Do you like linen?" Austin
asked wildly, then hastened to add, lying, "I do." He was chattering
out of fear and embarrassment.

"Yes, it's a noble material."

By now Austin had learned that Julien liked cotton, linen and silk,
that he revered natural wood and stone, especially marble but even
the ubiquitous Parisian sandstone extracted from this very quarry
in the last century, that he despised brick and concrete—oh, Austin
thought, I'll miss him.

Maybe because Austin was a foreigner and what he did and said
were thrown into relief, if only through contrast, or maybe because he
would soon turn fifty and was seropositive, he now had a heightened
sense of the swathe his life was cutting. In the past he'd been casual
about himself. He'd never wanted to shine. He'd never been known
for anything—neither his books, which were ordinary, nor his accom-
plishments, which amounted to nothing more than a nearly photo-
graphic memory of particular pieces of furniture and ceramics and a
low-energy charm that allowed him to pass hours with the rich idlers
who usually owned those things. Although he'd done well in everything related to the history of furniture itself, he couldn't talk a good
line about Louis XVI as a great patron, about Mme de Pompadour's
"rapacious curiosity" or her "exigent tastes," which constituted an
"enlightened tyranny"—no, he wasn't a phrasemaker nor was he
ambitious like those chaps at Sotheby's in London. And he preferred

spending an evening with his overgrown adolescent friends than with the countesses who owned the last great bits of eighteenth-century furniture in private hands—*finding* the furniture was always the problem. It sold itself. Over the years he'd acted as a middleman between countesses and museums in a few transactions, but he wasn't interested enough in money to persist—or rather he was too quickly bored by grown-ups, officials, heterosexuals (or rather by all those people, straight or gay, who kept their sexuality hidden).

No, he'd always seen himself as an amateur and his life as formless, but now, today, here in this suddenly hot sunlight and grass laid like velvet over the raw, gouged surfaces of the old stone quarry, Austin was alive for the first time since his high-school days to the question of his "destiny." Yes, he probably would die soon, probably in France in a charity ward since he didn't have French insurance nor the official residency that would entitle him to national health coverage. He had a panicky fear that he'd forget French, that his brain would start bubbling like alphabet soup, scrambling all the words he knew in the reverse order he'd learned them, so that French would be the first to go, then the language of furniture, next all adult conversation until he ended up with just a few nursery rhymes, the song his mother had sung him to make him sleep, "When Johnny comes marching home."

Julien was chewing a blade of grass and squinting up at the bright hazy sky. With his right hand he alternately tugged at Austin's seersucker lapel and smoothed it, but he wasn't looking at Austin. The gesture appeared isolated from his thoughts and the immobility of the rest of his body. Julien even stopped chewing. The rancid, cooking smell of grass reminded Austin of bitter Japanese green tea, the tang so inherently rank that sugar seems laughably inadequate to it.

For the next few days Julien was sick with a bad case of the flu. He called Austin every day to tell him he was getting better, but each time he stayed on the line only a moment. The one time he did linger was to tell him the plot of a *Fluide Glacial* he was reading. Like so many adult Frenchmen he read comic books filled with grotesque sex scenes and anarchistic violence, an art form that had largely replaced fiction for many Latin men in their teens and twenties. At the giant music and literature emporium, the FNAC, enraptured solitary men, unemployed no doubt, stood or sat cross-legged on the floor for hours in the aisles of the section for comics, reading and chuckling or sucking in their breath with amazement.

At last Julien was better. Once again he started coming by several evenings a week for dinner. One night Austin took him along for a formal dinner at the house of Marie-France, a woman he'd known for five or six years. They'd met when Austin had written an article about her vast apartment along the Quai d'Anjou on the Île Saint-Louis, twelve rooms with lamps, tables and even bronze bookcases that had been designed by Diego Giacometti, the sculptor's brother. The apartment was on the second floor and the drawing-room windows looked out on the Seine through leaves—the movement of the wind-stirred leaves and the racing, faceted water created a pointillism of living light.

It was a formal dinner for twenty served at two separate tables by two Filipino servants but Marie-France made it all seem comical, even improvised. Julien and Austin were seated apart, each beside glamorous divorcées "of a certain age." Austin's dinner partner kept raving about everything—her key words were *"sublissime,"* which he gathered meant "very sublime," and *"la fin du monde"* ("the end of the world"), which also seemed to be a sign of enthusiasm. Philippe Starck's new toothbrush was *sublissime* and Claude Picasso's carpets were *la fin du monde.*

Marie-France and all her friends were so civilized that they smiled discreetly and benignly when Julien and Austin stood by the piano after dinner drinking a brandy together. On the phone the next day Marie-France said her old uncle Henri had been delighted to meet them and thought he'd bring his own boyfriend to the next gathering, which had never occurred to him previously in half a century. "Of course *his* friend is a gardener whereas yours is an architect and so amusing." Although she was tall and sturdy (her ex-lover, a polo-playing dandy, used to call her "the good soldier"), she used some of the social words, if somewhat less frequently than her women friends. Marie-France could say, "You're a love" or "You're too adorable," if he'd rendered her the slightest service, but she wasn't mannered, her expression was lively and self-satirical and she was quick to shrug off

even the most reasonable compliment. Nevertheless, he wasn't certain she returned his affection until one day her cousin said, "You
know, Marie-France considers you to be one of her best friends."

He knew that Marie-France had married an aristocratic twit very
young and divorced him soon after their second child was born. She'd
raised them without remarrying, though she'd always been open about
her modest succession of lovers (three in fifteen years). She had the
soul of an artist and had decorated her apartment and her house in
the Luberon with exquisite taste and a quiet sense of the dramatic.
She respected Austin's opinion, though she collected only things from
the twentieth century, and she was delighted when he pressed her to
explain how she'd restored a painting, refinished a split-straw table
top by Jean-Michel Franck or mended the white calf-skin wall panel.
Her convent education and her very old, strict father had made her
yearn, when she was an adolescent, to meet foreigners and bohemi-
ans and anyone connected, however peripherally, to the arts; at the
same time, her considerable fortune and her name were privileges
she was preserving, in a near-custodial fashion, for her children. She
could laugh at her stuffier friends, but she always invited them back,
though she mixed the dukes and the financiers in with pretty
actresses, famous writers, even an American. Austin had been stung
when he overheard an old aristocrat, who was deaf and speaking
louder than he thought, say to someone, "I'll never understand why
Marie-France invites her suppliers to the house."

"Your Julien is delicious," she said now. "Please bring him around
as often as you can. My friend Hélène adored him and wants him to
advise her on her winter garden—please warn him that she's in hot
pursuit of free advice."

Sometimes Julien and Austin would wander through the narrow
streets of the Marais during the endlessly prolonged June twilight.
They'd go through the Jewish Quarter and often they'd eat at Jo Gold-
enberg's, a deli up front and a restaurant behind, full of cozy booths
and paintings of rabbis and of old women in babushkas. Violinists ser-
enaded each table in turn and a gypsy told fortunes. For Austin it was
like a distorted dream version of a New York deli—it took him a second to realize that *cascher* was the French word for "kosher."

As they ate their kasha and derma, Julien said, "I thought it over.

You must understand, I'd never met someone before who was sero-positive. For me it wasn't part of real life."

"Not even in Ethiopia?"

"Well, I suppose there are lots of cases there, but I think it's other parts of Africa, Black Africa—"

"The Ethiopians aren't black?"

Julien smiled with a smile so superior it was pitying. "Don't let *them* ever hear you say that. No, they think they're an ancient tribe, close to the Pharaohs, the Pharaonic Egyptians, and they look down on their black neighbors. It's true the Ethiopian elite is rather light-skinned, the men plump and often balding, their features quite small and regular, the women truly beautiful. Of course the Ethiopians *pretend* they're black when they think they can get some political mileage out of it. It's a clever, sophisticated nation—only in Addis Ababa do *all* the Western powers keep embassies."

He talked on and on about Ethiopia, while Austin waited for him to come back to their love and its future. Austin was soothed by this absurd reprieve and Julien, essentially a kind-hearted man, seemed happy, too, to avoid what he must have prepared to say.

But finally a densely packed poppy-seed cake, heavy as an ingot, was served as though it were a black curse in a fairy tale, and they both fell silent after Julien's pell-mell speech on the subject of Ethiopian pride.

"You said you'd thought it all over?" Austin prompted, determined to make it easy for this tactful young man.

"You must understand that I was thunderstruck when you told me about yourself. I'd never thought about it, I'd never met any-one . . ." Perhaps he saw from Austin's look of vulnerability that to insist on the singularity of Austin's condition only made it sound more monstrous. He ran out of energy and once again was caught in a brief moment of stasis, like a gymnast who has twisted and turned in every direction on a sawhorse and then balances upside-down on his hands for a second, before choreographing a military-sharp descent to the floor.

But now Austin couldn't help him out anymore. He couldn't be expected to fabricate his own walking papers.

"In any event, I realized you could—you *will*—become ill and it's a long illness . . ."

Austin felt he was being lectured at by an aunt or the Episcopalian minister back home about the ghastly consequences of his excesses, and his thoughts emigrated inward. He was caught out not paying attention when he heard Julien saying, "Anyway, I've decided I'm going to stay with you. I'll take care of you."

"You shouldn't be too hasty—" Austin protested.

But Julien interrupted and said, "No, that's what I've decided. I can't imagine leaving you. I'm already too hooked on you." Austin felt a warmth spreading through his whole body, as though he'd rushed naked through snow into a sauna.

Chapter Seven

Austin had dinner with Henry McVay at least once a week. The ritual was always the same. The butler, Michel, would answer the downstairs door and show Austin up. He'd say, "*Bonsoir*, Monsieur Smith," which he pronounced "*Smeet.*" They'd run into each other once in a gay bar and had a long chat and after that, one or two times, Michel had said, "*Bonsoir*, Ostend," and even peeled off his right glove to shake Austin's hand. But since the friendship didn't really take, Michel soon enough went back to calling him "Monsieur Smeet." Not that Austin didn't admire the powerful hands that barely fit into the gloves or the strong arm that could be detected through the white uniform sleeve when he bent forward to serve at dinner.

Henry liked his guests to arrive at precisely seven forty-five. That would give them a full hour to eat pretzels, passed in elegant silver bowls by Michel, and to drink a bottle of champagne from a crystal flute for the guests and a normal glass for Henry, who didn't like glasses with stems. Henry would invariably sit under a portrait of his grandmother by Sargent in which she had just turned, as though answering a startling call, toward the viewer, her cheeks flushed but the rest of her face white, two strawberries surfacing in a bowl of cream. Her hair was swept up simply from her narrow, surprisingly contemporary face. Henry had her pale blue eyes and a small, almost prim mouth like hers.

He didn't like to talk about his "things," his furniture and paintings and his irreplaceable collection of snuff boxes and other *bibelots*, all scattered in profusion on the old marquetry. Or rather, Henry's natural pride as a collector and his desire to confide all the juicy details of his skill in obtaining a treasure conflicted with his equally strong reserve as a gentleman. If some heavy-breathing New York dealer with a nipped-in waist and wide silk tie asked too many questions ("Tell me, Hank, where did you find this adorable miniature bronze Bacchus?"), Henry would roll his eyes toward Austin and say, "Oh, it was just something my grandmother gave me for my twenty-first birthday."

"The grandmother in the Boldini?"

"You mean the Sargent. No."

Henry was a rich man who had been kicked out of some of the best prep schools and two second-rate Ivy League universities for bad behavior and who'd arrived in Paris at the end of the war as everything the French wanted an American to be—handsome, wealthy, French-speaking and humbled before the monument of French culture. "You know, I met Gertrude Stein almost immediately," he'd say, "and I remember I thought, 'The old cow has been here forty years and she *still* has that frightful American accent!' And here I am, all these years later, and I'm no better than she. I live in an entirely French world—you're virtually my only English-speaking friend—and I'm completely comfortable in French though I'd never dare write anything in it other than a personal letter unless I had a friend go over it, but even though I now sometimes forget a word in English and have to look it up in a French-English dictionary—"

"Me, too!" Austin exclaimed.

"But I *still* have this weird accent. I even took a course in phonetics—all to no avail."

"But no one," Austin said, "has a problem understanding you. And that's what counts. Look at poor Yves Montand who tried to play in movies in America, but no one could understand him, though his English was otherwise very fluent."

Henry nodded, smiled, said, "More bubbly?" He called champagne "bubbly" or "champers" and it wasn't too clear whether those were words natural to his class and age or whether he was making a humorous allusion to old, dotty dowagers he'd known as a boy, so Austin always laughed just a bit in acknowledgment of a possibly witty allusion. There was just a fifteen-year age difference between them and Austin would gallantly say, "People our age—" but Henry would always interrupt him and drawl, "You're *hardly* my age, Sweetie."

"Of course your accent in English is equally bizarre," Austin offered.

"Bizarre!" Henry thundered. "How do you mean, bizarre? I speak like a normal American guy—"

"From the Philadelphia Main Line circa 1935, possibly."

"It's true I don't have your elegant Tidewater drawl."

"Do I really drawl? I thought only when I was drunk." They liked exchanging these mild, amicable insults, which only proved the efficiency and the elasticity of their friendship, trial signals sent out to test the lines. Austin was regarded as the father by his other friends, all of whom were younger. To them he was the source of favors and approval, occasionally of information. Only with Henry could he play the good student, eager to work his professor for hints and anecdotes. Or the favorite son, invited out by Dad to dinner in a good, old-fashioned restaurant.

A grand silence descended over them. Austin always feared boring Henry, especially since Henry was interested in such a narrow range of topics—gallery gossip (change of personnel and important upcoming sales, but no prices, please, unless it was a mythic sum), gay scandals (but no sexually explicit details, please), movies—and the past, the past, everything about Henry's own past, the occasional clarification Austin might be able to shed on Peggy's last Italian lover, the sports-car racer, or details about the secret queer life of a certain steel tycoon, though more often the past figured in Henry's anecdotes, recounted at length in response to Austin's persistent questioning. Maybe it was because he was an art historian, as fascinated by general truths as by minute iconographic details, but Austin could never hear enough about the people Henry had known, including all those he'd entertained at his historic house in Normandy in the 1960s, the Cecil Beatons and Garbos and Rothschilds.

Henry was always immaculately turned out in his tailored suits. But he was terminally bored. He went through his days systematically, with dignity and attention to detail, but it was never in doubt how tedious he found everything. His highest praise was "distracting" or "entertaining." "It's a wonderful evening, that film," he'd say. "Most entertaining. I found it marvelously distracting." He had a lover but no one had ever met him. If Austin went into the kitchen to make himself a drink, he'd see the lover's plate set for dinner and the prepared meal in the pot, ready to be heated up, but Austin knew nothing about him except that he was terminally shy, a discouraged painter, in his mid-forties.

Henry could become fussed, but only when the gay butler accused the straight chef of stealing, padding his bills, double-ordering meat and fruit so that he'd have extras to take home to his own family. The chef, a prima donna who'd worked at a two-star restaurant in the Perigord, refused to help Michel clean the silver or run the sweeper; he would do nothing but cook, but unfortunately there was precious little of that. "He'd be delighted if I had eight people to dinner every night. Then he could strut his stuff. He'd like nothing better. But I hate eating at home. I like going to restaurants—it's more gay and you never know whom you might run into."

Right now Henry looked so bored that Austin said in the isn't-this-exciting tones of a kindergarten teacher, "Well, my dear, I'm going to meet the wife tomorrow."

"What!" Henry exclaimed, miming shock. "Are you *mad?*"

"Possibly, but Julien absolutely insists."

"I hope it doesn't turn out to be a cat fight."

"Oh, I think she must know how to behave. Her father's a diplomat of sorts. And she *loves* old furniture. I told Julien indignantly that I'm not exactly a *bergère*, though I am slightly *bombé*," he said in allusion to his tummy.

Having mimed laughing, rocking forward and throwing his hands up, then slapping his knees, Henry screamed, "No!" He mimed stifling a laugh with one hand pressed over his mouth and eyes and with the other he blindly groped for Austin's knee and slapped it, too, for good measure. "Stop it!" he shouted. "It's too killingly funny." Mentally, Austin overheard a dim echo of Peggy Guggenheim, who'd been much more imperturbable, but who'd always greeted a shocking story with the routinely thrilled words (phrased as a schoolgirl interrogative), "Really? Truly? No! That's *most* amusing."

"Aren't you *afraid* of her?" Henry asked, suddenly soberly.

"Yes, a bit," Austin conceded. "I keep feeling I've stolen her husband away from her and that she'll never forgive me."

The next day they met at the Bistro de l'Alma, just around the corner from the Théâtre des Champs-Élysées; Austin had chosen it as a point midway between his apartment on the Île Saint-Louis and Julien's office at La Défense. Julien was already there in a booth with his wife, the two of them smiling. They stood for the introductions. Austin said, "It's fantastic to meet you at last. Julien's said so much about you."

What he'd neglected to say was that she would be dressed in a short black leather jacket, the motorcycle kind that the French call *"un Perfecto"* and that has snapped-down epaulettes, a fitted waist and a belt with a chrome buckle. Her hair was dyed a bright magenta and chopped off to expose her nape; her lips were painted a fire-engine red. Her unexpected punky look threw him off; all the comments he'd prepared suddenly seemed hopelessly conventional. So he said, "You lived in London for a while, didn't you?" because at least her *Perfecto* would look more normal in London than in Paris, where there was no youth culture and girls wore pearls under their printed silk scarves.

"Yes, did Julien tell you that?" she asked in French, delighted—or was she wary?

"You can speak to each other in English," Julien threw in proudly, though Austin knew he'd have been furious if they'd actually excluded him by speaking anything other than French. "Christine," he added, still proud, "was the girlfriend of the lead singer in The Quick." Austin assumed The Quick must be or have been an English band. If he admitted he'd never heard of it, they'd ascribe his ignorance to age, whereas at no time in his life had he ever known the names of pop groups; his unfamiliarity with The Quick might also "rumple" (*froisser*) Christine, as the French said, as though he was suggesting her one brush with fame hadn't been so close after all.

"But you speak lots of languages," Austin continued in French, "even certain languages of Africa, no?" In fact, Julien had said more than once, the *five* languages of Ethiopia, but since Austin didn't want to seem to be verifying Julien's word by turning to Christine, he left his remark vague and a question.

Christine nodded and said, "My father works for the World Health Organization, so I grew up all over the world. For instance, I spent my teenage years in Rome and Italian, I guess, is my best language after French." She had a well-brought-up young lady's way of deferring (and flirting) with him, the Interesting Older Man and Foreigner, but every once in a while she appeared to remember her *Perfecto*, her slutty make-up and Bad-Girl dyed hair, and she'd thrust her chin out and pucker her mouth into an expression halfway between a snarl and a moue.

But they were all three, he realized, caught between two roles or more. He, Austin, wanted to win Christine over but not collude with her against Julien. For his part, Julien was half-proprietary about Christine's skills as a linguist and intellectual, but on the other hand he was introducing to her his fascinating older lover who, if he wasn't fascinating, would have no appeal at all, since he wasn't rich or famous or handsome.

After they ordered, Julien told a joke about four nuns trying to get past St. Peter into heaven, a long story that dealt with holy water and various body parts. When he'd finished ("The fourth nun shoved the third aside and said, 'Before she sticks her cunt into the holy water I've got to gargle'"), Julien laughed enough for all of them. His big booming laugh rang out, which made Christine only smile complacently, since she was obviously used to it. "Now you tell a story, Austin," Julien said.

"I can't think of any."

"You used to have such great stories," Julien complained. Austin pinched off a little smile; he'd never told anyone a joke in his life. He was totally confused. What did these young people want, from him or from each other? Apparently they really were getting divorced, although Julien had said they still spent many evenings together—nights, too, he suspected. When Julien talked about Christine he complained bitterly of her *"petit-bourgeois"* family and of her tendency to put on weight. They'd pass an obese woman on the street and Julien would say, "There's Christine in five years." But obviously he wanted to keep her friendship and even arrange for her to shine in public.

Maybe, Austin thought, he expects me to help publish or publicize her books on those Italian soldiers under Mussolini who stayed on in "Abyssinia." If Christine was published, would Julien feel less responsible for her future? And would he then continue to be just as interested in me? Of course, as Austin knew, he had no power, no influence and not even any contacts in French publishing.

Austin accordingly brought the subject around to her thesis. She said that she had interviewed nearly fifty of the remaining soldiers, all very old men, who'd stayed on, usually for the black girls. "With their tiny soldier's pension they can live—not *well* but they can *survive* in Ethiopia, and they often live with young, pretty girls. They say about themselves they're '*sanded* in,' the way we might say someone was '*snowed* in.' *Insabbiati* in Italian; *ensablés* in French."

She talked about how many of the men had left wives behind in Italy, some of whom were living. "One old guy was sick and wanted to go back to his wife in Ancona and be nursed by her, but she wrote him a bitter letter saying, 'Where you have summered, there you must winter.'" Austin nodded and repeated the words, as he would have done after one of his Virginia aunts told him a mildly funny story.

They chattered on about one thing or another. Christine had a way of lingering over her words—especially Austin's name, which she pronounced with an impeccable American accent—as though she was afraid he wouldn't understand otherwise. The effect was, however, slightly menacing. Was she drawing out what she said in order to expose, or at least suggest, the threat to him it might contain? She cocked her head to one side and squinted when he said something, almost as if she were facing the evening sun; he didn't know whether she was frowning or whether, like a German, she felt no need to produce little social smiles. She'd delivered a talk on Ethiopia at the

National Center for Scientific Research; perhaps her frown was a way of indicating that as an intellectual she took nothing in without skepticism. She had to analyze everything before she assimilated it.

After he'd paid the bill Austin remembered he knew a rich woman nearby, up towards Passy, who had some extraordinary Coptic art—or was it Nestorian?—from Ethiopia, hanging in her hallway (in the *salon* she had several Renaissance Italian masterpieces). Austin promised to arrange a visit—probably just a drink. He also said he'd get an editor he knew at Gallimard to read Christine's thesis. In truth, the "editor" he knew was an ex-trick of Little Julien's, and he was not working at Gallimard but at Grasset.

Suddenly they were all on the sidewalk saying goodbye. Christine kissed Austin on the cheek but not Julien, an omission that probably indicated unreflecting intimacy between Julien and her rather than an intentional rebuff. She'd left a trace of her scarlet lipstick on Austin's cheek and she rubbed it off with the back of her hand.

They all laughed suddenly as though admitting to one another how sophisticated they were, and how easy it had turned out to be. But as Austin walked away he thought, Yes, but it's not over. Will she be angry if she has to hand him over to me for good? Austin knew that he thought about Little Julien at least twice a day, and he wondered if Big Julien or Christine had similar sessions of quiet longing for each other.

Maybe not. They were so bitter. At least Big Julien railed against her all the time. That night over dinner he seemed genuinely pleased that Austin had found her attractive and intelligent, but a second later, as though he were discussing someone completely different, he said, "You know I never really mourned my mother's death until now. I was finishing architecture school, and then I went to Ethiopia to teach, then we married, and years have gone by, I never let myself feel anything, but now—" He ran his hand over his face.

"Now?"

"Maybe it's because all that's come to an end and my marriage is collapsing, but now, suddenly, I miss not Christine but my mother. You know, we were everything to each other, my mother and I. I sometimes wondered why we didn't have more friends, my family, but we had each other. My mother, my father, my brother and me. We did everything together. My father had a boat on Belle-Île and we'd go to Brittany, to the Morbihan, where my grandmother had an old, primitive house on a river—the house didn't even have electricity and you could reach it only by water. Our mother did everything so well— she changed the decoration of our house in Nancy every few months. Her cooking was superb. And of course she played . . . the classical piano. We'd go on car trips together to La Baule or Honfleur or down to the Côte d'Azur—how my mother loved the beach! She and my father would go to a nudist beach at La Baule. I remember one of her friends was walking nude down the beach one day with handcuffs around her wrist and the other half around her husband's penis and scrotum."

Austin had to remind himself that Julien's parents were his age and, like him, pure products of the 1960s. "Did your parents walk around the house nude?"

"Oh, yes, of course!" Julien exclaimed, honestly happy to be recalling something—anything at all—about his happy childhood. "Everything we did was very natural. No false modesty."

Austin's own childhood was remote, and both his parents were dead; it was difficult for him to remember that he'd ever been given over to thoughts about them. In fact, at no time had he ever taken himself so seriously as this young man did. It was part of his appeal, this gravity of Julien's, this certainty that every old score must be settled, every memorial visited, a flower placed before every fond thought. Julien was a legend in his own eyes. If Austin had been French he might have been bored by such self-centeredness, but at least half of what attracted him to Julien was that knowing him represented a total immersion into France. Austin not only had to read Julien's favorite adult comics, but he also had to learn songs such as *"Paris est une blonde"* and *"Douce France, cher pays de mon enfance."* Not that Julien ever knew the lyrics after the first line or two, but that didn't keep him from singing along with made-up nonsense lyrics. He belted every tune out vigorously in his stentorian baritone. Before, Austin had thought of France as female—as perfume, cooking, Renoir mothers in the garden, as silky underthings and fancy fashions, as the soft valley of Paris itself, lying, inviting and seductive, below the stiff male lingam of the Eiffel Tower. Or he'd thought of *his* women—the Princesse de Lamballe and Marie Antoinette—women who acted through strange alternations of piety and snobbishness, who out of faddishness received the very philosophers whose ideas would soon enough cost them their heads. Women who rejected the stern standard of magnificence from an earlier epoch for the comfort of grace and intimacy. Bluestockings. Taste makers.

In this roseate vision of a France ruled by a feminine sensibility compounded out of caprice and pleasure, men had always struck Austin as playing the duller role. Only since meeting Julien with his very male curatorial concern with women's clothes, minds and manners had Austin glimpsed the male hands straightening the corsage or clasping the pearls at the base of the swan-like neck or rotating the naked woman on her raised pedestal so that she might present the painter with a better angle. Like landscape architects in a formal French garden, men were shaping and disciplining women, torturing them into unexpected forms.

Julien wasn't terribly traditional (after all, he'd lived in Ethiopia, he was at least partially homosexual and he'd entirely rejected the Church). But he was French in his tics—his fear of drafts, to the point of changing his seat two or three times in a restaurant if need be, his knowledge of cheeses, wines, mushrooms, his old-fashioned, deliberate way of speaking—all these habits and practices seemed rooted in the soil of *"la douce France,"* a soil he so cherished that he always defended the "peasants" when they marched in Paris in protest against the tumbling protectionist barriers raised to keep out foreign livestock and produce. Julien, who'd never spent more than a summer day in the country and then usually at the sumptuous *châteaux* belonging to his friends, could still go misty-eyed once *la campagne* and *les paysans* entered into the conversation. Austin was reminded of Colette's Julie de Carneilhan and the moment when this middle-aged aristocrat who has lived a slightly sordid bohemian existence in Paris for years is awakened one morning by her country brother, the squire, who's down below her window with horses, one for her. He's come to take her back to the family *domaine* now that war has broken out. Behind all the fads and follies of Paris lies the country.

Of course Austin recognized that he was constantly applying more and more layers of mythic lacquer to his idea of Julien, but a love affair between foreigners is always as much the mutual seduction of two cultures as a meeting between two people. Julien was an exception to the normal French way of doing things (even the assumption that such a norm existed), but with every eccentricity he confirmed or revised Austin's sense of the national character. If Julien said he liked artificial Parisian vamps, not big-toothed, tanned American gals, it was Baudelaire—the first aesthete in history who'd preferred artifice to nature—who was speaking through his lips, even if Julien had never read the essay on cosmetics. If Julien loved Paris with a young man's conviction that it would confer wealth and glory on him, he was echoing (at least to Austin's ears) Balzac's Lucien de Rubempré. And in Julien's constant pronouncements on the merits of this orange juicer design over that one, this Andrée Putman chair over that one by the thoroughly American Charles Eames, he was only indulging in the national pastime of judging—of feeling required and *licensed* to judge—everything from a mantelpiece to morality. If he was unsmiling and grave in talking about "design" (the French invoked the English word) he was shockingly irresponsible and unconcerned in discussing ethical questions. "Why *not* rape the child?—she's probably begging for it," he'd say of the latest Belgian atrocity, arousing Austin to genuine fury. Austin had a Kantian (and probably American) certainty that he was a universal legislator of morals; Julien knew perfectly well that the positions he took would affect no one and so should at least be "amusing." Maybe that was the reason *amusant* was the French word that sounded the most supercilious and disgusting to American ears.

He took Julien into the bedroom, which he'd prepared carefully. They sat on the edge of the bed and smoked some of the marijuana that Austin had mailed himself the last time he was in Florida in an ordinary business envelope without a return address. After Julien had come, he flopped back on the bed and said, "I never experienced anything like that before." He swallowed. He was staring at the ceiling. One nerveless hand briefly rumpled Austin's hair. "What about you?"

"It was great for me, too."

"But don't you want to come?"

"Not now. Maybe later."

But Austin hadn't enjoyed it so much. He knew exactly what Julien had experienced. And he did like having Julien so completely in his power. Nor could Julien worry that their sex hadn't been safe.

"I never knew—I'm amazed," Julien muttered as he stretched and Austin covered him with a sheet and a light blanket. Austin went into the bathroom, undressed, jerked off, washed up, stopped off in the kitchen for a glass of milk, then stumbled back to bed, consumed by the objective melancholy of the sadist.

Austin was able to garner for Christine a serious reader's report at Grasset's and a polite, encouraging rejection. When he sent the evaluation along he asked in his note if he could read the manuscript.

"I *told* her she had to make it less academic!" Julien exclaimed. "Should you be wasting your time reading it? I doubt if you'll find it interesting."

"I'd be surprised if she'd care what a furniture historian thought about Italians in Algiers—I mean, in Abyssinia. . . ."

"No, of course she'd like your opinion," Julien said, unaware of Austin's irony and the nuances of self-deprecation. "After all, you're the only professional writer she knows, even if your field is somewhat different."

Julien had just come from work, still in coat and tie, his face drained from twelve hours at the drafting table. The three-day spell of hot weather had been swept away by the coarse, scratchy broom of wind, wetness and cold that had descended on them overnight. Austin had always been alive to the appeal of the young male office worker in a starched white shirt with the sleeves rolled up to reveal muscular arms, the silk tie at half-mast, the top button pushed open by clamorous chest hairs that need to escape, the smell of effort breaking through the fading decency of a deodorant. Perhaps because Julien was so slender, the plastron of his shirt falling straight down from his breastbone like a plumb line, perhaps because he was so poor (Austin now knew he earned just two thousand dollars a month, got meal tickets from work for lunch and wore the green linen jacket every day because that was all he had), these vulnerabilities, physical and material, made all his posing just that much more touching.

Despite the strange, extenuating details—an intellectual for a wife, another man, much older, for a husband—Julien was still the Latin male, not the shoulder-rolling Italian model but the French version, elegant and refined, though masterly nevertheless. Austin loved the way Julien, exasperated on the telephone, raked his hand through his straight black hair, raised his eyebrows above disabused eyes, drained cheeks and a chin of resurgent black whiskers, and then scolded his brother or Christine. Austin admired the way this man spoke in such a low, resonant voice that it shook his entire frame whenever Austin held him in his arms, as though the life force was boiling water that made the whole kettle throb.

Austin registered, with some relief, that their new sex games never got translated in Julien's mind into anything psychological. It didn't occur to Julien to want to be Austin's slave. Not even during the drama of the moment did Julien ever roll Magdalen-bright eyes up at Austin. No, all he was relishing were the new sensations pouring through his body. His egotism was so sturdy, so carapace-hard, that he was incapable of imagining that his status, his own sacred status, could fall. When he looked at himself in the mirror during sex it was with intense fascination and only after he'd come did it occur to some responsible part of his mind to notice that Austin was still dressed and to wonder if he had felt any pleasure.

Austin's pleasures were all performative—the sort he imagined a straight stud must feel when he's racked a woman with yet another orgasm; he walked away with much fingernail-buffing vanity at having provoked such ecstasy and gratitude. Perhaps because Julien himself had always been encouraging Christine to flutter up to higher and higher sexual perches, he'd never stopped to wonder whether his own body was capable of the same buoyancy. Now that he knew it was, he, too, was grateful. He followed Austin's movements with big, adoring eyes, though the adoration wasn't pathological. It was frank, the same kind of admiration one athlete might feel for another.

Julien and Christine had fucked at least once a day since they'd met; sex was the one uncomplicated thing they'd retained from that first night in the bush beside the stalled jeep, the one thing that had weathered all their fierce arguments and their present hostile truce.

Austin just knew that in his place his other gay men friends from the States would feel compelled at this juncture to ask, "Well, are you and Christine *still* doing it? Now?" He suspected they were, and since that possibility excited rather than alarmed him, he didn't want to spoil something good by making Julien choose between them. He didn't want to force Julien's hand—what if the poor guy really was heterosexual? Anyway, most likely he and Christine would reconcile and break up at least half a dozen times more. There was no way to speed up the cycle.

Austin knew he'd be a lot less understanding if he was consumed by passion for Julien.

He wondered when the divorce was going to take place. Hadn't Julien said, "in a month," when he'd first met Austin?

And *why* were they getting divorced? Julien said she'd disfigured herself by gaining weight, but in fact she was slim and sexy. Anyway, wasn't *weight* a pretty frivolous reason to like or dislike someone? Austin was close to fat, but Julien reassured him by saying, "*Mais, Petit,* you're perfect like that. You're the way a man your age should look. I don't want a starved little queen."

Julien said they'd been happy in Ethiopia until she'd returned to France and her *petit-bourgeois* family, but her father was a distinguished diplomat now stationed in the Ivory Coast and Christine could be considered an intellectual or even an ex-punk—anything but a greedy, conservative, lower-middle-class prig.

One day Austin convinced Julien to call in sick and to join him in a limousine hired by *Vogue* and drive to the Normandy coast. *Vogue* wanted Austin to do a thousand words on Yves Saint-Laurent's new *dacha* at Deauville, designed by Jacques Grange.

Austin was more than used to the luxuries France could provide, though he enjoyed none of them at home, but he was delighted by Julien's obvious enthusiasm. His very way of sitting in the car, resting his chin on the back of his hand to afford passersby the best view of his profile, attested to how he reveled in the momentary glamor of the car.

"I hope you don't mind that I dragged you away, but I need your expertise as an architect. I can look at a building and see nothing. Just tell me everything you notice, even what seems to you laughably self-evident." The sky had clouded over. They had to squint and even when they weren't looking up they were aware of the deliberate progression of these big gray rollers turning over their heads, as though they and the other people around all these buildings below were inked type and the clouds moving paper. The coast had been fairly well spoiled by massive vacation apartments built block after block right up to the water line. Neon, billboards, fast-food places selling mussels, gas stations—and then, suddenly, a word from the chauffeur into the intercom and the gates to the estate were opening. "Over there," Austin said, "is Saint-Laurent's house, the Proust House I think he calls it, and out there is the landing strip where Pierre Bergé lands his helicopter, but we're heading over to those birch trees and the *dacha*. It's just been finished." Austin raised his eyebrows and laughed: "*Vogue* has an exclusive. . . ."

The *dacha* looked authentic from the outside, a wood house raised on stilts, with brightly painted shutters, set at the edge of a stand of trees, but inside it was a charming hodgepodge of stained-glass windows from Morocco, low settees from Edwardian America, stag's antlers on the wall, a white porcelain corner stove from Sweden and, scattered on every table surface, hundreds of framed turn-of-the-century photographs of Slavic aristocrats sporting Vandykes, monocles and gold-epauletted white uniforms or slender girls with long hair and unplucked eyebrows in long, gauzy summer dresses. Austin held his little tape recorder up to Julien as they walked around the *dacha* and he recorded everything Julien said. Later he made Julien pose in his shirt sleeves on the front porch. But Julien wouldn't smile or look directly at the camera. Someone must have told him that direct regard and a grin were unbecoming. Plebeian, perhaps.

On the way back Julien spoke for the first time in his halting English. Austin suspected it was to impress the driver. Although the sky directly above was still roiling with gray clouds, the low, early evening sun had an unimpeded access to every passing object—a medieval, honey-colored, time-pitted church porch, a 1940s shop front, pedestrians escorted by their own long shadows, a warmly glowing farm-house.

For a while Julien spoke of his mother, her way of treating Julien and his brother Robert when they were teenagers as though they were already adult men and she was an older sister, ready to laugh at their misadventures and to wink when their grandparents lectured them. "My brother," he said, "was a tall, slender boy who dieted fre-quently, never took the sun and wore black turtlenecks to frame his pale face. He wore a curious, long-waisted coat from England with dark brown velvet trim. He'd worked out a peculiar, gliding way of walking. His hair he brushed three hundred times a day and groomed with Yardley's lavender-scented brilliantine. He hated our father and refused to speak to him. He called him a *Philistine.*"

"I thought you said the four of you were so happy." A village glided past, looking in the warm, late light as though it were leaning slightly toward them, awake and shining for a Sunday snapshot. The driver, it turned out, was a Pole in his fifties who liked classical music and had tuned in a plangent Beethoven violin sonata.

"When we kids were younger, everything was ideal, but my brother infuriated my father when he became so . . . *styled.* I suppose he was already sleeping with adult men. I myself received a love letter from a man, but I'd never even smiled at him, he'd just become obsessed with me. Our parents read the letter, which for some reason sounded as though I'd actually slept with the man. Our father was furious. I promised my father I'd never done anything like that and he was eager to believe me. I was his favorite. He took me flying with him. He and three other men owned a two-seater plane together and he liked to scare me, dip and show me all the sights of Nancy and the countryside. He was born in a village in the Franche-Comté."

"Did you sleep with your brother?"

"No, he liked men, not boys. He never talked about it, one way or the other. He was very sweet to me—he's three years older. My big brother. But I was always a good student, being some years at the very top of my class, and Robert was never any good at school. He couldn't do math—"

"—Me, either," Austin blurted out, but he saw right away that he'd been foolish to suggest there were parallels between the tale of Julien's family and the accidents of his much more ordinary life—an American life, what's more, and therefore a bit comic and folkloric, in any event too far off the map to be as eternal as the Lives of France. The countryside had now lost its glow and was turning blue and shadowy.

"He was disastrous as a student, he wouldn't play sports, he refused to speak to our father, he glided around with his strange gait almost as though he were ice skating. One day our father lashed out at him, hit him with his fist between his shoulder blades. But Robert never said anything and the next day he was gone."

"Where did he go?"

"Our grandmother paid for him to go to a cooking school, a pastry school, in Saint-Paul de Vence. He was just sixteen. That's when he met Fabrice, his lover. They're still together, years and years later. But he didn't much like cooking. Then he worked in a men's clothes store in Cannes. At last he was able to indulge his taste for designer clothes, including hats and scarves."

Day after day Julien told Austin the story of his family. Sometimes there were new details about another subject such as the guys at work or the time in Ethiopia, but Julien never pursued them with the same zeal he lavished on his family chronicle. Austin wondered if he weren't a little bit in love with Julien; how else could he concentrate on all these stories? He heard about Julien's father's mother, a widow who lived with her daughter, Julien's aunt, a maiden lady who never said she was going to the toilet but rather, "I'm going somewhere" (*Je vais quelque part*). She and her mother wore navy blue to Mass every Sunday and would inspect each other for a full ten minutes before leaving the house, checking for lint and collecting it with a sticky roller.

Austin heard, again and again, about the two-seater plane, the boat on Belle-Île, the holiday that one time in Alicante—and especially, endlessly, painfully, about his mother's suicide on Belle-Île. Once when Austin said he was going to go on a strenuous diet, Julien said, "Don't, *Petit*, you're perfect as you are. Diets frighten me. Our mother was on a long diet, a fast, really, when she disappeared." The French used the word *disappeared* for "died" or "passed away." "You can become severely depressed if you diet." He thought about it, about her. "The poor woman. She thought if only she was a bit more beautiful our father would come back to her. But she was perfect, exquisite already."

Austin liked this new way Julien had, now that he'd started to talk about Robert, of saying "our mother," "our father." Maybe he sounded just a bit less isolated.

One day an old friend of Peter's named Herb Coy, an American who lived in a houseboat and worked as a secretary to a rich, prolific but unpublished writer, called to ask if he could make a short film about Austin. It was just a twenty-minute black-and-white film, a silent, which he needed to hand in as his Master's thesis. Austin agreed.

In one scene Herb, seated in a wheelchair and holding a camera, was pulled by a friend backwards as Austin walked, in a long "tracking" shot, toward him and along the back of Notre-Dame and its massive flying buttresses that looked like the scaffolding surrounding a rocket that would fall away during blast-off.

Austin, pretending he was alone and carefree, suddenly lit up with amateurish, overdone excitement. A second later he was pounding on the back a young, handsome Julien, dressed in a suit. Julien wasn't feeling well that day and had had to be talked into acting. They smiled at each other. The wheelchair was jerkily pivoted, the camera swooped and dipped and then settled down long enough to show the hammy Austin, chattering away, walking off toward the Île Saint-Louis with the modest, beaming Julien.

When Herb was about to reload the camera he realized the used film had unspooled in the magazine and been exposed to light when it was unloaded. He feared the film might be destroyed.

Chapter Eight

They went to Nancy for a weekend but they stayed in a hotel and never met Julien's paternal grandmother, much less his father. They walked all over the beautiful small city and again it wasn't the history of the Dukes of Lorraine they pursued, not even the sites sacred to the École de Nancy, the local Art-Nouveau movement propounded by Émile Gallé, Louis Majorelle, Victor Prouvé and the glassmaker Daum. They had almost no time for the Place Stanislas, a public square laid out like a chessboard and one of the most perfect ensembles of buildings from the eighteenth century, nor could they even visit the famous Gothic church of the Cordeliers. No, they had to see all the various apartments Julien's family owned or had ever owned, the studio here, the two-room on the fourth floor rear there. They had to walk through the big verdant nineteenth-century park with its formal statues to public figures and see the very steps where Julien had kissed his first girlfriend.

"By the way, when did you sleep with your first woman?" Austin asked.

"Girl or woman?"

Unprepared for the distinction, Austin blurted, "Both. Tell me about both."

"The first girl was Clémence, the one I kissed here." They both looked up at the step leading to the fountain as though they might see the scene replayed if they stared hard enough.

"How old were you?"

Julien shrugged, then turned toward Austin, frowning either from the sun or impatience. "Twelve?"

"And the first woman?"

They sat down on the step, as though they'd already forgotten about Clémence. "Her name was Monique and she was our mother's best friend. Even as a very little boy I admired her intensely. I always had to be near her. I played on her lap. She showed me all of her playing cards, sewing things. We never spoke out loud but whispered in each other's ear. That was our little game—whispering in each other's ear. And then when I was fourteen I became friendly with her son Étienne. I was always going over, asking after Étienne, although I guess I hoped I'd find Monique alone. She wore white linen trimmed in red and blue and drove an American station wagon and had an old-fashioned dog, a collie. There was something of the 1940s about her. Inside her house she even had indirect lighting. Well, I finally found her alone and almost immediately I was kissing her and then she was pulling me into her. It was less romantic than it had been with Clémence, maybe because she needed me and knew it. She wasn't fooling herself. We kept whispering into each other's ear—it was our only way of communicating."

If Austin asked for erotic details Julien merely smiled right through him as though he'd just gone both deaf and partially blind. Austin remembered that heterosexual men sometimes had a quaint "gentlemanly" reserve about appearing caddish. They preferred their private pleasures—and the immunity in which to pursue them—to any gross advertisement of their conquests. Of course only a few men had such scruples, but they were precisely those who deemed themselves and one another of the better sort.

"What happened to end it?" Austin asked. They were eating lunch under an awning at the entrance to the Place Stanislas; Austin suspected that Julien both feared and hoped he'd be recognized by a school chum or a relative. A city of just one hundred thousand, Austin thought, must be unbearably stifling. Back in America he'd wondered why French novelists and poets, decade after decade, had railed against the *bourgeoisie*. Surely the middle class wasn't all that oppressive, he'd thought, and weren't the artists themselves from middle-class families? But once he'd moved to France he'd discovered that, first, the word *bourgeoisie* did not refer to the middle class, not in the American sense, but to the very rich, the people who could and might buy their way into the aristocracy, and that this class was much more static and self-satisfied and exclusive than its American counterpart. With his usual vagueness Julien never explained how or why his affair with Monique had come to an end. Probably he'd hurt her and that wasn't something he'd want to tell another lover, who was also much older and just as vulnerable.

"Why can't I meet your grandmother?" Austin asked.

"No, I don't want anyone to know we're here. You don't understand about French families. It's all very . . . complicated."

As they walked one more time through the center of town, Austin asked, "Has your family been here for long?"

"Centuries. On both sides."

"Were they merchants?"

Julien frowned. "Many different things. One thing's certain—I couldn't join the Knights of Malta; to do that you need to have at least sixteen relatives who are aristocrats."

Austin thought he should look Julien's family up in the social register, but he recognized he was too lazy. He was too lazy to pursue any interest, truth be told, and he'd learned to sneer at his American infatuation with titles. As a boy he'd daydreamed endlessly about someday discovering his mother or father was descended from Huguenot nobility, but since his university years he'd sublimated this fantasy into a concrete study of the French families for whom the greatest furniture had been made. He knew that half the current French titles had been invented. "Was your family noble?"

"Minor nobility. *La petite noblesse*. See that church tower over there?" He pointed to a Gothic belfry. "My ancestors paid for it to be built, but the part of the story that always interested me was the architect's fate. The tower started to settle and—see?—it tilts slightly. It tilted the first time the bells were rung. The architect committed suicide, though as it turned out the tower has never had another mishap in several centuries."

On the train back to Paris Austin suddenly became impatient with all the mystery and, after Julien had drunk half a bottle of red wine, decided to clear up at least one thing. He said, "I must know why you're getting divorced."

"Christine is so *petit-bourgeois*—"

"So you've said. But in what way?"

"She was fine in Ethiopia, but once she was sucked back into the gravitational pull of her greedy parents—"

"Greedy? What do you mean by greedy?"

"They were the ones who thought she should be the co-owner of my apartment."

"What apartment?"

Julien blinked, perhaps for once astonished by his own secretiveness. "Why, do you mean you don't know that I have an apartment of my own?"

"Where you live with Christine?"

"I don't live with her anymore. My grandmother bought me my own apartment in Montreuil."

"Where?"

"It's a working-class neighborhood; it's actually an independent community, not part of Paris. They have a famous flea market where they sell a shoe without its mate, old magazines, lighters that don't work, that sort of thing, though they do have—"

"But Julien, you mean you bought this apartment when you were still happily married and you didn't want Christine's name on the—" He didn't know the French word for *deed*.

Julien withdrew into an offended silence. As their train hurtled along past a village apparently devoid of inhabitants, Austin drew a breath and queried his own vexation. He rather admired his style in defending Christine's rights when to do so was against his own interests. No, he didn't *have* an interest, since he would never inherit anything from Julien, nor did he want to. He wanted for nothing, he'd probably be dead in two or three years—or in a year, if he was less lucky. Yet even if he had been negative and in perfect health, even if he'd been younger than Julien and likely to outlive him, he'd never want to enter into one of those grotesque French family squabbles over an inheritance.

His mind slid away from the painful subject of the future. He had no future, which meant that he couldn't fully immerse himself in the present. He'd signed a contract to write *the* book on eighteenth-century French furniture, in which six long, heavily illustrated essays were meant to be followed by entries on each of the principal furniture-makers of the period, the *maîtres ébénistes*, though few had worked in ebony. But he couldn't bring himself to write the book, even though he'd long since spent the sizable advance. He knew that some people were galvanized by the prospect of an imminent AIDS death, but he'd become even lazier and more disorganized than previously. He couldn't even convince himself that he was the only man for the job; there were at least three other "experts" who were as qualified as he. Nor would such a book sell many copies, since the great French furniture of the eighteenth century was already in museums all over the world and investors needn't bother with it. Riesener desks could hardly be considered "collectible."

As a peace offering he pawed Julien's leg. They sometimes did that: held their fingers pressed together and slightly curved and then touched the other's leg or body gently, clumsily as a dog might seeking attention. Austin pawed Julien just once, humbly, but Julien broke into a smile, though he refused to look at Austin. Finally Julien voiced in a rush all the things he'd been thinking: "You don't understand. It was my grandmother's money. After the way my father pushed our mother to kill herself and now he enjoys her apartment on Belle-Île and the house in Nancy—why should my grandmother give anything to that *garce?*"

"Christine? Well, you're not committing suicide. She's your wife."

"But we're getting divorced. I supported her the whole time she was working on her thesis. We have no children. I owe her nothing."

"But if you'd put everything fifty-fifty in both your names, maybe you'd still be married."

"Things don't work that way in France. In America everything is the married couple, but in France it's the . . . dynast."

"Dynasty?"

"Many wives sign prenuptial agreements renouncing all interest in the husband's property."

Suddenly Austin was bored by the discussion. He didn't want to fill his mind with questions of succession over which he'd have no control. He'd always been generous in love; he still paid Peter's rent and bought him clothes and sent him a few hundred dollars every month. He couldn't imagine letting a marriage turn sour over whose names were on a deed. He lost respect for Julien—or rather he told himself never to count on him for anything. Then again, when he made an effort to understand, he conceded that a member of an old French family could hardly be expected to have a devil-may-care attitude to something sacred like property. Aristocrats didn't usually *earn* money anyway; the most they could do was preserve, hand down and improve property. He suddenly felt that the American entrepreneurial spirit was more manly, "bigger," as his mother used to say.

A few days after their return to Paris Austin had a chance to see two aristocrats in action. He introduced Julien to Vladimir d'Urbino. Vladimir's grandmother had lived in a twelve-room apartment on the Avenue Victor Hugo that looked down on an immense reservoir in which the Eiffel Tower was reflected at night. It was rent-controlled under a law that had been passed just after the war, and she paid less than the going rate for a studio. The only problem was that she'd died two years earlier, but Vladimir kept her "disappearance" a secret and paid the rent every month with a money order in her name. Most of the time he himself lived in Geneva or in the house he'd built at Évian on Lake Léman.

Vladimir had changed nothing in the Paris apartment. It remained an embalmed specimen of pre-war taste—rickety side tables decorated with sentimental panels of rosy-cheeked shepherds courting pale shepherdesses, frayed beige silk oriental rugs, paintings of Paris street urchins by Bastien-Lepage framed in heavy gilt and suspended on dusty ribbons from the cornice, a *chaise longue* upholstered in blue silk that was soiled and worn at the arms, a white marble fireplace soot-yellowed by a century of updrafts. The apartment smelled of face powder and unemptied garbage.

Vladimir was only thirty but Austin had already known him for more than a decade. They'd met in Venice where Vladimir (the son of a Serbian princess and an Italian baron) was just emerging out of adolescence.

He was tall, well-made, slender, and his green eyes, glowing above his slightly crooked nose, looked out at you with intimacy and impertinence. His lips were a light coral and tipped down at one end, as if they'd been torn when he was a child and skillfully mended, and his tenor voice had a slight nasal quality, which Austin later realized was the true sound of the French nobility.

Three years after Austin met him in Venice, Vladimir was living in New York for sixteen months in order to perfect his English and, more importantly, to frequent Studio 54, since the years were 1978 and '9 and he was under twenty-five, too handsome and slender to suit New York tastes until he opened his mouth and revealed he was a foreigner, a prince or something, possibly Russian—at which point he could do no wrong. That he liked women and seemed flattered by the attentions of other men doubled his popularity. Austin remembered seeing him once at someone's house on Washington Mews and a lady beside Austin asked, "Who *is* that young man entering the room like a prince in a Turgenev novel?"

Austin had known Vladimir in Venice, New York and now Paris.

Vladimir and Julien hit it off immediately. They were the same age and they seemed to have the same romantic notions, as though they'd read the same Frederick Uhlman novel about boyhood friendship. They liked the same vulgar jokes about "pussies" and "cocks," a bawdy taste that alternated with a twilit respect for art, the afterlife and good manners. They liked the same tacky music of the early 1980s, especially the songs of Princess Stephanie, they automatically dismissed any major film from Hollywood as a vulgar crowd-pleaser, and as adolescents they had each kept vague, poetic journals in which they nursed unnamed sorrows. They both went for long walks alone.

It wasn't a mutual sexual attraction, of that Austin felt certain. Perhaps their peculiar mix of values was so seldom encountered nowadays that what drew them to each other was the simple reassurance they weren't alone. They were cultured, rarefied aristocrats but not effeminate; they were sexually ambiguous but by no means about to clarify the mystery they'd created; they could laugh cruelly at what they considered petty, but they weren't cruel; they were as refined in bawdiness as in their elegiac dreaminess; but only they knew exactly where to put the accent according to a private scansion they alone could hear or work out. Of course they didn't discover this complexity, even congruity, right away, but by the end of their first encounter Julien was almost completely under Vladimir's spell. Julien had been impressed right away by Vladimir's mixture of elaborate attentiveness and a certain breeziness. *Arrivistes*, Julien said, could be mannerly and servile or brisk and rude; only a *gentleman* (he used the English word) knew how to indicate he was conceding none of his proud independence by showering his guests with constant acts of kindness.

Nothing much happened during that first meeting on the Avenue Victor Hugo beyond Vladimir's lengthy (really *too* lengthy) explanations about his current career impasse. Austin didn't pay much attention and he was certain that Julien was too busy absorbing everything from the oddly pastoral view of the Eiffel Tower beyond the reservoir to the sheen on Vladimir's old, hand-made shoes to listen to what he was actually saying. Not that Julien would have objected to Vladimir's self-absorption.

As they were leaving Vladimir's, Austin said, "You know, I should introduce Joséphine to Vladimir. They'd make a beautiful couple."

"Joséphine? Why her? She's terribly common."

"But she's not at all. I once introduced her at the Opéra Comique as the Princess Radziwill and everyone believed the imposture."

"No one, *mon pauvre petit*, who was an aristocrat himself would believe she was anything other than what she is, the daughter of schoolteachers. Anyway, family background is absurdly unimportant in itself, but Joséphine . . . she's sweet. But she's not exactly the most stimulating conversationalist. Nor is she so beautiful. She has that strong jaw and those wide, paranoid eyes."

"If people talk about her the way you do," Austin said, vexed, "she has good reason to be paranoid. I think she's beautiful, kind and entirely natural."

The next afternoon Austin called Joséphine. They talked for a while about their friends. Then Austin said, "I think I've found some-one perfect for you. He's an Italian aristocrat but he speaks French as well as you do, and you're from Tours. He's only a year or two older than you, tall, slender, funny when he's not going on and on about his investments. Then he can be rather decorously dull. Why don't you come to Geneva with us at the end of the month and meet him?"

"Is he gay?" Joséphine asked.

"Of course not. I *said* he was dull." They laughed and Austin went on. "I met him ten years ago when he was just a boy and he was already in love with Diana, a Venetian woman I know who heads up a foundation, and then I knew him in New York where—no, he's defi-nitely not gay."

"You have the worst gaydar," Joséphine said, using the new word from America she'd already learned from Gregg. It meant "gay radar." She pronounced it "guy-dah." She said, brightly, "The odd thing is that Gregg will be in Geneva that same weekend. He has a Spanish boyfriend, José, who's teaching aerobics there."

Austin phoned Vladimir in Geneva, who seemed happy to receive them all, but Austin insisted they'd be staying at a hotel, where he'd already made a reservation. Austin said, "My friend Julien was delighted to meet you. I don't think he's responded so enthusiastically to any of my other friends. He found you so—do you know the word *dashing* in English?"

"*Darling?*"

"That, too," Austin laughed. "Yes, you are darling. Now, listen, I'm coming with a beautiful blond girl from Tours, she lives in Paris, her name is Joséphine. . . ."

"I'll be delighted to encounter any of your friends, darling Austin," Vladimir said in English. Austin wasn't sure that Vladimir had regis-tered she was coming in order to meet him, or that Austin was offer-ing her as a serious candidate for his hand.

No matter. Better he should think it was his own idea. And given his present financial difficulties, perhaps he couldn't afford to choose a beautiful, appealing but poor woman for love alone.

They took the train from Paris to Geneva where a festival, "Say It With Flowers," had festooned every balcony and doorway and bus shelter with roses and attracted thousands of people to a city which otherwise struck them as an empty, dead expanse of banks—in fact, the flowers, already beginning to rot, seemed like arrangements piled high on up-ended coffins. Holidaymakers, quiet and strangely unexcited, were gliding tranquilly in boats across the lake, as though they were painted in a canvas by Böcklin, Hitler's favorite painter. "The Isle of the Dead," wasn't that the name of that foggy, kitschy work?

After their lunch in a restaurant in the city center, Joséphine said she was very impressed by Vladimir. But she said, "Are you *positive* he's not gay? He's so refined, so charming, even elegantly dull."

"Dull!" Julien thundered. Then he twisted his mouth to one side sarcastically, "I suppose you *would* find him dull. . . ."

"I don't *know* him, Julien," Joséphine wailed. "I was only repeating what Austin said. Why do you attack everything I say?"

"I'm surprised, that's all, that you find one of the most refined men in Europe to be *dull.*"

"Anyway," Joséphine said, confused, "I like him. It was Austin who said he's dull. I like him very much. . . ."

They had dinner that night at an Alsatian restaurant. Joséphine invited Gregg (and José if he was free) to drop by the restaurant around nine-thirty or ten for dessert. During the meal Joséphine felt slightly nauseous from the smell of the cooking sauerkraut and of the canned Sterno heat under their platter of meat and sauerkraut. Vladimir showed her such consideration in ordering the food to be whisked away (which Austin was sad to see disappear before thoroughly consumed) that soon Julien was also imitating his courtliness. "Yes, yes," he said, "Alsatian food is much too heavy for this season. Anyway, as Byron said, a woman should never eat anything in public but lobster and champagne."

"*Really?*" Joséphine asked, astonished.

"He meant a lady," Julien said, lapsing back into rudeness.

"Then he must have had you in mind," Vladimir added, smiling at her with his gentle, teasing smile. Soon Julien and Vladimir were competing to shower Joséphine with the choicest compliments, attentions which only made her more suspicious and paranoid than usual.

At that point Gregg and José came wheeling up on bicycles. They were wearing sweatshirts with stretched-out neck-holes and cut-off sleeves over flimsy, shiny basketball T-shirts. They were in black Lycra biking pants molded to their powerful thighs and wore fluorescent green bracelets and anklets. They had on baseball hats turned back-wards, the bills curving down over their tanned, sweaty necks. Gregg displayed his usual, shoulder-rolling, gum-chewing arrogance; his eyes were hooded and a satirical smile was playing over his beautifully carved mouth. José was much shorter, darker, younger and stared out at the world through two huge black eyes like bullet holes singed into his face under a shiny cloche of black hair. They didn't touch each other, Gregg and José; they didn't even look at each other; but they shifted their weight from foot to foot almost in rhythm, unconsciously echoing and accommodating each other's movements as though they were colts in the same herd.

Vladimir had turned pale. He said, with an intensity focused on Joséphine, "I hope you'll forgive me, but I've taken some sort of malaise and I must be up by seven tomorrow morning." He stood, took her hand and said, "Julien will tell us we're not supposed to kiss a lady's hand in public, but maybe he—and *you!*—will forgive me if I take this precious liberty." He even brushed her hand with his lips, which wasn't done, and waved vaguely at the others and stumbled off into the night.

Jose whispered something to Gregg, who then burst out laughing.

"What? What is it?" Joséphine demanded, fairly spooked by now.

"You guys crack me up," Gregg said.

"How?" Austin asked.

"Well," Gregg continued, sitting down, shaking his head, thrusting his gym shoes out into the aisle so that the white-aproned, black-vested waiters had to step over them, "well, José says that your friend is a little crazy."

"Fou comment?" Julien asked, already offended. "Crazy in what way?"

Gregg laughed and literally slapped his knee. "What's his name?

Vladimir d'Urbino? The count of Urbino? Well, José knows him very well—"

"You *do?*" Joséphine asked.

"Yes," José said, "he paid me to sleep with him."

"Sleep!" Gregg snorted. "Is that the word you're searching for? You told me you had to pee on him. He'd sit in the bathtub and—"

"No details!" Joséphine said. Then she turned to Austin, "So *this* is your famous heterosexual fiancé you hand-picked for me!"

Julien was so irritated with everyone that he stormed off alone and walked half the night before he came back to the hotel silent, cold and grim. Austin pretended to be asleep.

A week later, back in Paris, Julien arrived late at a dinner party. When he'd come in, Julien had whispered to Austin, "It's donc. I'm divorced."

"What!"

"I had to spend the whole afternoon at court. In six months it will be finalized. We don't even need to go back there."

"Where is it?" Austin asked with wild irrelevance.

"The Île de la Cité. Everyone gets divorced there. It was very easy. Christine and I had worked everything out in advance. I paid the court costs."

"Did you go out with her afterwards for a drink?"

"A drink? No. Why?"

"Do you feel all right? Should we just slip away now?"

"I would never do that to Henry. He organized everything, didn't he?"

"As you wish. . . ."

Their murmured exchange had already attracted curious glances and smiles of complicity; Julien broke away and made his rounds. He refused to kiss the proffered cheeks and merely shook hands. He looked startled, even a bit hunted, when Henry patted the empty space on the couch beside him. Austin couldn't help noticing the contrast between all of these sleek, rested, satisfied middle-aged men and this exhausted young man in his creased green linen blazer, with his oily, inflamed forehead and his dark, sunken eyes.

A bald man in his seventies named Bébé drew Julien down beside him. For an instant Julien, smiling out of embarrassment, half-resisted, but Bébé was stronger than he, at least for the moment, and Julien, clowning, made a big show of losing his balance and falling onto the couch.

"Hmnn," Bébé said, "so here's the married man. And do you really like to travel both by sail and steam?" (*à voile et à vapeur*), which was the French way of referring to bisexuality.

Austin said, "He just got divorced. In six months it will be final."

"Oh, Austin," Bébé exclaimed, "what a heavy responsibility for you! What's the English expression: *home-wrecker?*"

"Except we don't say that to our friends," Austin reminded him, smiling.

"And does your wife know she's been abandoned for a *man*?" Bébé had no eyebrows to arch, but his voice performed the job nicely for him.

"Very warm day today, isn't it?" Julien said drolly.

"Very?—Oh, you sly devil! *Quel diable malicieux.* No, that's not fair. We want the full story: Was your wife *au courant* about your steam side?"

"She's a very sophisticated woman."

Austin could see Julien was becoming cross and hastened to add, "Christine and I know each other and like each other. She's a fine writer and ethnologist."

"*Ethnologue!*" Bébé chortled. "And have we queers become *une ethnie* now? *Une tribu?*"

"It's true," Horace, an old poet, interjected, slurring his speech, "we do wear rings through our nipples now—"

"And eyebrows!" Henry called out.

"And foreskins!" Bébé added. "Why are they called 'Prince Albert,' Austin? Is that why Queen Victoria mourned the prince's memory for decades?" Bebe narrowed his eyes and pursed his lips flirtatiously, as he leaned toward Austin. Then he swiveled back and returned his attention to Julien. "Do *you* have such a ring in your foreskin?"

"*Very* hot today," Austin interjected. Everyone laughed uncomfortably.

By the time they'd all adjourned to the bistro on the corner Julien had retreated into a stormy silence, which no one but Austin noticed, but during their walk home to the Île Saint-Louis the silence was maintained. They walked through the Place Dauphine, where a few stragglers were still seated at outdoor tables sipping their coffee while their tired-looking waiters glowered at them, wishing them away.

"That's where I was this afternoon," Julien said in a small voice, sketching a feeble gesture in the direction of the massive, white, late-nineteenth-century Palais de Justice, which formed an ugly side to this otherwise sober triangle of residences and awninged cafés.

"Was it very depressing?" Austin asked.

"Depressing? No. Why? No, the only depressing thing was that I had to pay the court costs."

"But no alimony? No settlement? The apartment still belongs to you?"

"Of course! Why do I owe her anything? I supported her for many years while she worked on her thesis. She was so lazy. I was the one who made her work. I drove her to work—but I'll never do that again. I think I damaged our marriage. That's why I never get after you to write *your* furniture encyclopedia. But—"

"Yes?"

"Nothing."

Austin was touched that Julien had made such an easy link between him and Christine, even if it was to scold him. That must mean Julien thought he'd exchanged Christine for Austin. Between two men, Austin believed, no union could ever be a matter of course. Everything had to be invented, reimagined—unless one of those two men had Julien's sort of background and confidence. Julien wasn't harried by the homosexual's lurking fear of offending society, of being denounced or mocked or excluded or ever so gently chided—or, worse, "pitied" by well-meaning Christians who'd decided to love the sinner while castigating the sin. Or, still worse, "accepted" by liberals on a politically correct field trip in search of new, previously over-looked minorities. Only in upper-class French life had Austin found the exact shade of inclusion he had craved for. Maybe it was natural in a society where a king had been surrounded by cute boys, his *mignons*, and in which the brother of Louis XIV, *"Monsieur,"* had maintained an all-male shadow court. Or maybe acceptance was characteristic of a class that made a shared randiness—which was rigorously sealed off from all outsiders—a sign of its coherence and exclusivity. Whenever Austin had to go out to dinner with a *Vogue* or *Architectural Digest* editor from the States, he had to remember to censor his dirty stories and suppress the casual sexual banter he was accustomed to, though the same talk had long been his passport into the exalted circles of France that these very Americans craved to crash. Or thought they did. The bawdy tone of French aristocrats would undoubtedly have shocked them.

Julien believed he shared nothing with other gay men. In fact he rejected all group identity—as an architect, as a Frenchman, even as a minor aristocrat. His independence of spirit, however, was something Austin ascribed to his status as a privileged French man. Julien was a romantic individualist, whereas Austin was an amateur sociologist. Julien thought he'd invented himself, whereas Austin saw him as simply an unusual recombination of herd traits.

Austin gave Julien a glass of red wine once they were back at the apartment on the Île Saint-Louis. He rubbed Julien's shoulders; though he disliked them for being hairy, he loved this man. Austin was convinced that his own squeamishness about hairy shoulders was something puritanical and body-hating that persisted in him. The randy, big-hearted, life-embracing men he admired in books and movies would have kissed every follicle, tongued every black pore; only a stinting *petite nature* like his own would object to this sign that the beloved wasn't an eternal boy.

The night was cool, even foggy on their island, and Austin held Julien in his arms. He could feel Julien's heart beating in his chest and when he stroked his face in the dark there was the nail-file rasp of his beard and there, shockingly, the hot slipperiness of his mouth (he was sucking Austin's little finger). The pulse in the long, lean neck, the intermittent warm streams of breath on Austin's left shoulder, the moth-like brush of his fluttering eyelids—here was this vulnerable life in his hands, as mysterious as was his own. Austin strove to like himself, but the very familiarity of his habits of mind, the perfect-attendance pin his eternal physical presence had won, revolted him or, worse, bored him so much he was repelled.

In spite of himself Austin farted, whispered, *"Pardon,"* and Julien murmured drowsily, *"Petit . . ."* with a thoroughly indulgent tone of reproach. Later, they both seemed to wake up. Their embrace turned sexual.

Chapter Nine

In August Austin rented an apartment in Venice, one that was so many stories high that even though it was on the Grand Canal it was relatively quiet. Julien had never been to Venice, but he said he was sure it would be *"majestueux,"* and he was delighted to be going, if only for a week.

Although Austin and Julien spent almost every night together, they hadn't said, "I love you," nor talked about their future. All along Austin had felt he couldn't exact (or express) any promises until Julien's divorce had gone through. Perhaps if he'd been more insecure, or more desperately in love, Austin would have demanded reassurances.

Austin had accepted a position teaching the history of European furniture at the New England School of Fine Arts in Providence, Rhode Island, a job that was due to begin next January, just five months off, but he hadn't asked Julien yet to accompany him to the States, even though Julien knew Austin was leaving Paris. Julien's English was very approximate. Would he want to trade in his sure-fire job with a big Paris architectural firm for something vague in Boston or Providence? Would he need a work permit? A visa? And what about Julien's HIV status? What if he turned out to be positive? Weren't people who were known to be positive denied entry to the United States?

Austin had also invited Peter, his old lover, to fly from New York to Venice. Peter and Austin had been to Venice many times before in the previous decade and Austin hoped it would cheer him up. Venice suited Peter with its quiet strolls in back streets, its vegetable stalls under tents baking in the August sun like an African village hastily thrown up in a square bordered by settling, tilting palaces and the unseen but overheard lapping of out-of-sight canals. Hordes of tourists shouted and shoved into one another around San Marco and the Rialto, but San Trovaso and Santa Margherita and a dozen other back-water *piazzi* were so quiet and empty that sometimes the only sound was of two old women lazily talking together as they strolled home for lunch with their shopping carts rattling along behind them, one wheel in need of oil.

Peter wasn't working, his health was deteriorating and his mother told Austin that his prospects of living more than a year were dim. Though apparently he was rather frail he could still get about. He clung to his status as someone who had ARC, an AIDS-related condition, not AIDS, although that distinction was now dismissed by scientists as meaningless. He had only 103 T-cells and it was an anomaly that he hadn't already come down with a major opportunistic disease. Austin knew Peter was taking a risk by flying to Europe and back (long flights were supposed to be bad for the immune system) but he had to give Peter a treat. Peter wasn't a realistic, hard-headed sort of guy anyway. He lived for treats, surprises, parties, sprees, even miracles.

Austin loved him and wanted to be with him. Many of their friends, especially women, accused Austin of loving Peter like a son. That was a comprehensible relationship, father-son, and given their age difference it put a respectable gloss on a visual disparity that if it were simply sexual might have seemed indecent. But Austin wasn't clear and convinced enough about his own experience to assume the paternal role. Unlike a straight man of forty-nine, his own children hadn't ratcheted him year after year another notch toward death.

Austin didn't like ordering anyone around, or teaching anyone, and without an appetite for authority where lay the interest in being a father? If he were a genetic father of a real son, at least he'd enjoy the

benefits of being a recognizable player, but no one except a few indulgent friends were prepared to take their hats off to an aging queer and
his thirty-something ex–toy boy. Real fathers must feel a steadying,
nurturing pleasure in instructing, correcting, guiding their offspring,
but such a pleasure started with being certain about what constitutes
good and bad, about which values to inculcate. Austin didn't like traditional values (or thought he didn't).

Anyway, when Peter and he were together they were both kids,
not even venturesome teens but timorous tots, little kids unconsciously
holding hands as they stumbled toward the unknown. They assumed
nursery voices with each other, reassured each other in a fantastic but
pleasant way, baby-talked in an embarrassed parody of their very real
affection. True, Austin was the one who had always worked and supported Peter—maybe that was the only kind of paternity that society
could grasp: the economic.

Peter flew into Milan from New York, then changed planes for
Venice. He even took the boat all alone from the airport to San Marco,
but perhaps because he was frail and tired and a bit less eagle-eyed,
someone knocked into him as everyone was surging off the *vaporetto*
onto the pontoon landing—and stole his wallet. He found the empty
wallet twenty feet farther along with his passport and credit cards
inside but plucked clean of his money.

Not that he had much. Through planning and sacrifice Peter had
managed to accumulate three hundred dollars—"getting-around-town
money," he called it.

He looked taller and older. As he stood in the repeating volleys
of tourists who were following their flag-wielding leaders, his hair
gleamed white in the bright midday sunlight. His eyes shone a paler
blue as though the sea were now flowing faster and shallower over
whiter sand. Even his hand felt bony and breakable when Austin
clasped it.

"I can't believe the bastard—*all* my money—I *know* which one he
was, too." Peter's eyes filled with tears and a few vaguely curious
passersby stared for a second at a rising drama, their sympathy almost
stirred.

"Don't worry, Pete," Austin said, "I'm loaded."

"It's just so *damn* frustrating. If you only knew how for weeks and weeks I rationed myself to just one beer at the bar when I went out, saving, saving, or how I never had anyone over for dinner or went to a movie, just so I'd have a little getting-around-town money and not be a complete burden to you."

Austin hugged him and felt the delicate ribs and exposed backbone jutting their way through his clothes. "Poor Pete, don't worry." He grabbed his bag and scooped him onto the local *vaporetto* that would deposit them in front of their *palazzo* on the other side of the Grand Canal. They stood on the central deck as the boat zigzagged up the canal from side to side (the Salute, the Giglio, the Accademia . . .) and passengers pressed around them at every stop, leaving or entering the *vaporetto*. Peter looked more and more frightened and angry, as though these hostile foreigners might steal his suitcase next.

"You're just tired, Pete. That's a wicked flight." Austin had put on his baby-talking voice.

"Actually, it wasn't bad," Peter said in a grown-up, matter-of-fact way. "I slept a little and the movie was some sentimental thing that made me cry. I don't understand why I cry all the time now."

Austin knew not to ask him the name of the film; Peter forgot so many things these days, which bothered him, since he'd always been proud of his grasp of pop culture, as though he'd been preparing himself for the ultimate trivia quiz. He wasn't like Austin, who'd sacrificed his knowledge of the twentieth century to his mastery of the seventeenth and eighteenth and who, by living cross-culturally, was never expected by his compatriots to know much about recent American crazes, nor by the French to recognize the names of their pop singers or movie stars. The funny thing was that Austin could recall the very name of the court ballet Louis XIV had danced in when he was twelve (the first time he'd dressed up as the Sun King), but he'd never knowingly heard any house music or techno or whatever they were calling it.

When Austin got Peter down the alleyway at the bottom of an architectural chasm six stories deep and just three feet wide, and through the surprisingly grandiose door of their palace and into the elevator just big enough for two passengers, then down the windowless corridor upstairs and into the ultra-modern apartment with its woven brown leather and chrome chairs, then and only then did Peter begin to relax. He opened the windows giving onto the Grand Canal and peered out with a fragile invalid's hesitant, carefully dosed curiosity at the plash and play of gondolas floating four abreast while an aging, wobbly-voiced tenor sang *"O Sole Mio"* into a microphone for Japanese tourists.

From this high window he could see half a dozen churches and the very top of the Campanile as well as a few of the lacy spikes bristling along the domes of San Marco. The mysterious topography of Venice, typified by street signs that pointed both to right *and* to left for the path to the Rialto or to San Marco, suddenly looked decipherable from this height.

Peter turned back from the window, a thin, very thin silhouette pressed like a tall, unlit candle against the Venetian sky, Tiepolo blue with fleecy Bellini clouds. "You look great, Pete," Austin said, hoping to sound casually convinced that nothing had changed, that he didn't even notice the twenty pounds shed since the last time they'd gotten together. His reassuring noises weren't a lie if taken to mean that a new, birdlike nobility had descended on his features, as though the victim, before he was sacrificed to the gods, had to be encased in an avian mask.

"When is Jules—" Peter asked.

"Julien. He's arriving two days from now. In the evening. He's taking the train from Paris. It's his first time here, in Venice," Austin added, hoping to avoid the whole awkward business of having a new lover by directing his old lover's attention to some minor matter, the surprising fact that Julien had never been to Venice before.

Peter perched on the chair beside Austin. His breathing was shallow and fast and his eyes were racing here and there. With the force of a falling stone it came over Austin that they were occupying entirely different places. Austin, though positive, was still bloomingly healthy, making enough money to travel and invite his friends along, embarked on a new love affair, whereas Peter was markedly ill, frightened and disoriented by the all-night flight and the pickpocket who'd welcomed him to Venice. Possibly Peter was alarmed by Austin's busy life in Paris, crowded more and more with men and women he didn't know.

Austin had a present, even a future, whereas Peter had only a past in which Austin bulked large.

While Peter slept Austin hurried out to the Rialto and bought fruits, vegetables and a white, flat fish with tiny, lusterless eyes, as though they were just pale photosensory pores rather than proper image-isolating eyes. In the backed-up bilge of August, everyone moved slowly through the viscous heat. The greengrocers under the Rialto open-air market, which was held aloft by squat columns topped by dolphin capitals, misted their lettuce and basil with a garden hose, but even so everything looked parched. Someday August would be over, the aimless, milling three-day bargain tourists would be hauled away in their buses, the real Venetians would come back from the Dolomites, the rich international gay and social population (*i settembrini*) would alight once more for the season. Once again the shopkeepers would walk briskly, sliding wood crates of produce off barges, smiling and waving at their regular customers, calling out their marvels in their husky dialect, all hollow, resonant vowels deboned of every last shaping consonant and the market would smell of shameless white truffles in rut and the poultry butcher would hold up soft brown feather puddles of tiny game birds, as though offering fistfuls of molding autumn leaves as a delicacy.

Now Austin contented himself with the albino fish, some fresh, pliant eggy tagliatelle, a bag of tomatoes and onions and a bottle of olive oil for the sauce, an overblown lettuce the color and cut of a glam-rock singer's hair *after* a three-hour concert (he smiled at his rare contemporary comparison). As he hurried home high-up shutters closed and a disembodied hand pulled a canary's cage into the cool, marble-lined fastness of a dim apartment before bolting shut curious, cut louvers, jig-sawed to fit the flame-shaped window frame. Two cats hissed and growled, squabbling over a small bundle of garbage neatly tied in a transparent blue plastic bag and dumped, all by itself, in the middle of the pavement. Shop after shop, all selling *commedia dell'arte* masks and kitschy Murano glass, filed past; metal grills were rumbling down over the display windows. The long, sweaty reign of the afternoon siesta was beginning, a time for desultory family squabbling, suffocated sex, tiring, dreamless sleep.

By six in the evening Peter had awakened, showered and shaved and was sitting up, lean and dressed-up and sipping a chemically correct martini. He'd always looked like a New England patrician but now his higher cheekbones, whiter hair, bonier shoulders and the birdlike way he cocked his head from side to side made him resemble the patriarch of a ruling clan, someone outraged by *fin de siècle* depravity or the immorality of abroad.

But in fact he was none of these things. He only looked that way. He was still a kid—the ultimate boy with his sweet seriousness and his steadily gazing concentration on the people around him. He could also be silly with his entranced enthusiasm for TV soap operas, his long, overly detailed stories of personal martyrdom, all the ways former friends or deranged relatives had done him in; it was hard to know where the hopped-up resentments manifested by the soaps stopped and his own real travails began.

Austin had cashed a few traveler's checks and stuffed Peter's wallet with a sum that matched what had been stolen. Peter got tears in his eyes and said, "You're so nice, Austin, you've always been so nice to me. My life wouldn't have been half so fun without you, and you're steady and loyal, you don't forget your old friends." They sat side by side in the wide, matching leather and chrome chairs and held hands intermittently, though they each had a certain fastidiousness about prolonged touching; Austin associated it with an unwanted display of affection even when, as now, he wanted it.

He knew Julien couldn't fathom this American puritanism, mixed as it was with American licentiousness.

They went for a stroll down the echoing pedestrian walkways that contracted into a sordid little path smelling of cat urine, then dilated into a proper *calle* lined with elegant shops selling marbleized paper, men's silk pajamas and, further on, multi-hued summer sweaters of silk and wool. A standing gondolier glided past, but neither the canal nor his barque were visible and he looked as though he were a moving target in a shooting gallery. It was a city of unchecked fancy—the doors were large or tiny, grilled or painted, the knocker a bronze fist or a Moor's turbaned head or a sword-pierced heart. No two bridges were alike, not even any two street lamps. Austin wondered if Julien was the sort of architect who thought form should follow function; if so, he'd be sure to detest Venice.

Now that the long siesta was ending the streets were reviving and even the shopkeepers' faces looked sponged clean by an oblivion that renewed all the necessary illusions. The evening tide would soon inundate the whole system of canals, even the narrowest and most remote, and the eccentrically shaped chimneys, widening as they rose, and oddly cut crenelations of the city roofline were casting their mysterious shadows across the treeless squares and sidewalks and the sealed marble wells, their polluted waters capped.

Austin bought Peter a beige silk sports jacket and a belted raincoat and three dress shirts on sale. When they emerged from the shop with its English look—the polished wood shelves, green library lamps and brass-fitted counter—they were plunged back into the true Venice, the constant murmur of a thousand muted human voices ricocheting off stone pavements and walls, of stray sunbeams irradiating a window display of colored glass trinkets and projecting rainbows, of sweating tourists in shorts, their faces baked red. Darting quickly through them were elegant locals already in evening clothes as they rushed, bejeweled and coiffed and perfumed, towards an early dinner before an opera at La Fenice, a house that had burned down so often it had a stake in its name: the Phoenix.

Austin cut short their walk when he felt Peter losing strength. As they were threading their way through the narrow chasm leading to the door of their *palazzo*, Peter bent down stiffly to stroke a puppy muzzled with a little wicker cage over its mouth and nose. His master was trailing not far behind. Peter looked like a very old general tousling the hair of a child who'd brought him flowers.

Once upstairs Austin set to work making dinner while Peter perched on the roomy windowsill, sipping a wine so pale it resembled water. He was looking down at the Canal, its noise and activity so far below they were generalized into a picturesque haze.

Peter went to his bedroom to hang up his new jacket and raincoat. He came into the kitchen, tears standing in his eyes, and said, "I'm sorry I'm being so emotional, but you offered me new clothes and that suggests you think I'm going to go on living for a while. . . ."

• • •

When Julien arrived two days later it was in the evening. He'd boarded a *vaporetto* at the streamlined Mussolini-era train station and now, as he descended the boat at the Stae stop, he was exuberant, as though the brightness dancing in his eyes and his quick, excited movements were assembled out of the lights fractured by the myriad currents and cross-currents of the flowing, sloshing Grand Canal.

He looks so young, Austin thought. Then he glanced over at Peter in a cruelly unconscious instant of comparison. Peter looked so—well, it wasn't old, exactly, but *dry,* as though Peter were the white-haired, stiff-jointed, desiccated version of this brunet young Frenchman with his full lips, rounded rump, his clear dark-blue gaze focused on some distant point of pleasure whereas Peter's washed-out blue eyes were blurred by the indistinctness of all his present woes.

Austin was so happy to be with Julien. For the first time since coming to Venice he was light-hearted.

Although Peter spoke some sort of pidgin French, he was too tired to summon it up, or maybe he'd forgotten or found it embarrassing to test out. Julien scarcely registered this linguistic problem. He was so exuberant about being in Venice that he stormed the city, rushing across bridges and plunging into the Piazza San Marco, which, if it was the drawing room of Europe, was at once more tattered and more solemnly majestic than any other *salon* one could imagine. Old-fashioned floor lamps with fringed silk shades had been dragged outdoors and lit above each of the competing string orchestras and the lights lent a slight credibility to the drawing-room idea although the guests nibbling ices and the streams of shadowy passersby sauntering along under the dim arches were dwarfed and even mocked by the enameled church domes, the great brick upthrust of the campanile, the solemn entrances and exits of the huge Moorish figures of the corner clock, the soaring columns supporting saints and a crocodile, the illuminated stonework of the Doge's Palace like patterned fabric stretched above the tent pegs of the short, squat columns and the distant moonlike glow of the neoclassical church of San Giorgio on its own island, looking on but muted, really exactly like a moon on a foggy, unhappy night.

Austin and Peter were silent, somnambulistic tourists but Julien was the excitable kind who had to share his impressions, half of which Austin translated into English more or less at random and half of which he let skip like stones across the lagoon. Peter nodded encouragingly, smiling, his head lowered and his eyes rounded—maybe he was a bit attracted to Julien, since he was being ever so slightly seductive, or maybe coquetry, after all, was his only way of showing friendliness to a man.

They ate at the little restaurant Harry's Bar had opened over on the Giudecca, *spaghetti alle vongole* and grilled *bronzino* and silver cups of raspberries in sugared lemon juice. Peter drank too much and tried to interest Julien in his unhappy childhood and lonely if glamorous school years in Florence but Julien, though kindly and well-intentioned, didn't know what he was supposed to do with all the information, which wasn't exactly urgent or even recent. Austin kept hoping that Julien would understand that Peter didn't have much to live for and that, after all, Austin would be sleeping with Julien later tonight and poor Peter would be alone.

Although they never really found a topic that first night together, Julien was a good sport and was even happy to go along for yet another drink to Haig's Bar, for if Venice was a crowded museum by day, at night it was nearly as deserted as a museum. English aristocrats and successful French decorators and rich Milanese businessmen—all the people who owned apartments here and were willing to endure the city's dullness for the sake of its chic—were laughing and talking loudly as they raced along, hoping to get to the Accademia for the midnight *vaporetto*. Most bars, the stand-up zinc-counter kind, had closed long ago, but Haig's carried heroically on into the cool hours after midnight, perhaps exempt from the usual laws by virtue of its English name. Here Julien was happy to see the last remnants of an earlier Italian era consecrated to mindless pleasure. He watched with sympathy the bored, stylish young people in rumpled evening clothes, a black tie undone and dangling like an unfinished joke, a fragile chain-mail evening bag slung carelessly from the back of a chair, thick black hair curling over a sickly forehead, the drinks—brought up on a salver in eccentric stemware—chosen for their colors: garnet, chartreuse, cloud.

Back in their rented apartment Peter was almost falling asleep standing up and crouched a bit so Austin and Julien would kiss him on the forehead, as though he were their son; then he toddled off and Julien rushed to the window for one last glimpse of a passing *vaporetto*, projecting its yellow lights in every direction as it zigzagged up the Canal.

In the evenings Julien would put lavender-scented brilliantine in his hair and tie a complicated ascot for himself out of a blue silk scarf printed with gold hunting horns. Peter lifted an eyebrow fractionally at each of Julien's efforts to emulate the Haig's heroin-and-Campari crowd, but he also seemed amused by so much boyish posing.

As the days passed, Austin and Julien became intensely romantic in their lovemaking (back in Paris sex had been rougher, even brutal). Austin's only worry when they embraced in the dim *salotto* was that Peter might surprise them en route to the bathroom or kitchen—he was sure he was feeling what parents with young children must feel, but like a young parent his desire overcame his misgivings.

Because he was a Southerner, and a Southerner whose mother had been a Virginia lady, Austin always needed to know what his friends thought of each other; any reservation someone might express he considered an insult, any criticism a betrayal. Julien had figured out how much Peter meant to Austin and made vague but approving sounds. One night, when for professional reasons Austin had to dine with the Cinis and the Montebellos, Julien and Peter ate alone at the Grappa di Uva and came back laughing and stumbling drunkenly, arm in arm.

Austin was thrilled. For weeks he'd been brooding about his new job in Providence, Rhode Island. Now he thought that he could invite Julien to live with him. Of course Peter wouldn't want to leave New York for Providence, but he might have to spend longer and longer periods of convalescence with Austin—and with Julien, if they should stay together. Maybe because Austin was a product of the unpossessive 1970s, he'd always thought gay men shouldn't pair off in little monogamous units. They should stay loyal to their old friends and lovers and take them in when necessary, not reject their former mates like heartless heterosexuals.

Anyway, Peter and Austin had promised that they'd take care of each other and now the time for honoring that pledge was speedily coming due. Austin had felt guilty about lingering on so long in Paris after Peter had gone back to live in New York, but he was comfortable with his cozy life on the Île Saint-Louis. As long as Peter was still able to go out and meet the preppie black men he liked as they stood around the piano singing show tunes at the Town House, right after work, still dressed in coat and tie, then he wouldn't really want to share the East Village studio apartment again with Austin—he wouldn't like to have his style cramped. Peter was looking for a last lover as frantically as if he was searching for a cure.

And Austin couldn't really afford to rent a second studio for himself. Besides, as long as he was based in Paris he could work regularly for several American magazines as a journalist fluent in French, but if he lived in New York would the same editors think of flying him down to do a story about a Key West Eaton Street renovation or sending him up to Litchfield to write about a neoclassic *atelier?*

Now this teaching gig had come along and Austin would be a useful but discreet distance from New York; he'd be teaching just three days a week and could devote the rest of his time to Peter, if Peter needed him.

In bed that night Julien whispered, "What do you and Peter have in common?"

"Nothing, really," Austin said, "but I've always loved him and wanted to take care of him. We lived together for so long—*that's* what we had in common, our life together."

"So being in love means you want to take care of someone? For you that's what it means?"

"Peter just wasn't made to work. He never had any ambition. When he first returned to New York with that degree from the Louvre, I got him interviews with half a dozen decorators in New York, but nothing came of it. He doesn't make a good impression. He can't really follow a conversation. He dresses far too young—he thinks he's still a kid, but he's white-haired and in his mid-thirties. Certain gay men fall for his little-boy act, but it makes straight women want to throw up, and they're the customers. They don't mind if a guy is gay so long as he's virile and smooth and intensely interested in them and even a little autocratic, but an aging sweet little boy who's self-centered and speaks in a high voice like a girl—well, that doesn't play."

Julien laughed and said, "You certainly have no illusions about him."

"But I love him. I feel bound to him. He's the witness to my life. I call him every few days from Paris. If he's sad I think of treats to cheer him up. The last time he came to Paris, it was last summer, we had lunch at the Bagatelle. We looked at all the roses and we took photos of each other beside the ponds and the weeping willows and that greenhouse where they have Chopin concerts, then we sat in the shade and ate a long, complicated lunch that was so light it left us hungry. We drank a bottle of Chassagne-Montrachet, the best white wine in the world, and we were so happy that we held hands under the table, because even if AIDS wasn't going to kill us this year or next, we knew it couldn't be far off and we were entirely happy."

Austin went on thinking about that day in the Bagatelle even as he stood naked on the cold marble floor (for they had gotten out of bed one more time to look at the Canal) and held Julien in his arms. Their room was lit only from the illuminated boats below and the unique street lamp with its three clear panes and its single pink one—the basic street furniture in Venice, like everything else, was irregular and strange. The water traffic had at last abated and most of the palaces were darkened—though soon enough low-riding barges powered with outboard motors would be bringing small dark-green melons to market, the melons the size of children's heads.

After a week, Julien took a morning train back to Paris and his job. He thanked Austin rather formally, at least with an unusual degree of politeness for someone of his generation, and Austin realized they still hadn't spoken of living together. They weren't yet a couple, nothing could be taken for granted.

Peter and Austin lingered on another five days. "You really love him, don't you, Austin?" Peter said when he saw how Austin lit up whenever Julien phoned.

"Well, I don't really know him that well, but—"

"Come on, Austin, admit it."

"Peter, I've never played my part so carefully. I just think about winning, I scarcely stop to wonder how I feel, really feel, inside."

"Well, it's obvious he adores you. He told me, that night we had dinner alone, he said he thought you were . . . what does *pour* or maybe *tour ghetto* mean?"

"*Hors ghetto.* That means I'm not a typical fag—I'm out of the ghetto, I'm non-scene, as the English say."

"Mary, you could have fooled me. Miss Girl . . ."

There was a seafood restaurant way out toward the Arsenale, a place that had been trendy a decade ago partly because it was so hard to find. As they strolled home after a charred, greasy meal of squid, they skirted the Lagoon, up bridges and down, past the church where Vivaldi, the red-haired priest, had been the composer, past the Daniell, where Byron had stayed, past the Piazzetta; when they reached Harry's Bar they went in for a last Bellini. Peter was a little drunk and said, "Austin, I don't completely trust Julien. I hope he doesn't hurt you. You say you're playing cool and fast just to win, but I think you're out of your league, just as you were outclassed by Little Julien."

"There's not a day that goes by when I don't think about Little Julien. And you know he's becoming a wonderful artist—everyone in Paris is talking about his furniture. His own apartment had six pages in *Elle Déco*—I'll show you, I kept it. I wish he'd loved me more or, failing that, I wish I could have done more to help him along in the world. I wish I'd been famous or rich—God, he was the best sex I ever had."

"Don't worry, Austin, Little Julien will come back to you. You used to be his lover and he cheated on you. Now he's Marius's lover and he'll cheat on him with you. Don't forget I slept with Marius that one time six years ago when I was dazzled by his mansion and servants and paintings, but he's not a nice guy and he's got a minuscule dick, really tiny."

"Well, mine's no great shakes. . . ."

"Compared to Marius you're a sex machine."

Peter's comments had soon raised a rather different doubt in Austin. He thought that as long as he'd been courting Julien, his gaze had been turned inward toward the thrilling, unfamiliar machinery of all these new sexual experiments. But now that they'd become more romantic, which Austin considered far more intimate and exciting, Julien might just be stifling a yawn. Or he might suddenly have become unpleasantly aware of the furry, sagging, graying body beside him.

That night in bed Austin couldn't sleep. He got up and sat naked in the window and looked down at the commotion on the Grand Canal, boats traversing streaks of light like water insects trampolining the surface tension. He wondered if he was so superficial, even now, as he was approaching fifty (as he was approaching death!), that he didn't know what he really wanted. Little Julien had been confused when they were together; he was still dating girls or at least flirting with them and saying he wanted to get married. Now he was living happily—or at least openly—with Marius; of course when Marius traveled to India or Egypt he always invited along two or three women, possibly as a cover.

Big Julien was different—less self-sufficient, more vulnerable. He was suffering over his divorce and a decade ago he'd been cruelly disoriented by his mother's suicide. The divorce was bringing back all that old pain. Maybe Julien associated women with pain now. He was grateful to Austin for cooking him dinner, listening to the long, maniacally detailed stories of his past, laughing at his jokes, even if his humor was more malice and Rabelaisian excess than wit. Considering he was more a practicing bisexual than Little Julien, whose attraction to women seemed mainly theoretical, Big Julien was much less confused. He knew what he wanted: Austin. He loved Austin and called him *mon chou* and *petit* and said he was the leading expert on French furniture. If Austin mentioned that he didn't have a doctorate and that his reputation in America was shaky, Big Julien would set his jaw and become angry on his behalf. "What do these Americans want? They know nothing. We French are in awe of your expertise—you must be given the Légion d'Honneur! Get Henry to recommend you; he knows Élie de Rothschild, who's an officer. It's only a matter of time. Those Americans should get down on their knees before you, kiss your feet with gratitude. . . ."

Most important, Big Julien had said he'd take care of Austin if ever he became ill. *When* he became ill, rather, since no one escaped AIDS, it seemed. Austin mustn't entertain false hopes. He must train himself to accept the inevitable. Big Julien would be a devoted nurse, he was sure, as long as it took, although he'd certainly be tyrannical as well, fussy about schedules and expenses and critical of every doctor. Austin hoped his position in Rhode Island would become permanent, even tenured; he needed the health insurance. He had to be cool-headed and prudent, although his first instinct was to kill himself, quickly, cleanly. Austin had always taken care of other people, his alcoholic father and Peter, all his young friends in Paris; he couldn't bear the prospect of depending on someone else. And for what? To grow old overnight, turn into a precocious skeleton, lose his strength, sight, mind?

After their five extra days alone, Austin put Peter on his plane to Milan and New York, then boarded the Cisalpine Express that ran through Switzerland on the way to France. He felt more and more invigorated after Chur as they ascended the snow-covered mountains and the air became thin and cold. He dismissed Peter's warnings about Big Julien; they were too transparently self-serving. Julien wouldn't reject him; Austin had become his sidekick, his only friend. Maybe he'd also become something like Julien's mother, but that wasn't something you could say. Not to anyone.

Chapter Ten

By the middle of December everything had been decided. The six-month wait for Julien's and Christine's divorce to be finalized had flowed smoothly by and she even invited Austin and Julien over to a nearly inedible dinner on December fifteenth, not exactly to celebrate but at least to solemnize the occasion. A month earlier Austin had put her in touch with a Paris-based Brazilian-born cinematographer who had obtained for her a small *bourse* from the National Center for Scientific Research, which would enable her to go with him, Carlito, to Ethiopia to make a half-hour film about the Italian soldiers who'd stayed behind in Abyssinia. Austin enjoyed helping her, as if his assistance would stave off the day when she'd denounce him for destroying her marriage.

Christine had met in Paris an Italian restaurateur from Calabria. Her second-best language, as she'd said, was Italian, since she'd lived in Rome from the age of ten to sixteen; even more important, she added, she preferred being an Italian and couldn't help remembering that Stendhal had said a Frenchman was an Italian in a bad mood. Well, she wanted to be constantly in a good mood. She liked drinking and laughing loud and dancing all night. She liked running her hands through her thick hennaed hair and wearing a top cut so high it revealed her slightly pudgy stomach and the gold chain she wore around it like a tummy anklet. She said she knew it was "naff" and she didn't care. He was short, her Italian, Angelo, just her height, but he had deep-set dark eyes that were ever so slightly crossed, which made him look mysterious, and his face was so unusual that he resembled three entirely different men depending on which angle you looked at him from. He used orange-water to wash his face every night, and the smell made her feel calm, since when she was a child her mother had always given her *fleur d'oranger* tea at bedtime.

"I went to Calabria with Angelo and stayed on this ghastly little farm with his mother."

"How did you get along with her?" Julien asked.

"She treated me exactly as one of her own children: like shit."

Julien laughed a long time.

"I'm going to have Angelo's baby," Christine said.

"Congratulations," Austin and Julien chimed in almost together.

"If it's a girl I'll call her Allegra."

"My favorite name for a girl," Austin said truthfully, though the name had a sad association—Byron's daughter, who'd died young.

For a moment Austin felt old and sterile next to this ripe young woman. He wondered if she thought that, too; that this gay couple at her table were stiff and bachelorish, sapless. He wondered whether Julien was regretting losing her. Julien, however, appeared sincerely happy, but mildly so, as though he was no longer magnetized to her fate. The only question he asked was, "When is the little girl's birth expected?"

"The little girl! *La Petite?*" Christine exclaimed, delighted, scandalized. "How typically male to assume it will be a girl. . . ." Her laugh died away and she said in her firm, emphatic way, "June. She's due in June." Christine spoke with all the pedantic clarity of a reformed stammerer, not just now, but all the time. Austin thought she'd make a very bad actress; she'd sound as though she was reading her lines with great deliberation, off a teleprompter.

"Are you sure Angelo is the father?" Julien asked.

"A hundred percent sure."

The walk back from the Bastille, where Christine was living, to the

Île Saint-Louis was barely ten minutes long. Austin said, "When I think of all the beautiful women in Paris like Joséphine who can't find a man, I'm stunned that Christine's already found her Angelo."

"She's always been surrounded by men, even when she's overweight and pasty-faced and in a foul temper."

"What's her secret?"

"She's very involving. Almost immediately she's got you sitting front row center watching her personal drama. She knows how to make you feel everything she's feeling. She's never coquettish and she's never self-pitying, the two worst female sins. And she plays her tigress sex card—she's very passionate and leaves scratch marks on your back. It's an absurd, corny act, and it works every time." He said "corny" in English, a word Austin had taught him, though its meaning was as difficult for a foreigner to grasp as *camp* or *nerd*.

Austin looked for signs that Julien wished he'd stayed with her or that he might be the future father of little Allegra, but Julien seemed entirely, almost unconsciously happy with Austin. He didn't talk about Christine or Allegra.

The next day Julien went alone to his farewell party at the architectural firm. He came back very late, toward three a.m., quite jovially drunk and full of tag-ends of stories. Bizarrely, Julien had never told his co-workers he was married until now, when at last he was getting divorced. He'd shown his new divorce certificate to everyone; one of the secretaries, who'd been courting him for the whole year he'd been there, became retrospectively jealous. Petulant, she left the party early. The draftsman he often worked with late, who was called Christopher McMahon after a Scottish grandfather though he couldn't speak more than two words of English, seemed relieved to know that Julien was— or had been—a married man. At the party they kept hugging each other, and *le Petit* McMahon, after they'd stained their teeth with Bordeaux, even kissed Julien on the lips more than once, as though he'd just been waiting for evidence of Julien's heterosexuality in order to make love to him. *Le Petit* McMahon ("Mahk-Mah-OWN" was how it came out) was married, too, of course. When Austin asked if McMahon was handsome, Julien came out with the usual consolation prize, "Not handsome, but he has a certain charm." Austin was sure that's what his French friends said about him.

Clumsy with drink, Julien pulled a big flat balloon out of a paper bag. It had been his farewell gift from his office chums. It was an inflatable sex doll, a female one, of course, with red hair (perhaps, after all, he had told them Christine was a redhead or maybe he'd just said he was drawn to them). It wasn't quite life size and it had a hole for a mouth and big startled eyes painted on (the red hair, too, was painted on). It had another hole, just one, between its legs. Julien held it up, half-inflated, and laughed his big, booming, unfunny laugh. Austin smiled weakly, but he did smile; he'd learned when he was a kid and his father had come back home from a party stumbling, laughing, then shushing himself and trying to tiptoe comically through the darkened corridors though he could scarcely walk—little Austin had learned then to come sleepily to his bedroom door with a big grin, as though joining in with Silly Daddy, though Daddy's violent way of crashing into things and the sharp oak-cask smell rising off him had been scary. The rule down South was never to be a spoilsport.

Julien had given notice to his firm six weeks earlier; he'd said he was off to New York to serve an apprenticeship with a major architect (he was not yet at liberty to say which one). He and Austin had in fact flown to New York for a lightning visit to see a pair of gay Hungarian architects in their forties who lived in Brooklyn Heights in austere penury and were revered by a handful of other young architects for the highly conceptual designs they'd submitted to international competitions. They were currently building a model that showed how they would turn the ugly nineteenth-century monument to Christopher Columbus in Genoa and its crowded square near the train station into a peaceful pedestrian island with great symbolic significance by installing three towers of different heights (allusions to the three masts of Columbus's fleet).

Over drinks Austin cut the crudest deal he'd ever concocted. He told the Hungarians, though not in so many words, that he'd write an article on their house in the Heights (virtually their only piece of "realized" work) for *Elle Déco* if they'd fill out a U.S. government form saying they needed to hire Julien in order to enter the big, lucrative architecture contests in Paris; no American would do, since only a French architect would be familiar with the thorny Parisian building codes and could write up the proposal in French. The exchange was as imaginary as any of their building projects, given that they hadn't a penny to pay Julien.

The Hungarians looked willing but frightened. They obviously needed the journalistic "exposure" in the States but as intellectuals who'd only recently left a Communist state they were wary of attracting government attention. "But you don't understand!" Austin cooed with a giant, reassuring grin. "There's no follow-up in America. Getting in the first time may be a slight problem, but once you're past Immigration no one ever looks at your documents again. After all, we're all immigrants over here." Istvan and Laszlo (now "Steve and Larry" to their forty-something gay neighbors in the Heights) nodded warily. They looked very hungry and when they left the room for a moment Austin whispered in French to Julien not to eat their hors d'oeuvres, since the chunks of Cheddar probably also constituted their dinner.

Julien was applying for a professional visa, a much more delicate affair than a three-month tourist visa, which Europeans could obtain on the plane over if they declared they had no intention of working in the States, had no criminal record, were not pregnant, Communists, homosexual or HIV-positive—and if they could prove they were solvent and had a return ticket. For a foreigner to obtain a professional visa, however, he had to convince a genuine American resident to sign a statement saying he or she would be hiring the foreigner—and that the job could not possibly be performed by an American. The safest career for an immigrating Frenchman was pastry chef, since everyone in official Washington circles apparently believed that no native-born American could make a convincing coffee-flavored *religieuse*.

Julien and Austin had been carefully coached by Austin's Paris lawyer, a French woman educated at Harvard who handled Americans' tax problems and their real-estate deals in France. Mathilde had little experience with U.S. immigration matters, however, especially those concerning a French citizen moving to the States.

Julien even found a student, his grandmother's lover's great-niece, to live in his apartment for the spring semester and cover his expenses. Julien said she had a perfect upper body but an enormous butt; she wanted to be a sports instructor and to open her own gym in Nancy; and she appeared to be in love with Julien. She even said she was studying English since she was planning to travel to New York to enroll in a high-impact aerobics course and would arrange to see him there, possibly stay with him. Whereas Austin would have panicked in the same situation, Julien liked having women fall in love with him. He thought it was normal. And he was usually flirtatious in return. Apparently a real love, the unique love, the sort he'd felt for Christine and felt now for Austin, differed in quality as well as in strength from all these other flirtations.

Austin decided to give up his Île Saint-Louis apartment. His landlady's daughter, a dynamic, warm French businesswoman his age who lived in New York, had been begging him to move out for some time. She wanted to redo the apartment entirely in travertine and with recessed lighting so that she could rent it for five thousand dollars a month instead of eight hundred. But year after year he'd persuaded her to give him another stay of execution until he finished his furniture encyclopedia. He lived surrounded by two hundred reference works, all his books on Martin varnishes, on the *bergère gondole* and the *fauteuil à dossier écusson*, the *chauffeuse* and *duchesse brisée* (a "broken duchess" wasn't a medieval martyr, just a sectional *chaise longue*). Now she was audibly relieved when he announced over the phone that he was at last moving out. The books he wasn't shipping to Providence he gave away to friends; he even had a book party where the guests could raid his shelves. His pictures came down, leaving ghostly dust frames on the white walls. All the sheets and towels and linen were his, as well as half the furniture, including a round drop-leaf table (peasant, eighteenth century, pear wood) and a few Louis-Philippe chairs he and Little Julien had re-covered with a cheeky checked fabric they'd found in London. Austin tried to be indifferent to the loss of his little hold on Paris; such indifference, after all, was appropriate to someone facing death: good training. He called a chatty moving man who'd been recommended to him. The man spoke with a voluble American accent that Austin found ridiculous and reassuring.

Austin had a farewell lunch with Joséphine. She complained of her dull life in which she had to work so hard just to survive that she had no time left to devote to the illustrated books for children that brought her such pleasure. On an impulse Austin invited her to come to Providence "for a year or two" and stay with Julien and him, rent free.

She kept asking him if it was really a serious offer. When he convinced her it was, she said she couldn't come until the following autumn—until then she was engaged to teach kindergarten (in a *maternelle*).

One night after dinner in the half-denuded apartment in which the dust had been so stirred up it made them sneeze constantly, Big Julien made him sit still in one of the Louis-Philippe chairs. He handed Austin a flat, heavy box, wrapped and beribboned. Inside was a picture frame suspended from a brass bar. The frame could be flipped so that one could see the pictures on both sides. On one side was Julien's pen-and-ink sketch of the great stone volute on the church roof across the street opposite their window; on the other was an old photograph of Julien as a seven year old with his brother, sitting in the back seat of their father's single-engine plane. In the front passenger seat was their mother, stylishly coiffed (she looked like one of the models of the late sixties with her hair chemically straightened, wrapped around her skull and lacquered in place). Their father, the pilot, was undoubtedly taking the picture. Julien was holding their wire-haired fox terrier in his lap and laughing. He looked cute and innocent. The French had taught Austin to despise innocence as nothing but an impediment to exciting adventures ("In a French novel," someone had said, "if the heroine is innocent she's debauched on the second page so the reader can move on to the good part, the scenes of *la volupté*, whereas you Americans can write a whole book about the tragic loss of innocence: what a bore!"). Nevertheless, Austin still was attracted to Julien's sparkling eyes, his frank, fearless merriment, the absence of all irony in his seven-year-old, plump, round-cheeked face.

Austin was thrilled with this gift. He and Julien had lain in bed so many nights looking at the church roof. Its inward-turning spiral seemed of more mystic significance than other symbols, such as the Crucifix or the Star of David, maybe because it was their very own emblem. He knew that Julien had taken many snapshots of it and now he understood why. "I'm a lousy draftsman," Julien said. "I've never been able to draw. I worked from the photos. But I did it for you, so you'd always have something—something portable—of the Île Saint-Louis."

"And the photo of you and your mother and brother!"

"That's a sacred picture to me, *Petit*. Do you remember that day in Nancy I left you alone for an hour?"

"Yes."

"I went to visit my mother's grave. Now I wish I'd brought you along."

Austin didn't ask why; he'd learned not to ask too many questions.

Finally Julien said, "Just to introduce you to her." He paused. "Do you believe there's . . . something after all this?"

Out of respect for Julien's feelings for his mother, Austin said, "Perhaps. How should I know. Possibly." But then he thought a while and decided he owed him the truth: "No. I'm sure there's nothing after this."

Julien swallowed and said, "Probably just as well."

They went to bed.

Austin could hear Julien breathing in the dark. He didn't move. Well, he'd said he and his family were all atheists, hadn't he?

Or had that just been braggadocio?

"I'm very moved by the drawing, *Petit*," Austin whispered. Julien smiled at the ceiling but didn't move or even open his eyes, as if he was under doctor's orders.

Because he had a wart on the head of his penis that wouldn't go away, Julien went to the Hôpital Saint-Louis, which specialized, among other things, in venereal diseases. The doctor who saw him said he wouldn't treat him unless he agreed to be tested for AIDS. He wasn't intimating that Julien seemed *likely* to be positive; it was simply that no man in Paris today with a venereal wart on the head of his penis should go untested. This logic induced Julien to do, six months later, what

Austin's physician, Dr. Aristopoulos, had failed to persuade him to
accept.

The only problem was that Julien wouldn't have the results until
four weeks had gone by, and by then they'd be in America. "It's just as
well," Austin said, "since if by some chance you should turn out to be
positive it would be better if you already had your work visa and were
living in Providence."

"But why should I be positive?"

"God knows, I'm not saying you will be." Austin paused. "But did
you never have relationships with men?"

Julien left the room. Later Austin heard the toilet flush. When
Julien reappeared he said, "I can think of two things. When I was a
child I always wanted to have a monkey. My parents said no. So I
decided to head off for Africa to be a veterinary. I was just seven or
eight—"

"The age you are in the photo of the plane?"

"Yes. And the postman found me miles from our house. He was
gentle and asked me where I was going. I said I was going to catch a
plane for Africa where I'd be a monkey doctor. He drove me home.
Anyway, twenty years later when I finally got to Ethiopia, someone
gave me a green monkey. At first I was delighted, but then it bit me—
look, you can still see the marks, here, on my hand."

"Don't they think green monkeys are the origin of AIDS?" Austin
asked dutifully, not believing for a moment that this explanation
applied to Julien.

"The only other thing I can think of is that once, in Ethiopia, I had
an infected ear and the African doctor gave me a shot of penicillin
with an old needle that he didn't even dip in alcohol."

"Why didn't you stop him?"

"It's idiotic, but I didn't want to be impolite."

"Ah, that's your *ancien régime* side," Austin said, smiling admiringly.

They worked for three days packing up their separate apartments,
paying the post office to forward their mail, giving away the electric
appliances that wouldn't work in the States without heavy, clumsy
transformers, presenting the little black-and-white television to the

Spanish maid, the set that Austin had bought to improve his French comprehension and which he'd ended up being addicted to, carting the remaining books to the *bouquiniste* on the Left Bank across from the Tour d'Argent, stuffing nine U.S. duffel bags with his scholarly books and paying one thousand dollars extra in overweight at the airport. The talkative mover came for his furniture and his trunk, which was so heavy that four men (including Austin) were needed to drag it downstairs.

They decided to leave France in mid-January so they'd have two whole weeks to settle in before Austin had to start teaching. Julien, of course, would be going out for job interviews.

They staggered onto their plane without having slept a full night's sleep in a week. Following Austin's suggestion, Julien dressed conservatively, in a dark jacket, white shirt and silver tie. "That intimidates them," Austin said. "They feel like saluting someone who looks like a gentleman. It sets you apart from all these tourists in gym clothes. Or from the homeboys." Austin had just read an alarming article in *Newsweek* about this new phenomenon, homeboys, and was ready to lecture a wide-eyed Julien: "The States is very dangerous. It's not like Paris—"

"The métro can be dangerous after midnight in the suburbs," Julien objected.

"America is dangerous *all* the time. Or can be. You never know. Homeboys are black teenage guys who wear baseball caps backwards—"

"And do breakdancing."

"Julien, I'm not joking! They wear gold chains and slinky basketball shirts and huge gym shoes untied and they travel around in their cars in gangs with sawed-off metal pipes in their hands and play the radio loud and beat white people."

Julien rubbed noses with Austin and said, *"Mon petit* homeboy." He loved it when Austin exaggerated.

At the Boston airport they were separated. Julien had to go through the line for foreigners. He was carrying his big black artist's portfolio, five feet by three, zipped up. In it were plans for all his major architectural projects. He looked very respectable, if pale. Austin, of course, had been waved through Immigration and he waited impatiently just on the other side for Julien before they went down to pick up their luggage.

To Austin's horror Julien, whose English was still very approximate, was held at the Immigration desk for many long minutes. The stony-faced guard kept typing numbers or letters into his computer and studying the screen. He then asked Julien to step aside for a moment. Julien was smiling and nodding, even bowing, but he looked deadly pale. Another man in a business suit, tall, slightly balding, thin, finally appeared and led Julien into an office. There were no windows in the office; Austin couldn't see what was going on.

Peter's sister Meg had driven over in her station wagon to meet their plane. She was going to load up the back of her car with their things and drive them the fifty or sixty miles to Providence. Austin had met her just once. He went downstairs to the baggage room and piled high two carts with the duffel bags. He didn't touch Julien's luggage, since he thought he might have to identify his bags to the authorities. Maybe they'd mixed him up with someone else, a smuggler.

Austin worried that once he went past Customs he wouldn't be allowed back into the Immigration area, but he couldn't keep Meg waiting, either; she'd see from the "Arrivals" monitor that their plane had come in on time. As soon as he went through the last doors, which swung open automatically, Austin spotted Meg, a young woman as handsome as Peter but younger, less careworn. She was entirely healthy in appearance, the sort of sporty New England girl who looks uncomfortable in heels and as embarrassed as a boy in make-up. She wasn't masculine; there was even something fawnlike about her narrow face and big gray eyes; but she would have appeared more relaxed with a hockey stick in her hands than in her camel-hair coat with a black leather handbag dangling from her forearm.

Austin said, "I don't know what's happening. They're interrogating my friend Julien. You shouldn't hang around. We can always get a taxi."

"A taxi? That will cost you a hundred dollars!"

Six hundred francs, Austin thought. "That's okay. This could go on for hours."

"I'll stay here with you for a while, at least."

Austin thanked her. Shaking all over, he told himself to stay calm. Meg guarded his two carts and nine duffel bags while he went over to a Bureau de Change and cashed three one-hundred-dollar traveler's checks. He'd need money in any event. The people who were letting him their house had mailed him a map and the keys; he'd bought their car from them, sight unseen. Once he got there he'd have the car—

But what about Julien? He suddenly saw the balding man in the business suit hurrying along and Austin rushed up to him. He explained that he was traveling with the Frenchman who was being detained. "What's wrong?"

"I'm not at liberty to say."

"Well, will he get through?"

"I can't tell you that."

"When will I know something? I left his baggage on the carousel."

"The luggage has been brought up to my office. It's safe."

"That young lady is waiting to drive us to Providence. What should I tell her?"

"She'd be best advised to leave. This could take some time."

"That means he will be coming on through in a few hours?" Austin raised his eyebrows and produced what he thought was a faint, ingratiating smile.

"No, it doesn't mean that at all. It doesn't mean anything."

"Can't you tell me what the problem is?"

"What is your relationship to the gentleman?"

"Friend."

"No, in that case no."

"Should I just wait here, then?"

"That's entirely up to you."

"Could you be so kind as to come back eventually, I mean after everything's been decided, and tell me what to expect?"

The man, who refused to return Austin's social smiles and seemed impervious to Austin's charm or even his quandary, looked at him coolly and said in French, "We'll see."

"Merci infiniment," Austin said. It seemed grotesque that two Amer-

icans in America were speaking French to each other. Did he think
that Austin was really French? Was he, this official? Why wasn't he
wearing a uniform? He looked like an Interpol agent.

Reluctantly, Meg looked at her watch after an hour and said, "I've
got to get home eventually and prepare dinner for my husband and
kid. Dick . . . you remember Dick? He took the day off to look after the
baby, but he's hopeless in the kitchen. Unless you need me?" Here she
patted his arm in a psychiatric way, at once reassuring and distant.
Austin felt sorry for her; she'd wanted to do a favor for the man who'd
lived with her brother so many years. He knew that all the sisters
had grown closer since they'd found out Peter had AIDS. Perhaps
Meg had planned to discuss Peter's health with him. She was barely
thirty and she already had to accept the imminent death of her only
brother, the only boy of the five children, this strangely unsuccessful,
unmotivated, Europeanized problem in an otherwise hardworking
American family (Meg was an award-winning kindergarten teacher
with her own weekly educational television show in the Boston
area; Alice had taken over her grandparents' pharmacy; Ellen banded
migrating birds in a Tidewater reserve; Toni was a Chicago fabric
wholesaler . . .)

But Meg's kindness, even her clearly indicated American "concern" in the way she knitted her unlined, silken brow to suggest how
she felt for him, irritated Austin; irrationally he blamed her for "America's" rejection of his lover. Austin's heart was pounding, he'd soaked
his way through his shirt and he was caught up in alternating gusts of
frenzy and lassitude. He'd start to gossip in a chummy way with Meg,
then suddenly erupt in a panic over what was happening. "What do
you think it could be?"

"Maybe there's something funny about his passport?"

"That's it!" Austin exclaimed, snapping his fingers. "Ethiopia! He
lived in Ethiopia and these Boston goons are going bananas over the
stamps—a spy! A bomb! Communism!" But then Austin immediately
regretted what he'd just said; what if Interpol had highly sensitive
directional microphones picking up everything he was saying? For
their benefit he added, just in case, "Of course I'm joking. It must be
something else."

At last Meg left. Austin was secretly relieved, because he feared that if and when Julien came out he'd be too shaken to make polite conversation with a stranger in English. Nor would he like to find Austin smiling and nodding while he, Julien, had been so anxious. More than once Julien had accused Austin of being more concerned about pleasing a stranger than loyally helping a friend—or his lover.

Eventually the sign on the big board announcing the arrival of their plane was effaced. A popcorn machine somewhere (he couldn't see it) filled the warmed air with its distinctive movie-theater smell. A family of redheads, speaking with penetrating *R*-less Boston accents, was standing next to him. They looked as though they'd been dressed by Goodwill: the mother wore a dirty gray parka with a hood lined in orange quilting. Her black stretch trousers were covered with cat hairs and her black boots had been bleached in patches by snow-melting salt. Her hair was flattened on the side where she must have slept. The older boy, dressed in a shirt stiff with dried orange juice, was coolly dribbling an imaginary basketball and, when their mother wasn't looking, quickly socking his little brother in the ribs. The little boy would start wailing each time. His face was filthy from crying and from rubbing snot over it. "Jason!" the mother shouted. Outside, through the plate-glass windows, he could see that night was falling rapidly. Car lights were pivoting as they turned through the thickening darkness and shone on the slushy road.

After two hours went by the same balding man came up to Austin and said in French, "He's being sent back on the next plane to Paris at his expense. You can talk to him for ten minutes. Come with me." The man led him and his luggage cart not through the baggage and Immigration section but by a back corridor; they had to stop three times while the man tapped a code into a lock and swiped his badge through a magnetic-band detector. At last they arrived at a higher floor and a hallway of plain metal doors and curtained windows. It seemed deserted. The only smell was of Lysol. A uniformed soldier armed with a rifle was stationed outside one door. The balding man unlocked the door and let Austin in. "I'll be back in ten minutes," he said.

"What a warm welcome America has extended," Austin said. Julien looked smaller and dirtier, his beard growing in quickly. They held hands for a moment but Julien, looking around nervously for a concealed camera, drew away.

"What went wrong?" Austin asked.

"Our stupid lawyer didn't tell us that if you apply for a professional visa you can't come in on a tourist visa while you're waiting for it to come through. You really should demand your money back from that madwoman. You like people like that, you think they're funny, but look at the mess she's gotten us into. When I was going through the line they typed in my name and saw I'd applied for a professional visa. Thanks to your advice I was all dressed up as if for a job interview with my entire portfolio under my arm. If I'd had on shorts and a Hawaiian shirt they probably would have waved me through."

"When do you go back?"

"On the very next plane. Which we have to pay for. It's the same plane we arrived on. It won't be ready till tonight."

"Can you pay with your credit card?" Austin had made him a partner on his American Express account.

"They'll accept the return ticket I already had."

"*Petit*, don't worry," Austin said. "I'll call my landlady and get my apartment back for a few days and I'll fly back to Paris in a day or two. I'll call the president of the college here and get him to put pressure on our senator to hurry up your visa. Here, take this money." He gave him the two thousand francs he still had in his wallet. "Was that man difficult?"

"He made me speak in English for hours and then only at the end did he say something in perfect French. I think maybe he *is* French. The bastard. . . ."

"Where will you go in Paris?"

"I'll stay with Christine," Julien said.

Of course he had no choice, since he'd already sublet his apartment, but the words crossed Austin's mind, *I'll lose him to his wife.* He knew she had only a double bed and her couch wasn't long enough or stable enough to sleep on. In another week Julien would be learning his HIV test results. He'd given up his job, his wife, his apartment, his country and his language—maybe even his life—to follow Austin, but it hadn't worked out. "I'll call Christine to tell her you're on your way. She should be there tomorrow morning when you arrive."

"Tomorrow?—Oh. I'm so tired. Anyway, I have my own key."

"You do? To her apartment?"

"It was also *my* apartment. She never changed the locks. Why should she?"

The man came to the door. Austin stood up. "I'll call you tomorrow when you're back in Paris."

He had to load up his nine duffel bags in a taxi. Night had fallen, even though it was only four-thirty in the afternoon. The driver was a turbaned Sikh. Austin sat huddled in a corner of the back seat, hating the Sikh and his loud voice as he shouted in his language into a radio phone. He sounded furious but from time to time, amazingly, he laughed, so apparently it was a pleasant conversation he was having with another Sikh. Austin tried to imagine the dog's dinner of dirty hair under the pomegranate-colored turban—they never cut their hair, did they? And how the hell did *he* get into the U.S. of A. with his dog's dinner hairdo and gold teeth, shouting away in his own language, when a well-dressed, well-behaved French architect was kept under armed guard and sent home over a technicality? They should never have applied for a professional visa. During all his years in France Austin had been a tourist.

They were traveling on the very dark, forest-lined highway toward Providence at just fifty-five miles an hour, which seemed unbearably slow compared to French speeds. Luckily the Sikh's telephone signal had faded. Austin told him the story. The driver said, "Yes, Immigration is a bother. But don't lose faith."

"How did you get in?"

"My wife is American."

"How did you meet her? Was she a tourist in India?" Austin imagined a blond hippy.

"It was an arranged marriage. She's Sikh, too."

The highway, which had been dug ten feet lower than the surrounding town, wound gently through the outskirts of Providence. All the houses were of wood and looked huge. Despite their size they had almost no space between them, though he could scarcely see anything, so dimly lit were the streets. Here it was, just five or six in the evening and the streets were deserted. It was much colder than in Paris. The streets had been cleared of snow, which was piled high in banks on the sidewalks. Now they'd turned off the highway and the driver was looking for someone he could ask directions from. But there was no one around. Presumably this was the downtown, but half the stores were boarded up. They went all around a three-block-long esplanade between unlit government buildings—Austin had forgotten Providence was the state capital. Someone had said Rhode Island was one of the poorest states in the union, but then again *Time* had ranked Providence as among the ten most livable cities in the country. The thought made Austin laugh ghoulishly. Finally they spotted a brightly lit chrome diner, or rather it was a take-out truck; several white teenagers were standing in front of it, blowing on their hands and stamping their feet against the cold. "We'll ask them," Austin said, but in a moment the car was surrounded by the kids, who were pounding on the roof.

"Lock the doors," the driver said.

"Go home, Towel Head." The Ayatollah had recently aroused American ire, Austin had read in the *Herald-Tribune*. When they drove off, the teens shouted, "Faggots!"

"Very nasty," the driver said.

At last a filling-station operator gave them directions and they arrived at the proper address. The house belonged to the Professor of Aesthetics at the college; he and his wife were on a sabbatical in Italy. Austin's key worked. The Sikh helped him with the duffel bags. Austin paid him and he left. "Cheerio," he said. "Best of very good luck with your friend."

The aesthetics professor had left a long list of instructions on the dining-room table. It would be necessary to feed the green leather couch, but not the brown cloth one, with "hide food" once a week. All the flowers in the kitchen and the green plants in the "sitting room" were plastic, so they required no care, although Mrs. Professor had mixed in some real moss with the fake tiger lilies in the big brass bowl in the "sewing room," so would he mind terribly "moistening it from time to time—if it comes to mind?" There were very worrying paragraphs about what to do in case the water system flooded—all sorts of green-marked levers and two red ones to turn counterclockwise in closets on different floors. The tub in the bathroom above the entrance hall must not be filled more than halfway, since the water that slopped over into the safety drain went directly into the crawl space above the "balloon-suspended" ceiling (classified by the historical society) and would fissure it if it accumulated and would flood the parquet and the oriental carpet below—and to "refloat" the ceiling would cost "thousands, if it could be done at all." There were fifty-two channels available on the three television sets and a closetful of classic films ("everything from Dreyer's *Joan of Arc* to *Rashomon*").

Austin stood in the dim house. His body was convulsed with sobs, which drove him from room to room like spurs dug into his ribs. "What arrogance," he said. "I thought I could live anywhere. I built my perfect little life in Paris and I threw it all away to come to this shit hole." He found the heat and turned it up to seventy, though the instructions warned that to "maintain the house above sixty could run into the hundreds! Wear a sweater. The English do."

"*Pauvre Petit,*" he said, staring at his own drawn face and red eyes in the downstairs bathroom mirror. He didn't know whether the "*Petit*" was Julien or him. "The arrogance," he wailed. "The sheer arrogance."

He went out to the garage, unlocked the door and rolled it back, for the first time saw his four-year-old Volkswagen Sirocco (rather ominously, someone had told him it wasn't being manufactured anymore). He figured out how to make it work and drove it to the supermarket, following the professor's map. He thought, "I must get some food or I'll go hungry. There probably aren't any restaurants open after sundown." He half-imagined that the homeboys were turned loose after the sun set. He rolled his cart up and down the aisles, looking at the cellophaned meat and pallid vegetables and the cans of "chunky" soup and loaves of packaged "whole-grain" bread and he wept when he thought he'd given up his butcher with his pot of rabbit in mustard sauce and his *Veau Orloff,* the pastry shop with the *croissants au beurre* and the greengrocer with his five kinds of mushrooms and the fishmonger with his smoked mackerel for salads; he could hear mentally the way one would call out cheerily, "*Bonsoir, messieurs-dames,*" on entering a shop, even though it was vulgar to do so. Now he was approaching the checkout girl who, he could see on drawing closer, had set tiny brilliants in her fingernails and painted swirling white lines radiating out from each gem through the purple gloss. He looked at her narrow, pimply face under a tumbleweed of sprayed hair, stared at her nails again and burst into sobs. The girl looked right through him and said something to the boy who was "bagging." In France one bagged one's own groceries; Austin was slightly scandalized by this babying service.

Back "home" he saw that all the houses on his block were completely dark; the patch of woods across the street was frighteningly black. He unpacked his bags and put his clothes away in the emptied chest of drawers. Straight pins and even a stray paperclip were wedged into the cracks in the corners of the wood drawers, which smelled very dry. In the bathroom the professor's wife had simply pushed all her ointments, sprays and beauty utensils to the back of a six-foot-deep shelf. She'd erected a barricade of cardboard shirt boards, leaving the front of the shelf—painted but chipped and greasy—for his toiletries. He thought, Julien is *still* at the airport, with nothing to read, nothing to think about except how I betrayed him.

On every wall in every room were lace "paintings," collected by the professor's wife. She was Polish and, according to a monograph she'd left out for Austin, these works were embroideries and laces that Polish women had made over the centuries—"A Portable Matrimony" was the title of the essay ("matrimony" was considered to be the female form of "patrimony"). One sentence read, "Tormented by wars, pogroms and Cossack raids, such laces were the sole matrimony beleaguered Polish women, proto-feminists all, could carry with them in a single suitcase. 'Lay not up your treasures on earth'—unless they can fit into a suitcase, we might revise the saying!"

The professor and his wife, it turned out, were devout Catholics. He had been decorated by the Pope and there were photos of the Vatican ceremony everywhere, and a nearly life-size wood statue of the Virgin beside the bed. She was dressed in a gilt robe and wearing a detachable gilt crown set with glass "jewels." Austin tried it on. He wondered how the professor and his wife must feel about two men sleeping in their bed—they must have been desperate for a sublet, he thought.

He called Peter in New York and told him the whole long story.

"Don't worry, Austin, it will all work out. Tomorrow morning you can phone your Paris lawyer. Then call the president of your school."

"Oh. I will."

"Then call Jules."

"Julien."

"Sorry. So how does it feel to be back home?"

"Appalling. Everyone seems to be sleeping all the time. The only living creatures are giant squirrels bounding insolently over the lawn. This house is huge and hideous. There's the locked-up wine cellar in the basement, the locked-up computer room in the attic, everything else has a film of grease on it."

"Why are you being so brittle?" Peter asked.

"Because I'm so unhappy." The minute he was no longer able to be satirical he felt old and tired, as though he'd been brightly lipsticked and someone had sponged off all his make-up. He cooked sausages and instant mashed potatoes and ate them in the dining room under another lace picture. The Master Bed was so high he had to climb up on it by means of a three-step wood ladder; he fell asleep on top of the impeccably white chenille bedspread while the furnace roared somewhere far below and poured its costly heat up through the floor vents.

Next day he rang Julien to say that he'd be flying back to Paris the following evening and that they could stay in the Île Saint-Louis apartment. The provost of his college in Rhode Island had told him that America wasn't a "banana republic" like France and that if Austin tried to pull any strings he'd be hanged by them (a curious image, Austin thought). "No, seriously," the provost had added, "I wasn't able to do anything to get Dubuffet in years ago, and I had Sargent Shriver himself on my side. Pull doesn't work here. You've got to be patient. I've consulted the school's legal counselor and he says you could demand an instant hearing from an immigration judge but it could easily backfire and your friend might *never* get in. If you just wait for things to take their own course, he'll be here with us in Providence within a month. So just relax and enjoy all the cultural advantages of our city. Oh, and how does it feel—are you glad you gave up Paris for Providence?"

Austin laughed a dry laugh, a hard laugh of pained regret and humiliation. He'd always thought that someday he should move back to America. He'd thought that even before he'd tested positive. Maybe because the French commented on his accent he'd never stopped thinking of himself as a foreigner. He voted nowhere since he'd been a tourist in France and without a proper long-term visa he couldn't vote through the American Consulate in stateside elections—or so he thought (he'd never bothered to inquire). He'd lived an irresponsible life, the foreigner in France, the expatriate in America.

That night he walked restlessly through the rooms in Providence. Here he was in this cold, empty city with its boxy houses, their windows glowing dimly at night, this city with its abandoned, windswept downtown, with the dark, dangerous woods across the street. He was exhausted from jet lag. For him it was three in the morning. The house with its smell of mildew, its plastic poppies, its framed Polish laces, spoke of other people's lives, the poverty of an academic couple who'd raised two children and sent them to expensive universities and never modernized the kitchen. There were few books beyond the brittle paperbacks they'd bought in college thirty years ago—all those Turgenevs and Dostoevskys, for a Russian Lit. course, probably, and the vogue books of the 1950s (*The Outsider, The Man in the Gray Flannel Suit*) and of the sixties (*Growing Up Absurd,* Marshall McLuhan).

It was an outpost of an alien culture and for the first time in his thoughts about Americans he could hear himself saying "them." He even said to one of his colleagues, "Americans don't like that sort of thing." The remark won him a funny look.

Chapter Eleven

He arrived back in Paris four days after he'd left it. He went to his old apartment on the Île Saint-Louis and called Julien from the street (the phone had been turned off). Julien rushed right over. Without a word they went to bed and they made love with a feverish desperation that precluded pleasure or at least sensuality. It had been years since Austin had had sex in which every kiss stood for an effort to swallow the other person, every fluttering of tongue on nipple could be deciphered as laying balm on a sore heart, and the simultaneous explosion of two orgasms meant marriage.

Even after they'd come Austin kept feeling critical (as when an accident victim is said to be "in critical condition"). He needed love or was it help, and he butted his head under Julien's arm and into his side, he hooked his fingers, critical, searching, onto and over Julien's small, white lower teeth. He closed his eyes and felt his way into his wet fingers and thought he was pulling a hard, bony baby out of a bloody womb.

"*Petit,*" Austin said, "I'm so miserable without you. I keep worrying that you're going to go back to Christine."

Julien laughed a laugh of recognition and in the dark involuntarily shrugged his shoulders in a complicated Gallic way that seemed

half-apologetic: "It's true she's so kind to me and the whole experience of being rejected by the Americans was so humiliating—in Europe
we have the false idea that Americans are sweet and kind, but I never
saw such unsmiling, hard faces—real fascists. And who are they to
assume we're so desperate to get into their country? We're not Haitian
refugees on a raft. Our standard of living in Europe is higher than
theirs and France is such a garden, so rich and varied with its crickets
and olive groves in Provence, its mist and castles in Brittany, its *thousands* of castles—they have nothing to compare with it."

Austin was happy that at least Julien was railing against *them*, not
against a *you* that would include him. "No, it was disgusting; I just
hope it won't turn you off America forever. Someone told me if we'd
come through JFK in New York you would have been shooed through
in all the confusion. But Boston in January? Not exactly thronged
with European tourists."

Suddenly Austin could seriously envision Julien staying in France
and even reuniting with his wife. Perhaps she'd won him back after all
just by calmly waiting. Or had she been the one to reject Julien originally? Austin would never know. She'd certainly wasted no time finding an Italian lover and becoming pregnant. If she'd been waiting for
Julien to come back, would she ever have become pregnant with little
Allegra?

Austin wasn't a fighter. The prospect that Julien might leave him
hardened his heart. He pulled away from him, ashamed that he'd
showed so much emotion to this man who wasn't the convinced lover
he'd imagined, the person with whom he could finally feel safe. No,
Julien was weighing his possibilities, still hesitating, and that symp-
tom of the famous French realism sickened Austin.

They were ghosts who'd come back to haunt their former lives;
some higher dispensation allowed them to inhabit this old apartment
for just five days, but it, too, was ghostly—shabby without its soft
lamps and bohemian throws tossed over the mammoth metal heater
that no longer worked. The apartment was dusty and resonant. Given
how small the rooms were, the resonance sounded odd, as though
they were in the antechambers to a mammoth cave. The windows
were curtainless, the worn carpet denuded of the two sumptuous silk

rugs Austin had brought back from a holiday in Istanbul, the kitchen empty of its dishes and cutlery.

And the city, too, was ghostly, since none of their friends knew they were there. They called no one and just walked and walked, visiting all their favorite places, crunching along the formal gravel paths at the Jardin des Plantes between beds of dead flowers, all neatly labeled, or descending the escalator under the Louvre's glass pyramid into a necropolis of art miles and miles long, or standing under the high, illuminated glory of the narrow Sainte Chapelle, its walls of stained glass housing a precious holy relic, a single splinter of the True Cross. When they jostled their way through the crowds under the arcades of the rue de Rivoli, Austin was disturbed to see the buses in front of ParisVision disgorging so many fellow Americans, as though he feared being confused with them. He spoke loudly to Julien in French to insulate himself against this confusion.

"I only have to teach two days a week, Petit," Austin said. "You could stay two weeks in Montréal, which is supposed to be beautiful, and I could fly up twice and spend five days with you each time. By then things will be sorted out and you'll be coming to the United States."

Julien looked at him with a flash of intensity and said, "D'accord." He had a sharp way of biting into that word, which in his mouth became a form not of aggressiveness but of conviction. Simple, matter-of-fact acceptance, so at odds with what Austin had perceived the previous night as a wavering commitment to their love and the move to Providence.

In one way he knew Julien well, his erect but supple posture, his deep voice and hollow, mirthless laugh, his sensitive nipples, his pain over his mother's death, his anger over his failed marriage, his romantic posturing, his dandified distance from all moral questions, a disdain which often made him seem capricious, even cruel, his fascination with other people's glamor, not as an abject admirer but as a powerful generator of personal glamor himself. Austin knew inside-out everything about Julien's intense secretiveness. When Austin would press him on a point he didn't want to talk about, he'd smile and turn his head slightly to one side with a sort of royal unreachability.

They walked and walked through the crowds, past rich Arabs followed by their silent, shrouded women and their fashionably dressed children, big black soft eyes in open peony faces. Past old tourists from the provinces, stiff-jointed, blinking but smiling good-naturedly despite their feeling of sudden disorientation as they entered a swirl of gypsy girls, rushing around and through their group, whining and jabbing open hands at them. Julien and Austin walked and walked past the smell of heated chocolate wafting out of Angelina's and the half-glimpsed movement of waitresses in white aprons darting between the Louis XVI chairs, past the windows of a men's shop and the sight of the tailor in vest and shirtsleeves, a yellow tape measure dangling around his neck, standing alone, apparently entranced, in the center of the empty room, past the English-language bookstore with its windows piled high with a local bestseller, *French or Foe*. Then the arcade ended and opened up into the immensity of the Place de la Concorde with its seated matronly statues representing the cities of France gathered in a serene circle around the Egyptian obelisk and the tangle of revolving traffic and the distant gold glow of the Tomb of the Emperor and the columned splendor of the Madeleine, at the end of a wide street, the rue Royale. Maybe because there were no buildings on the west side of the square, the eye was led up, up above the massed chestnut trees to the gray skies, as intricately contoured as the brain's thinking cortex and as active.

Austin felt intensely uneasy. He couldn't, wouldn't stay in Providence alone. Only two people living as a couple could survive there in one of those big, dim, lonely wood houses. He'd already slept on the high bed twice, listened to the furnace, pulled back the blind to look at the leafless trees across the street. He wouldn't eat Grape Nuts alone under the ancient fluorescent lamp in the grease-impregnated kitchen and then drive in his Volkswagen Sirocco alone to the campus or to the supermarket to push his cart up rows of unripened vegetables.

He loved Julien and wanted to be with him all the time. If Julien came they'd have fun—Providence would be an adventure, or at least a big laugh.

Austin flew back the evening before his classes began. After the bourgeois propriety of Paris, where girls strove to resemble their mothers and wore suits and low heels and stockings and garter belts and painted their nails with pearlescent pink polish and twisted a scarf elegantly around their shoulders like a heavy napkin around champagne, the students at the New England School of Fine Arts and Brown University with their loud voices ("*Ex*-cellent, Dude!"), their layers of ripped and stained clothes (they looked like dirty, creeping haystacks), and their prickly politics shocked him. He was told that some of these kids were from rich families, often of the English or European aristocracy, and when he'd find himself alone with one of them, especially if he or she was French, the youngster would slip into an Old World deferential politeness and virtually drop a curtsy. But whenever the students were in groups they were loud, rude, hilarious and in the classroom they were witch hunters in full cry after the slightest sign of political incorrectness, especially in their professor.

Austin had scarcely heard about political correctness while he was in France throughout the eighties. The French, probably wrongly, thought it was retrograde to focus on the rights of special interest groups since everyone, every abstract, universal citizen, was theoretically equal in the eyes of the French state. For the French to talk about the rights of blacks or lesbians or Asians was only to reduce their legal and political equality (their "freedom," as more than one French person had put it to Austin, though he never understood exactly what they meant). At the New England School of Fine Arts during his course on eighteenth-century French architecture and furniture-making, Austin angered the young women in class by stressing the importance of French women during this period of history.

"Only aristocratic women!" one red-faced fat girl in overalls shouted.

"Yes. Naturally," Austin replied.

"Why naturally?"

"Because they were the only ones who hired architects to build their *châteaux* or cabinetmakers to make their—"

"Are you denying male oppression in this period?"

"In *all* periods," a bubblegum-blowing girl, slumped deep into her chair, snarled, not looking at anyone, her bubbles bursting angrily.

"Look," Austin said, "I'm not interested in sexual politics—"

"When you say French women were privileged or powerful you're making a political statement, buddy, even if it's wrong."

"Shall we go back to our discussion of André-Charles Boulle and to his four sons, Jean-Philippe, Pierre-Benoît, André-Charles and—"

But three of the women in the class had walked out of the room, slamming the door behind them. Austin felt like running after them and shouting, "But I'm *gay*, I'm not the enemy."

A few days later he received a note in his box (which he would have ignored had the department secretary not told him he *had* a box and that a very important message was in it). It was from the Dean of Sexual Harassment and Gender Infringement Issues (Austin tried, unsuccessfully, to turn it into a funny anagram). He was told that three "female" students (he winced since in French only animals are designated as *femelle*) had reported his "sexist reading of history" and his "insensitivity to feminist issues."

Austin bridled at the injustice of it all, he who had never had any designs on women and had offered them only disinterested friendship, he who had published important monographs titled "Woman as Taste Maker in Eighteenth-Century France" and "Madame de Pompadour—Slut or Savant?" Indignant, he showed the letter to a gay colleague over lunch, who shook his head and said, "Boy, are you in a fine mess!"

"I am? But I was just making a simple historical observation, which has the advantage of being *true. En plus*, why wouldn't feminists be *pleased* to know that women once reigned over the crucial domain of taste?"

His colleague, a bearded man who, incongruously, wore a ring on every finger, even his thumb, waved his decorated hands over his head as though fighting off bees (or the Furies, Austin thought). He said, "Just send a contrite letter to the Dean admitting your error and promising to reform. Imagine you're in China during the Cultural Revolution and have just been accused of bourgeois pseudo-objectivity. No way to win. Just crawl and eat dirt and maybe it will all blow over. Maybe you should organize a discussion group after class on "Sexism in Historical Hermeneutics" and announce that you hope to *learn* from it. No one will come to it, least of all those disruptive cows who walked out of your class, because they're all too fucking lazy here, but it will look like you're eagerly soliciting to be *re-educated* after your years of wandering through the Black Forest of European pre-feminism."

"But what about academic freedom?"

"Forget it. These are battles you can't win. If you're accused of racism, anti-Semitism, child abuse or just flirting with your students or if you're perceived as a male chauvinist, you've already lost, it doesn't matter who's right or even if you've been falsely accused. Just give in, submit to a humble re-education, and hope the harridans move on."

"The funny thing is that I actually believe in feminism," Austin said, staring gloomily into his mug of watery coffee.

"You *do?* Whatever for?" The other man raked his beard with his ringed hands.

"No, I love all these French women in the eighteenth century, the first feminists such as Olympe de Gouge and Thorigny de—"

"Never heard of them. I'm a potter and I just show them how to throw pots. If they want to see Astarte's wide hips in a pot, I *encourage* them. I've been properly re-educated."

Austin jotted off a short letter of contrition and kept all traces of jocularity out of it. After three in the afternoon he had the much more serious problem of going back to the house at the end of the street, just where the woods began. When he had told the bearded colleague where he was living, the man had sung, "There are fairies at the bottom of your garden."

"What?"

"That's the biggest cruising ground in town, the woods across the street. Don't tell me you didn't know that when you rented there."

"Honestly. . . ."

"The man you're renting from, Hal Devereaux? He *hates* the fags down there and is always running in the woods chasing them off in the name of Christian decency."

"You mean all that still goes on?"

"More than ever. You're in Reagan country now."

When he got home Austin put in a call to the Hungarian architects, Istvan and Laszlo, to make sure they'd sent in their promise to hire Julien, but they hemmed and hawed (they were each on a different extension, proof of how little work they had or perhaps how upset they were). One of them (Austin couldn't recognize their voices, just their accent, which was the same) said, "We're too worried . . . we spoke to our lawyer . . . our own status . . . and now you say that Julien is having immigration troubles . . . best to lie low."

Austin cried, frustrated and frightened. The worst of it, he realized in his bitterness, was that these cowards and traitors would get their *Elle Déco* article out of him after all; it was too late to reverse the process without arousing the editor's suspicions and, anyway, the photos of their Brooklyn house had already been shot.

It was ten in the evening in Paris; he couldn't contact Howard, his Paris lawyer, who wouldn't be in his office. He could call Henry McVay, who might know how to help.

"What a mess!" Henry exclaimed. "Why don't you call my friends Phil and Bob—they're architects. You remember Phil Bluet, who's the heir to the Bluet soap-powder fortune? No, listen, Sweetie, I'll phone him myself. I'll sort of . . . *feel* him out." His voice suddenly took on a confidential tone and Austin could picture him squinting and wriggling his hand in the air as if to demonstrate how he'd auscultate his friends. Austin admired Henry's worldly competence, something Henry himself, with his normal bashfulness, would have dismissed completely if it had been brought to his attention. "No, it's nothing, don't be silly," he'd say, casting his eyes down and to one side. Then he'd look up to see if Austin had been taking the piss out of him.

As Austin waited for Henry to call him back, his mind raced like hands playing scales—methodical and irritating. Any day now Julien would be getting his test results: what if he was positive? They'd be together a few days in Montréal and Austin would be able to comfort him then. But how would Julien make out alone two or three days in a big, unknown, winterbound city, with no one to call and nothing to do but brood?

Henry called back and talked to Austin with a calm decency, a grown-up sobriety so at odds with his usual spluttering (Henry's favorite mode was comic indignation). "Phil is out on the West Coast but Bob—

you remember him? Tall and handsome as Gary Cooper?—well, Bob will be driving up to see a client in Concord, Mass., and he said he could have lunch with you this Friday afternoon at the Olde Concord Inn."

"Do you think he'll sign it? He isn't really committing himself to anything, my lawyer assures me there's no government follow-up and the—"

"*Your* lawyer," Henry said reproachfully.

"Yeah. Incompetent fool."

"Well," Henry sighed, "I hope to *God,* Sweetie, that he does help you and darling Julien, but you won't blame him, will you—"

"Lord, no," Austin said, the soul of generosity, although in his heart he loved everyone who helped them and cursed everyone who failed to do so.

Austin had moved easily, hand over hand, through the last decade, and if he complained less than his contemporaries about being gay and fifty it was because he had never tested his mettle at a bar or sauna but lived inside his charming circle of young, affectionate friends. Now, here he was, in Providence, alone, separated from his friends and Julien—and if he had to go out to find a new lover, here, what would he find?

His colleague's mention of the cruising across the street piqued Austin's curiosity. Not because he was feeling desire; the trauma of returning to America had frozen his libido. No, he wanted to see if he could attract anyone. And what if Julien could never get through Immigration?

Austin walked for an hour through the cold, leafless woods, kicking up dead leaves and the smell of soil and mold. He thought that only in America would one find, even near the heart of the city, these big, neglected woods. In France the trees were planted in neat rows, like crops. But everything in France had been observed and regulated for centuries; only America was so shaggy, so unsystematic, so full of surprises.

Austin's surprise was a twenty-four-year-old six-foot-four guy with a forehead that sloped back and heavy jowls as though his brains had fallen out of his cranium but couldn't pass through his narrow neck. He carried around a swollen, round belly on his otherwise normal body. He was wearing trousers in which the cuffs had been let out— not for him, certainly. They'd been let out for someone else, the previous owner—that's how old the pants were. Even remade, the trousers stopped at mid-calf, like pedal-pushers. He had the look of someone who'd been dressed in hand-me-downs by an orphanage, for his shirt was plain dark-blue wool, unbuttoned to reveal a classic white T-shirt stretched over his belly (maybe the shirt wouldn't button up over this mature watermelon). He wore a standard-issue Navy pea coat, also unbuttoned. The trousers, a gray cotton, had a big hole in front through which the white pocket fabric could be seen, spotlessly clean. The trousers were carefully ironed and pressed, even if they were too small all over, not just too short. The waist was pressed down and partially folded back by the weight and heft of the belly, the zipper was bulging. The thighs looked gigantic in the stretched fabric. His hands were small, almost blue from the cold; they appeared to be boneless. His ears were also surprisingly small, as if they hadn't grown at all since childhood.

The man kept walking deeper and deeper into the woods, looking back over his shoulder from time to time. At last, at a turn that smelled of sewage for some reason, he stopped and just stood there. This sort of tentative, step-by-gradual-step cruising was something Austin had thought had vanished from the world.

"Hi," Austin said, more huskily than usual.

"How's it going?" the man asked, unsmiling, his eyes crinkled as if from the mental effort of talking. Or was he, too, apprehensive?

"Getting cold, huh?" Austin said.

"Sure is."

"You work around here?"

"Looking."

"What?"

"I'm looking for work."

"What do you do?"

"Transportation."

The woods, the failing light, the distant sound of a slow, rumbling train and its whistle, the smell of sewage, the wariness of this man so pale he looked bled white—Austin suddenly felt plunged back into the snot-nosed, sandy-eyed squalor of childhood, that age when you don't choose your company but accept whoever comes your way.

Austin stood so close to the man while they talked about the weather that it was a provocation. The man backed away. He seemed uneasy.

"You live near here?" the man asked.

"Yeah. Just up there. The brown house."

"You live in that big house alone?"

"No," Austin said. "My wife and son are out of town but they're coming back next week." Austin thought that would sound more normal, less intimidating, to the man than the idea he was a self-declared fag all on his own. Anyway, the guy wouldn't try to drop in for a visit, a handout or blow job after next week; if he saw Julien he'd assume he was Austin's son.

"Want to come up for a coffee?"

"Sure. It's cold as a witch's tit out here."

"Not much work out there?" Austin asked. It was 1990 and lots of Americans were out of work, especially in the Northeast.

He said, "I've had some bad luck."

"That right? Mighty sorry to hear it." Austin was saying lines, as though he were in a stage adaptation of *Tobacco Road,* but he scarcely noticed. He was a born seducer of strong men, which meant he was gifted with abundant negative capability. Now that he was older, he was attracting a different sort—big, husky working men who picked up on something well-spoken and sober about him and who found his white hair, barrel chest and black glasses reassuringly paternal, married, as if he were the neighborhood dentist.

They drank their coffee and then Austin said in a soft voice, "Wanna go upstairs?"

Austin felt mildly guilty, but Julien's rule of discretion gave him a certain immunity. Julien would never expect him to confess anything; he'd probably even stop him from telling. And this cloak of discretion, possibly, had been drawn over Julien's own adventures. He was young and virile; he surely wasn't waiting chastely in Paris for Austin.

The man stood up, stretched nervously and said, "Lead the way."

But when they got upstairs he asked where the "bathroom" was; he left the door open and the sound of his pissing excited Austin. He came into the bedroom and unconvincingly mimed weariness by stretching first one arm, then the other above his head; his mouth formed a circle but not in a genuine yawn—he wasn't even inhaling.

He climbed up onto the bed, still fully clothed and shod, and stretched out and closed his eyes. Austin undid the man's laces, removed his shoes, then unfastened his belt and inched the tight fly zipper down, afraid to snag it in his underwear. Even though the man, "Herb," was pretending to have fallen asleep, as if a wand had been waved over him, he still obligingly lifted his pelvis from the mattress so that Austin could slide his trousers off.

Later, they drank a beer together. Herb said he'd just gotten out of prison for writing bad checks and had nothing, no one, and no hope except for a beat-up truck an uncle had given him reluctantly. Austin said he'd pay two hundred bucks if they could drive into the Boston airport together and bring back his trunk. "It weighs a ton—I mean, almost a ton, seriously."

Herb said, "The load don't bother me. I'm strong enough. But I don't know if the truck can make the round trip. If it breaks down we'd be up the crick."

"Yeah, but what's the use of having a truck if you can't make money off it?"

Austin noticed that Herb was unsure of himself, disoriented, fearful, and Austin thought, Prison doesn't harden men but weakens them, eats away at their confidence.

Herb promised to come back the next day around noon, after Austin's class. When he'd gone, Austin said out loud, "So, that's what you've come to, Aussie," which is what his mother had called him. He was left with nothing but the man's coal-tar smell and a sense of bleakness, as though the world's wattage had been cut, as though he'd been returned to his American past, but a black-and-white small-screen version of it. He kept feeling he was dreaming a feverish half-dream which took place in the dim, shabby, empty corridors behind the brilliantly lit set.

Herb showed up the next day at the very moment Austin was on

the phone with Julien. Austin realized that sexually he preferred ser-
vicing this big fat man who smelled of defeat to dominating Julien, but
the comparison became irrelevant, even ridiculous. He *loved* Julien
and he could hear in Julien's voice his pleasure and excitement. "That's
the driver," Austin said in French, "who's going with me into Boston
to pick up my trunk from U.S. Customs."

The mention of Customs drove Julien into another diatribe against
America, which excited him so much he didn't ask details about the
driver.

"What was that stuff you were talkin'?" Herb asked when Austin
had hung up. "Spanish?"

"French."

"Ooh-lah-lah. But you're American, right? Canuck?"

"No, just plain old American. Scotch-Irish. Heinz 57 variety. Mutt.
No, I just lived in France. For business reasons."

"Oh."

Herb was so nervous about his truck and how it would perform on
the highway that his thoughts seemed remote from sex. The truck was
big, very big, but it could go no faster than forty-five miles an hour.
The motor coughed twice, then lurched back into play. Cars that were
backed up behind in the slow lane, preparing to turn off, honked at
them. "Fuckin' bastards! Goddamn rich bitches!" Herb shouted. But at
last they reached the long metal shed where arriving goods were
stored and an official, not even looking at them because he was talking to another Customs officer, stamped Austin's form. Herb backed
the truck up to the loading dock and wrestled the trunk into the back
of the truck. Austin noticed the big, burned hole in the wood floor,
through which the pavement was visible. On the way back Herb
talked rarely, and then only to the truck.

Once they arrived at the house, he relaxed, smiled. Austin made
him a ham sandwich while he showered. Then, once again, he pretended to sleep on the high bed, while Austin knelt between his legs.
When Austin glanced up his body, his head was entirely blocked out
by his immense, swollen belly. They ate and drank beer and Austin
gave him the two hundred dollars, which he'd put loose in his pocket
so that he wouldn't have to display a tempting wallet in front of Herb.

They had talked for a while over their beers and the conversation had been bluff but easygoing. Now, however, when Austin paid him, Herb retreated back into sullen servility. Herb would be going off to sleep in his truck, whereas Austin would remain in his big, heated house, presumably awaiting the return of his wife and son. In Herb's eyes even a family looked like an acquisition beyond his means.

On Thursday night Peter arrived by train from New York and on Friday they drove over to Concord together. Austin was terribly nervous about the meeting with Bob, Henry McVay's friend. They'd met only once before, in Paris, at one of Henry's cocktail parties. But there was all the difference in the world between a *soirée* in Paris and the request of a large personal favor in Concord.

The Inn had so many rooms tacked on that Austin, nearly feverish and out of control with anxiety, was worried that Bob wouldn't find them. He kept hopping up from their table to make another tour of the Inn—up two steps, down one, racing around and around through all these women with their wide hips in black trousers below hand-knit cardigans, their strong jaws and lined faces framed by glossy, pure white pageboy haircuts.

At last Bob cut through the crowd like a tall ship sailing gently into a harbor full of anchored dinghies, and indeed everyone bobbed in his wake, gawking at this elegant country gentleman, so poised, so quietly virile. Austin of course noticed right away that Bob appeared fractionally less effusive than he had been in Paris, as though steeling himself to refuse the favor Austin would ask.

They ordered iced tea although it was cold and windy outside. The waitress served them crusty, steamy chicken potpie. Peter said, "My family lives here in Concord. When I was a kid I'd do grave rubbings and sell them to the tourists. And I'd take them out to Walden Pond."

They chit-chatted during the meal, as businessmen do, and after the dishes were cleared Austin said, smiling easily, as though it were all a matter of just a detail between gentlemen, "We're so grateful you're willing to sign this form for us."

"Well, what is it exactly?" Bob asked, looking at his watch. He had an appointment with his client.

Austin explained as quickly and as offhandedly as possible that Bob and Phil would need to sign the document (it's right here!) promising to hire Julien to help them submit plans for major French building competitions.

Bob read through everything, his face suddenly as severe as that of his Puritan preacher forefather, the famous one who'd known Emerson and who'd been photographed by Brady, his body held in place against blurring by scarcely visible metal clamps. Here, in this Inn, which had been reconstructed, rewired, redecorated countless times, Bob's expression was the only authentic Concord antique, a genuine heirloom. At last he said in a voice that was noticeably softer, "I'd like a Xerox of this."

"No problem!" Austin shrieked, grabbing the paper out of his hands and racing to the restaurant's hostess, then, following her directions, running coatless down the street to the copy shop two blocks away. Within ten minutes he was back, red-faced, panting. He was sorry to appear so desperate—that might scare Bob off. In fact, he was convinced Bob was going to refuse, which of course was the prudent thing to do.

But a day later Bob phoned and said, "I don't really like doing this, since it might jeopardize our business if we're ever investigated, but Henry asked us to help out and Phil and I are incapable of refusing him anything."

When Austin called Julien in Paris to tell him the good news, Julien's voice sounded very small. Austin was sitting upstairs in the Providence house.

"What's wrong?" Austin asked.

"It's just that—I talked to the doctor at the Hôpital Saint-Louis today and he wants to redo my tests, but he says they're not very promising."

"He thinks you're positive?"

"Not just positive, but my T-cells are way down, just above one hundred."

"A thousand, you mean. Normal is one thousand."

"No," Julien said, irritated, frightened. "No."

"But I don't see—"

"How many do you have? How many T-cells."

"Seven hundred," Austin said. "Something like that."

"I guess you're lucky. You must be one of the rare lucky ones."

"My time will come," Austin said. Austin looked out at an old woman who was walking her dog. She refused to slow up when the dog began sniffing. She dragged him along, angrily, it seemed.

He wanted to ask if the doctor had said how long Julien must have been ill, because suddenly Austin was overwhelmed with a sense of guilt. He tried to remember all the times they'd had sex. On perhaps five or six occasions they'd been seriously stoned. Could he have slipped up and touched Julien's ass with a fingertip which he'd doused in his own precome?

"Well, they need to verify their tests." He didn't want to say it would probably all turn out to be a false alarm. He blurted out, "You must be . . . devastated."

"No, why?" Julien asked brightly. He had regained his steely poise.

Austin paused, lost in thought, then said, "I wish I could be there with you." He disliked the sound of his own voice, as if the only problem was sincerity or its convincing simulacrum.

Austin had rented a room in a gay guest house in Montréal, and when they arrived a week later, at the end of January, the neighborhood of two-story turn-of-the-century buildings looked like the dreary outskirts of Milwaukee, not the "fun" city he'd heard so much about. The snow on the sidewalks had melted and refrozen several times until it appeared glazed and dirty and nibbled from within, as if by arctic termites. Julien was repelled by the manager, a short, tattooed, bald Munchkin with a handlebar mustache who smelled of garlic, and by his young, willowy boyfriend, who slumped to hide his height and who constantly feigned amazement because someone must have told him once that his eyes were more attractive when wide with wonder.

"Why do we have to stay here?" Julien asked. Guiltily, Austin realized that he'd always chosen gay hotels, no matter how sordid, out of a fear that he and his kind would not be welcome elsewhere and a prejudice that with gays he'd be closer to "the action," even though now the clubs opened only after his bedtime and if he could get past the doorman he'd be shunned by the young clientele. Austin had a lover, a married bisexual who detested most gays, certainly those who lived within the ghetto.

Austin had heard so much about the Gallic "charm" of Montréal that he was shocked to see that it was just one more medium-sized North American city with tall buildings, elevated highways, neon, a rusting port and outlying miles of small, nearly identical houses. Carefully preserved, like the remains of a saint in a crystal coffin at the center of a modern brick church, was the historic district with its narrow streets and antique stores and imposing Hôtel-Dieu. The cathedral, Notre-Dame, had a glowing, starry blue ceiling; it seemed the home of a church entirely devoted to the cult of the Virgin. God the Father was nowhere to be seen and Christ only as a child and then only to picture Mary at work as the Blessed Mother.

Julien had cut his hair penitentially short; he'd also let his beard grow an inch long and the effect was hearty, masculine, in keeping with the swirls of snow that kept *rising*, curiously, through the lamp light, as though snow were steam. He wore a knit, blue-black merchant-marine cap, which he could roll down over his ears when he and Austin went out walking, and fleece-lined gloves which hung straight down from his shoulders as if weighted.

He wanted to see Indians, which made Austin cringe, since he'd already been through all this with French friends in America. He'd taken them to a housing development near Albuquerque and cruised slowly past the shoddy bungalows. They'd caught a glimpse of a paunchy middle-aged man in jeans and T-shirt and had seen some kids coming out of school laughing and shoving each other. One of the French tourists had turned big sad eyes, confused, toward Austin, sprouted two fingers behind his head like feathers and made a slow, mournful war whoop with the other hand fluttering over his silent mouth. Austin, unsmilingly, had shaken his head firmly. *"Non?"* the disappointed tourist had asked.

"Non," Austin had said.

Today it was the same story, although on the "reservation," a colorless suburb, someone at the filling station directed them to a small factory where Indians were making snowshoes (*raquettes*). The wet, varnished wood, careening past on an assembly line, rose up into a windowless loft where the shoes were unloaded and left to cure. An old guy, who had one blind eye that had turned blue, showed them around; Julien was elaborately polite to him, as if to make up for centuries of oppression and to mark the difference between a liberal Frenchman and racist North Americans. Everything smelled of turpentine.

The following weekend Julien was waiting for Austin at the airport. "I can't bear this city another second," he said. "Those stupid fags at the guest house are planted every waking hour in front of the television. And they hate me because I speak normal French, not their ghastly, sing-song *joual*. In Paris everyone says how open and kind the Canadians are, but they're not—they're Catholic fanatics, they detest English-speaking Canadians, all Americans, all real French people, and the only things they like are their inedible *saucisses de Francfort*. Anybody who likes frankfurters, as my father says, has never visited the factory."

"What have you been doing?"

"Sitting in my room and thinking."

"About what?"

"About how I'm going to spend the rest of my life. I called my doctor in Paris. He had the results of the second test. It's certain: I am infected. And my counts are even lower—ninety-five."

Austin had a strong urge to turn on the car radio, to tune in the loudest possible rock music. He wanted to say, "Oh, but T-cells go up and down, most doctors pay no attention to them," but he knew that was a lie Julien wouldn't believe.

"Anyway," Julien said, "let's just drive north to Québec City."

Julien was the worst driver Austin had ever known but now, instead of cringing at every misjudgment or infringement, Austin welcomed the heightened sense of danger, of lost control.

Soon they were on the highway in the big new American rental car. It glowed and bubbled in the dark like a jukebox. Snow began to fall so thick that it created in the beams of their car lights a rippling white banner. Cars descending from the north crept past, tiny under thick white carapaces. The radio warned of snowstorms, but Julien and Austin were too excited to pay any attention. For so long they'd been hemmed in by legal restrictions, for so long almost everything they'd done had been according to a schedule or to advance their interests, for so long they'd sat in dim rooms feeling alone and scared that now they surrendered to a surge of energy, a loud, boyish joy, archaic, rude. "Yes!" Austin shouted, pushing half his body out the window and giving a power salute to the elements.

Soon the snow was falling so fast and heavy that they could no longer see the road or the place where their lane spilled over onto the gravel embankment. Austin got out of the car and walked ahead, locating the gravel edge with his steps. Julien drove the car slowly, following Austin. After twenty minutes of inching along, Austin on foot and Julien behind the wheel, they were overtaken by a team of snow-plows, wheeling red and yellow lights and sweeping both lanes clear. They followed in the path of the plows, their radio station consecrated to Motown's greatest hits, which they turned up louder and louder. Julien—his face bright under his knit cap and his smile all the whiter framed by his beard coming in so black and full—laughed and looked younger and happier. He was still just a young guy, just twenty-eight, and all this talk of dying seemed suddenly pretty abstract. The music was so loud they couldn't talk but they kept looking at each other, their smiles cinematic in the whirling brilliance of the plow lights. Austin decided they should never talk about AIDS; it was an abstract thing that would never take hold if they ignored it.

Around ten o'clock they entered Québec at the height of its winter carnival. A parade of little kids tootling on small, one-note trumpets marched past in red parkas. People were selling "caribous," a hot mulled drink, and crowds surged into and out of bars, which were covered with tiny, twinkling lights, and carried off plastic cups. Floats rolled down the steep, stony streets—here was a Styrofoam Asterix with his pals in striped blue and white trousers, all wearing blond, drooping mustaches and silver helmets, seated on a papier-mâché camel, heading across the desert away from an onion-domed palace toward—well, the sign read "GAULE CMX. KM."

The buildings, as best they could see by the electrically wired gas lamps, were all constructed of stone from which protruded wooden window frames that housed small panes, frosted over. Icicles dangled from the gutters and one long icicle even hung from Snoopy's giant cheek as he glided past on a float.

Julien's face lit up from within. His eyes sparkled, even his skin shone in the flash of lights and cameras, and there was something solid in his bearing as they threaded their way just beyond the city's old fortifications. All around them were giant ice sculptures carved and molded by artists from every arctic land, including Siberia and Iceland—ten-foot-high ice tables and chairs, a bathtub-sized ice replica of the Queen's crown, an ice ski resort complete with ice lodges and ice figures descending icy slopes.

They wandered through the streets, getting drunk on caribous. The little kids, no longer marching, blew their trumpets at random and laughed. All the picturesque guest houses were full but they found a room in a twelve-story modern tower outside the gates and from their balcony they could look down on the entire town twinkling with fairy lights as whole families, cocooned in their matching quilted down coats, moved like gaudy, segmented caterpillars across the white streets under a sumptuous black sky.

Chapter Twelve

After that happy weekend in Québec City, Julien flew home to Paris. There, three weeks later, he received his American papers and once again headed for Boston. Austin met him at the airport—this hateful prison he knew too well—and drove him in the Sirocco to Providence. Julien was fascinated by the big, wooden houses; he said, "In Paris there were so many fires in the Middle Ages that wood was made illegal. Here, if things aren't wood they're made of brick, but back home brick isn't considered a noble material, although at the time of Louis XIII it had a brief fad. No, for us stone is the only acceptable material, the only noble material."

Austin said, "That's because the French were building for the centuries to come. Americans once believed in the future, but that was two hundred years ago and they were too poor to build anything big and ambitious."

Julien added pleasantly, "You have to be religious to build for the future." He was struck—even disconcerted—by the big lawns that flowed over from one house to the next with no walls to fence off each property; this lack of wariness seemed unnatural to him.

He had nothing but contempt for the aesthetic philosopher's house, which he saw as jerrybuilt and filled with junk. He was appalled by the "formal" dining room with its ten chairs placed symmetrically around the oak table. He decided if things weren't so symmetrical they'd already be better. He took up the frightening orange rug and then pushed the table against one wall.

"But, Julien, you're destroying the parquet!" Austin shouted. "You've gouged it—look!" He could already picture the philosopher's bill for damages.

"Parquet? These are just slats (*lattes*)."

Austin tried to convince Julien that this ugly store-bought furniture was expensive in America and that even if he held it in contempt it was obviously precious to the professor who, after all, was an aesthetician.

Julien just snorted and assured Austin that no one could conceivably have reflected even an instant on this odious decor. He banished several armchairs to the dank, sooty basement, stabbed wildly at the stereo controls until he'd broken something, even attempted to take down Mrs. Professor's lace pictures but discovered that their frames were screwed into the wall and ended up covering them with brown wrapping paper.

Through a rich friend of Austin's they'd been lined up with the leading AIDS specialist in New Haven. Julien drove them into the city, though he cursed the low speed limit and the inadequate or misleading road signs.

Dr. Goldstein's AIDS research laboratory had received a major gift from Austin's friend and so he was extremely deferential, though he would have been warm in any event because he was that kind of guy. Tall, slim, sixty, he told them that he swam a mile every morning at six, that he taught at Yale, that he'd just come back from Israel, where he'd lectured and toured with his son. He pointed to a photo of his son in which the kid was dressed in a dark suit with an embroidered prayer shawl around his shoulders and a white yarmulke hairpinned in place.

He became more and more expansive and Austin's powers as a simultaneous interpreter were put to the test. Julien never once looked at Austin and even seemed annoyed by his translating, as though he were interrupting. He nodded and smiled and drank in everything the great man was saying and even murmured, "*Merci, Docteur, merci infiniment.*"

When the conversation devolved toward AIDS, Dr. Goldstein gave them a tour of his lab, which involved twenty technicians at work on different floors of the hospital, including one sterile zone where the technicians had to be gloved, masked and even vacuumed clean on the way in. On the way out their paper clothes, once shed, were put into sealed coffins and their street clothes and especially their shoes were meticulously sterilized.

Austin in all fairness couldn't imagine how the doctor could be more human, attentive or informative; maybe Austin resented him only because Julien was so obviously under his spell. He then examined them separately. When Austin had stripped off all his clothes, the doctor looked him up and down and said, "A fine figure of a man," which surprised Austin, since he was convinced he was nothing but a collection of flaws, starting with his age.

He spent much more time with Julien, then brought them both back to his office for a final chat. "Do you have health insurance?" he asked Julien.

"No. I—no."

"Don't worry. We'll figure something out."

"*Merci infiniment.*"

"Think nothing of it. You know, AIDS is no longer the death sentence—"

"*Le SIDA n'est plus la condamnation à mort que c'était autrefois,*" Austin whispered as unobtrusively as possible.

"*Ah, non? Tiens,*" Julien said coolly, as though he'd just learned a surprising if incidental fact.

Dr. Goldstein talked about the important work that was being done, not just in his own laboratory but even (here he smiled ecumenically) at the Institut Pasteur.

"Pasteur," Julien said, nodding with pleasure in advance of Austin's translation.

"Today we think of AIDS as a serious but by no means necessarily fatal disease, like diabetes."

Austin translated the words, but in his heart he knew they were false.

Dr. Goldstein prescribed AZT for Julien as well as a Pentamadine inhalation every two weeks as a prophylaxis against the kind of galloping pneumonia associated with AIDS. Julien was sent off to have a blood sample taken. While they were waiting Austin asked, "Don't you think Julien must tell his ex-wife that he's positive?"

"Yes, of course."

"She's pregnant," Austin said. "Presumably not by Julien. At least she says it's by someone else." He paused. "But he and she have . . . made love until very recently." Austin wasn't sure at all of what he was saying. "Is there a chance I might be the one who infected Julien?"

"Yes," Dr. Goldstein said. "An extremely remote one."

On the way home Julien said, "I feel so much better. He's a great man, isn't he?"

"Yes. He agrees with me you should phone Christine."

"I will. Of course. I must." He drove silently for a while, mile after mile of forest scrolling past them on the highway. "It's just very difficult."

"Of course it is." Austin realized he'd never seen Julien so ill at ease. Usually he'd just push a situation aside, scornfully, if it made him feel guilty; certainly he never admitted he might be wrong or have endangered someone else.

Now he squirmed and smiled as he spoke into the telephone, said *"Oui"* solemnly, many times, lowering his head and voice, started to defend himself, then interrupted his high-pitched objection and sighed, "You're right. Of course. You're perfectly right." When he hung up he said, "She's very worried about little Allegra. If she's positive she may try to abort, even though she's in the second trimester." He didn't eat dinner and went to bed early. When Austin tiptoed into the bedroom three hours later he saw the pale street light reflected in his open eyes. He blinked. Austin left quietly and slept in another room.

Two weeks later Christine called back to say she was negative and the baby would be safe. Now that she was relieved about her own future she had the leisure to become concerned about Julien's. He said, "My future? Six months of it. I've had it." But then he laughed and said, "We're going to buy a dog."

During the academic exam period in early February, which came soon after Julien's arrival in Providence, they hopped a small plane to New York through a storm (Julien was airsick all the way and vomited three paper sacks full). At La Guardia they met Peter and flew in a 747 to Miami and from there they took yet another flight to Cancún in the Yucatán. Originally Austin and Julien were going to travel to Mexico alone, as a couple, to relax after the ordeal with the Immigration authorities and Julien's discovery of his HIV status. But Peter had been so palpably hurt that Austin had felt bad. "Are you going to push me out of your life now that Julien is finally by your side again?"

Their hotel, which looked as though it had just opened, loomed over the beach, balcony after balcony. On each balcony a hot tub bubbled and steamed, lit from within.

Most of the rooms were dark and empty and the few tourists in the lobby were speaking French Canadian. A mile inland tiny Mayans with silky black hair and wizened faces were sitting and sweating in the dark, eating tortillas in a smoky room with a beaten earth floor. Along the coast these massive hotels, which looked like battle stations that had just landed from alien solar systems, throbbed with air-conditioning and glittered with lights beyond open ditches smelling of sewage. A few of the Mayans in uniform crept timidly across the vacant lobby wielding brass dustpans and brass-handled brushes, but all of the waiters and bellboys were big, laughing Americans with sideburns and sunburns.

The next morning Peter drove them in a rented Volkswagen down the coast. It was hot, in the nineties, and he opened his window. Julien, who was in the back seat, said, "Would you mind closing it?"

"*Closing?* Why? It's boiling hot."

"I'm not well. I have very delicate . . . *poumons.*"

"Lungs," Austin translated.

"The fresh air will do you good," Peter said. He turned to Austin for a confirming smile, but Austin just raised his eyebrows ambiguously. He wanted to stay out of it. He pointed out the occasional entrances to ranches, marked with unobtrusive hand-painted signs. "Do you think they have cattle? The underbrush is so thick—it's really a jungle. Why would anyone call this jungle a ranch?"

Austin kept translating bits and pieces into French, but Julien stared stonily ahead and once Peter made a little click of irritation with his tongue, as though French had been an understandable weakness in Europe but now Julien must stop being indulged.

Julien was wearing two winter scarves and had his collar turned up. At last, his voice choked with emotion, he said, "I'm asking you once more to close your window. You're endangering my health."

"Why? How?" Peter snapped. "Look, we're all three positive, and I have AIDS or at least ARC, but if you're worried that fresh air will cause pneumonia you're wrong. That's just some crazy French superstition about drafts. What's *draft* in French?"

Austin stared at his lap and muttered, *"Courant d'air."*

"You *told* him I'm ill?" Julien spluttered, glaring at Austin. "You promised me you wouldn't tell him or anyone else."

"Look," Peter said, driving faster and clenching the wheel so hard his gaunt knuckles turned white, "we don't go in for that secrecy here."

"I won't tell anyone else," Austin said, "but since we're all three traveling together for ten days . . ."

"Merde!" Julien shouted. *"Merde!* Austin, you do break *la promesse* you made me. Do you think I want—" he stretched out his hand toward Peter, toward the back of his head, silvery, the hair thinning— *"him* to know my life? It's *my* life. *My* death."

"Don't be melodramatic," Peter said.

"I won't say nothing if you closes *la fenêtre.*"

"The window," Austin translated dully.

"It's ninety *degrees!*" Peter wailed in his high, girlish voice.

Julien put his hands over his ears, lowered his head and kept up a low chant of *"Merde, merde, merde, merde. . . ."*

"Close the window, please," Austin said. "We can open the vents. Close it for now."

"Jeez," Peter grumbled. He rolled it up, *nearly* to the top, leaving an inch open, however. His face was blotchy red with anger, his jaw set and his chin poking forward.

They arrived at a luxurious house Austin had rented for two nights. It was part of a gated compound that had its own well-lit, curving suburban streets named in English after North American birds (Robin,

Bluebird, Oriole . . .). It had a food store stocked with Coke and hamburger buns. The only Mayans to be seen were roaming the carefully raked, white sand beach selling ponchos slung over their shoulders. No one bought them. It was too hot for ponchos.

The main bedroom had one wall, on the sea side, that folded back so that one could sit on the mammoth, sybaritic bed and gaze out at the water, but Julien bolted it shut since he preferred excluding Peter to contemplating the waves ("So childish!" Peter hissed).

Austin went first with Julien, then, while Julien slept, with Peter for long walks down the beach.

Julien said, "You *promised* me. Do you think I want that little *girl* with his squeaking little voice and his old man's head and his bird brain to know the details of my personal life? How can you do this to me?"

"I'm sorry. I had no idea you disliked Peter so much. I would never have—" Austin wanted to say "invited you to the States," but he said, "—invited you both on the same long trip. As for your secret, you have to realize that we've been apart for several weeks and I've been frantic about getting you into the States and I've been worried about your health. Peter has been my only *confidant* all this time. He's my ex-lover, he's my best friend, he's very ill with AIDS himself, so of course it seemed natural—"

"I don't care. *Merde!* It's my life. Once you break your promise you could find another reason just as convincing—to *you!*—to tell another person, then another." They sat on the white sand beach and looked out at the evening sky. Julien sighed, smiled slightly, then said, "I've seen the sun set over the sea all my life. It's so strange to think the Atlantic lies to the *east* of us now and the sun is setting behind us."

On his walk with Peter, Austin said, "You're so used to having your own way all the time, but you and Julien are both brats and one of you has to compromise and adjust a bit, just a—"

"So it should be *me*, I guess, who adjusts," Peter muttered angrily, "since he's your boyfriend and he's *schtupping* you."

Austin was shocked by the Yiddish word. Too much New York, he thought.

Day after day they drove along the coast of the Yucatán, then one afternoon they headed inland to a half-buried Mayan site. When they got out of the car Peter went off in one direction, plunging down a faintly marked path that was being taken back by the jungle, almost visibly. It was hot and humid but the sky was cloudy and the light a dull gray. Lizards shot across the path. Julien had found a pyramid no more than twelve feet high and was sitting on a wide, crumbling step halfway up, his face lifted to the light, his eyes closed. He was posed as if for a photo of the sensitive young man communing with the feathered serpent. Wasn't that what these Aztecs (or Mayans) worshipped? Perhaps he was daydreaming about human sacrifice, Peter's.

Austin felt an unbearable tightening of his shoulders. He didn't know if he was supposed to follow Peter into the jungle or stay behind here with Julien. They scarcely spoke to one another now beyond the simplest exchanges at the table and even in the domain of politeness things had broken down. Last night Julien, going through the dining-room door before Peter, had muttered, *"Pardon."* It was his tenth *pardon* in half an hour, as though he wanted to prove that not even his distaste for Peter could make him abandon his aristocratic politeness.

"I hope you're not going to say *pardon* every five minutes for the rest of the trip. It's not necessary. It's even very annoying." The whole dinner was spent in silence except for the weak enthusiasm generated by the headwaiter who made them a flaming dessert and cut the orange peel in a long, unbroken ribbon with a certain sullen flourish.

In bed Julien had hissed to Austin, *"Merde,* he can't force me to give up my manners. I'm sorry, but that's the way my mother brought me up. That's who I am."

Austin had wanted to say, "We were all brought up only too well, Peter as a little Concord patriarch, me as fallen Virginia gentry, you as a member of the *petite noblesse* of Nancy. Perhaps one of us would be a bit more accommodating if only he felt a jot less *entitled.*" But Julien was incapable of understanding the concept of an "American aristocracy" and had once sneered and guffawed when he'd heard those two words pronounced together.

Now as Austin stood in the jungle he wished he *could* be torn in two so that one part could joke with Peter, jostle against him, talk like a speedy but flaky kid about the "neat" ruins, and the other part could muse with the more romantic, serious Julien over the evanescence of human glory.

Neither of them would accommodate the other. Peter suspected but hadn't fully grasped that he no longer ruled over Austin. In the past other guys had gone rapidly through Austin's life and, like Little Julien, had maintained a distance and didn't want to spend all their time with him. Peter imagined he reigned over the harem if not always over the sultan's affections.

But even if Peter were to understand that things had changed, that he'd made himself unwelcome, nevertheless he was so given to collecting and preserving grievances, he so relished and resented his martyrdom, that he'd simply go off bewailing the injustice of it all rather than try to repair the damage. His horror stories about Mexico would soon enough provide him with choice dialogue in his finest soap opera performance ever. The pity, Austin thought, is that a soap, like life, is fated to go on and on. Even the most zealous fans forget earlier episodes and eventually people stop objecting when one actress replaces another in the same role.

That night they stayed in a peaceful, nearly deserted hotel built around a pool on which bright bougainvillea blossoms floated, like little gifts for the dead. Even after the sun had set and the sky had darkened with tropical speed, the purple flowers glowed with more and more intensity, as though they were paper ships lit by candles within. The rooms were cool and austere, monks' cells—high plaster walls, unstained but varnished wood desk, door, ceiling, worn-down terracotta tiles, scrubbed so clean the grouting shone bone-white around them in squares that seemed to advance in the quickly dying light, a bed raised high on spindly metal legs and covered with mosquito netting floating like a bridal veil down from a gathered point on the ceiling. The air smelled of grilled corn. Outside, a dog barked in the humble village between the hotel and the archaeological site.

Austin and Julien lay in the thickening darkness side by side on the bed that squeaked every time they moved. The dog barked with the sort of persistence that Austin had devoted to crying when he was a child.

Julien said, "This is a nightmare. This is the worst trip of my life."

"I'm sorry," Austin said. "It's pretty terrible for me, too. You and Peter are the two people I care for the most—"

"Well, I don't care for him. I just hope I have the satisfaction of seeing him die before I do."

Austin was stunned. He lay in the windless night that had finally descended over them and stared out through the gauze mosquito netting at the dark room. It felt almost as though a cone of ether were being pressed down over him, as though he might swoon into a sleep, never to awaken.

Austin wanted to die. He'd always half-believed he could charm anyone into doing anything, but Julien's hatred for Peter now appeared to be unshakable. Peter was lying in his room down the tiled corridor that was open on one side to the big onyx-smooth slab of the pool, scummed with its wilting flowers. Peter was frail and coughing, spindly, fragile, even breakable, yet his spirit was strong, blazing, stubborn. He could, if happy and relaxed, cock his head to one side, smile with his blurred smile and let his eyes wander, embarrassed and tender, somewhere along the floorboards up to the chair rail. But if he was vexed he could become angry and righteous as a patriarch and his new leanness, as well as the white whiteness of his hair, only made him blaze all the more indignantly as he stared up at the ceiling in exasperation.

Here was Austin, entering his fifties, making a new start in life back in America, infected but healthy, even chubby, and he had invited along Peter and Julien, both years younger than he but much more immediately endangered. He wondered if he'd infected both of them—it was certainly possible. Maybe his virus was benign to him but lethal to everyone else.

Right now he couldn't bear the tension. If only one of them were a bit more diplomatic! Austin had spoiled Peter for so many years, always indulging him, reassuring him of his love, that now, as a result, he was incapable of any self-restraint—

No, Austin wasn't being fair. Poor Peter had no one except Austin to look after him now that he was approaching death. They'd made a pact, not sworn in blood but in time, a more solemn fluid, to look after each other. But now Austin was reneging—not because Julien was *"schtupping"* him (he wasn't)—but because he feared he'd been the one to infect Julien. Austin was acting out of guilt.

And Austin couldn't forget that soon after they'd first met, Julien had promised to nurse Austin all the way through to the end. Back then Julien had just assumed he himself was negative.

There was nothing Austin could do.

In the silence broken only by the dog's tireless barking, Julien said, *"Merde!* I haven't gone through all this just to share every waking moment with this stupid—he *is* stupid, you know. Profoundly stupid. Cretinous. I've made every effort to be polite, but now he's called even that into question. Does he think I want to emulate his quacking voice, his rudeness, his stupid shopgirl talk?"

Austin laughed experimentally and said, "There, there," as though he were a mother calming down an angry child, but the tone irritated Julien even more, who whispered, in the perfect blackness of this high-ceilinged room, "You can see him all you want but he can't come to our house."

"That would break his heart."

"Well, he's breaking my balls."

Austin wished he'd never met Julien. He wished he'd devoted himself with more generosity to Peter during the last year and returned to New York then, twelve months ago. If he'd obeyed his contract with Peter to the letter he would never have had this tragic dalliance and he wouldn't be facing this lacerating dilemma now.

Maybe because his father had been an alcoholic, given to alternating hug fests and the accelerating drums of rage, Austin had never trusted people who didn't possess what he called "a court of higher appeals." People who mainlined passion scared him. He wanted to be able, as a last resort, to call on some cool, unfluctuating sense of justice in them.

Maybe Austin was now too afraid of losing Julien to love him. Maybe he preferred to think of him as a charge, a foreign visitor, even a patient, rather than as a lover. People praised Austin for the "maturity" that had allowed him to survive the deaths by AIDS of so many friends, but he knew that the minute someone became ill he began, secretly, to withdraw larger and larger sums of love from that person's account. Oh, Austin went on being kind and confiding and amusing, but he no longer counted on that person for anything except gratitude.

Not that things were so clear with Julien. He loved Julien—and he certainly resented him.

Julien didn't have a court of higher appeals. He had so many other qualities—loyalty, self-respect, charm, a taste for beauty, vividness, good manners—but he had no more a sense of justice than he had a sense of humor. Perhaps a sense of justice was the gift of Protestants, those people who set themselves up as universal legislators for humanity. In a Catholic country like France where the state did everything for its citizens, they were never called on to be fair or fine. They could alternate between being fiercely partisan or bovinely passive.

When they were driving the next day through the countryside toward Mérida, the capital of Yucatán, Austin was musing in the tense silence within the Volkswagen about Catholics and Protestants in France. This led him to think about André Gide. He recalled that when Gide betrayed his wife Madeleine by staying away from her too long with a boy, the first boy he was truly in love with, she took her revenge by burning all his letters to her. Gide had always delivered himself on the page to her fully and intimately, and he'd counted on assembling those letters into his finest book. But she burned them, acting like a woman in a Greek tragedy, knowing that in doing so she was committing the worst crime imaginable against a writer. With this one act she evened the score and needed never to talk about her grievances.

That was it! he thought. He would act like Madeleine Gide. This half-effaced memory of what a woman had done sixty years earlier would guide him now. Austin decided that if he never ever made love to Julien again this absence of physical affection would mark the exact spot where he refused to accept Julien's cruelty toward Peter. Julien might puzzle over Austin's coldness but he couldn't ask him why he was being so distant. Julien was too discreet or too proud to mention it. He might think it was because he'd lost his looks or Austin's love, but he'd never know and Austin would never tell him why. Or he might think that by becoming positive he, illogically, was scaring Austin off. If Austin made this one resolve he wouldn't need to reproach Julien or even say how appalled he was by his lack of magnanimity. No, Austin could go on being pleasant, kind, even loving to Julien. Obviously he couldn't abandon Julien now, nor would he forgive himself if they lived together with a palpable hostility between them year after year, or however long it would take. They could sleep side by side, hug, spoon, kiss, but everything must remain familial.

Once he'd made that decision he slept peacefully.

Chapter Thirteen

When they were back in Providence, Julien wanted to find work as an architect, but he and Austin quickly discovered that the Northeast was in the grip of a recession, that unemployment in general was high and nowhere more so than in the building trades. In every office architects were being let go. Austin thought, How stupid we are. How out of touch. Anyone else would have known about the economy or found out about it before moving. All this anguish over Julien's work visa was pointless. He's never going to be able to work.

Through *Elle Déco* Austin lined up a story on a prominent Israeli architect who had an immense *atelier* in an old brick factory in Cambridge, Massachusetts. The architect walked them through his many projects, past the impressive models, and touched their shoulders with warmth and politeness as he guided them around corners. But later, as they sat in his office, he explained that he had *no* American projects and was able to keep his large staff on thanks only to his foreign commissions. But even for him, the most successful architect in the region, the immediate future looked grim.

Through that long cold February and March Julien stayed in bed in a silent, shaded room. It was as though he'd decided that if he expended the least amount of energy possible, the virus would become drowsy, dormant.

Or perhaps he was just depressed.

He found something that resembled a café a few blocks from cam pus and he'd go there in the afternoon after an elaborate *toilette*. He'd arrive in a tweed jacket with leather elbow patches, a coat he wore over many layers—a waistcoat, a shirt, a T-shirt and his aquamarine silk scarf from Ethiopia decorated with gold hunting horns. He would sit at a corner table, sipping his coffee and sketching the people around him or reading a two-day-old copy of *Le Monde*.

But more often than not when Austin would come home from art school he'd find Julien stretched out in bed, lying on his back like a *gisant*, a recumbent figure on a tomb. He was motionless, as though under a mud pack or in a trance.

"Are you sleeping?" Austin would whisper.

Sometimes Julien wouldn't respond, even though his eyelids would always flicker. Occasionally he'd say in a soft voice, "I'm resting."

After years of idleness—or rather undisciplined bursts of activity that followed his whims alone, alternating with naps and squalid bouts of TV watching—Austin was overwhelmed by the demands of teaching. He had to prepare two two-hour lectures every week. Other professors, he found out, filled the time by raising easy-to-answer questions and calling on students to hazard an opinion, but Austin couldn't remember their names and he was afraid of their feminist denunciations. He had spent so many years entertaining his young friends in Paris that he now confused the classroom with a dinner party, feared boring his "guests" and hopped lightly, amusingly, from one topic to another. He spoke so quickly, so glancingly, that he'd exhausted his entire knowledge about French furniture in the first class, at least every general idea that could be turned into a snappy summary or droll anecdote.

Of course he remembered that his own professors thirty years ago had been foully dull, had reeked of pedantry, had said everything twice and filled up blackboards by jotting down at random a few of the nouns they'd happened to say. They'd called on students solely to catch them napping or daydreaming. Down time hadn't troubled them in the least. The sweating, squirming kids stammered and struggled to get a word out while the teacher walked about predatorily, rapidly thrumming his fingertips together. Those teachers hadn't had friends the age of their students and they never worried about entertaining them or even winning them over—that was long before the era when students evaluated their professors at the end of the semester.

Exhausted, in a panic, squeezed in behind the wheel of his Volkswagen Sirocco, Austin would come home trailing student papers and lecture notes to find Julien lying in bed, the six grandfather clocks in the house ringing out the hour in slight discrepancy. Julien, like any good French husband, expected two hot meals on the table every day, each with a starter, a main course, a cheese and a sweet. And he wanted Austin to do the shopping every day; he refused to eat anything frozen. Luckily, in the first few weeks they were in Providence, a luxury supermarket opened that sold nothing but organic food. They dubbed it "The Healthy" (*Le Sain*) as opposed to the big chain store, "The Unhealthy" (*Le Malsain*), where they had to go for white flour, white sugar, white rice—in fact, anything white. The Healthy they liked not because the products were pesticide-free but because they had a bit of flavor. The apples weren't brightly lacquered, one could hope that someday the cheeses might ripen, the fish was fresh, the chickens had been allowed to run through a barnyard at least once.

Julien stopped drinking and Austin followed suit. From one day to the next they became entirely sober. At first Austin had a hard time sleeping without wine, but after two weeks he was sleeping more profoundly than at any time since childhood. So well that he had the impression he was never fully awake. His vision began to cloud up with floaters, not just vagrant specks but larger, roiling bits of milky tapioca that swirled as restlessly as the snow in the paperweights Joséphine collected. If he'd sit down to prepare a lecture (and that was virtually all he ever did when he wasn't cooking) the white paper boiled and sank away as though seen through a rain-speckled window. His half-asleep brain seemed no better than his eyes. Feeble, unfocused impressions floated by, leaving him untouched. Silly thoughts loomed closer and waned, all of them fuzzy around the edges as though his mental prescription needed to be revised, sharpened. He had more and more difficulty remembering names—but those lapses he blamed not so much on age as on living, more than ever, in two languages at once. Every thought, every reference, every experience had to be filed away (and retrieved, even if with difficulty) in French and English—oh, sometimes his head ached from the effort. Even his research for his lectures (and for his long delayed and now indefinitely deferred book) was invariably in French, which he had to translate instantaneously.

His students, he discovered, were interested in something they called "theory," some post-structuralist (or had they said "post-modernist") gobbledygook. One guy—who was studying at Brown but who'd signed up for his course—had said, "I'm not really thrilled to be wading into all this *detail* in your class. I'm a semiotics major and I've had five semesters of theory—*Topology and Topos in Proust* was last semester."

"Oh, I *love* Proust," Austin gushed. "Don't you? That scene in which Charlus becomes King Lear—"

"Uh, I've never read Proust, actually, but I've read Derrida, Sontag and Gérard Genette on Proust."

"Sontag?"

"Maybe that was Barthes. I took a course on Barthes's *S/Z*, too, and that was way excellent."

"So you were expecting to learn the semiotics of furniture from me?" Austin asked with acid charm, though the student missed the edge.

"Yeah . . . or, you know, deconstruct furniture. . . ."

"I'm afraid I'm only interested in how it was *constructed*."

"I figured as much. Guess I'm going to hafta drop the course."

Several other students followed suit. Austin realized that now he'd never be offered a permanent position. He'd lived abroad too long in a chatty, self-deprecating *milieu* in which even the most pro-found knowledge had to be worn lightly. His students, he thought, had picked up a smattering of French thought but nothing of *salon* manners. In America, he discovered, people believed what they were told. When Truman Capote (or Frank Sinatra) had said, "I'm the greatest living stylist," everyone in the States went on repeating this bizarre self-promotion for the rest of time. Or when Austin said, "I'm not used to simplifying my humble scraps of knowledge into a few generalizations for eighteen year olds," a colleague, nodding reproachfully, said, "Oh, so you don't know that much about your field? You did too much facile journalism over the years, I guess." Austin had no doubt that he and two French fruits he knew who worked for Didier Aaron, the *antiquaire,* were in fact the only three people in the world who could date and authenticate eighteenth-century French furniture with absolute authority—but *he* couldn't make that claim for himself, now could he? In France enough people knew something about his subject to be able to recognize his perfect expertise, but in America the whole field was too exotic to measure.

His friend, the beringed bearded potter, said over coffee, "These really are the last days of civilization."

"People have been saying that all my life," Austin objected with a smile.

"And people were right. Things *were* going from bad to worse and now they have arrived at worst. These kids *never* read anything. They wouldn't even know which end the book opens at. If you suggest they look at a reference work they smile at you with indulgence, as though you'd suggested they consult an astrolabe or a map of phrenological bumps."

"And what *is* all this about *theory?*"

"Of course these theories are all such rubbish that not even their professors could say what they mean. They just throw abracadabras in each other's teeth and wait to see if it goes down—or *passes,* as my mother used to say about hard-to-digest food. Naturally they can't read French, they don't bother to read any of what they quaintly call texts . . . and *theory* of the French sort is far from the most harmful kind. Where it's really lethal is when it touches on feminism or queer theory."

"I never needed to *theorize* about being queer," Austin said, batting his eyes.

"Don't for a moment imagine that the fact you actually are queer gives you a leg up. In fact for most of them the idea that their professor is a sexually active being amounts to an admission of rape or at best sexual harassment. How's your own case going?"

"Well, I did exactly as you suggested. I organized a study club devoted to a feminist re-examination of eighteenth-century taste—"

"And no one came?"

"Well, one woman came."

"Tough luck. But she'll desist soon enough; they don't like to do anything singly. Once they've looked you in the eye they get this uncomfortable inkling that you might be a human being, too, which queers all their theories."

Julien drove them to New Haven at the end of March for his half-hour Pentamadine spray session, a treatment to prevent PCP, the "gay pneumonia." Dr. Goldstein also examined them both. To Austin he said, "Have you noticed anything about your weight?"

"Uh, no, not exactly."

"You've put on thirty pounds in two months. And you know at your age it may never come off again."

"In Paris I didn't have a car and here there are such big servings—"

"No portion control," Dr. Goldstein nodded.

"And Julien likes big French meals but then he never eats anything and I end up taking seconds and thirds. Portion control be damned!"

Dr. Goldstein didn't smile. He said, "I swim a mile every morning at six in the university pool."

And read three books by noon and have two perfect orgasms to your wife's four by your nine o'clock bedtime, Austin thought bitterly. Oh, and treat two hundred sick fags.

On the way home, as the dark forest of evergreens rolled past, Austin thought, I'm fat so that I won't be tempted to have sex with anyone else. America has neutered me. No, I've done it to myself.

Julien said, "Do you think I've lost my looks?"

"Not at all. You look exactly the same. Even better. More rested. Why?"

"Because when I go to the café no one ever looks at me. Nor on the street."

"In America only New Yorkers cruise each other. They have a special dispensation. In any other American city it's a Federal offense." Austin had never really thought about it before, but of course it was true. This lack of lust or at least inquisitiveness meant that no one expected anything to happen on an American street, except rape or murder.

In Paris people thought you might be a celebrity or a connection or a possible fuck—or at the very least they hoped to borrow a few fashion hints from you. In the métro Austin had seen a seated girl slip her phone number to a standing man. In a queue hands were busy— not such a pleasure for women, perhaps, although Austin had never heard any Frenchwoman complain of it except good-naturedly.

"In France," Julien said, "we believe in the art of seduction."

Later when he came to think of that late winter and early spring in Providence, Austin saw the big wood house with its many windows staring out at the leafless trees like Lot looking back at all the still nearly human pillars of salt. He thought of Julien stretched out on his sepulchral bed. He remembered his own frantic sessions late at night as he scribbled down more and more notes for his less and less well-attended courses. He pictured Julien, pale and big-eyed, dressed in silks and cashmeres and an intricately tied ascot, descending the wood staircase to the dining room. There he'd taste the asparagus experimentally, holding each stem between his fingertips in the elegant French way while like a true American Austin sawed away at his. In a soft, back-from-the-grave voice Julien would ask him about the day's adventures ("Of course I don't have any," he said, "on a day like today when I didn't go to the café").

Julien thought Austin had lost his talent as a "cooker," as he said in English, and he appeared to find his gossip less spicy than in France; Austin couldn't make him understand that the local ingredients were inferior. Julien was, of course, quick to concede that everything that happened "over here" was simply material for future anecdotes to be told later around the Paris dinner table. Austin didn't think of it that way. This wasn't a half-humorous field trip for him. He was back among his own people. He realized, when they invited the bearded colleague for dinner and the instructor from the Brown French department along with his boyfriend, that in America (at least outside New York) people didn't feel the Parisian necessity to be "brilliant" in conversation—and Austin's efforts had a chilling effect on the others. In fact, the table talk kindled only when Austin left the room to slice the free-range turkey. When he returned, he cast everyone into a fit of self-consciousness; he interrupted, he translated, he wheeled out a sure-fire old Paris anecdote that fizzled without provoking any response other than confusion. The professors began to discuss an enemy of theirs, someone who'd chained an undergraduate to a radiator and thrashed him. When the boy had complained to the Dean of Sexual Harassment and Gender Infringement Issues, the professor had impenitently insisted that the boy had "begged for it" and the Department of Humanities had tried to hush everything up since the sadist was a leading Elizabethan scholar—irreplaceable, apparently.

Despite the juicy possibilities of this gossip, the professors didn't know how to serve it up. They got bogged down in detail, they introduced too many names, and they never told the end. Their main activity was to work up indignation over the minor players. Although the French professor spoke French to Julien over drinks, at the table he reverted to a voluble, joky English and frowned when he caught Austin mistranslating him.

Most nights they were alone and watched TV from the revolving chairs. Since the aesthetics professor specialized in popular culture the TV was state-of-the-art and, as promised, fully loaded with fifty channels. Julien was specially fascinated by the shopping channel—all those ropy, arthritic hands displaying diamond chips, the strange household appliances, the ghastly pantsuits in fabrics that resembled shower curtains. He laughed with his bass rumble.

Julien said, "In France we have only five channels, but here, where you have fifty, people don't even have the focus of the same few programs to discuss the next day at the office. In France there are a handful of cultural events everyone must know about and discuss—

the Goncourt Prize book, the latest Alain Resnais movie, a William Forsythe ballet, a Bob Wilson staging of an opera. But here you have so many cities and so few national newspapers—in fact there's not much press."

They were going past a kennel in the Massachusetts countryside when Julien begged to stop. They'd already discussed the possibility of buying a dog. Julien picked up a basset hound puppy. "Look how he presses his little pink belly against me. Let's get him!"

"What will you name him?"

"Ajax. I've always wanted a basset. But you wanted a collie, *non?*"

"Only because I had one as a child. But they're rather stupid dogs."

The tiny puppy staggered uneasily about the big, drafty house, stepping on his long ears. Julien was delighted with Ajax; he declared him the most intelligent and affectionate dog who'd ever lived, almost human in his sensitivity.

But he wouldn't eat. Julien was certain that he'd been weaned too early. "*Merde!* He's just a baby! These people are criminals! I'm going to sue them!"

"Spoken like a true American," Austin said. "You're learning quickly."

One of Austin's students, a girl with a classically beautiful face, red hands and split, over-treated blond hair, came by from time to time. Eleanor had a fascinatingly hoarse voice and a sly, dirty laugh; she laughed all the time as though Austin had just said something ironic and nuanced, although his years of living abroad had made him, on the contrary, wonderfully straightforward—"You're wicked," she'd exclaim and point at him with a badly bitten nail. She had a reputation for drugs and lying. She'd dropped out because she was shooting heroin and this semester was her first back in school after a year-long hiatus. Her stories about her father sounded possibly exaggerated. "He'd stolen away a big Mafia type's girlfriend. Oh, no. Unh-unh. Hel-lo-oh! I mean: *please.* So, he was, like, with her in some fabulous suite, like, overlooking the Mediterranean, fourth floor up. He was out on the balcony in his cool smoking jacket, like, sipping champagne. Suddenly the girl, like, wasn't there anymore. She'd, like, vanished. No one ever saw her again. And Dad was suddenly, like, on the sidewalk below—splat!—he's a hopeless quadriplegic now. That's how he got into drugs, helping him fight the pain."

It was hard for Austin to look mournful about a cliché that had occurred to a figment, but Julien, who couldn't follow the story but appreciated its setting on the Riviera, smiled with alternating bursts of sympathy and pleasure. He also liked Eleanor (who'd been in the weaving department) because she wore an old Chanel suit and a pillbox hat. Her very high heels, her bare, scratched legs, the soiled suit with the trademark gold buttons (they were sewed on very badly and one was missing), the Jackie Kennedy hat, bobby-pinned into her over-processed hair, her splashed-on Shalimar—oh, even Austin could see it was all supposed to be a big camp, but Julien just assumed this poor misguided American wanted to be chic in the authentic French manner but hadn't yet mastered a few crucial details. Her grown-up clothes failed to disguise her extreme youth, and her constant tremor. She had a boyfriend—a lean, pasty-faced, long-haired boy who *slithered* when he entered a room—whom she called "Dybbuk" for some reason. Maybe he was the one who'd infected Eleanor with the idea that lurking under every bland statement was a dangerous steel trap of irony, since he punctuated every burst of mumbled speech with a bass chortle. He painted big scary canvases that were partially burned. Eleanor assured Austin that Dybbuk's erections were "alabaster hard" since he'd started shooting up. Austin found it hard to believe that such an exhausted youth, who sat whenever he had a chance or just hunkered with his back to a wall if no other resting place presented itself, could manage even the most cursory Play-Doh erection.

Austin liked her because she wasn't a PC harpy and because she saw him as an equal. She had tidbits of gossip about people they knew, about herself if necessary, and she assumed that Austin's life (or at least thoughts) must be agreeably scandalous.

Two days after they bought Ajax Eleanor came by and saw the puppy lying mournfully in its wicker nest.

"He hasn't eaten a bite since he got here," Austin said. "I'm afraid he's going to starve to death."

"Let me handle this," Eleanor said. She warmed up some milk and sugar and then fed the formula to him with an eyedropper. Suddenly he came back to life, tail wagging, nails slipping and clacking on the linoleum. Julien had tears in his eyes.

"He was weaned too early," Eleanor said.

"Yes, I am of . . . agreement," Julien said loudly. *"Mon pauvre petit bébé,"* he said to Ajax, cuddling him. "Can he eat something solid?"

"Do you have any turkey?"

"Turkey?"

"Dinde," Austin translated.

"I'll drive over to the Healthy, right now." Julien raced around the house looking for his keys and sunglasses. He dashed back into the kitchen to kiss Eleanor on the forehead.

Ajax never stopped eating after Eleanor, as Julien put it, "opened his appetite." "That is a woman," Julien declared. "We men are nothing beside the powerful maternal instinct. Only Woman can save us, civilize us, give us life."

Nor was Julien ever far from his dog after that. He took him out for long walks. "Jax" would pull on his leash toward the sound of children's voices. There was a preschool playground nearby and Jax would begin to whine and tug as soon as he heard that constant high hum. The kids would pretend to be scared of him, which was absurd, he was so small; their high-pitched cries would send Jax into ever more vigorous paroxysms of barking and yearning.

When they'd come home Julien would recount their adventures ("An old lady came down off her porch and offered him raw hamburger, but I told her he'd just been fed. Ajax was furious with me, but you can't be too cautious"). Julien treated Jax as an invalid, though one who'd made a splendid recovery. He'd wash his ears, especially the tips which had dragged through the dust. He loved his paws and marveled over their four-leaf-clover pads. "Look at his giant curving nails, he's like a pterodactyl. He's a very primitive animal, one of the very first dogs." On the first sunny day, though it was still cool, Julien took his nap with Ajax in a big ecru hammock they'd brought back from Mexico. Austin took pictures of a dozing Julien and a wide-awake Ajax peering out over the taut fabric.

They visited the vet for vaccinations and heart-worm pills. "Heart-worm" was the one English word calculated to defeat Julien (since it contained an initial aspirated *h,* an unfamiliar *o,* two hard *r*'s and too many other strong consonants in strange places), but he said it often out of anxiety. Ajax was outfitted with a thick, metal-studded leather collar to which an ID tag was attached giving their address and phone number. Julien said it was a very "butch" collar; Austin was surprised he knew the word and wondered if he'd learned it from a gay American.

The very next day Julien was walking in the woods with Ajax off the leash when the puppy heard the cry of children and took off like a bolt. Julien ran as quickly as possible after him but Ajax had soon outpaced him. By the time a panting Julien came jogging up to the playground, Jax had terrorized all the little kids. He would run toward them, jumping up on them, which would set them off in spasms of screams. He would then become all the more excited, turning and turning, looking for new playmates. As he wheeled around, his protruding tongue spattered the children with drops of saliva. His eyes were intelligent but vulnerable; his mouth appeared to be smiling. A teacher had come out with a broom to drive him away. Julien intervened and dragged Jax off on the leash. He was spluttering with rage against the sadistic teacher, but he hadn't known how to denounce her in English.

"Pauvre petite bête," Julien crooned to an exhausted Jax when they were back home. He wrapped the dog in his arms as Jax lightly snored. Every few seconds Julien swooped down to kiss his pink, freckled stomach. "He smells like hot popcorn," he said.

"A boy I met out walking with Ajax," Austin said, "told me he'd known lots of bassets. He says they are the most stubborn dogs alive. And always running away."

"What nonsense!" Julien said, indignant. *"Le pauvre petit* just thinks he's a human child. That's why he wanted to play with the other children. But these neurotic American children just start to scream when they see him—what's *wrong* with them?"

"Ajax is American, too, Julien."

Julien kissed his stomach again as Ajax dozed on. *"Mon pauvre petit américain.* And he's black, too. That's why he wants to move to France. He's heard that American blacks are better treated in France. I've already read him the life of Joséphine Baker."

Austin had never heard any whimsy coming out of Julien's mouth before, but now it never stopped. Julien decided that he would raise Ajax to be the next pope. He was constantly on the lookout for pious deeds and minor miracles, which would confirm his calling. Julien started calling him Pius VII, which in French was pronounced *"Pissette"* and also meant "little pisser." The whole idea was mad and in the worst taste, but Julien clung to it so long that Austin suspected he took it half-seriously.

One day, while talking on the phone in his office at school with Peter, Austin mentioned Ajax. It just slipped out.

"Who's Ajax?"

"A dog."

"Whose dog?"

Austin didn't want to say *ours* so he said, "Mine."

"Your dog? You bought a dog?"

"Yes."

"So it's really a dog you and Julien bought."

"You could say that."

"A puppy?"

"Yes. It's a basset hound."

"How old?"

"Probably just two months old."

"That's a big commitment, isn't it?"

"Not really."

"Dogs live to be twelve or fifteen years old. It must have been Julien who wanted it. You're too egotistical to want a dog, though I suppose you're attached to him by now."

"How do you know?"

"Who wouldn't get attached to a puppy? Anyway, I know you. If you're in love the person can talk you into anything. Although you'd never buy me a dog. When we were together you refused to buy me a dog."

"Well, at first we were living in a one-room apartment in New York, then in two rooms in Paris. A third-floor walk-up."

"I would have walked him. It's good exercise. Good *cruising*." Peter said the word *cruising* with a bitter explicitness, as though only by making such a sexual allusion could he hope to communicate with someone as depraved as Austin. Peter was silent for a moment, then Austin realized he must be crying.

"What's wrong?" Austin asked.

"You never loved me enough to give me a dog. For a gay couple a dog is like a child. You and Julien have a child now. I guess he's won."

"Won what?"

Suddenly Peter was angry. "Oh, nothing. If you can't figure that one out you're even more out of touch than I thought." He hung up.

Austin didn't know what to do—send him flowers, call him back, fly down there? Now that he was far away from his Paris friends (and given that almost all his New York friends were dead), Austin contemplated with horror his new break with Peter. His world was shrinking rapidly. Soon he'd be all alone, and for Austin aloneness was the equivalent to death. He felt bad that he'd hurt Peter in so many ways—but he was even angrier that Julien should have treated Peter so high-handedly.

Julien, Austin thought, had bad, heterosexual values. As the new wife he, Julien, assumed he had the right to insist that Austin never talk to the ex-wife, Peter, much less shower the castoff with attentions and presents. Only heterosexuals could be so cruel; among male homosexuals friendship ruled supreme.

In France Austin had had a busy sex life before he met Julien. He'd gone from one affair to another, the most exciting and memorable (and longest) one having been with Little Julien. He'd frequented a sauna for older men and their sometimes much younger admirers. He'd made love two or three times a week, just as when he'd been twenty years old, except now he couldn't just walk out the door and trick; now he had to plan ahead, buy a few opera tickets, cook a few meals, be prepared for rejection, go somewhere that had a special clientele.

He'd fallen in love with Big Julien, perhaps just a bit because Gregg had told him Julien was "husband material." If Gregg hadn't suggested that Austin invite Julien away for the weekend and "hold onto that one, hon," would Austin have made a play for him? Maybe not, since Austin was still pining over Little Julien and still, even here in Providence, jerked off thinking about him. When he'd called Little Julien once from Providence he'd said, in a romantic tone, "I think of you often."

"Yeah, every night just before going to sleep," Little Julien had said with his wicked laugh that almost submerged his words in a rushing flood of hilarity.

Austin felt less alive than he had in years. It was as though his pulses were racing (so many department meetings, private conferences, lectures, so many papers to grade) while at the same time his feelings had never been so dim, so nearly extinct. He longed for sleep. When Julien fell asleep, Austin would sneak out of the room into one of the other bedrooms. If Julien complained, Austin said, "The other rooms feel neglected," but so much silliness only concealed his need to be alone. Once Julien said, "I suppose it would be wrong if I . . . made love to someone now that I'm positive." It was his only acknowledgment of their chastity, which he ascribed, possibly, to Austin's fear of "reinfection." He once said something that revealed he chalked up Austin's sexual indifference to his own becoming positive. Did he think Austin was repelled by infected meat? Julien was so close-mouthed there was no way of knowing what he was feeling.

Back in Paris Austin had had hours and hours every day to marinate on his daybed but here, in Providence, he was always expected to be on tap. Only in bed in the spare room could he masturbate and recall every detail of Little Julien's body, as well as his coarse sensuality, which coexisted so neatly with his civilized behavior. Or he'd replay erotic encounters that went back all the way to his early adolescence in Virginia. . . .

Some nights he was too tired even to masturbate, though he was convinced he needed to, not because he required the physical release but because he was thirsty for privacy, introspection, for the lavish pleasure of looking inward.

He who'd stayed young because he'd had so few responsibilities was now hurtling through time, as a meteorite scorches its path when it enters the earth's atmosphere, burning his way into maturity and beyond, into age.

His students never looked at him as a human being, except Eleanor who, when she'd been a freshman at a college in New York, had had an affair with an ancient English philosopher and cultivated the knack of regarding her elders as contemporaries. But otherwise no one ever commented on his moods, clothes, remarks. Nor did Julien, who now spent more and more time with Ajax walking the gray sidewalks under gray skies. Julien loved him—loved their sexless good-night kisses, loved it when Austin came home from school, loved watching TV in the matching bucket chairs, Ajax belly-up across his lap, whiskers twitching to the broadcast roar of a gunfight, his long, silky ears quickening into life when Lassie barked on screen in an ancient rerun. But Julien didn't study Austin or even really notice him; he had been as surprised as Austin that Austin had gained ten kilos and even made a show of indignantly denying it, not just out of kindness but also out of indifference or rather inattentiveness.

Sometimes, of course, Austin's days went well and he felt happy to be dashing about campus, but then he'd catch himself as he commented on new departmental regulations and schedules or he'd realize that this was a life, yes, but a lesser one. Paradoxically, he'd never felt so understimulated intellectually as here, at a university. Professors produced books and papers, but they had no idea how to serve up their ideas in conversation. They were specialists, not intellectuals. They'd even looked especially worried when Austin once referred to them unthinkingly as "intellectuals." They reacted as though the word carried a nerdy, rabbinical weight and suggested something unwashed and unathletic. They were all just regular guys, and those who'd been born in Europe were particularly dull, as if they'd taken the pledge not to introduce anything tricky or insufficiently bland into a social evening, much less something stimulating, which they would have called "pretentious."

Perhaps because they never talked about their work to nonspecialists, they never submitted their writing to a standard of common sense. They were alone in a private hell populated only by

graduate students, loyal colleagues and spiteful rivals—
nom would ever have said, "Hey, wait. What does all this
vhat earthly application does it have?" Austin thought
of scholarship, concerned with dates, methods, attributions, was unimportant but at least honest.

The bigger problem was what he'd just heard described for the
first time as "the dumbing-down of America." He recognized that precisely in the years he'd been away Americans had lost interest in the
game of high culture. Europe concerned them not at all except as an
optional but fun theme park. People no longer pretended to a wide
general knowledge; each academic had his specialty, which he learned
as a baker might learn baking, but no one claimed now to have mastered all the culinary techniques of culture.

One afternoon Austin found Julien talking to a young red-haired
woman who resembled Christine, not just because they shared the
same coloring but in something particular—the large mouth, perhaps,
or the deliberate way of talking.

The woman's name was Lucy and she was from Hot Springs,
Arkansas. She was a graduate student at Brown in creative writing,
even though she was already forty-two and a professional accountant.

"But, Lucy, how can you *learn* writing?" Julien asked as he poured
her more tea. He'd taken extra pains with his *toilette* today, Austin
noticed. He was wearing not one but *two* scarves around his neck. He
had on his heavy, ankle-high, pale brown Church shoes with the brass
side buckles, polished to a high gloss. He didn't seem as interested in
the conversation as in the pose he was striking.

Lucy said, "What do you mean? What do you mean, *learn?*"

"Yes," Austin chimed in, "we French people are convinced literature is divine and is inspired directly by God or Racine, we're never
sure which."

"Racine?" Lucy looked confused.

"Just teasing."

"Oh. You were teasing?"

"Moving right along," Austin said, standing up. "I have a few
quizzes to grade. I'll leave you two youngsters to your tea party and
literary conversation."

After that Julien was constantly crouched over pots of jasmine tea with Lucy. He liked her because she liked him, because she resembled Christine—and because she spoke very slowly. Her talk was as slow as her metabolism. In fact, Julien learned English from Lucy. She was never in a rush and quite routinely expressed the same thought in two or three slightly varied ways, as an Italian woman might. Instead of over-articulating or shouting, as Americans usually did when addressing foreigners, Lucy just kept buttering a thick salve of words over every subject that came up. She reminded Austin of his paternal grandmother, who'd always said, "Now take your time telling me about it. I want all the details."

Lucy had a big white BMW which she'd bought second-hand. She drove it with just one hand in her lazy, soft-boned way; Julien was very good at imitating the way she held her hand, the elbow close to her breasts, the wrist curved like a swan's neck. He even learned her way of checking herself out in the rear-view mirror, of letting her face go inert in a professional model's deadpan.

He said he found her to be a bore, a *chieuse* ("pain in the ass" was perhaps the best translation), and whenever the phone would ring he'd call out, *"Bonjour, les chieuses!"* He liked to complain about Lucy, about her whiny chicken-farmer accent, her fake ladylike airs, her limp hand on the steering wheel, but he loved it when she prepared him a genuine Southern goulash (though he hated the result). "Inedible!" he whispered rudely when Lucy went "to the little girl's room," as she called it. Her mother and aunt were identical twins, bony Southern ladies with white hair they still wore in the same cut. Julien adored studying their photo and marveling over their interchangeable looks. He liked to hear about the South, although he would have preferred more plantations with Greek columns and fewer twisters, trailers and red-neck atrocities.

Lucy was his first real friend in America and a thoroughly intimidated, besotted woman friend at that. She fell for their French allure and she often said, *"oui, oui,"* in the midst of an English sentence. Donna, who was one of Lucy's friends and Austin's student, said, "Gosh, I hear Lucy has learned French from Julien. She runs around saying, *'oui, oui,'* all the time now, then clapping her hand over her mouth as though it just slipped out. Then she says, *'Pardon,'* with a French accent."

Julien talked to her for hours and hours about his mother and wicked ex-wife. Lucy wanted to hear all the sordid details and was expecting an American-style confession, but Julien had his own way of telling a story and certainly wasn't soliciting sympathy. He didn't want to "spill" about his mother, have a "good cry" and "get it all out." No, for Julien his mother's death was his identity. He had made mourning a way of life. Although he wore his bright scarf, he'd sewn black ribbons to his innermost soul.

Nor was he hoping to "let go" of his rage against his wife; he hoped for revenge and, as he liked to say, "Revenge is a plate to be eaten cold." Or rather, on some days he was angry with Christine, though on others he wondered how she was faring and he hoped her pregnancy was going well. When he was alone with Austin, he liked to talk about sex with women; it amused him that Austin had never slept with a woman. *"Pauvre petit,"* he chided, using a deep voice and pursing his lips. *"Il était mignon,"* he said ("He *was* cute"), that weird third person and past tense French grandmothers used when addressing a baby. Austin would blush and that would make Julien laugh even harder. Austin suspected that most gay men of his generation were embarrassed by women, and elaborately polite to them, because they didn't desire them; they'd insulted women by not wanting to make love to them. Younger gay guys, who'd grown up in co-ed dorms with women, treated them casually, guiltlessly, as sisters. But Julien liked them not as sexless sisters but as horny, lusty ladies.

Ajax took months to be housebroken and left piles of shit on all the carpets which, as luck would have it, were pale. When at last he'd been trained, he started to chew everything. He was teething, and soon he'd sharpened his teeth on the legs of every chair and the upholstery of every couch and armchair, even the sacred blue bucket chairs reserved for television viewing. Summer came and Julien was always outdoors with Ajax in the hammock or sprawling on the lawn in very tight white shorts and no shirt. A teenage boy—one of those Rhode Island kids who'd never left the state even though it took only an hour to drive from one end of it to the other—hung around for hours on his bike, chatting up Julien. He was obviously attracted to Julien, who encouraged him until one afternoon the boy, aroused, said he was hungry and slouched into the kitchen and went through the fridge.

That night Julien was outraged. "How dare he take things out of our *frigo?*"

"Americans do that," Austin explained. "At least kids do. It's called 'raiding the icebox.'"

"Have they no education?"

"No. None."

But despite this fit of pique Julien had been pleased to see he could still attract someone, a young man, irredeemably American, an idiot who thought Paris and France were two separate countries, but who had velvety eyes set in a baby-fat face covered with blond down, someone whose short, wide erection showed through his shorts when he looked at Julien too long. Julien was still in the running.

They spent June and July in Providence. Austin had forgotten about hot, humid American summers but he and Julien enjoyed sleeping late in the air-conditioned bedroom, then taking long walks in the sticky early evening with Ajax under the huge, leafy trees past the big wood houses, which seemed even less inhabited in summer than in winter. No one was around, although sprinklers rotated on lawns and garbage was collected and sometimes the radio, tuned to a baseball game, crackled through an open window. Julien said it reminded him of Addis Ababa.

At night, after darkness fell at last and a breeze came up off the river, they'd eat a *salade niçoise* made of seared fresh tuna from the Healthy. They put out mosquito-repellent citronella candles in tin buckets on the porch, which Julien called *la terrasse*, and they'd set speakers on the windows and listen to Mozart CDs and stroke Jax's tummy as he dozed after a strenuous day of destroying the furniture. "Did you notice how he never barks?" Austin asked admiringly.

"Of course he doesn't bark—though one day an ambulance went past and Jax started to bay, exactly as though he'd heard a hunting horn. The hunt is in his genes."

In August they rented a beach shack on an island nearby. The shack smelled of kerosene and every dish in it was chipped. The construction had obviously been done half a century earlier by a ship's carpenter—the staircase was snug and Austin, at least, had to turn sideways to mount it. The upstairs windows were portholes and the night lights were beautiful old port and starboard lights glowing a dull ruby-red and a dirty emerald within verdigrised brass fixtures.

When it was foggy they'd walk down the empty beach (*"la plage sauvage,"* as Julien called it, to distinguish it from a raked beach with cabanas for hire, the kind one found in Nice or Cannes). Ajax was afraid of the water and fascinated by it; it was a moving, noisy thing to chase but he didn't like to be wet. He looked abashed and licked his salty coat with deep chagrin.

One morning they awakened late to see through the porthole a man on a wood barge hauling cages up out of the water. Ajax was barking joyously on the muddy shore, turning round and round as if to reel in this big, unknown catch. Austin and Julien slipped on shorts and strolled out to see what he was doing. The day was so calm and misty that no one was around.

"Hey, how you doin'?" Austin said. He was surprised how his voice carried.

"Good."

"What are you fishing?"

"Eels."

"Seems like you got a lot of them."

"I'm the only one round here fishes for 'em."

"Whatcha do with 'em? Sell 'em to rest'rants?"

"Hell, no—folks round here won't touch 'em. No, I pack 'em on ice and we fly 'em direct to Brussels. Them Belgians pay top dollar for eels, don't you know?"

"Right. Sure we know. This fellow here's French. We know all about eels. They're great. Smoked. Or in green sauce."

"Wouldn't know myself."

He went back to his work without any need, apparently, to wind up what they'd been saying. He was a big man, Austin's age, grizzled, wearing grease-stained overalls. He was so close, at least so audible, that Austin could hear him breathe as he dredged the cages up out of the cold, silted water. Austin wanted to change places with him. He thought of his young, fat truck-driver, the guy who'd driven him to get his trunk in Boston. Ajax looked solemnly up at them as the mist laid down strip after strip of softening gauze over the scene—this wound—for Austin thought the morning light was achingly bright.

That night in bed they could hear Ajax gnawing feverishly at the base of his tail, harvesting fleas. "Have you heard about Lyme disease?" Julien asked.

"No."

"It's very dangerous. It's from *tiques*—"

"Ticks."

"The kind on deer."

"Deer? But there are no deer on this island."

"Oh." He was silent. Austin could almost hear him blinking beside him. "Are you certain?"

"Yes."

Lucy visited them for a weekend. Julien arranged her clothes so that he and she looked alike. He tied her blouse in such a way that it would expose a bit of her stomach. They both wore French sailors' berets that Julien had found in a harbor-front store, dark blue with red pompoms. He made her buy expensive lizard-skin sandals like his. He tied a red silk neckerchief around her pale throat, as he tied one around his own swarthy one. They rode bikes the five miles into town and Lucy made him buy her a chocolate soda from an old-fashioned soda shop decorated with a black counter, chrome stools and a pale-green neon-bordered wall clock. Julien was outraged that in America dogs could not go into restaurants. When Austin explained that they were excluded for reasons of hygiene, Julien said, "But Ajax is much cleaner than most of their clients."

Back home they barbecued swordfish and ate it with béarnaise sauce off a card table they'd hauled outside. Lucy drank too much white wine. A foghorn was hooting. The big lighthouse just across the straits was like a geometer turning a compass round and round, one that drew on the air with cheerful futility. Lucy became kittenish and asked Austin to go fetch her sweater from the cottage. When he came trudging back up the short hill to the promontory that looked down on what they now called "Eel Bay," he saw their faces illumined from below by a match as Julien lit them after-dinner cigarettes; they looked like children staring down into Japanese lanterns. Ajax was stretched out, his black chin balanced on a white paw; he seemed troubled because it was obvious he didn't approve of the dew settling on the grass or of the fog rolling in in palpable waves around him, as though there were a ghostly atmospheric surf that moved to its own independent tide.

"Are you happy?" Lucy asked Julien. She was a self-conscious girl, never very spontaneous, and made these strange stabs at depth from time to time. Of course Julien liked her way of talking, maybe because no one French would risk such a gambit. Austin could also tell she was awkward because she felt so much. She was sweet and sensitive, which made her oddly remote despite her Southern gush; obviously she'd learned not to show her feelings. She seemed in love with Julien.

He said, "Of course I'm sad I have to die, but I love Austin so much. I'd rather live with him for just two or three years than live a whole long life without him."

"And you, Austin?"

He was staggered by Julien's honesty and the simple, manly certainty with which he'd talked. He wanted to be just as honest and loving. He found himself saying, "I could never really give myself to someone before. Not really. Maybe because I wasn't sure they needed me or maybe I was afraid of being suffocated. But now, because our love, Julien's and mine, is short and intense, I'm not afraid of it, even though if I outlive Julien I'll probably be terribly—not just hurt. Cast down. Destroyed." Austin was surprised by the honesty of what he'd just said. Strange that Lucy's questions should have made him speak so clearly and feelingly, whereas his private thoughts were just turbulent murk, like this fog rolling in.

"*Pauvre petit,*" Julien said. "You'll have Ajax." He whispered to the dog, while holding one front paw in each hand and staring into his eyes, "You'll be a *brave toutou,* won't you, and take care of Papa, won't you? Won't you?" Ajax looked very solemn for an instant, then embarrassed. He pulled free and walked away.

Chapter Fourteen

Early in the autumn Austin offered to take Peter anywhere he
wanted. "We can go to Paris or San Francisco or Rome or London—you name it."

"Disney World."

"In California?" Austin asked, his heart sinking.

"No, dummy. Disney World is in Florida."

"Do you want to stay there just a night or two and then go on
down to Key West for the weekend?"

"Gosh, no, are you crazy? Disney World takes a whole week to do
properly."

"What is it, exactly? Rides?"

"You don't know anything, you're not even a real American.
There's the Epcot Center, for instance, which is made up of pavilions
from all over the world. It's like traveling to Asia and Africa and
Europe without ever leaving America. Each country has a fabulous
restaurant."

"Oh."

"You don't want to go, you offer me my choice, then when I
choose a place *I* want, you're too snobbish even to *try*—"

"Don't be absurd, Peter, I'm delighted to discover Disney World."

Julien had said repeatedly that Austin was free to see Peter anywhere he liked, so long as he, Julien, would never have to lay eyes
again on that "whiny little girl" (*cette petite fille pleurnicharde*). Now he
could hardly object to the trip to Orlando, though he said, "You could
probably go to London for the same amount of money. It seems a
waste. But I guess Peter wants to ride on the rides."

Austin would be away only for a week. He left plenty of money
with Julien (who also had the American Express card Austin had
given him). "I'll call every day," Austin said. "Lucy has instructions to
look after you."

"I don't want that *chieuse* around the house all the time," Julien
said; he routinely insulted all his friends. For him only the family
existed. Friends were seen as false gods, sacrilegious rivals to the true
cult of Mother-Father-Brother—or now, under the new dispensation,
of Ajax and Austin. Julien allowed himself to find friends "amusing"
or "diverting," as though they were *saltimbanques* in a perpetual circus
of wasted time and distracted feelings. But he could drop them in an
instant and thought he owed them nothing.

"Well, you might get lonely. Let her prepare you a meal."

"Her? *La chieuse* can't cook, all those dreadful spices that make you
cry and give you a stomachache. When I was still healthy—"

"In Addis Ababa?"

"Precisely. Then I could experiment with spicy foods, but not now,
not one of Lucy's little bayou gumbos, oh, no, that I can't survive.
Besides, I want to be alone. With my thoughts. My past. Thoughts of
my mother. Now, no one exists for me except my brother and you and
Ajax. And my memories of my mother. My wife is dead for me. And
so is my father."

Austin flew to New York, changed planes and according to a pre-
arranged plan found himself sitting beside Peter on the New York–
Orlando flight. Peter was noticeably thinner but carefully dressed and
groomed. He was testy with Austin, although Austin was calm and
resigned to everything. He'd dedicated this week to his old friend.

They had a rented car that came with the package—flight, hotel,
amusement park admission. Their hotel was one of the more modest
ones, but Austin still found it expensive. Of course he realized that all

these big families came to Disney World for their dream vacation and, if there were five of them, spent five thousand dollars in a week, a fifth of a normal salary. Or so he imagined. Perhaps there was a save-in-advance layaway plan. Perhaps a normal salary was fifty thousand.

Peter and he were the only pair of adult men in what was otherwise a world of strollers and harnesses, diaper-changing areas even in the men's toilets, high chairs at table and unbreakable plastic glasses in the bedrooms. They parked their rented car and had no further need of it, since they were ferried from the hotel to the rides in Disney buses.

Because they'd come during the last week of September the crowds were smaller and they seldom had to wait more than twenty minutes to get on a ride. Peter and Austin sat in a boat that was just inches above water level and were jerked and dragged by chains through a fun house—except the displays weren't scary, unless you found dolls singing songs about world unity frightening. All the dolls were singing the same jingle in high, chipmunk voices that later he couldn't get out of his head. He kept picturing the dolls—Chinese in coolie hats, Russians in white fur toques—tilting forward in a sudden glare, singing the words in various ethnic accents.

They spent a whole day in a special section devoted just to the movies. Disney cartoon characters were impersonated by costumed youngsters in mouse or dog heads (Pluto made Austin think of Ajax). They ran up to children and cavorted with them. For Austin, these encounters were highly embarrassing because he could hear the heavy breathing of a real, smaller human being under the frozen smile and could see the round, unblinking eyes through the plastic nostrils and he wondered what the performer looked like, what was his name, if he was an actor with aspirations.

"How's your boyfriend?" Peter asked one afternoon as they were returning to the hotel on the bus.

"I should call him—oh, he's okay."

"What does he do all day? Watch soaps like me?"

"He spends a lot of time walking and grooming Ajax. He even engaged a dog trainer—he calls him *le professeur,* remember how even a gym teacher in France is called *le professeur de sport?*"

"Obedience training."

"Yeah, well, it didn't work. Ajax learned nothing, not even the commands to sit, certainly not to come when called. Julien believes Ajax will someday obey, but only if he says the words of command in English—'cawm,' 'seet,' 'gude boh.'"

"I know," Peter said. "We had a basset when I was a kid, named Relentless. My mom had to give him away. He was too destructive. And she said all she ever saw was his fat butt as he was waddling away while she screamed herself hoarse."

Austin resented the callous way Peter was talking about his basset—and then, for no reason at all, Austin felt, as if an elevator had just dropped a floor, that soon (in a year?) he'd never hear Peter's high-pitched voice again nor see his lopsided, loopy expression, one blue eye bigger and higher than the other gray one, never again would he be so pleasantly jostled along in the rapid boil of Peter's bubbling chatter, nor feel Peter's indignation burning steadily under it. Time was meant to be lived patiently, one step at a time, and those who lived in it were meant to walk with their eyes trained on their feet. But something about being here, in this unreal place dedicated to such cheerless, standardized pleasure, a place that was just a hot, sunny void in central Florida, a joy that was paid for, dollar by dollar, as a meter ticked rapidly and chains tugged the boat violently around the corner and yet another wall of dolls lurched forward in a brightening, then dimming light, their mechanical mouths timed to the high, wailing song about a small, small world—something about this place made time break into shards, bits of the regretted past lying next to bits of the feared future.

"Are you worried about the future?" Peter asked him.

"You mean taking care of Julien, watching him become more and more ill?"

"No, going on living without him, after his death."

Austin laughed. "Honestly, I don't think that far ahead. I just rush around to my classes and prepare him meals. I live from day to day, not wisely like AA people but as though I'd been stunned." He then asked, "Are you afraid, Peter?"

"Of dying? I'd like to have one good affair before I die—I still look all right, don't I? Tell me. Do I look AIDSy? If you saw me at a bar would you be scared off?"

"No, not at all," Austin lied. "But that's not a very self-affirming attitude. You should go to the Body Positive dances and meet a student who's positive—an African American, of course."

When they went to the Epcot Center, Austin felt his ire rising as if it were vomit. It tightened in his stomach and scalded the back of his throat. There they were, in "Paris," and part of "Paris" was "the Île Saint-Louis," and Austin had a snobbish reaction to this silly simulacrum—the ridiculous berets and baguettes and the Edith Piaf sound track, the beveled windows and lacquered walls containing half a café, cut open in a longitudinal section ten feet away from a baby Eiffel Tower. Austin was also frightened by it, as if it meant to suggest he'd never gotten out of America, never lived on the real Île Saint-Louis for eight years in its cold rains and on its deserted, windswept *quais*, never stood at the stone railing and looked down into the klieg lights of a passing *bateau-mouche*, never befriended the ruddy-cheeked, full-jowled butcher in the tight swaddling of his bloody apron. He felt like one more American in bermudas browsing over this parody of his past. When his drunk father hadn't been able to pay their utilities bill and the lights had been turned off and he had lit dirty stubs of candles set in a dusty old chandelier dangling big, fat lusters and had tried to pass it all off as a joke or a "period" adventure—oh, that feeling that their very existence was imperiled, that their house would be dismantled room after room by bill collectors, *that* was how he felt now. Didn't Peter see that he, Austin, had given him something authentic, something precious, three years on the Île Saint-Louis? Really, Peter was such an airhead he seemed to prefer this county fair, this vile fake, to the historic heart of the world's most civilized city.

Only the "Moroccan" section retained its authenticity because as they ate their couscous in the high, blue-tiled restaurant with its stalactite ceiling of intricately tooled white resin, the young, brown-skinned waiter flirted with them. He spoke to them in French, he winked at them, he took their money after the meal with a long, lingering smile. While Peter and Austin looked at the brass hookahs and hand-painted ceramics and tooled leather footstools on sale in the Moroccan "bazaar," Austin said, "The only thing that's authentic here is that waiter flirting with us, which would happen in exactly the same way in the real Morocco, the real Marrakesh, don't you agree—"

But Peter had already run out to the central reflecting pool, where the closing fireworks display was illuminating his upturned face. "Oh, Austin, *thanks* for bringing me here. I know you hate it, but I wanted to come back one more time in this life."

"*This* life?" Austin asked as they walked down the wide esplanade to their bus.

"I don't know, don't challenge me, I'm a Catholic, Austin, you know I was raised a Catholic and Father Frank, my mom's priest? His brother died of AIDS and he's very understanding and not very doctrinal, he never talks about the Pope or sin or homosexuality, he just— well, I guess he wants to comfort me." Peter looked at Austin and said, defiantly, but with a put-on How-Am-I-Doing? boldness, "And, brother, I'll take my comfort where I can find it."

"Of course, Pete, you know I don't hate religion or—well, anyway, I'm happy for you. And it must mean a lot to your mom."

"Hold on, I haven't crawled back into the arms of Holy Mother Church, I'm just talking to a priest. He's given me a little devotional book I read whenever I'm feeling blue."

When they got back to the hotel they went along the outdoor corridor and over three bridges before they arrived at their room. Everything smelled of chlorine and heat and decaying plants. The red message light on the phone was blinking. "It's Lucy," Austin whispered, as he listened to the voicemail, "she says Julien's in a New Haven hospital. He had a massive outbreak of herpes across his face. They're trying to keep it out of his eyes, his brain. I've got to call her."

"Oh, no, there goes our time together. It's almost as though he'd planned it," Peter said. "I never get anything. I can never have you two minutes to myself. Maybe I have to be hospitalized to get your attention." Peter threw himself face-down on his bed and sobbed. The wine, Austin thought, looking at his back working in rhythm with his sobs. He had drunk too much Moroccan rosé. Austin felt guilty—for him guilt was a physical thing, a dread in the guts, a panic headache, a moral cold sweat. Guilty that he had to leave Peter here alone. But there was no question that he must fly back to Providence tomorrow morning.

Lucy said, "Oh! I'm *so* relieved to get you on the phone. You can't *believe*—okay, okay, I'm going to start, *calmly,* at the beginning." She drew a deep breath and let a moment go by as she collected her thoughts, though it all sounded as stagy as some New Age guru's "centering" of "Self."

Austin didn't want her to begin at the beginning—he asked, "Where is he now?"

"Connecticut State."

"Do you have his phone number?"

"Sure. Hold on. I'll tell you in a methodical way—"

"Of course, but first: how is he?"

"They've got him on a Zovirax drip for the herpes, and they've brought his fever down. He's comfortable and cheerful. It looks like— I mean, it looks *as if*—it won't damage his vision or get into the brain, but you can't believe how close it was, it wasn't like any herpes I've ever seen, it doesn't follow a single nerve but it's splattered across his face like he'd been thwacked by a red pepper bush."

She told him how he'd called her at home and seemed bizarrely cheerful— "And he kept slipping into that crazy French, *not* like any French *I* know," which was pure folly, since Lucy didn't speak a word of French of any sort, as everyone agreed.

"He sounded delirious, so I *rushed* over there."

Sure you rushed, Austin thought, picturing her trying on two skirts and three tops before "coordinating" them sufficiently to drive, limp-wristed, over to see Julien, whom she now called, half-seriously, her "French lover." He imagined she'd even spent some time applying make-up to her large mouth—but why was he being so vile in his thoughts toward this girl, who'd undoubtedly saved Julien's life?

"I'm so grateful to you, Lucy, you're such a friend."

"My pleasure, I'm sure," she said in a little-girl singsong, a parody of her real feelings and manners.

"I'll fly directly to New Haven or, I guess, New York tomorrow if I can get a plane. By the way—"

"Oh, I almost forgot, *he's* Austin."

"What do you mean?"

"I mean that since he has no health insurance someone at the hospital decided to register him under *your* name."

"That was very nice of her. Or him," Austin said in a soft voice.

"It sure was. He could be arrested."

"Arrested?"

"Well, sure 'nuf, 'cuz that's *fraud,* Austin. It's exactly as though you robbed a bank. Julien and you and that person at the hospital could *all* be put in prison."

"Isn't that shocking?" Austin asked. "A man falls gravely ill, far from his country—"

"Well, that's just the way it is," Lucy said matter-of-factly, as though to complain were unrealistic and childish. She was right. It was.

After he'd made all his flight arrangements, Austin sat on the edge of Peter's bed and gave him a half-hearted massage, comfort disguised as physical therapy, but Peter was inconsolable. He even shrugged Austin's hands off his shoulders. Austin thought it was so unfair that he'd come to this appalling place just to please Peter and now he would never receive any credit for it.

He flew the next morning early to La Guardia airport and took a train and taxi to the hospital. He gave his own name, Austin Smith, as the name of the patient he wished to visit. Upstairs he found the room number easily, knocked on the door timidly and then let himself in. There was Julien in bed, watching TV, a splash of red welts across his face, extending up his cheek, just narrowly missing his eye and ending above his right eyebrow.

"You see, *Petit,*" Julien said. "You can't ever leave me. See what happens."

Austin sat on the edge of the bed and pawed him, his hands like a dog's paw. He was careful not to foul the Zovirax drip and said, in English, "How are you, Austin?"

"I'm fine, Julien." He laughed, delighted with this game of reversed identities. He explained how he'd told the Irish nurse, Meg, the one who joked so much and treated him so well, a whole story about his father the American, his French mother, and about how he himself had been raised in France and had never really known his father after age three, when his parents had divorced. "I had to explain why I had such a strong French accent," Julien said so solemnly that Austin—the real Austin—burst out laughing.

"It's wonderful to see you looking so well."

"Thank God the hospital was willing to take me in under these . . . special conditions."

"Yes," Austin said, "the clerk's obviously a great-hearted man. Others would have politely explained why it was impossible and thrown you in the street. . . ."

Julien held his finger up to his lips.

"How's my sweetheart?" a fat, breathless nurse called out in an Irish brogue. "How's my Austin? And were you named after the city in Texas?"

"No, no," Julien said, confused by the question but smiling over the whole game, "I think it was an American war hero—my father was a soldier."

"To be sure. And who might this be, love?"

"Julien," Austin said, though he pronounced the name in the English fashion.

"Julian and Austin, such old-fashioned names. Nothing *common* here, I see. Just two old-fashioned toffs."

On the train home Austin watched the ponds and trees glide past in the cold, dying light, the whole haphazard landscape, the turning leaves, halfway between solemnity and slum. If the slender trunks rose and branched against the silver and sable clouds, flexible as dancers, underfoot there was a pile of compressed, rain-soaked cartons, their metal bindings rusting into the pulp, or here, now, an automobile graveyard flickered past, the feeble sun spiderwebbing through a broken windshield.

He'll have to go back to France, he thought. We can't all three, the hospital clerk along with us, be packed off to prison. And I don't want Julien to have to live through this uncertainty. Austin pictured Julien's smiling face, still handsome under its scarlet brand—his smile summoned up the memory of a cousin whose face was heart-stoppingly pure and white if only the right side was seen, but who was transformed into someone else, nearly a monster, when he turned and revealed a long, purple birthmark, which had somehow melted his left nostril and thickened the left corner of his lips.

Chapter Fifteen

Ten days after Julien was released from the hospital, his brother Robert flew over to the States with his lover Fabrice for a two-week holiday. Julien met them in New York where they spent a long weekend, then all three came up to Providence on the train.

Austin had rented a ski house, an A-frame, not far outside Bennington, Vermont; he was certain the French guests would be staggered by the colors of the Vermont leaves changing.

Ajax slept in his corner of the back seat while Robert caressed him constantly, almost unconsciously. If he heard another dog bark outside, Ajax would instantly be on the alert, his eyes on stems, a yearning treble mew in the back of his throat. He was playful and charming with human beings, but other dogs awakened in him fear and fascination. In that way he was like a snob at a reception, kind to everyone but mesmerized only by a glimpse of another Hohenzollern.

Julien wore dark glasses but still found the brilliance of the leaves in full sunlight painful to look at. He appeared healthy otherwise and was thrilled to have his brother with him. They went walking down country roads; Austin felt they were inside a badly bombed Gothic cathedral, half of the stained glass shattered and on the ground, the rest still clinging to the leadings. Austin was happy to be with Robert and Fabrice; he'd spent two weeks with them in Nice a year earlier and felt very comfortable with them.

Julien had decided to say nothing to his brother about his illness—yes, the herpes, though he called it chicken pox, but not AIDS. "Just imagine what that would do to the poor boy," Julien said. "He's already had to live through our mother's death. What if now he had to accept his little brother's death, too? No, he'll find out about it all too soon."

What did Julien think about what he was living—or dying—through? He seemed to have aestheticized his fate. He struck Austin as someone who'd rocked back on his heels and raised his eyebrows in an appraising, epicurean posture; he was ignoring the dangers all around him. He was the bowler hat descending into the live volcano, the spats seen through the cobra-quick underbrush. He'd laughed his way through the hospital and had learned how to tease his nurses in the best American manner. He had nothing but praise to offer an American hospital—although he must have realized that, as Austin Smith, Visiting Professor, he was receiving special (and very expensive) treatment.

Was he afraid?

Austin knew that herpes was horribly painful but Julien never spoke of his suffering. When they first met, Julien had moaned as loudly as any French mama's boy when he scratched his finger or pulled a muscle or came down with the flu, but now that his martyrdom was finally beginning, he said nothing. He joked like an American—and redoubled his affection toward Austin, who saw he'd become the steadying point, like a father talking his son down from the roof where he'd sleepwalked before awakening.

Julien's dark glasses were Italian although, to be fair, he'd never been one to collect brand names or to buy costly or original baubles. No, he was able to confect a look out of scarves, tarnished brooches, an old felt slouch hat, a satin vest as brightly striped as a Christmas ornament under a corduroy jacket worn down like the bark on a rotting log.

Robert and Fabrice admired everything—the white church steeples pointing up through the gaudy autumn leaves like a pure ivory tusk in a jumble sale, the broad highways, the country inns and little restaurants with their Brown Bettys and carrot cake—so *exotic*, all of it, especially the friendliness of waiters and families at neighboring tables, which they observed with the puzzled indifference of the deaf at the opera. They spoke no English although Fabrice, a born communicator, was always ready to make a smiling, gesturing effort or pantomime his frustration.

Robert was thirty-one, three years older than Julien, though he looked much younger. Whereas Julien had his father's "villainous" skin, sexily scored with acne scars and permanently oily, Robert looked as if he'd just been unmolded and glazed. His hair had been mounted under a blow dryer, his nose had been thinned and restyled, his face may have been sanded—certainly it was flawless and he held it up to the world as if to show off something fragile to its best advantage and with no glare. His narcissism made him no less attractive to Austin.

Robert seemed to be dreaming most of the time, lost in vague thoughts. He wasn't subjected to the passage of time, only to the movement of the elements. He'd blink, locate the incoming signal and start any reply with a bass, rumbling elegance, with a deliberation worthy of a monarch: "Perhaps you would like to know," he'd say, or "Are you perhaps wondering if. . . ?" At first Austin thought Robert could scarcely understand a foreign accent as heavy as his own, but then he realized that anyone at all, even another Frenchman, struck Robert as an alien.

In Nice, he had few friends and never varied from his routine. He rose late, he cooked plain rice for breakfast and mixed it in a bowl with cooked egg whites for protein (the yolks he threw to the birds who swarmed over the gravel roof of the next house down the hill). He clipped the sculpted bush in the window with fingernail scissors. He endured a two-and-a-half-hour workout at the gym, then put in four or five hours helping Fabrice out at the garden store or delivering plants. He never read anything, although sometimes he went to the theater or the opera at Nice or Monte Carlo. Usually he and Fabrice arrived home late, toward nine, and boiled some fish and mixed a salad, which in the summer they ate out on the verandah, which was large enough for a table and four chairs, with a panoramic view of Nice and the old port below and, in the distance, the twinkling Promenade des Anglais. In the winter they sat indoors and watched TV or listened to Fabrice's old 78s of French *chanteuses*.

A native of Nice, Fabrice could speak the local dialect, which was closer to Italian than French, and when he strolled through the open-air fruit markets he stopped to chat with old friends in Niçoise. Though he was outgoing, what in New York would have been called a schmoozer, he was at heart a loner. As an adolescent he'd gone to Paris where he'd done advanced studies in landscape architecture, but his fellow students had mocked him for his southern accent and he'd never been serious about a career. "You know," Julien whispered—in English—when they were in bed that first night in Vermont, "Fabrice was a child prodigy. He did beautiful architectural drawings, he could play the accordion, even tap dance, he was a genius at math, but he was always lazy. You see how they are. I love them but if I don't insist they are unable to get out of the house before noon or eat dinner before ten or eleven."

Fabrice wore a strange wig that no one, not even Robert, had ever seen him without. It was a pale, chemical brown, synthetically straight, although his real hair, around his ears and down his neck, was graying and curly. He told jokes constantly, mainly peepee-caca jokes, but pussy and cock jokes, too.

And yet their love of Julien and Austin, certainly Ajax, was sincere and intense. They were kind people whose lives had been turned down so low, the flame sometimes threatened to go out.

But their lives weren't static. They were living through a dramatic change, although one that was creeping by so slowly that only the participants took heed of it. As Julien had told Austin, until three years ago Robert had remained the skinny, stylized, perfumed boy who had so infuriated their father, the businessman and amateur pilot. Until three years ago Robert had starved himself still skinnier and had used Fabrice's bulk and cheerfulness and endless anecdotes about the stars of the past to fill every corner of silence and space around him. In Nice, while Fabrice laughed with a client over the phone and set up appointments to redo a lawn or a herbaceous border, Robert had looked down on the old port at night or trimmed his box tree. Most of the time he lay on the couch with his hands behind his head and daydreamed so poetically that strangers were startled to hear his rumbling voice and his pedantically well-turned sentences.

Then, nearly three years ago, Robert had joined a gym near the Cours Saleya. Perhaps he'd noticed he was turning fewer heads, not only because he was approaching thirty, which for gay men is the Cape of Lost Hope, but also because his kind of stylized elegance was no longer sought after; it had been replaced by body-built buffed broncos, hot little guys (*les p'tits mecs*) with stretch T-shirts, black jeans, power boots, bald heads, a gold earring or two, and a bull tattoo.

There were minor choices, parachutist or grunge, basketball or (as the French said) "destroy," but no matter where the accent was placed over the syllables, the word remained the same: muscles.

As Austin had observed during his fourteen days in Nice, Robert brought an unexpected fanaticism to his workouts. He admitted that within six months he'd gained fifteen kilos, all in the chest, shoulders and upper arms, without adding a centimeter to his waist (he despaired over his legs, which refused to bulk up). At the gym he spoke to no one at first, then began to joke with some of the women in their forties and early fifties, bleached blonds in leopard-skin body suits and lipstick-pink tights who wore extra-long false eyelashes and applied their lipstick with brushes. They "revived" their tans in the winter with an iodine-colored bronzer. If other gay men asked him to partner them in precarious squats, he apologized in his thrilling voice but said he was on far too rigorous a schedule to be able to participate in someone else's program—all said in his most "Old France" manner, so polite and severe it froze the blood of the imprudent.

Before long he found he was making *sotto voce* jokes with the blond ladies about the little fags. He agreed to escort one of the ladies to a Beauticians' Ball in Cannes but hinted that he lived with a woman closer to his own age who was very jealous. He moved out of the bedroom where he'd slept for thirteen years beside Fabrice; or rather he found he'd fallen asleep yet again on the couch and then, when Fabrice complained, Robert said that now that he'd put on all this weight he was too hot and big to bunk up with someone else. He liked the couch. He let Fabrice wash his back every night. In Vermont Austin glanced through the half-open bathroom door and saw Fabrice, special sponge in hand, working over Robert's mammoth back. Robert sat perfectly still in the water, leaning forward to unfurl the full cape of his lats. Fabrice, completely clothed, a cigarette in his mouth pouring smoke into his left eye, sat on the edge of the tub, proud, content, delighted with his role. Austin for some reason thought of those steers in Japan that produce Kobe beef—weren't they massaged day and night to render the finest marbleized meat?

Julien whispered to Austin that he found Robert's Mediterranean machismo tiresome, although there was no question about the depth of Julien's devotion to his brother. "He was never like that in the past. He fought violently with our father to defend his way of being, but now he makes faggot jokes and turns his head to follow the passage of a provocative woman. It's all so silly. He's never been to bed with a woman—he's like you, *Petit*, a *purist*." Austin had to admit to himself that he found Robert's machismo sexy.

One day, Austin tweaked Robert by referring to Fabrice as "your lover." He asked, "How long have you and your lover been together?"

Robert blinked his gray-blue eyes and said, "Whom might you have in mind when you refer to my lover?"

"To Fabrice, of course."

Fabrice himself mimed a tiny curtsy.

Robert, unsmiling but patient, as if speaking to a confused child, said, "But Fabrice is not my lover. That word would totally misrepresent our relationship. For me Fabrice is more like a father. Fabrice is, yes, my father."

As soon as the words were out of Robert's mouth, Austin regretted he'd ever provoked the discussion. Fabrice was obviously hurt; he hadn't needed to know this bitter final truth. Austin touched Fabrice's shoulders when he walked past him.

That night they ate quail and venison in the restaurant a mile away with its great chef and countrified waiters, reedlike, red-faced teenage boys who seemed weighted down by enormous feet as if someone had poured too much lead into the tin soldiers' boots. At every window there was a fake candle, just an up-ended scroll of ivory cardboard and a forking, flickering filament in the light bulb, but the effect, seen from the road as they approached, was welcoming and calm. The Frenchmen liked the plain board floors, redolent of beeswax, the faded hooked rugs and the big fire in the old stone fireplace. Of course they also liked the self-conscious boys with their clip-on ties and white shirts, the cheap kind through which their thin torsos could be seen, boys as crushed by their high calling as acolytes at Easter Mass. Their own waiter, "Bob," turned out to be a history major from Bennington, which puzzled the foreigners. "Even the servants go to university here?" Fabrice asked.

"He's not really a servant," Austin said. "The very word makes us laugh. He's just earning some spending money. His father could even be rich—in America rich parents want their children to work."

"How cruel," Fabrice said. "He inherited, he didn't make it—"

"But perhaps he did make it," Austin said. "You forget how many *nouveaux riches* we have."

"But can't you *tell* if that boy's rich or poor?" Fabrice asked. "In France I would know right away, just by the way someone talked and moved, not only who his parents were but who his grandparents were as well."

"No, in America there's such a general style—"

"But his table manners, *Petit*," Julien objected, "his way of holding himself at table."

"No, no," Austin laughed. "There's absolutely no way of telling. I know how essential all that is to you, to families like yours—"

"Quail, I want quail," Julien exclaimed, almost as though he was heading off a delicate subject, any mention of their noble family's history. "Do you like quail, Fabrice?"

Fabrice told a long story about his grandfather, who'd hunted quail in the Alpilles and who'd covered himself with glory as a *maquisard* sniping at the Nazis.

In bed that night Austin stayed awake, looking at the high, pitched ceiling of sloping wood beams. He couldn't sleep because he kept remembering Fabrice's silly smile and the panicked expression in his eyes with which he'd greeted Robert's remark, "For me Fabrice is more like a father." Fabrice was barrel-chested, but even so thinner than Austin, who was so heavy now that all his clothes felt tight on him, even the roomy Yamamoto jacket he'd bought precisely because he'd swum around inside it a year ago. And Fabrice was still out cruising every night on the Montburon above Nice, at least if Robert's jokes were to be believed, whereas Austin had given up sex altogether. He masturbated occasionally but only because the eternal flame cannot be allowed to go out—that would be a bad omen, surely. And this talkative, endlessly congenial Niçois had been forced to hear and swallow that he wasn't his lover's lover but rather his father.

"*Petit,*" Austin whispered experimentally in the dark.

"Yes?" Julien was awake, too.

"Do you think of me as your father?"

"Of course not, Austin. Oh—I see. No, but Robert's lying. He doesn't think of Fabrice as his father, either. He's completely dependent on him. *Petit?*"

"Yes."

"When I die I want you to promise me you'll do everything to make sure Robert stays with Fabrice. Robert is such a dreamer, such a child. He can't earn a living and now he's too old to learn how. He may be attracted by some younger man he meets at the gym and have . . . an affair. Why not? But promise me you won't allow him to leave Fabrice, who truly loves him and will care for him as long as he's alive."

"I promise—but you're not going to die, Julien."

"Yes, I am. The end is already beginning. You must accept that, *Petit.*" He drew Austin's balding head to him, to his chest, which did feel fractionally leaner, harder. Julien might be a *poseur,* just a bit, but why not? His affectations might see him through all this with a few tatters of gallantry to clothe his suffering—well, if not all the way to the end, then at least far, very far along the cold way.

In the beginning Austin had been thrilled to have such a handsome, mature young man paying him court, or rather accepting his, Austin's, attentions. Then, before Austin had had time to transpose his affection up a fifth into love, the tune had changed. Julien had learned he was not only positive but already well advanced into this fatal illness. They'd been separated by Immigration, reunited only after great difficulty, and then Peter and Julien had quarreled. . . .

Austin had never shirked his duty toward Julien (a *grave* duty if Austin had been the one to infect—say it!—to *kill* him). But moving back to this farcical America, to this witless academy and its Savonarola students, had thrown him off balance. When he came back to the house after a long day ("Who's heard of Chippendale chairs? No one? Sheraton? The Bauhaus? Foucault?—Ah, that's better"), he sometimes resented Julien and his siestas, his elaborate *toilettes*, his sepulchral tone as he whispered, "I'm just resting."

Now all that was past. Austin felt committed to Julien, joined to him: married.

Julien winced in the autumn light filtering through all these brilliant falling leaves, but he took long, happy walks with his brother and an Ajax as excited as a slum child on a farm. The two brothers—one dazed, massive, trudging under his howdah of musculature, the other slender but sparkling with electricity—leaned into each other, laughing and chattering as they had during their childhood in Nancy (Austin dubbed them the "Nancy Boys," but they didn't get it). They walked down the dirt road between maples on fire, touching off sudden gasps of recollection and easy laughter.

Later, when they all drank tea inside the gloomy A-frame and looked out through glass at the intensely glowing embers of the leaves, the brothers' eyes glazed over. They forgot Vermont and were transported back to the pop songs of their adolescence, which they bawled out, though neither could hold a tune. Robert was bigger but dimmer, whereas Julien burned with a feverish excitement.

Julien was proprietorial about America in explaining it to Robert. When they'd go off somewhere in the car, it was Julien who would have to speak to the waitress in a diner or ask directions of a passerby. They'd spend hours "doing" the antique stores—and at every point Julien demonstrated the advantages of America (its friendliness, its efficiency, its charm and variety) and especially its natural beauty.

Julien was fascinated by Shaker furniture. He discovered a factory not far away in New Hampshire that still followed the old Shaker designs, and all four of them toured the workshops. "Oh, sure," one of the workmen said, "we get lots of the French here, don't you know?"

"It's so strange, *Petit*," Julien said when at last they'd bid farewell to their guests, "but when I was married I always dreamed about how wonderful it would be to spend time as part of a gay couple with Robert and Fabrice. They used to tease me all the time about Christine; they never really liked her. She was too smart, too argumentative, not glamorous enough. Too sexy in a female way."

"And now?"

"Of course, it was wonderful, and thank you for renting the house and taking everyone out to dinner, but Robert's macho nonsense—*enfin*, you see, I thought we'd be two gay couples together, two brothers with their older lovers, but now, *bon bref*, Robert has decided he's straight. You know, most of the guys at his gym are afraid of him. They think he's a queer basher."

Every week Julien took the car into New Haven and Dr. Goldstein examined him and ran more tests. Never for an instant did Julien forget that he was being cranked up the first high Russian mountain of the roller coaster and that any moment now he'd start his steep, fatal descent. But at the same time he wanted to enjoy every hour that remained.

He decided to be completely open about his HIV-status, if not with his brother then with the young Americans he was meeting. He said, "It's easier that way. You showed me the value of honesty, Austin." He told Lucy that he was positive, which she had of course already suspected. He had met several students in the French department and he confided to them the nature of his disease. Perhaps America itself didn't seem quite real to him. Would he be this honest back in France?

He and Austin joined an exercise class that met three times a week. They continued with their total abstinence from liquor and tobacco. Even when the cold weather blew in, they spent hours walking Ajax. Gradually they came to know every street of Providence, or at least the area around the universities.

Joséphine came to stay with them just before Christmas. When Austin had originally invited her to move with them to Providence he'd felt that her presence would make things easier for Julien and take the curse off his having to live openly with another man. He and

Julien never discussed her arrival, no more than they ever talked about their lives together. Julien had been married before, and though he may have announced to his classmates that he was homosexual when he'd just been sixteen, the avowal had probably sounded to them more like a manifesto than a confession. After all, that had happened in the 1970s when kids, even in the conservative French provincial town of Nancy, had taken weird stands. Julien had never had to live out his homosexuality as a public act, as a declared member of a despised minority. No, he'd been the married man, half of an attractive, dynamic couple in the professions who'd spent their two years in exotic Ethiopia and returned to Paris with an advanced degree (Christine) and a job as a gifted architect (Julien). Now he'd turned into the unemployed foreigner, the young, skinny partner of a portly man in his fifties who himself enjoyed no prestige beyond his unwritten credentials as a furniture expert. Of course Julien would prefer living in a household that included the blond, beautiful, talented Joséphine.

Of course. Except Austin had figured everything out wrong. Almost within a day of Joséphine's arrival Julien was irritated with her. She smoked and he thought her habit endangered his fragile lungs. She flirted with every man she met—or rather, since she was afraid Austin and Julien would mock her if she cocked her head to one side and cooed, she stared at her victims and hoped her housemates wouldn't notice. Julien did notice, of course, and warned her off the young man she liked the most, an Israeli architectural student named Aaron who was engaged to someone back home.

Joséphine pretended to like Ajax but found his long, licking kisses disgusting and his constant desire to sleep on her lap, though by now he weighed almost a hundred pounds, less than endearing. He mounted her leg and unsheathed his penis as if it were a new lipstick shade, Glamorous Glans. Ajax had picked up a peculiarly funky smell, something reminiscent of pea soup, that was concentrated in his hindquarters, possibly in a gland near the root of his tail. At least that's what Austin's uncle, a hunting and fishing man, had said over the phone: "A basset? Hell—" (pronounced "Hail")—"them bassets ain't dawgs, them's *hounds*. And if'n a hound dawg ain't hunted he starts to stink."

He let out a muted rebel—well, not a rebel *yell*, but a hoarse Confederate grunt. He dropped the cornpone accent, lowered his voice and said, "They store up stink in a gland near their tail, which they secrete so the rest of the pack can pick up their scent. But if they're not out running they can get real *high*."

Julien refused to acknowledge it and Austin liked it, but poor Joséphine washed her hands ten times a day and sprayed the air with "Jacky." When she came home from a walk one day, Ajax leapt up on her and tore her tights with his claws. Finally her exasperation came flashing out—which excited Julien into a rage.

"He was just being friendly—he *loves* you," Julien shouted. He squatted to kiss Ajax's unperturbed, smiling face. *"Pauvre petite bête."*

When Austin saw Ajax's silky brown head from behind with its narrow skull and notched occipital bone he thought of him as a retarded child. That image touched him but made him feel guilty; he thought there was something cruel about turning a much less intelligent creature into Man's Best Friend, something akin to the King's pleasure in his Fool. When they'd all be talking Austin would glance down at Ajax's eyes straining to comprehend, the small, feeble brain more nose than knowing, the warm eyes sympathetic, baffled.

But Austin had guessed right that Joséphine would make them all more accessible. People seemed to call more often, invite them to dinner more readily, as though a woman were a door thrown open into the previously sealed house. Frequently Austin would come home to discover Joséphine over tea with Lucy and Julien, for even though he complained of the noise and smoke and confusion Joséphine had introduced into their lives, Julien liked that she was the one who arranged everything; now he could get up suddenly, pleading weariness, and vanish to another floor of the house and Joséphine would be stuck with these lingering American students. Unlike French people, they didn't know when to leave. Austin said, "Well, we're so close to the soil, to our farming past, that when we visit we make an occasion out of it—" but he suddenly realized he didn't know how to explain either *canning* or *sewing bees* in French.

In bed one night Julien asked, whispering, "Why did you invite her to live with us?"

"For your sake. So people wouldn't think we were lovers."

"But I'm proud to be your lover."

"But you were married—"

"I'm not the way you imagine. I'm much more evolved (*évolué*). I don't give a damn what people think. I chose you, *Petit,* and after that there were no more choices to make."

They had to give up their house at the end of December. The Professor of Aesthetics and his wife were coming back from Spain. Austin panicked when he looked around at the damage. He found a carpenter who sanded down and revarnished the many chair legs Ajax had gnawed on during his teething. A young woman from the weaving department found fabric that roughly resembled the couch upholstery and attempted to darn the holes. A team of house cleaners dusted, steamed and swept. "You're going too far," Julien complained.

But the professor was furious. He wrote that he'd been tempted to sell the house, it was in such bad condition. "I've hated to bring it up and have spent many an hour (this will no doubt slay you) in prayer seeking guidance (that's the kind of guy I am)."

Austin showed the letter to Julien, who instantly started disputing it, line by line. "But it was all just Salvation Army junk and—he thought he could take advantage of you, you're too naive, the house looks better now than when we moved in, then the floors looked like a bowling alley, all varnish, we added some character, we're French, we know real parquet, the so-called balloon ceiling is just a normal hallway—"

"Okay, okay."

Austin wrote out a check for eight thousand dollars. He realized that his American year had cost him money; he'd earned nothing and spent almost all his savings. He begged Julien to respect the new house they were moving into for the spring semester, small, elegant and built at the beginning of the nineteenth century with a chimney in the center that opened up on three sides to fireplaces in the main rooms. The living room was just two steps up from the sidewalk on a busy street and when Austin was reading the paper he could hear students hurrying past, shouting and talking—a relief after the furtive silence of the cruising woods. Upstairs, next to their bedroom, was suspended a glassed-in porch perched in the treetops, looking out over the slanting, snow-hung roofs and the neighbor's black cat slithering through fence pickets as if patrolling the back alley. The Christmas season was dark and cold, but their new house, with its bright red front door, had put a jolly frame around the dour picture. The furniture was Shaker-austere to the point of spindliness; Julien admired it and sketched one particular highback chair again and again.

During the six-week vacation in late December and all of January they drove to Key West in the Sirocco, taking turns scrunched up with Ajax in the back seat. Later Joséphine confessed that it was during this trip that she had come to love the dog. He was such a fine doggie, naturally she'd given in to him. They saw an exhibit of Erik Fischl's works on paper in New Haven, a big Francesco Clemente retrospective in Philadelphia, a great Titian exhibit in Washington. They stayed with friends until they arrived in the outskirts of Charleston, South Carolina, and, the next day, Daytona, Florida—in both cases they sought out obscure, understaffed motels where they could drive Ajax right up to the door at night and no one would notice or complain when they ushered him into their room.

They took turns driving, singing songs, lapsing into long silences. In Georgia they turned off the I-95 onto a country road and ate in a family-style restaurant that smelled of kerosene and that served salty ham and grits. "We could live here," they'd say, "or here," every time they'd see a quiet town that looked as if time had soared right over it. But all the while they knew that what they lacked wasn't a place to do their living in but life itself.

When at last they pulled into Key West, the weather had gradually changed from freezing to hot, the trees from bare oaks to luxuriant traveler's palms and crumpled pink hibiscus party favors. The clothes of passersby on the street had gone from parkas to shorts. Austin sighed, happy to smell the unclean brackish sea all around them, to look at the sloppy, slow walk of a black woman idling down the sidewalk, her heels gray as an elephant's knees above the soiled blue of her worn-down slippers. He sighed to observe a big yellow cat crossing Whitehead Street, ignoring everything—cars, tourist buses, the rush of clouds overhead—everything in order to concentrate on a clump of weeds in an empty lot that was vibrating to a suspicious rhythm.

Their rented house huddled under a big tree that the neighbor, an old hippy with a sparse white beard and bad teeth, called "a tourist tree" because "it turns red and peels." The garden was composed of gravel, white and dusty, and schefflera plants that were twice as large as any Austin had ever seen, as if nourished on plutonium. Strings of miniature white bulbs festooned the trees; they cast a pewter glow onto the new tin roof and made the painted porch pillars look like perfect sticks of blackboard chalk fresh out of the box. The earth smelled of mildew; it was so wet that the dead just a block away in the cemetery had to repose in sealed cement vaults above ground.

For Austin Key West was the South, or something like the South. He recognized the house trailers hoisted up on cement blocks and the gray hamburger patties soaking through slices of Wonder Bread, the Sno-Queen stand squatting under a giant plastic cone, two fat ladies seated, overflowing the peeling planks on a park bench as they waited for the bus, the sound of a Hammond organ bleating inside a narrow Pentecostal church. All this was smalltown Southern life as he knew it, but it was tucked in the corners or around walls of tumbling bougainvillea, purple as a Mardi Gras cloak, coconuts rotting in their husks at the tide line and buckets of little rock shrimp boiled in beer, their spicy shells a mortification to greedy fingers.

They rented bikes and sped down shaded streets bordered by the white wooden houses with their high crescent windows—"eyebrow windows" people called them—and their jigsaw porch frieze of sawed-out gingerbread men or starfish. Old cars rebuilt out of fenders of different bleached colors chugged past without silencers under lianas dangling from trees worthy of Tarzan. Cuban sandwich shops reeked of frying pork and plantains. At the end of a road lined with street lamps and squeezed between luxury hotels hung the sea, a dull gray panel of mist streaked green, like an infusion of tart spring herbs in a tarnished cauldron.

As they threaded their way down the Keys a transformation came over Joséphine. She put aside her little-girl politeness, tucked a cigarette behind one ear, suffocated Ajax with fierce affection and switched into a T-shirt white as baking powder that revealed she wore no bra. She rolled up the sleeves. She squeezed into faded jeans that emphasized her boyish butt and snaky hips. She painted her lips a faded purple. When she drove she squealed around corners and at the lights she pushed the accelerator to the floor.

Within a day she'd met a local painter who did big canvases of voodoo altars—bits of leather, beer bottles, even cigarettes were offered to black-skinned gods and goddesses with thick hair standing on end; sometimes the gods were mounted on the backs of horses with red eyes. Thomas was a light-skinned black man with blue eyes, delicate caramel-colored hands intricately rigged and triggered with blue veins and fine muscles visible through the thin skin. He had no buttocks at all—he was forced to keep tugging his trousers back up to his waist, which was no thicker than Austin's upper arm. Thomas had a strange gait—nothing noticeably wrong if you focused on it but if you observed it from the corner of your eye it was a movement that seemed partially paralyzed or even performed by a plastic knee or hip replacement—or perhaps it was just the effect of his hipless body stiffly casting forth his legs as he walked.

Thomas was in his early forties, or so he said, though he appeared to be ageless. He was interested in their French-speaking household and invited them to come to his studio, an old house in Bahama Village, the black part of town. He said his mother was Haitian and he could speak some of the *patois* but not proper French. The walls of his house were built out of thick planks of Dade Pine separated by white lines of cement or caulking. Voodoo candles were flickering in the mouths of sun-shaped scrap-metal disks; the air was thick with the acrid smoke curling off a green mosquito-repellent coil.

Joséphine lingered that first evening and said she wanted to study the paintings more thoroughly. She began to sway interpretively to an old recording of Steve Reich's "Drumming." She'd adopted the ostensibly inward but actually exhibitionistic motions of a woman who knows she's being looked at with desire. She'd be fun to tease later, Austin thought ("Of course you slipped out of your shoes, Joséphine, it was part of your Graham training"), but for now she didn't care what Austin and Julien thought, she was obviously glad to exist once more as an exciting body in the pale blue gaze of this heterosexual man, a black artist who must have his pick of all the ofay tourist chicks. She closed her eyes and threw her head back, bobbed up and down in place, letting her arms weave the air around her; all her movements were calculated to make her breasts rise and fall inside her T-shirt.

Before they'd left Providence, Joséphine had asked if Aaron, the Israeli architecture student, could come down and stay with them. Julien had said no, absolutely not, he was a cold, cruel man, that was obvious, who didn't even like Joséphine. And besides he, Julien, had to have some peace. "I don't have much time left," he said. "I have to be selfish with every moment."

Joséphine went cross-eyed with stubbornness, or rather she was so hell-bent in her obsessiveness that she just set her jaw and jammed every incoming signal. So they shouldn't have been surprised when one afternoon Aaron—black curls crawling down his neck over his T-shirt collar, affable, confident, showing a bit of sexy paunch—showed up in a rented car. Joséphine put on her best debutante manner, as if she were wearing a large blue satin bow; maybe she thought by holding her head high and steady she could induce a tone of good manners that would preclude any surliness on Julien's part.

It didn't work. Julien was furious. He shouted at Joséphine in French, which Aaron didn't understand. "I told you, no guests: you have absolutely no respect for our privacy. Nor for my health."

Like a goddess Joséphine flashed anger from her beautiful fierce eyes: "You're just a brat! I must lead my life! Your health has made you a tyrant." She turned to Austin. "If Aaron goes I go, too."

Aaron, hearing his name, shrugged. Then he stretched and yawned, showing his gold fillings and his pink, healthy tongue. Although he was just twenty-three he had the majestic Babylonian look that suited a man in his forties—the heavy, immobile forehead, the big, ice-cutter nose, the sprouting beard filings that swarmed below his Adam's apple to join the ringlets rising up from his chest. What was pathetic, Austin thought, was that Aaron didn't care one way or another about the outcome of this argument, which was tearing their little family apart. Even Ajax managed to hold his usual effusiveness in check and to study the newcomer with his head cocked to one side.

Austin refused to decide for or against Joséphine. They'd always been so fond of each other, even if Austin's feelings of affection, as was usually his way with his women friends, were more willed than spontaneous, or rather slightly ceremonial, based on constant declarations and very public reassurances. Of course Austin thought that *all* of his friendships had something remote about them. One of the things he liked about aging was that those young people who needed an older man to approve of them were so easily satisfied. They were convinced by the frail, gloved hand vaguely sketching a sign in the incense-heavy air and didn't require the close huddle of sustained warmth. Or he frequented people who were themselves removed, even remote. Julien, for instance, was dandified and cool, at least in his outward manner, which suited Austin. Who knew, would ever know, what Julien was feeling inside?

A lot, it seemed, this evening. He rushed about the house shouting, *"Merde!"* Austin, who'd only lose by saying anything, retreated to the kitchen to trim and steam some vegetables. When he emerged with a big bowl of brown rice he discovered the house was empty. Julien's bike was no longer chained to the front porch pillar.

Austin ate. Hours went by. Joséphine had no doubt taken Aaron with her to the gay tea dance. They'd eat a burger on the dock and come straggling home at midnight, giggling and drunk on rum punches, secretly amused by all the gay eccentrics they'd danced with.

But Julien? He never stormed off like this. He wasn't warmly dressed—just his skimpy white gym shorts, the very ones he'd been wearing when they first met in Paris. And a Virginia Woolf T-shirt, the name and portrait nearly worn away from repeated washings. He had on sneakers—no sweater. Maybe he'd taken some money with him, slipped into his jockstrap.

Where is he? Austin wondered. Julien could so easily kill himself. He could swim out to sea. After all, he has nothing to lose—he'll be dead two years from now in any event. Why not die now, while he's still handsome, intelligent, intact? His brother would even think he'd died in imitation of their mother rather than from a disease, a banal disease, the disease of the moment. Of course that would be harder for Robert to accept—but would also strike him as more glamorous.

He'll swim out to sea—that's the sort of fool-romantic fate he would embrace. Where is he? He has no identification on him, no one on the island knows him, no one would be able to identify his body. And Joséphine would rather put her own pleasure first. Well, wouldn't I? My mistake was to give up sex, put on weight. Better to be the least little housewife in one of these trailers getting banged every night than a full (very full) professor of design who has forsworn sex.

He realized that both he and Julien resented Joséphine. She was having sex with Thomas, now with Aaron. Julien called her a "nympho," but she was doing what they wanted to do.

At last, toward three in the morning, after the bars closed, Julien returned in a horse-drawn carriage. He was very drunk.

"Where's your bike?" Austin asked, instantly hating himself for bringing up something so petty at a time like this.

"I left it at the harbor. I was too drunk to ride it home."

Austin paid off the driver, an English young man in shorts and top hat, a lock of blond hair hanging down his forehead. "Cheers?" he said as his horse clip-clopped away. Julien stumbled, laughing, into Joséphine's room.

"Julien, I was so worried, I kept imagining all the worst things—what are you doing?"

Julien was pulling Joséphine's clothes out of her drawers and stuffing them into her duffel bag. He threw the bag out into the street along with Aaron's suitcase.

"What are you doing?"

"There!" he shouted. "They're no longer welcome here."

While he was still shouting, Joséphine and Aaron drove up in his car. The smile faded from her face the instant she saw her things protruding from the duffel bag: "*Julien! Quand même! Tu exagères—vraiment. . . .*"

When Julien laughed wildly and hung all his weight from the white porch pillar, turning and turning, she came to a quick decision and said, "Very well. We're not welcome here, Aaron. Let's go find a motel room."

"But you said I was invited to stay here. I don't have much money with me. If I'd thought I'd have to pay for a room I would never have driven all the way down here. You promised me—"

"We can stay with Thomas, the Haitian painter, the one you met at Sloppy Joe's. He's a nice guy—*il ne fera pas toutes ces histoires, lui.*"

"What are you saying? Talk English," Aaron said. "You promised I could stay down here for my holiday—"

"But it's not up to me."

"Get out! Get out!" Julien muttered. He then stumbled and fell. He picked himself up and went over to sit on the swing at the dark end of the porch, as if he were an actor who'd just left the stage and fallen out of character. He nursed his knee. The tree behind him on the neighbor's lot was lit with a pink spot; Julien's dark hair was in the shadows but, posed against the pink light, it picked up a red halo.

Aaron didn't have his French friends' sense of drama. They were willing to make proud, noble, possibly foolish decisions, but he wanted to hash it all out. He didn't want to be inconvenienced for the sake of a gesture. Anyway, Joséphine seemed to mean nothing to Aaron; Julien was right about that: he was engaged to a woman back home who was finishing her military service.

Two days later Aaron drove on to Naples, Florida; he'd been invited there by a rich uncle who owned a garment-manufacturing plant in Indonesia. Joséphine moved back from Thomas's studio, where she and Aaron had been camping out.

"So," Julien said, his face frozen in a hard smile, "did you get your *foufounette* fucked by a big circumcised dick?"

Joséphine shook her head sadly and screwed her face up into a nauseated expression. "You're sick," she said. "And truly disgusting." But Austin realized that by using the child's word for the vagina, *foufounette,* a cute word, Julien was in his meager fashion trying to apologize or at least send out a friendly signal. And Joséphine, by responding to him as a little sister would to her irritating big brother, had broken through the formality of hate.

They stayed in Key West for three weeks. Julien never drank again—in fact, his one night of wandering around town in his gym shorts was the only time he interrupted his sobriety. Joséphine shifted her affection back to Thomas and didn't mention Aaron again, but it was obvious she was brooding about him. She worked every day on the illustrations she was doing for a children's book—big, bold pastels, some in extreme close-up, of two snowy-haired, full-aproned but remarkably agile grandmothers, capable of turning somersaults and doing handsprings and drawing a little neighbor girl into their network of crime-fighting.

Julien and Joséphine had promised to drive back with Ajax five days before the end of the vacation; they were supposed to cede the house to Peter and Austin, but as it turned out they didn't want to leave Key West until the last possible moment. Austin rented them a suite in an old house on Eaton Street and told them firmly not to come by the little house with the tin roof and the tourist tree. "This is Peter's time with me."

Peter was even thinner but he was more sharply focused than he'd been at Disney World. He wanted to bike to the beach on the army base every day; he was an experienced tanner who knew how to work his way efficiently toward less and less sunblock. They rode past the military guard in a narrow house in the middle of the road, paid their few dollars, glided under the wind-twisted pines and spread their towels on the narrow strip of sand beside the blue-green, rapidly flowing water. The beach was not far from a narrow channel that led into the harbor. Sailing boats glided past just thirty or forty feet away, their white sails strangely close and all out of proportion, like monsters in bad process shots in old Japanese horror films.

"Oh, Austin," Peter said, once they were lying calmly side by side, "I'm determined to live as much as I can. Thanks for bringing me down here. I know you're still not drinking, but I hope you'll go with me to the bars."

"It's years since I've been to a bar. And look at me, how out of shape I am. Won't they turn me away?"

"Oh, but people like a bit of heft now, Austin. It shows you're not sick."

"Everyone says that," Austin grumbled, smiling, "but it's not strictly speaking true."

He rubbed oil on Peter's narrow shoulders and even up his long, long neck, on which his elegant, white-haired head was posed, regal as a bewigged young woman's seen from behind in a Fragonard. His head was at once stubborn and vulnerable. That was the strange contradition that characterized Peter. He was this slightly dazed kid, like a cartoon character who'd just been slammed on the head with a massive hammer and stunned out of malevolence into a goofy affability. Austin could almost see the stars dancing around his head. But he was also willful and the least contradiction sent him spinning into paroxysms of outrage. He not only collected injustices but had also invented new ways of making them pay handsome dividends.

"Anyway, won't you go with me to the bars?" Peter asked. "I hate going alone. I get attacks of vertigo. The doctor says it's nothing that can be controlled. It's the virus working directly on the central nervous system. I guess I always was a dizzy blond."

Austin said, "Sure, I'll go. It'll be fun. Maybe I'll even get laid. Peter, you're my tempter."

Austin was stunned by Peter's way of talking about the virus so candidly. It was easy to forget that there actually was a virus that existed, grew, outwitted its enemies, invested its host, had designs on new hosts, ate nerves and polluted blood. Usually the virus controlled its empire only through intermediaries, through *ukases* relayed along synapses or by orchestrating the slow collapse of immunities as it inched past the inner sanctum of the blood barrier so that it could reorder—simplify in some monstrous, radical way—the chemistry of the brain. But if the effects of the virus could be felt everywhere, in the dimming of an eye, the whittling down of all the fingers so they couldn't fill out their old rings, which just slid off, or in temporary gusts of deafness that reminded the invalid of the long, reverberant silence to come, the virus itself was seldom referred to and even less often did it make a "personal" appearance. It was the silent partner, the unnamed investor, the power behind the throne.

Life was easier with Peter than with Julien. Peter didn't draw attention to himself. He dressed with conventional good taste, a taste which Americans called *preppie* and the French *BCBG* (*bon chic bon genre*). Peter was thankful to the waiters, he was efficient and self-effacing when buying something in a store, soft-spoken in public places, never obscene, full of "thank yous" and "you're welcomes," a bit colorless. Around him Austin wasn't expected to come up with an opinion on every aesthetic topic, nor were people themselves treated as "amusing" or "elegant" or "beautiful." People (unless they belonged to the very narrow band of black men Peter cruised) were classified as "nice" or "not specially nice." In the disco on Duval Street Peter could be counted on to know the words to the songs, which he'd sing along to soundlessly, and the proper steps, whereas Julien made a wide swathe on the floor if he bothered to dance at all; his numbers were all show-stoppers.

Perhaps the real difference was that Peter respected gay life as it was—mindless, sexual if not sexy, procrustean—whereas Julien was too much of a lawgiver to accept the rules handed down by the tribe. Austin knew that gay life had little left to offer someone his age but he found it more restful, a reflex, to dance in the normal, invisible way, as he'd been dancing for some thirty years now.

That night Austin spotted Julien and Joséphine at the club, just a dim *instantané* in a strobe flash. Julien looked young, younger than such a strong personality would warrant. Although Austin wanted to take off with them, he didn't dare; he was worried about a repetition of the Disney World debacle. It made him nervous that they were lurking about at all. Poor Peter.

Peter and Austin went to the outdoors bar where some Virginia college boys, three of them, each six foot three and skinny, hair in brush cut, pressed khakis, buffed penny loafers, were talking loudly, a whole mouth full of . . . if not exactly mush, then something coarser, of oatmeal. One of them was trying to get an older man, a stranger, to arbitrate a dispute. He kept asking the man politely to help settle the matter but the boy was making no sense at all and the arbiter was shrugging with a grin.

"Austin," Peter said, "all I can think about is Alex, my new beau."

"What! And you haven't told me a thing." Austin was drinking tonic without the vodka but it still brought back the old exhilarating bar taste. "Who's Alex? Black, of course. . . ."

"I hate when you say that."

"But he is black, right?"

"Yes, but you make it sound so kinky, like a fetish, like a *thing*: Peter and his preppie blacks. But it's not like that."

"It's not?"

"*No.*"

Austin wasn't sure how far he should go in teasing Peter, who liked people to notice him and talk about his habits, as though he existed in the eyes of observing friends as a character. But he didn't want to be typecast as a "dinge queen," as people used to call white men inebriated with blacks, as someone consumed by "Black fever."

"Anyway," Austin said, "so he *happens* to be black and a little bit preppie—"

"*Little* bit?" Peter exclaimed. "Oh, brother, you can't imagine how preppie he is. He's the Mayor's assistant, don't ask me what he does because I can never get that straight—" Peter was obviously very drunk. He'd turned on his smile, which hummed and glowed like a neon bar and his gestures—eyebrows raised, lips pursed, emphatic hands with the fingers spread so wide they almost bent back—were performed with the drunk's insistence on accuracy and order.

"Let's start all over: Who is Alex?"

Peter perched on a stool at the bar and patted the empty one beside him. "He's a native New Yorker. He's thirty-eight, shorter than me, just a *wee* bit paunchy." In his drunkenness Peter overdid his indications of "weeness." He stooped a bit to squint at an inch squeezed between thumb and middle finger. His face was rosy, his eyes beginning to cross, a lock of hair had fallen over his brow: he was drunk and happy. "*Not* that I mind. No, he's cute. He's interested in—he *designs* furniture. He has only one fault. He's a workaholic. No, two: he's negative and I haven't told him yet that I'm positive. Of course we're always very, very safe."

"Does he like you?"

Peter grabbed his hand. "Oh, I *hope* so, Austin, because I want to have one happy affair before I die. That's mean. You and I had a *great* affair. But we're more like family than lovers. Not that it isn't terrifically romantic being here in Key West with you under a moon—well, I *think* that's a moon over there someplace." He held his hand up over his eyes to indicate looking.

They drifted across the street and down a back alley to a bar known to attract an older set. Peter had nothing against older men, who'd always been good for buying drinks and handing out compliments. They'd make all the moves, which suited his nature. Nor did Austin mind his fellow seniors—in fact he sometimes said all his problems originated from his interest in kids.

The door to the bar gave access to an area open to the night sky but enclosed by ten-foot-high wood palisading. The lights were low, the music deafening. Most of the customers were in their forties. Inside, in the shuttered part of the club, a single bare-chested, barefoot boy in a kilt was dancing lasciviously on the bar. Austin watched him, mesmerized. He realized how long it had been since he'd even held someone in his arms or been kissed full on the mouth. Of course it was all the fault of the decision he himself had made in Mexico never to touch Julien again. Nevertheless, even if he'd been the one to choose physical solitude, it was hard to bear.

In the back room an old-fashioned mirror ball turned, casting its banal shards of light above an empty dance floor.

Austin exchanged glances with a man in a black cowboy hat who had on new jeans and old boots. Do I know him? Is that why he's looking at me funny? Austin said good night to Peter and left; Peter said he'd be home in an hour or so. But on the way out Austin noticed the man was following him. Austin slowed up and turned back to say, "That go-go boy was ready for Las Vegas, if you want my opinion."

"Yeah, he sure was," the man said in a very deep voice with a touch of a Southern accent, if not drawl.

"Where you from?"

"Dallas. You?"

"Virginia, originally," Austin said, to establish a Southern affiliation. "Right now I live in Providence, which ain't the same."

"Guess not. Like to get together?"

"Sure, why don't we grab this cab and go to my place."

"Why not."

Austin left his bike chained where it was in front of the Cuban Cultural Center.

In the back seat of the car Austin half-turned toward the man and smiled at him. He looked to be no more than forty, with a long, lean but underexercised torso, a wooden face that cracked and split audibly around even the most minor smile, and a voice deep and expressionless that reminded Austin of a closed cedar chest. When Austin took his hand, he surrendered it easily and even stroked Austin's thumb with his own, but he looked out the window simultaneously. Austin was worried they might stop at a light and Julien would come cycling up beside them. It was such a small town. At the same time nothing seemed more natural than sitting beside this man with the dry, warm hand. There was a simple no-bullshit manliness between them and not a trace of flirtatiousness.

Back in the house Austin offered him a drink. He said he didn't drink.

"Neither do I!" Austin exclaimed joyfully, as if it were the most extraordinary coincidence.

Peter had made Austin a joint. Austin asked dubiously, "Should we smoke this?" But by now the man had pressed his mouth onto Austin's. They kissed in the ordinary way, their hands explored each other's body in the usual fashion—but then, suddenly, Austin felt safe enough, *present* enough, to lean on this man with the full weight of his desire. It wasn't even that he was releasing his lust; it was more that he'd found it.

After a moment the man drew back. It was so obvious they'd each met his sexual match. Even in the old days not more than one in twenty men had been this hungry, this available. The man smiled hugely. "Wow," he said, like a diver coming up for air and, like a diver, shaking his head abruptly to one side to get his hair out of his face. "We better smoke that joint after all. Hell, I ain't got no right to but I want to."

At first when they were naked in bed Austin knelt on the floor between his legs, as if all he had to offer was an expert mouth and a discreetly absent body. But the man said, "Hey! You! C'mon on up here. Yeah. That's right. Climb up here. Right into my arms."

He was a very nice man—oh, Austin knew, he'd most likely turn into a humorless accountant if questioned, even a deacon in the gay Metropolitan Community Church, something solemn and ghastly, but as a creature, as a *guy*, he was relaxed and neighborly, a set of young muscles under skin that age had untuned just a bit. But he was a comfortable grown-up in his baggy skin suit, and this ordinariness, this

Southern ordinariness, which Austin had almost forgotten, struck him as miraculously sexy. He never thought he'd feel this big, roomy man covering him again, tongue a wet, muscular fluke mooring one face into another, hands taking root along Austin's back. Austin's nipples, his penis, his mouth, his arms were all glowing; a heat-seeking missile would have found five sites to bomb.

Because he was stoned he also became just a bit metaphysical. He floated here, above their writhing bodies and above the sound of their voices, too astounded to make much sense. He thought it was like a symphony, which existed up here, ideally, as a silent score, eternal and unchanging, and down there, as a performance, noisy, imperfect, plangent with feeling.

Chapter Sixteen

They returned to France. In Providence, things at the college had fizzled out. Although a few of his colleagues, mainly other art historians, had uttered regretful noises about Austin's imminent departure, no one seemed to mind it. After all, he'd made a few waves. There had been his sexist remarks. And then he and Julien had not been the sort of dotty, aging gay couple an academic community likes—great cooks, kindly uncles to faculty children, demon bridge players. And then AIDS (for they had made no secret about their health), didn't AIDS suggest that they hadn't been faithful? No one would say that, naturally; in fact everyone pulled long faces and spoke of the tragedy, the *holocaust*, and vaguely blamed the Reagan administration, but the presence of AIDS did imply, didn't it, that there'd been lurid promiscuity sometime in the past, not just the once-a-week domestic squirt-and-giggle that was usual on Providence's East Side. Austin was, shockingly, almost twice Julien's age, which hinted that Austin was susceptible to the charms of youth—*not* appreciated in a professor. And wasn't there something about Julien having been married? Did that mean Austin had taken him away from his wife and infected him?

Worse, Joséphine, though almost thirty, was endlessly walking

Ajax past Aaron's door, and he really was a student. Apparently Aaron had told her he didn't want to see her anymore, but she kept traipsing up and down Benefit Street on the off chance she'd run into him. Once she and Austin did see him puffing up Planet Street, but when he caught sight of their familiar silhouettes at the top of the hill—slim girl in a pea jacket, blond hair flying like a pennant; round bespectacled man trailing a long knit scarf; and fat basset hound straining at the very end of an extendible blue leash—Aaron had hid behind a tree. The only problem was that the tree was a sapling and Aaron was becoming more and more paunchy.

"Look, Joséphine," Austin said loudly enough to be heard by Aaron, "that tree is pregnant! Have you ever noticed a pregnant tree before? We call it the Coward Tree."

For Joséphine the joke was a bitter one. *She* longed to bear Aaron's baby, to learn Hebrew, to live on a kibbutz, to circumcise every finger if that would make Aaron look at her. One night she stood outside Aaron's door, buzzing and buzzing him, pleading to be let up. After Aaron stopped responding over the speakerphone, Joséphine began to beat her head against the lamp post. The people on the ground floor called the cops.

For Austin the presence of this suffering girl, driven by her longing, gave a beautiful face to his own shameful desires, which had been reawakened by the man in Key West. The night after they'd met, the man had showed up at the tea dance as arranged, but Austin had already promised to invite Peter out to a final dinner at Louie's Back Yard facing the sea. Austin kept regretting that he'd failed to tell the man how much he liked him and to line him up for another date, another life, a life to come.

In Paris Julien began to paint seriously. He wanted to make some small mark on life. He couldn't work as an architect again—he didn't even want his former colleagues to know he'd never been able to work in the States or that he was ill or that he'd come back to Paris, ingloriously.

He'd become interested in architecture as a painter *manqué*. When he was nineteen and had been living in the historic heart of Nancy in an unheated noble house with no electricity or running water or toilet except in the courtyard, a house that had been virtually abandoned, Julien had stridden about the decrepit *salon* over rain-damaged parquet missing slats, wearing tall boots, long hair and a flowing white pirate shirt. He'd painted by candlelight, standing before his easel while drinking mulled wine and trying to stay warm. He'd rented a floor of the house for just a few francs but let it be divined that it was a family property, for if to be an aristocrat was a good thing, to be a ruined one was even better. In England, say, a baronet might have felt dubious about practicing an art, but the French, used to a court society, forgave their aristocrats the possession of talent. Austin had seen some of Julien's arty photos from this period, foggy black-and-white shots of larval girls in leotards wrapped in fishermen's nets in the attic under the massive beams supporting the mansard roof.

Now Julien knew he had two more years at most to live and he wanted to leave a legacy of some sort. As a painter he would be free to travel—to London, to Zurich, to Rome, to the French countryside—to all the places Austin liked to visit in his own AIDS-restlessness.

When Austin thought of Julien's aspirations as a painter (for surely he wouldn't be content to paint and not to exhibit), his heart sank. Painting wasn't like writing, something you could do in hundreds of private ways. No, it was a narrow profession plagued by strictures and governed by just a dozen critics, not more. Sincerity, depth of feeling, flair counted for nothing. What was crucial was being resolutely up-to-date: original, but not too much so, and only in the approved manner.

Julien didn't think that way. He had a kind of sweet confidence in his own powers and an indifference to the market that amounted to suicidal ignorance. So much of any of his activities was playing the role, striking the pose, that now he was happy to sit at the Café Beaubourg and sketch and look interesting with a three days' growth of beard and a black turtleneck.

Austin, who'd painted in high school but who'd lacked the confidence to go on with it, envied Julien his pleasure and concentration. When they were alone Julien forgot about the impression he might be making and became, all over again, the serious kid constructing something with toy blocks. He could sit at his desk for hours drawing, hearing the African radio station, Radio Nova, without really listening to it; he'd get up from his work, blinking and merry and ready to eat. And he'd be unusually affectionate in his warm, one might say fatherly way. Working restored his equilibrium and gave him back that sense of purpose that even living with a fatal disease requires if one is to live at all.

Austin was glad to be back in France. Providence had been a wasps' nest, burnt over and nearly extinct but still feebly menacing. The houses pulsing in the dark, the eerie silence of the streets in which voices carried with the presence of sound across water, the deserted, windswept plazas downtown, slowly filling up with snow, the dowdy, malicious but nearly invisible professors—oh, he had to laugh at it from the safe distance of Paris with its glittering cafés spilling out into the street, its two hundred curtains rising every night on cabarets and theaters and opera houses, its exuberant populace overconfident about exactly how to eat and dress and make love.

Austin loved walking the streets again and buying prints and old books along the quais. He knew France was entering a major decline and for the first time he was meeting young people eager to emigrate, but he didn't care; his own prospects were too dim to trouble himself about the future. He lived in the eternal, pearl-gray present of Paris under slanting-cold rain, of dark-blue lacquer doors guarding graveled gardens and soot-streaked walls of pale sandstone. Once again he assembled his little band of friends who, unlike Americans, practiced the courtesy of almost impersonal gaiety, whooping with laughter, excitedly recounting their misadventures. Joséphine had already turned her unhappy passion for Aaron into a hilarious anecdote, emphasis on the Coward Tree.

They found a large place on a noisy corner between the Tour St.-Jacques and the Centre Georges Pompidou (the priory and the oil refinery). Although Austin was very short of money and even had to borrow some from Henry McVay, he wanted Julien to live in this spacious apartment with its back bedroom that could serve as a studio. The room had a white marble fireplace and casement windows looking out on stiffly pitched roofs; just across the way, a fashionably bald boy with beautiful eyes lived with an elderly—well, with a man Austin's age. They would sit up in bed, the bald boy and the elderly man with his full jowls and white hair, and watch television; at night by the flickering colored light Austin could see them holding each other, propped up in bed.

One night Austin read a novel by a French friend in which Dr. Aristopoulos, his old French general practitioner, was a character. At two in the morning Austin discovered, albeit from a piece of fiction, that Aristopoulos had died of AIDS. Austin was devastated. He said to himself in a comic voice, "What's the world coming to when even the croakers start croaking?" but he cried in strange spurts of sadness. At eight in the morning he called the novelist, who confirmed the news.

A friend from Boston lent them his two-room farmhouse near Vendôme and they spent July and August there. One long day stretched into another. In the main room Julien set up his easel, but most of the time he worked at a wooden table under the tall, open windows, drawing and looking up occasionally at the hay fields under a haze in the distance or at the barn to the left in the foreground, which two roofers came to repair with old tiles in the medieval tradition; Julien drew them crouched on the slanting surface, rebuilding the system of wood slats that supported the overlapping, weathered ceramic squares. In his drawings, dressed in their blue overalls, they looked like man-shaped jigsaw pieces that, when filled in, would be part of the seamless blue heavens.

Each room had a big Dutch door. Just outside one of the doors was a patch of stinging nettles ("Good for soup," Julien invariably said). An old wooden hay cart was abandoned in the nettles, tipping forward from its shoulder-high wheels and resting on its poles. When Ajax went exploring the cart, which was dozing under pinwheels of attendant butterflies, he stung his paw with the nettles: *"Mon pauvre petit bébé,"* Julien crooned as he extracted them.

The main room had a stone fireplace so tall a man could walk into it, and even in summer, especially after a rain, it smelled of ashes. It was one of those fireplaces that never draws properly; the wrong geomancer had been consulted, apparently. The narrow galley kitchen was perfectly functional, with its bottle of butane to fuel the stove and its ancient fridge, which had to be washed free of moss and fungus before it could be plugged in again. In the bathroom the tiny spiders and their fine webs had to be hosed down. It was as though the whole house was always about to be engulfed again by nature. In the summer minuscule wildflowers crept over the wide stone threshold.

Austin carted six boxes of reference books down to the country. He was determined to finish his long-overdue furniture encyclopedia. Only by doing so could he ever bail them out again.

The big day every week was Wednesday, when Julien and Ajax and Austin piled into their old but recently acquired Renault 5 and went to the village market. In temporary stalls erected on the graveled main square, merchants were selling hot quiches right out of the oven, thirty kinds of fish right out of the sea, vegetables right out of the garden, including loamy white onion bulbs, plump and sprouting grass-green shoots as stiff as paper fans. The local watery goat cheese, locally cured hams and bacon, even the perch out of the nearby river—everything was fun to buy, rush home and eat.

Other than that once-a-week excursion, they stayed close to home and worked. Sometimes Joséphine would drive over from her parents' house in Tours and stay with them two or three days. She'd draw her illustrations. Julien would be at his easel, she'd be bent over one table before one big window and Austin at the other.

Around noon the heat became more intense and the world seemed to hold its breath like a child hiding in a dusty closet. Bees hovered around the wildflowers, the heat-haze thickened over the fields, Ajax found the only cool, shadowed patch of the stone floor to stretch out on, the radio murmured on the only station they could get. Every day an announcer with a warm, soft, civilized voice recited another long, eventless episode from a novel about a happy if sometimes tedious family. When Austin sank onto the creaky old bed for a nap, he'd half-listen to that seductive narrative voice, making its reassuring distinctions ("On the other hand," "Not only . . . but also," "Needless to say . . .").

Julien and Austin had never been closer. In the late evenings they prepared their supper, slicing the ripe tomatoes and covering them with shredded mint leaves, which grew just outside the back door, or elaborating an old-fashioned chicken fricassee with mushrooms and pearl onions. Afterwards, while the light still held, they walked down the two-lane rural route with Ajax off the leash, past the fields where grazing cows, irritated by Ajax's defiant barking, loomed up to the barbed wire fence and sent him off, cowering, ears pressed back and tail tucked between his ample buttocks. They'd wander past the woods where an owl hooted and a slender moon was hanging like a Christmas ornament on the highest branches. Inevitably Ajax, hypnotized by a dried-out cow turd or a long-dead, thoroughly excavated rabbit's carcass, fell behind. He was so intrigued by these ripe, unfamiliar smells that his hearing clicked off and he could not pull out of his trance until, suddenly, he'd discover himself alone on a darkening strip of country road and he'd race back to them, heart thumping, ears flying.

Or Julien would want to walk through the garden of the nice woman who lived across the road but only came out once a week for a rendezvous with her married lover; he lived in another town, too. When she was not there, Julien used to lift the latch of the garden gate and visit the herb garden right next to the house, aromatic with thyme and tarragon, the rows of beans, potatoes, cabbage, carrots and the small stand of fruit trees. He admired the tidiness and freshness of the garden, and visited it with all the didactic seriousness any Frenchman devotes to a mineral collection, say; Austin even heard him instructing Ajax on the names of every vegetable. Each visit had the sweet dignity of a ritual, as when a grandmother shows a child all the treasures in her china cabinet, one by one.

Once they walked so far—just to see an abandoned Romanesque chapel at the crossroads they had glimpsed from the car—that night had fallen entirely and the walk home past the woods on the other side of the stream was frightening. They heard angry voices in the woods and saw the glow of a flashlight held by someone crashing through underbrush. Austin had goose bumps as if a dead hand had brushed across his nape.

At night they lay in bed and read to each other from an old warped book they'd found on the kitchen shelf, a dictionary of French insults. Whereas Americans were supposed to be friendly and popular and any nastiness was considered a treatable flaw, in France people admired those who had the courage to be tart or difficult; Julien read out the insults in his booming voice with obvious relish.

In the fall they were back in Paris. Austin had worked hard during the summer, inspired by Julien's example, and the encyclopedia was almost finished. He still had six months to go on the notes and bibliography, which would be difficult to reconstitute since he had jotted everything down on bits of loose paper, coffee-stained and inserted into a blotter.

Julien had finished five striking paintings of dark, brooding young men posed, often in silhouette, in an open doorway against a salmon-pink evening sky or along the girding of an industrial-era metal bridge. In one of them the man was walking a leashed dog, who was already straining halfway out of the composition. An American friend of Austin's who had a gallery in Passy met with Julien. She encouraged him to do more of his satirical sketches and fewer of his brooding paintings, although it occurred to her she might plan, for a year from now, a show of "Bitter Boys and Sweet Sad Men." She was proud of her title. Austin thought the date was perhaps tragically distant.

Julien responded to the possibility with a renewed determination to do his best work. This would be his one chance; he didn't want to miss it. He visited the Louvre—only a half-hour walk away—almost every day. So that he could avoid waiting in line, Austin bought him a membership card, which gave him special entry through the new French sculpture wing. Austin kept loading him up with art books that might excite his imagination—Aubrey Beardsley, John Singer Sargent, Francesco Clemente. Julien used them in an entirely practical way, not out of respect for each man's place in art history but for motifs they might suggest.

He was struggling to refine his taste in painting at the same time as he was wrestling to improve his technique. That was the dreadful thing—he knew he didn't have enough time to master this demanding medium and yet he was too honest to cheat. He'd become a passionately serious man. In Julien's neat desk and meticulous working habits Austin saw the architect he'd been, that professional who is half artist and half engineer. But what struck him was Julien's happy studiousness, his humming, arts-and-crafts independence and pleasure, as though he were a jeweler with his vice, pliers and blowtorch.

In November Austin was in London for a few days, authenticating a desk for Sotheby's, when he called Julien, who'd stayed home in Paris to work. "Things are sort of strange," Julien said in a light, bemused voice. "I got turned around in the street and couldn't find our apartment. I couldn't remember my brother's phone number this morning, though I know it by heart. Then just now I was trying to write something, but all the letters look as unfamiliar as hieroglyphics. . . ."

"Count backwards down from twenty," Austin said as calmly as possible.

Julien couldn't get past seventeen and he laughed, not in panic but as if he found his predicament droll, goofy. Austin decided to take his cue and said, "That's funny, but you may have toxoplasmosis—"

"Toxi—?"

"It's a parasite in the brain, but it's highly treatable. Can you get in a taxi and go see Dr. Verneuil at Hôpital Villejuif? Do you have money? Can you get there on your own or should I call Joséphine? I'll be back tonight."

Austin rushed back on the very next plane (the tunnel train wasn't working yet). In the apartment he found scraps of paper scattered around, covered with Julien's efforts to write normal, coherent sentences. One of them read, "This is very bizarre, but one no help why yes. . . ." (*C'est très bizarre, mais on pas d'aide pourquoi oui. . . .*)

Julien had been hospitalized. Austin barreled into a taxi and found him in the cheerful AIDS wing, the Hôpital du Jour, already less delirious, his thoughts slowly unscrambling. It was almost exactly a year since the herpes attack on his face.

Now he began to lose weight visibly. Austin would cook him all his favorite dishes—couscous, paella, *navarin*—but he'd become sick eating them and blame Austin. Although Austin followed the recipes and refrigerated everything when he wasn't working with it, Julien was certain that he'd let the meat spoil or used too much butter. Salmonella, botulism, maggots were only a few of the diseases Austin had courted with his American ineptness.

One day Julien looked at himself in the bathroom mirror and said, "I've lost my nice round, firm buttocks. You can see them in photos from when I was a boy in Alicante in Spain or a young married man in Ethiopia on the lake with pink flamingos in the background. Women always commented on them—they were narrow but rounded. And now I've lost them, I guess for good."

His weight had sunk from one hundred and sixty-five pounds to one hundred and thirty-five and though his face was not yet cadaverous his body would have looked blade-thin if he'd not dressed so carefully. He'd always favored the layered look but now he wore two or three shirts over a thermal T-shirt and under an unstructured jacket. His trousers were baggy, of wide-wale corduroy. Since his neck had become so scrawny his scarves and ascots had become more and more layered as well, tied with more and more extravagant knots.

He was always cold and after a walk with Ajax through the mist or a light December rain he'd come back trembling so violently that he'd huddle in bed under an eiderdown, wearing gloves and outdoor wool scarves. He looked like the gaunt Proust. He stopped shaving more than once a week; perhaps he thought his heavy black stubble would protect his face from the elements. Austin remembered someone had said Proust's face looked as if it was being "devoured" by his beard.

Austin took him back to Key West for the month of January to a house he'd rented because it had a jacuzzi. Julien would go into the tub for long sessions; the swirling water massaged his lower back, which had become intensely painful day in and day out, and finally warmed him up. Perhaps some of his medications made his skin photosensitive; he became as tan as a Mexican Indian even though he seldom went outside before evening.

The preceding year they had rented bikes and Julien had sped all over the island like a restless teenager just before he gets his first car. But this year he was so thin and weak that as he pumped his way up Elizabeth Street from the Waterfront Market with groceries in his basket, he lost control and fell. Austin came gliding up behind and scooped him up from the ground. "It's all your fault, giving me these groceries," Julien said. "And now I've lost control."

"You've lost . . . ?"

"I've shit in my pants." Julien was angry and humiliated.

Austin ran into the restaurant and ordered a taxi. He locked Julien's bike to a lamp post. The taxi didn't come, but at last a two-wheeled rickshaw drawn by a bicyclist came along empty and Austin hailed it.

Soon they were home and Austin stood naked with Julien in the big outdoor shower and washed his soiled body clean. Julien slung an arm around Austin's shoulder and let his knees buckle; he was ready to pass out. Austin put him to bed.

The bicycle-rickshaw man had given them his card. Whenever they had to go somewhere they called him. Riding behind him was a pleasure, watching his powerful buttocks bunching and uncoiling inside his pink shorts. He was Australian and kept up a stream of chatter that didn't demand answers. They decided to call the foot-powered vehicle a pedophile; whenever they needed to go somewhere they said, "Let's call the pedophile."

Julien became so thin, so dark-skinned, and his beard grew in so thick that as they headed back to Paris people in the Miami airport stared at him. In Key West, where everyone was familiar with AIDS, no one had made a fuss. In Paris, the rule of discretion (or maybe it was just big-city indifference) meant that no one gawked. But when they were in what surely counted as "the real world" they were exposed to a hostile curiosity.

Chapter Seventeen

All the time they were in Key West, Ajax had been boarded with Robert and Fabrice in Nice. Now they flew from Paris down to the Riviera to get their dog—and to tell Robert, at last, that Julien was dying.

Although the month was February the weather was bizarrely warm. Robert was standing in the airport, Ajax seated tranquilly beside him; Robert was wearing just a short-sleeved shirt, which barely contained his massive chest and shoulders. Austin looked for a sign that he was shocked by Julien's appearance, but Robert's beautiful face was impossible to decipher.

Soon Fabrice pulled up in his car and bundled them all in, but he seemed mildly offended when Julien asked him to put out his eternal cigarette. "I'm not well," Julien said. "I'll explain everything to you later."

Fabrice and Robert had moved out of their bedroom and surrendered it to their guests. They said they didn't mind sleeping on the two black leather couches in the living room.

Julien left with Fabrice, Robert and Ajax to go shopping and for an hour Austin was alone in their house. The winter sunlight was bright, pouring over the terra-cotta tiles of the roofs on the slopes below them. A few houses down, pale red roses were still flowering in the corner of a walled garden. A skinny gray cat with paws dipped in black ink lay stretched out, half on its side, one leg extended ahead as if it were doing the sidestroke in its sleep. The sun had whited out the details of the port in a generalized glare but had left in a few picturesque elements: the faded blue-striped awning over a *bouillabaisse* restaurant on the far side, the palette-knife brilliance of a taut sail entering the harbor, the gleam off the hood of a car turning out toward the Promenade des Anglais.

Here, much closer, just below the windows rose up the olive tree, which produced the small *niçois* olives. There was the gravel rooftop where Robert tossed the cooked yolks of his eggs every morning for the birds; here and there were a few orange crumbs mixed in with the little stones.

Inside he walked around the pyramid-shaped bush, which Robert trimmed every morning with manicure scissors; it was a fine example of French topiary, which mystified the English, who liked their nature shaggy. Austin looked at the grand piano and even struck a few notes, but it was out of tune. He lay on the bed and looked at the plaster garland on the ceiling. He listened to the distant churn of traffic as it drove up the mountain. He got up and stood in a side window that looked out over hundreds of white, gray or sand-colored houses that flowed over the hills.

He realized that he was always tense these days and had been tense for months. He almost never had a moment like this for daydreaming, and his old life, the life he'd led on the Île Saint-Louis, struck him as unbelievably carefree—but also shallow. He'd been entirely self-centered then and although he'd looked his age he hadn't felt it. He'd gone on and on, decade after decade, being a kid, though he'd filtered his boyishness through some later notion of Parisian pleasure, a notion that made pleasure take on the weight of an artistic pursuit or a proof of civilized elegance.

Now he was a "caregiver." That was the word he'd heard in America. Someone had asked him if he was Julien's "primary caregiver." Startled at first, he'd finally said, "Yes. Yes, I am." He was convinced that he had little in common with the old, irresponsible, endlessly joking gay men he'd known in America before he ever left for France. Of course they had died or changed, too. No one was the same. They'd all changed and that old world of gay men with snappy retorts who'd committed to memory every last lyric from a Stephen Sondheim musical was gone, had fled, never to return.

The boys came back and suddenly the house was noisy with Julien's and Robert's rumbling voices. "Bébert!" Julien called forth. A moment later they were in a clinch in the bedroom, both of the brothers sprawled across the bed, laughing. Then Julien rushed into the living room, swept down on Austin and said, *"Mon petit bébé d'amour,"* and Austin could see Robert behind him, framed in the doorway, trying to smile, but something stricken, something broken, in his glance.

Julien had told them.

Fabrice was brushing down Ajax and talking to him in a soft voice with so much tenderness that Ajax's eyes had gone huge and mournful. A light winter rain began to fall, in no way dimming the sun; squalls were blowing far out to sea and the palms were bending in the wind, although up here everything was calm. The rain was falling down in straight silvery lines.

The next day it was even warmer and the winds had scoured the skies clean with just a few faint swirls of cirrus clouds high, high above, as though an over-zealous housekeeper had scraped the blue enamel off the white bowl. They drove with Ajax all in one car out to Cap Ferrat and stopped at the very tip, near the Santo Sospir, the villa where Cocteau had lived so many years before. Inside, Mme Weisweiler, Cocteau's old patron, was still living, though she was ancient and an opium addict, thanks to Cocteau himself; she'd acquired his habit without picking up his habits (of hard work, curiosity, exuberant creativity). Austin could picture Cocteau with his turned-back jacket sleeves, his beautiful "son" Édouard Dermit with his black, wavy hair and upturned nose, Mme Weisweiler in heels, hat and white linen suit trimmed in dark piping. She who had once been so svelte and stylish, who'd been the perfect smiling embodiment of sleek feminine beauty in all those black-and-white French magazine photos of the 1950s—she'd ended up an immobilized old woman half-dead in this nearly empty, dilapidated mansion. Robert said he'd peeked into the windows more than once but had never seen her.

They descended all her stairs to the rocks and the sea. From here they could look back at the long, slow curve of the Nice beaches and the white turrets of the old grand hotels (*les palaces,* as the French called them, using the English word). The winter sea was dotted not only with pleasure boats but also with big, rusting ships hauling goods along the coast or produce up from North Africa. But they were all far away, as if this peninsula was held between cupped hands. Here, on Cap Ferrat, the massive white stone mansions glittered in the afternoon light behind dusty green umbrella pines.

Robert and Julien sat on the rocks, dangling their feet just above the water, while Fabrice stood, smoking, and Austin tipped back, stretching his whole length out on a chalky stone. He closed his eyes and absorbed the heat of the sun. Julien said to his brother, "Look at the jellyfish."

Austin cocked open one eye and glanced down at the gently lapping water, gray-green in its depths but colorless as ether here. He could see the large white medusas, nearly a foot in circumference, floating and pulsing with the waves. They dilated and contracted like optic muscles—at least Austin saw them as something like vision: crystalline, neural, sleepless.

"They're beautiful, aren't they?" Julien asked. He seemed fascinated by their pulsing; they contracted and relaxed constantly, all liquid and powerfully if invisibly muscular, clear as tears. If you didn't look carefully you wouldn't see them at all, so transparent were they. They were like sunspots in a lens, or subaquatic spider webs. They were oil on water, if the oil was squeezed from white roses.

"I'd like to be that peaceful," Julien said.

Fabrice, who was standing behind the two brothers, rubbed his left eye; maybe it was just irritation from his cigarette smoke.

"Bébert," Julien said to Robert, "I want to come back after I die as one of these medusas. You like to come down here all the time. I promise: I'll float by you one day. You'll know. They're so peaceful."

But then later he touched a jellyfish with his stick and tore it. He was shocked; he had had no idea they were so fragile.

As the two brothers talked, Austin and Fabrice went for a walk all the way down to the point of the peninsula. They sat for a moment on a bench and looked out across the expanse of the Mediterranean, as uniform as a field of wheat but exhilarating, an invitation to voyage, as heady as a great draft of cold vodka.

"Ah, Ostend, you can't imagine how hard we were hit by Julien's news." Fabrice rested a hand on Austin's shoulder. "We love Julien so much. Robert is truly shattered. I can see it in his eyes. We had our doubts, of course. First with the chicken pox so near his eyes—we thought that was strange. Then when he said he had a brain tumor—"

"—But he didn't have a brain tumor," Austin said.

"Precisely. No, but he told us he had a tumor. I suppose he dared not mention the toxi, the intox—"

"The toxoplasmosis."

"Precisely. So he said he had a tumor. But we talked it over with a doctor we know and told him that Julien had a brain tumor which had been *cured* and that now he was *normal*—and our friend said that was impossible. He said maybe it hadn't been a tumor at all. Then a mutual friend of ours, someone we've known for years, who used to be in show business and has nursed friends with AIDS, she said it sounded like AIDS, her hairdresser had had something similar, and Robert was so angry he hit the table with his fist—oh, Ostend, how could this have happened?"

"Was Julien often active with men?" Austin asked. He'd been curious for so long; now he had a legitimate reason to ask.

Fabrice looked disconcerted by the question and said, "Why did Julien ever get married? We were very opposed to that. We're so happy he found you. These brothers! They're extraordinary, aren't they?"

Suddenly Fabrice began to cry and Austin put his arm around him. He was such a kindly soul, Fabrice, and even his refusal to pay his taxes or even think about them Austin found *sympathique*. Julien complained about how lazy and disorganized his brother and Fabrice were, but Julien, too, half-admired their indifference to life's duties and tedious details. Fabrice told so many bizarre jokes, sometimes with a cruel edge to them, that it was easy to forget he was so full of

love and tenderness. His dog, his Robert, his cousins, a few friends
from adolescence in Nice—the circle was small, but his big heart constantly irrigated it with fresh, strong sentiments.

Julien and Austin hurried back to Paris; Julien had his painting to
do, his show to prepare. Austin was perpetually conscious of not wasting Julien's time, as if Austin was setting him up for eternity, as if the
thoughts he was entertaining, the information or impressions he was
storing up would be his to meditate on forever, mental food for the big
voyage. He forgot he was heading in fact for nothing but oblivion.

Or, more recently, Austin thought that Julien's experiences now,
since there would be so few of them, should be superior to the ordinary run, so mixed and compromised. But what did that mean? Superior? How? To what? Julien was in pain from his back almost
constantly. It was the result of pancreatitis, which a new drug, DDI,
had caused. The doctor had warned that one out of twenty patients
who took DDI developed pancreatitis, which could be fatal. American
and optimistic, Austin said the odds were overwhelmingly in their
favor and the danger infinitesimal, the possible benefits wonderfully
promising. French and fatalistic, Julien expected the worst but realized he had no alternative. Both he and Austin, being human, invariably talked about his getting better. That was the pattern they'd
absorbed since childhood: someone was ill, he submitted to treatment,
he got better.

Not for a moment did Austin imagine that he was required to
share Julien's pain. He didn't really have time to reflect on their condition. From early morning to early evening, when Julien went to bed,
Austin was running. Walking the dog three times a day. Shopping for
fresh food every day and cooking it. Accompanying Julien to the hospital for examinations and treatments. Receiving friends—for Julien
wanted to see people, but only for short spells. Accordingly, they had
worked out a plan: friends would drop by for a drink, then go off to a
restaurant with Austin while Julien ate his chicken soup and stewed
carrots and crème caramel in bed and watched a movie on video. The
friends were always impressed by how elegant Julien looked, how
warm and smiling his expression was. They said, "Usually when
someone in France becomes ill, gravely ill, he retires from the world

altogether. It's vastly to Julien's credit that he's stayed so open." Did they mean that as praise? Or were they shocked he imposed his illness on them?

When Austin came home, even if it was no later than ten, Julien had fallen asleep while the old black-and-white movie was noisily winding down.

For a long time Julien claimed he adored all the French classics— *Atalanta, The Rules of the Game, Dr. Knock*—but one evening he said, "I don't want to see anything old anymore."

That single statement, presented without preamble or explanation, read to Austin as a cry to survive, to live vividly in the present. He was right: the past was a luxury only the healthy could afford.

One day the doctor prescribed an estrogen patch, which was designed to revive Julien's appetite. He slapped a fresh one to his forearm every morning. "But he said a side effect was that it would probably kill off my sex drive," Julien admitted in a deliberately neutral, scientific, almost offhand voice.

Austin didn't say anything. He felt too guilty for having neglected Julien's body for so many months. If they'd continued making love, perhaps Julien would have fewer regrets now.

Julien said, "Well, I guess I can say goodbye to all that. To sex." Something in his tone made Austin wonder if Julien had gone on having occasional adventures, enjoying some of the countless erotic possibilities Paris offered its citizens every day. He hoped so.

Even though Austin accompanied him on every third visit to the doctor, Julien was remarkably self-reliant. He and the social worker who'd been assigned to his case filled out all the forms; Austin would have been lost if he'd been faced with this very French form of bureaucratic business. Not that the system wasn't benign. If a patient had fewer than two hundred T-cells (and Julien had never been tested with so many) the state reimbursed one hundred percent of his medical expenses, even his taxi fares to and from the hospital. In addition, Julien (and thousands of other out-of-work people with HIV) received unemployment benefits, which gave him pocket money. Even the man who came to the house to massage him was paid by a government agency.

Julien sold his apartment but with little profit—the market was bad and then, at the last moment, the Communist mayor of his township put in a low preemptive bid that could not be disputed or rejected. Even sold so disadvantageously, the apartment brought him in some money. He was determined to spend it all before he died so that his hated father would inherit nothing. (Under Napoleonic law parents could not disinherit children, but neither could children disinherit parents.) Julien bought the video machine, a full-length leather coat that was so heavy he looked exhausted just standing up in it, a luxurious white terry-cloth bathrobe for Austin that was so thick it filled an entire suitcase, then a holiday to Rome over Easter.

They stayed in the Villa Médicis, the Renaissance *palazzo* near the top of the Spanish Steps that belonged to the French government. In its huge reception rooms and extensive gardens the young French writers and painters and sculptors who won the Prix de Rome circulated for the two years they lived there. A friend of Austin's, a furniture curator at a museum in the south of France, arranged for them to stay at the Villa as guests during Holy Week. Julien paid the low daily fee as well as the airfare.

They were virtually alone in the great palace. The French had all gone back to France for Easter. A tiny, studded door set into a larger one let them into an impressive lobby ending in stairs that led up to a bust of Louis XIV before branching off to right and left and ascending on up to the reception rooms and ultimately the bedrooms. As for the artists' studios, they were each independent little buildings tucked away in corners of the huge garden.

Julien and Austin could come back at night after a dinner on the Piazza del Popolo and open the dwarf door set into the giant *portone*. The lights would spring on when they touched the timed meter. After ascending several floors they'd cross a slender, shaky *passerelle*, a suspended metal walkway, and then they'd reach their room, sober, barely furnished, although with a twenty-two-foot-high ceiling, coffered and as neatly carpentered as a ship's hull. The room's single wide window looked out on the garden. The first night they were there a bolt of lightning hit a hundred-year-old pine and splintered it in half. As so often these days, they said, "Too bad it didn't hit us. Instantaneous. Dramatic. A fine death." They'd become connoisseurs on the ways of dying and after a story someone would tell to invoke pity and terror, they would cock an eye at each other, smile and say, "That sounds attractive," or "Not bad. Quick and to the point."

The fiction was that Austin himself would die soon after Julien, even very soon. And some days Austin hoped that he would fall down a manhole or double over from a heart attack the day after he buried Julien. That would all be so much simpler. In that case he wouldn't have to rebuild a new life. The tackiness of survival—which led, inevitably, to forgetting and faithlessness—could be obviated. He had no savings, no one to look after him, no close surviving relatives, no job prospects; he was *counting* on dying quickly.

Julien still had sums of energy to draw on. There was so much they had to see: the Caravaggios in the French Church, Michelangelo's *Moses*, the dome of St. Peter's and the Pietà, the Forum and the Colosseum, the marble Renaissance vastness of St. John Lateran, the miniature medieval cloisters of a silent order of nuns who cared for the deaf at Quattro Santi Coronati, the lamp posts dangling baskets of pink azaleas around the bottom of the Spanish Steps, the creamy lubricity of Canova's nudes on exhibit in a museum along the Corso, the perverse splendors of the Carracci brothers' paintings inside the fortress-like French Embassy, the Palazzo Farnese (which a friend arranged for them to see). Julien was too skinny to sit on an uncushioned metal chair in a café. His face, gaunter and browner than a Navajo's, frightened the Romans; even the flirtatious young men around the Campo dei Fiori averted their eyes, they who invariably looked up from their fruit and flower stands with black eyes wincing from the vulnerability of narcissism.

In the mornings, Austin could tell, Julien was often tempted to stay in bed but then, by heroic dedication to experience for its own sake, he'd rise, dress, shake the rust out of his joints and set his slowly atrophying muscles once more in motion, for the only way to live at all was by pretending there was going to be a future worth preparing for. That future was so past belief that only the most grimly abstract sense of duty could prod him now through all this onerousness. He was a bit like a Frankenstein monster slowly coming unstitched.

One evening the Easter holiday was over and the *palazzo* began to fill up with the returning *pensionnaires*—pale Parisians in black, murmuring in hushed voices rich with insinuation and knowing, so different from the loud querulousness of Rome and its verbal shrugging. The French, who consider even the mildest day too hot and who have no stoic scruples about complaining, were all saying, *"Chaud . . . trop chaud . . . comme il fait chaud!"*

Then, the next afternoon, after a long, dreamy walk through the Pincio looking down on the entire city as it spread out all the way from the spun-sugar battlements of the monument to Victor Emmanuel to the opening crab claw of colonnades in front of St. Peter's, as they were ambling down the hill to the Villa Médicis, suddenly Julien doubled over. He said it felt like sharp needles piercing his eyeball, the left one, the one that had so nearly been blinded by herpes in Boston.

It wasn't too late to call their travel agent in Paris. They were locked into a low-fare air ticket that permitted no changes, but the agent phoned Air France and talked about Julien's AIDS emergency. Within ten minutes she phoned back to say they had two seats on the last plane of the day if they could be on it in an hour and a half.

They threw their clothes in a bag and rushed down the hill to the taxis clustered in front of the expensive German hotel on the street at the top of the Spanish Steps. Julien was in excruciating pain, writhing on the back seat of the taxi. Austin sat beside him, not even daring to hold his hand lest the pressure of his skin (or even the mere fact of his presence) add to the reality of his suffering, as though pain, like the atmosphere, could be measured in pounds per cubic inch. Julien had long since put behind him all play-acting, exchanging it for a woodenness worthy of the cigar-store Indian he'd come to resemble, so brown and hard was his skin, so inexpressive his features. But now he twisted and turned in his seat, grimaced and thrashed from side to side. If someone had dared to annoy Julien, even unintentionally, Austin would have gone for his throat. But now he could help in no way except to pray silently that they'd get to the airport in time.

They did. They'd even been upgraded to first class. As soon as the plane took off Julien felt better. As the cool, compressed air came rushing through the overhead nozzles and the soft voices of the French stewardesses were asking them with formulaic politeness for their choices, Julien's whole body uncoiled and stretched. He scarcely trusted his good luck, but it seemed he was intent on proving that pleasure, after all, is nothing except the cessation of pain. He smiled. Now he was at home only in this pressurized world of propulsion and purely symbolic comfort. Even when they landed the symptoms didn't come back.

Despite his greedy sight-seeing, he now admitted he'd been disappointed by Rome, although Paris, too, struck him as more pedestrian than he'd remembered. "It seems so colorless after Italy," Julien said. Everything looked standardized and well-maintained, compared to the baroque shabbiness of Rome, its broken pediments incised against the blue sky or its marble thresholds half-sunk into the red earth. It occurred to Austin that Julien was being so fastidious to justify to himself why he was unhappy in both cities.

They went to the Hôpital du Jour where Julien was welcomed exuberantly by the nurses and the shy Iranian intern; Austin realized with a slight shock that with them Julien was still being as charming as ever, whereas at home he'd long since given up the effort. The Iranian could find nothing wrong with Julien's eye.

Chapter Eighteen

Austin no longer slept with Julien. He'd put sheets on the couch in Julien's studio. The mattress was lumpy but Austin was usually so exhausted that he fell asleep immediately. No matter how tired he was he remained alert to the slightest signal Julien made. If Julien had a gasping fit behind his door, Austin was suddenly there, hovering in the hallway, listening, verifying. If the floorboard creaked, Julien would call out, *"Petit?"*

"Oui?"

"I'm okay. Go back to bed."

Only once in the whole long period of his illness did Julien ever say, "Would you sleep with me tonight? I'm afraid."

Austin stopped drawing the curtains and turned to look at Julien. He was so moved by this naked demand for comfort that he acquiesced without a comment. He realized how brave Julien had been on all the other nights, how brave in his endurance and silence.

Austin had bought some pornographic magazines and dutifully masturbated to them, even though he didn't like still photography of men (he preferred dirty movies or, best of all, stories). He said out loud, "I'm so physically lonely." Maybe he found sexual despondency easier to admit to than just plain loneliness.

One night at a reading someone gave at the Village Voice, an English-language bookshop on the Left Bank, he met an American gay man in his early forties who was in the audience and they'd exchanged numbers, not with the idea of sleeping together (Austin knew Rod wasn't attracted to him), but simply because they'd laughed so hard and in such an exhilarating, spontaneous, thoroughly American way while sipping white wine after the reading. "Oh, the best people," Austin told Rod, "are Europeanized Americans."

Now Austin phoned him at all hours during the night to laugh and whisper. He never had a free moment to see Rod and even forgot what he looked like, but they told each other everything, week after week, in those alternating joky and confessional riffs peculiar to Americans that no foreigner can ever successfully duplicate. Austin fell half in love with Rod and appreciated his way of diverting even the most solemn facts about Julien's illness into irrelevant or irreverent remarks. In Austin's place Julien would have been indignant at the "liberties" that Rod was taking, but Austin appreciated their softening effect, as if someone kept playing waltzes on the piano as the ship sank. He could tell that Rod was eccentric, a big reader who had had little formal education, a peddler of drugs at the clubs who maintained a strict regime of working out and homeopathic medicine, someone who was obsessed with what no longer existed: the deejays who'd died of AIDS in the eighties, the forgotten hit songs of the seventies, the magically seamless segue from one song to another on a certain night at the Saint in 1980.

Rod had heard of an acupuncturist in Toulouse who was supposed to work miracles with AIDS patients. He even produced a friend from the clubs who came by one day to sing Dr. Kado's praises to Julien and Austin. They flew down to Toulouse and saw the doctor. Dr. Kado was partially crippled. He told Julien that the world had been good when it was green, and at first they thought he was an ecologist. But no, he meant that the creatures, the dinosaurs, had been green and that then there'd been white people who'd "degenerated" into yellow people who were further degraded into the blacks. But not to worry. Through acupuncture and proper channeling, people were ascending back toward pure reptilian green and saurian virtue. Homosexuals themselves were degenerate forms but with proper therapy and meditation Julien could look forward to a cure. "A cure of AIDS?" Julien asked.

"No," the doctor said, "of your homosexuality. I've had a startling degree of success. You must eat only things that are—"

"*Green*," Austin said, interrupting. "Come on, Julien, let's get out of here."

One day Austin's aristocratic friend Marie-France invited him and Julien to tea. Her sitting room was situated between an inner and an outer garden—the inner one made up of trimmed boxwoods and raked gravel paths around a verdigrised fountain of a nymph, the outer one composed of twin *allées* of trees, leafless now, and enough varied ferns as ground cover to please any Victorian. Although it was almost spring the days were still short and cold and in the afternoon the French doors opening out from the *salon* looked like stretched panels of gray, watered silk, each slightly brighter or darker, fractionally different shades of twilight.

Marie-France was brisk and perfectly turned out as always in a Chanel suit, with a black bow gathering her hair up behind, her skin radiant and unlined. Nothing about her seemed rushed or artificial; her low voice was self-deprecating, alive to every possibility of wit, even at her own expense. She asked them all about Rome, as if they had been normal rich tourists, the sort she knew, seeking distraction, checking out their Italian cousins. "Did you see the Contarinis?" she asked. "Teeny and Dukie?"

She herself was more interested in actresses, writers and painters, people who would make her laugh and would cast a bohemian glamor over her *salon,* crowded as it inevitably had to be with old relatives and good tailoring and bank presidents who were, for once, intimidated by the commingling of so much artistic talent and so many aristocratic titles.

If Marie-France was shocked by Julien's protruding bones, brown face and stubble, his layers of shirts stuffed above his hipless jeans and slat-thin legs, she didn't let on at all. She was courteous, merry, light, although her deep voice made her frivolous remarks sound like fife music rearranged for the bassoon, and the gray light of Paris filtering through windows on two sides of the room crammed with row after row of white marble busts and couches upholstered in candy-striped velvet or pale blue satin imprinted with still paler peonies—this dim, liquid light in a room in which lamps had not yet been turned on lent a peacefulness, even a sadness, to every one of her starchy movements, even to her perfect posture. She always looked as if she was about to rise and tiptoe away.

Then Marie-France's sixteen-year-old daughter, Hortense, the one who hoped to compete as a horsewoman in the Olympics, came in. She would have let the two men kiss her rosy cheeks, as any upper-class girl was trained to do, but she shrank back, just a millimeter, from the ruin of Julien's looks and in blushing confusion half-sketched in a shy, comic curtsy. Immediately she curled up against her mother, as a much younger child would have done, and after studying them without seeming really to hear what they were saying, she hurried away, dropping another perfunctory curtsy on her way out.

The *shame* of disease, of their loathsome, terminal, *sexual* disease, overwhelmed Austin and he felt his cheeks burning. Marie-France even appeared to him to have turned fractionally colder, as if she regretted that her innocent daughter had been sullied by the contact.

Did Julien notice anything? No, he seemed very happy with their visit and several times on the way home said they must see more of Marie-France. When he'd gone to the toilet for a moment, she'd astonished Austin by saying, "Poor fellow. . . . Listen, if ever you need money, even a lot of money, remember, I have it." Austin was especially touched by her remark because he knew how painful it was for her to mention money at all.

Julien became extremely ill with a microorganism, a kind of tuberculosis, in the blood; it was called "avian micobacteria." His remaining cushion of flesh, no matter how slight, was boiled off his bones; he looked like a ramshackle infant. One day he was standing in the shower, studying his big, naked bones in the mirror beside the tub, and he said, "Look what's happened to my body. It's over."

But it wasn't. A new treatment for this particular disease had just kicked in and it was so effective that two weeks after he'd started it his raging fevers were calmed and he was eating like a horse. The weight flowed back onto his body and he looked better than he had in a year.

His energy came back, too, and when Lucy flew over to visit them he took a real pleasure in showing her Paris, though later he complained that she was sapping his last blood, snacking on a dying man's bones. He said she was a vampire and an idiot and he'd even heard her saying to her mother on the phone, "Now we have to go out for another *French* meal," spoken in such peevish, weary tones, as if this particular ordeal was well known back in *L'Amérique profonde*. But for Julien, complaining put him in high spirits; it was a form of creativity; it was even a form of affection. Lucy and Julien conferred for hours— on her poetry, her clothes, her decision to marry, her desire to have a baby. Julien insisted she have a baby; being childless was the one thing he regretted, he said.

He found out through a mutual friend that Vladimir had committed suicide. The friend didn't know the details but he said that Vladimir had lost his looks, his face had been covered with what appeared to be boils, all very mysterious, though he'd undoubtedly contracted AIDS. He just didn't want to admit in so many words that he was gay and dying of the usual gay disease. Nor did he want his friends to pity him. Julien looked often at the photo Vladimir had inscribed to him and created a minor cult around it. Austin would find him staring at it, tears in his eyes. Austin remembered Vladimir as he'd been as a young man in Venice, barely out of his adolescence, or in New York, when someone had glanced up to see him entering the room and had asked, "Who is this young man who looks like a prince in a Turgenev novel?"

Now that he'd seen death at such close quarters, smelled its sour breath and felt the twitch of its flank in the dark, Julien didn't want to be backed into a corner by it. Through Joséphine he met Patty, a South American poet in her fifties who was willing to help him out. Patty was unhappy, had gone through a mastectomy, her husband had left her, she drank too much and one of her two daughters had become very ill. To say that much, of course, to make a clear list of woes like that, was terribly American on his part, Austin realized. He'd found out whatever he knew about Patty from Joséphine. Patty herself wallowed in the *non-dit* of unnamed suffering. If anyone came close to formulating a question about what she was going through, she would dissolve into a fit of cigarette coughs and glide out of the room, mumbling something about the bottle of whiskey she was trying to locate.

She had beautiful manners, a proper Buenos Aires upbringing despite her foul language (so typical of the radical but bourgeois heirs to 1968), the overflowing ashtrays, the unkempt hair and badly bitten nails and the thin, flushed face of an alcoholic. Her apartment was on the edge of the Sentier, the garment district, anything but a fashionable address, but it was huge and furnished with fine old family things she hadn't polished or even dusted in ten years. She looked out at the world from under a fringe of hennaed hair, her huge eyes made bigger with kohl she'd applied with more expertise than her shaky hand would seem to vouch for. She liked them both, especially Julien, and welcomed them with a sympathetic glance that spoke of all she'd lived through and was too proud to talk about—or perhaps she was too disdainful of language to confide her feelings to words.

Often Austin would come home from walking Ajax to discover Patty and Julien "talking death." They'd be huddled over Earl Grey for him, Johnnie Walker for her, and the air would be pungent from her Gitanes (he never objected when she smoked at their place, as if she alone had earned the right). The afternoon sunlight, reflected off the top windows and the stone of the buildings across the way, would be applying knives to the rising entrails of smoke that twisted above their heads. She'd shake a little smoker's cough out of her pinched chest and mouth, which radiated lines out away from the opening. She'd laugh, or in a hoarse spasm indicate laughter, and she and Julien would wait almost silently, certainly nervously, until Austin was out of earshot.

She told Julien he should go to Amsterdam, where doctor-assisted death was legal for those suffering from a terminal disease, but when Austin telephoned a Dutch euthanasia society the man who answered was curt and possibly suspicious. "No, no," he said, "euthanasia is only legal for Dutch citizens, and a minimum of three doctors must sign a release form. Anyway, euthanasia is only administered to patients suffering from Alzheimer's and they usually belong to a club and have written a living will years before they begin to lose their mental competence." This was the same Dutch singsong complacency Austin had met years before in an Amsterdam leather bar when a lantern-jawed, gum-chewing blond with bad skin had asked him in a bored voice, "And would you like to be beat?" just as if he'd been saying, "And would you like more fries?"

When Austin mentioned the suicide problem to Henry McVay during one of their almost daily phone conversations, Henry said, "Yes, killing oneself is far more difficult than most people suspect."

"Have *you* ever contemplated it?" Austin asked. He suspected that Henry would laugh in his face, but on the contrary Henry said in a low, matter-of-fact voice, "There's not a day that goes by that I don't think about it."

"Oh?" Austin said on a high, cracked note. "You?"

"*And,* Sweetie, what's more: I've belonged to a Hemlock Club for over a decade."

"A hemlock . . . ?"

"What!" Henry exclaimed, surprised to the point of mild indignation, his strongest suit. "The Hemlock Society has meetings in every civilized city around the globe," Henry said in his old-fashioned, deliberate manner, one that foreigners, not incidentally, always prized; he was the opposite of a mumbler. He spoke in all-caps, even to a fellow American, which lent the present conversation a macabre emphasis.

"But why, Henry? Why should you of all people long for death?"

"Everything is fine up till now. I'm enjoying myself immensely. But what if I begin to lose my health, my mobility, my *faculties,* for God's sake!" He laughed, remembering, as a good Parisian, to add a frivolous note: "What if I become terminally *bored?*"

It was easy to blame Henry for being too much of a hedonist, incapable of devoting any heroism merely to enduring—but Austin couldn't think of any good reason to disagree with him or disapprove of him. Henry had always lived for pleasure. Even his connoisseurship had been a rarefied form of pleasure since it combined knowledge with possession.

"I'll give you the Hemlock booklet," Henry said, "but you won't find it of much use. The *cocktail,* if you get my drift, is maddeningly

vague. Has to be. Legal reasons. It appears some demented teens
began to kill themselves on yet another American death trip. They'd
discovered the formula from an earlier Hemlock Society publication—
completely crazy, of course, and a perversion of our purposes, which
are humanitarian."

Indeed, when Austin read through the reassuring, reasonable,
grim booklet he realized that there was no recipe for a fatal brew in
these sad pages.

Julien was in despair. "I no longer have the courage to throw
myself off a bridge into the Seine. I would have done it six months
ago, but I didn't want to leave you. Our life has been wonderful
together, *Petit*. But now that I almost died I know the horrors that lie
in wait for me. And it's a question of dignity. I admire Vladimir. I don't
want to be a victim just waiting for this virus to have its way with me."
Perhaps, Austin thought, he wants to join his mother as rapidly as
possible and in a manner worthy of her own self destruction. Dying
slowly from this disease, Austin told himself, is done by losing more
and more control, day by day, whereas the act of suicide is a way of
taking charge again.

"But, Julien," Austin said, "you've been so sick but now you're
well. You almost lost your vision and you've regained it, you almost
lost your mind and then it came back, and now you almost died from
your bird fever—" (that's what they jokingly called the avian micobacteria, *fièvre de l'oiseau*)—"but you're better than ever. Who's to say
they won't just keep finding one cure after another?"

"No, no, *Petit*," Julien said, kissing each one of Austin's fingers
with a dreamy indifference, as if he were telling beads while falling
asleep.

And then Patty came up with the pills. There were some thirty pills, all
sizes and colors, Valium blue, aspirin white, candy pink, held in a blue
silk Chinese bag that snapped shut and was embroidered with a gold
dragon. The dragon had red eyes. The bag was a sky blue, the color
called "cerulean." It probably wasn't even silk, just a shiny Taiwanese
synthetic—a cheap sewing kit but with pills instead of needles and

threads (needles to pierce the heart, Austin thought, and threads to snip). Inside were instructions typed with a bad ribbon on a smudged piece of paper, folded in with the pills; the pills felt heavy but yielding in the hand, like a scrotum. The instructions said:

1. *Take the Valium first (blue) to calm the gag reflexes.*
2. *Wait 20 minutes, then take the remaining pills with a glass of champagne.*

The pills were put in the drawer of the black Art-Nouveau desk with its legs as slender as a colt's, but Austin couldn't imagine Julien taking them. He couldn't picture coming home one day and finding Julien dead on the couch, his face bluish-white under his black beard visibly coming in, thicker and thicker.

Now that he had his pills Julien withdrew slightly from Austin.

He also went out for longer and longer walks and treated Ajax more as a younger brother whose loyalty could be taken for granted and less as a fat, impossible baby to be spoiled. Sometimes Julien seemed more than aware that other people found his cuddling of Ajax excessive, even repellent; people shook their heads when Julien talked of raising Ajax to be the next pope or called him *"Sa Sainteté Pie VII."* People thought it was disgusting the way Julien would throw half a broiled chicken on the parquet for Ajax to gnaw on and gulp. But Julien liked to show how *legislative* his love was; it set its own laws. And as Julien became thinner and more reedlike and more and more fastidious about food, Ajax, his creature, gnawed more and more fiercely at the fat bodies of cooked fowl. They complemented each other, the anorexic devil and his gross familiar, but they went well together, one all flesh and flesh-eating, the other a pile of shambling bones.

At a party Austin met someone who'd known Vladimir years before; she said that she had heard the business he'd started had failed and that he'd turned into a monster, with big lumps all over his body.

Despite his apparent recovery, Julien's stats were sinking—had, in fact, sunk. His medical appointments now devoured his days and when Austin peeked into Julien's calendar, just the abbreviated notes he carried around with him, Austin read about appointments with the "*pneumologue*" (the lung doctor?), the "*opthalmologue*" (he was taking three different drops for his eyes). In addition, he was taking one Bactrim a day (a sort of super-strong antibiotic, wasn't it?), Immodium to control the diarrhea (two in the morning and two at night), two Rifabutine a day, one Malocide every day except Saturday and Sunday, half a sachet of Actapulgite three times a day (but not with the other medicines), two Kaleorid morning, noon and night, five Zovirax pills four times a day (against herpes, Austin remembered), a Zovirax cream for the face, a child's dose of Humagel in sachet form three times a day, one Vivamyne every morning, one Osfolate per week, one Buscopan three times a day maximum . . . Austin reeled at the thought of keeping it all straight: once a week; not on weekends; thrice daily maximum; not to be taken with the other pills. . . .

There were notations about a Neomycine-Bacitracine pomade, about two Ciflox a day for one month only, about two Doliprane a day (a kind of aspirin, Austin thought), about Lexomil and Triflucan. There were blood cultures that revealed he had 0.7 T4-cells and just 23 T8s (the lab wrote *soit!* after each number, meaning *sic* or "this is the real number, not a mistake"). He had suppositories to insert, creams to spread, artificial tears to drop into his eyes, Retin-A to rub into the red skin stretched over his cheekbones. If the Immodium didn't stop the diarrhea he could swallow up to ten drops every four hours of deodorized tincture of opium. The last resort was a skin patch of slowly secreting morphine analogue.

Besides the prescriptions were all the forms from the social worker signed, "I wish you lots of courage and I beg you, *Monsieur,* to accept my distinguished salutations." The "distinguished salutations" were normal; what struck Austin as almost eerily human in an official letter was any mention of "courage." There were his applications to the French state for "medical aid" and "medical aid in the home." He had stickers to put on all his prescriptions from an organization called ARTS, which had nothing to do with painting or music but stood for "Association of Research for the Treatment of Seropositives."

Whenever Julien would go out for a while in the late afternoon, Austin would call Peter in New York. One day Peter was so choked up he could barely get the words out.

"What's wrong, Petes?"

"Alex, my beau . . . ?"

"The preppie guy? The Mayor's assistant? The furniture designer? Running for alderman . . . ?"

Austin had half-wanted to tease Peter about his paragon of a lover, the consummate young black man on the rise, but his words only made Peter cry all the harder.

"What happened?"

At last Peter pulled himself together sufficiently to say, "Alex has broken my heart. He's killed me."

"What do you mean, Peter?"

"I mean he was my last chance."

It took half an hour for Austin to reconstruct what had happened. Alex, apparently, had been an obsessive worker who seldom slept. He was managing his building, he was constantly dancing attendance on the Mayor, he had to stay up all night in his big studio in Queens where he and his two assistants were fashioning the prototypes for an entire collection of furniture which Bloomingdales might buy and manufacture, final decision pending. He loved Peter and admired him, but Peter, after all, wasn't working. Peter had lots of leisure on his hands. He wanted to spend "quality time" with Alex.

"I don't know which factors counted the most," Peter said solemnly. "But I told Alex one night I was positive."

"How long ago?" Austin asked. He thought this Alex must be one of the least observant people in the world if he needed to be *told* that Peter was positive. Probably only Peter could imagine his disease was invisible.

"Two weeks ago. I think. I'm having lots of trouble keeping track of things—of time. But Alex was great about that—he said he didn't mind, that he would take care of me. But I'm sure he *has* to mind. I can't remember: did I tell you his last lover died just a year before we met? He can't be too thrilled about nursing and burying another lover."

"*C'mon,*" Austin said. "You'll bury us all."

Peter sighed, didn't comment, went on: "Then, last Wednesday, brother, there's a date I remember, I invited him to dinner, just the two of us, I'd gone to Dean and DeLuca's for the first asparagus, I had bay scallops, a bottle of champagne, raspberries—and he didn't show up. You know I don't have much money. With a dinner like that I can shoot my whole week's allowance—*your money,* though my parents are helping me now and I get money from the city. Alex kept calling. He was in the Mayor's limo. It was nine, then ten, then midnight, some emergency. I lost it. I just completely went ballistic. I told him to forget it. *Then* I didn't hear from him for two days. Then I got this letter. Want to hear it?"

"Sure."

" 'Dear Peter—

" 'We're both in our thirties, we've always been honest with each other, we're grown-ups, I owe you the truth.

" 'Though in some ways you're perfect for me—you're interested in design, it's magic in bed, you've got the European sophistication I like—I'm afraid we have entirely different rhythms and expectations.

" 'You want someone around all the time, at least in the evenings, and given your health prospects you've got a perfect right to that. I, on the other hand, am very ambitious, busy and getting busier. If I make you unhappy now, you'll be miserable in the future as I take on more and more responsibilities. We must stop seeing each other—totally. Let's make a clean break of it. We weren't meant to be friends. Lovers or nothing.' "

"Oh, Petes, I'm so sorry. . . ." Austin took note of the gallant sound of "lovers or nothing," which just marked Alex's cowardice.

The worst of it was that the more Austin discussed it with him, the more he realized that this really and truly would be Peter's last stab at romance. He'd been hanging on, keeping his health and looks and cheerfulness as intact as possible, just barely remaining a member of the middle class, all in an effort to "bag" Alex. But now that he'd lost him he'd never try again—nor would he be able to. He'd lost his reason for living. Now he'd sink into the shabbiness and senility of AIDS, no matter how much Austin did for him. Austin could see that Peter had lost Alex because he, Peter, was too impatient, too subject to quick rages—too spoiled, which was something Austin had done to him (even that a child's word such as *spoiled* could be applied to Peter proved how thoroughly Austin had babied him). Peter was convinced that Alex hadn't been put off when he learned Peter was positive: "After all, he'd taken care of one lover with AIDS."

Precisely, Austin thought to himself. Maybe Alex couldn't face burying another lover and ending up alone all over again.

Over the next few weeks Austin phoned Peter every other day, but then Peter stopped answering during a whole long weekend in May. He'd been complaining of unbearable pains in his feet, which felt as if he were walking on hot wires, he said. The discomfort was caused by "neuropathy," which in Julien's case made his extremities go numb but in Peter's caused him to suffer agony. So violent was the pain that the doctor had had him try the same morphine-analogue patches that Julien sometimes resorted to ("analogue" because real morphine was too addictive? Or was morphine too hard to prescribe legally? Could addiction really be such a problem for someone about to die?)

Austin phoned one of Peter's friends, Mick, a big raunchy computer expert who was also very ill but would never discuss it, who virtually came running out of the hospital onto the disco floor, trailing IV tubes, exchanging his oxygen feed for a popper. "I don't know where she is, that saucy lass," Mick said casually, as if they were discussing nothing more serious than a deb's early departure from the ball. Throughout the anxious conversation Mick maintained his flippant tone and female nouns and pronouns for Peter ("Pierette"). That's one way of coping, Austin thought, though one that shades into insanity.

But Mick, despite his rigidly silly manner, made dozens of calls until he located Peter in a private room on the psychiatric floor of Doctors' Hospital.

"Psychiatric!" Austin exclaimed when Mick called to report in.

"Well, after Alexandra dumped her ass—"

"Alexandra? Oh, Alex."

"Then Pierette started slapping those morphine patches all over her body like they were beauty spots. She *claims* she got confused, but if you ask me she wanted to off herself; after all, she was *done dropped* and that can humiliate one of today's smart young career gals who's determined to have it all! Very Valley of the Dolls. . . ."

When Austin called Peter in his hospital room, Peter said, "Those patches are *dangerous*, Aussie. I couldn't remember how many I'd put on. The next thing I knew I was completely *delirious*. I'd wake up on the floor. Then some time would go by and the downstairs neighbor was having the door removed because I'd left the water on in the kitchen and flooded her out. I found myself at night in Harlem. Oh, Austin—" He burst into tears. "It's been such an ordeal."

It seemed the moment for Peter to move back home with his parents. He couldn't take care of himself any longer, obviously, and his sexual and romantic ambitions had burned out as if destroyed by fever. Now he had no reason to stay on in New York, sex capital of the States.

Austin phoned Peter's parents, who picked up on two different extensions, listened to everything Austin had to say and responded with a sweetness, a tender concern. They said they would set out for New York as soon as they hung up.

"But I wouldn't tell him to give up the New York apartment right away, if I were you," Austin said. "Nor would I say this move up to your place is permanent. He needs time to adjust."

Once he was living with them in the glass house in Concord they'd built for their old age above a stream in the woods, Peter sounded much more tranquil. New York, city of transience, had seemed all too evanescent to him, now that his hold on life was so tenuous. New York, city of ambition, had felt like a marathon in which he alone was walking.

Austin's six-hundred-and-twenty-page, heavily illustrated book, *French Furniture of the Eighteenth Century*, was at last published that fall, bearing a dedication to Julien; when it won a prize Julien framed the piece of parchment lettered in red. Julien's paintings were exhibited quietly in Passy in October and received three short reviews, two enthusiastic, one merely descriptive. Though his teeth were chattering and his face was nothing but teeth, cheekbones and glittering eyes, Julien stood for two hours at the reception and discussed his work with solemnity. Some of his friends hadn't seen him in a year or more and were visibly shocked by the transformation of his looks; everything he said they were quick to agree with, nodding constantly and murmuring a nearly unbroken hum of assent. He looked like the Ottoman Empire in a turn-of-the-century political cartoon.

He began to prepare to die. He became obsessed with the English woman he'd had an affair with so many years ago in Ethiopia. He wrote Sarah long letters in his broken but by now highly expressive English. He sent her some of his mother's jewelry; she wrote back, somewhat startled by this renewed interest and touched by the imminent death he faced. He'd apparently told her all about his love for Austin. That was the one way Austin had affected him—he'd made Julien more honest about his sexuality, even about the disease.

He talked all the time to Austin about his gold watch, one of the few things of great value he possessed. Should he change the gold-link bracelet for a crocodile band? Should he give the watch to his brother Robert? Now or in his will?

Now that his paintings had been shown (the exhibition had been accompanied by a catalogue Austin had written but not signed), now that he'd even sold two canvases to Henry McVay (who promptly put them in storage), Julien lost interest in his art. For him it had been a way to press his signet ring into the molten stuff of life before it hardened. He'd also redirected some of his energies as an architect into painting.

Not that he'd forgotten his first profession. He and Austin drove out to Levallois-Perret, one of the new middle-class suburbs to the west of Paris, to see a massive apartment block that Julien had designed and that only now was being erected. This rickety, shivering old man with the protuberant eyes, the thinning, dry hair, the huge rack of shoulders hanging out over a wisp of a torso was, after all, only thirty-two years old, under ordinary circumstances just a youngster coming into his own, not this shuffling ancient without hips and a twenty-seven-inch waist, shoes too heavy for his feet, belt too cutting for his tender skin, leather coat too heavy for his frail frame. He looked at the cold, concrete forms of the ten-story building beneath two slender cranes and partially sheathed in scaffolding, and blinked emotionlessly. His eyes registered everything, he even took half a dozen snapshots, but it meant nothing to him, the building—at least he had no feelings to spare for it or to express.

Julien was suffering more and more from the pancreatitis he had developed as a side effect of the DDI. Both he and Austin remembered the doctor's warning that the drug could be life-threatening, but only occasionally did they acknowledge that he could be expected to do nothing other than get worse and die. They clung to their ingrained notion of improvement, made almost plausible by the fact that each individual crisis caused by herpes, toxoplasmosis or micobacteria had in fact been treatable.

Julien had always been open to new experiences—new fashions, new arts, new countries, new friends—that Austin might present to him for his delectation, but now his energy wasn't sufficient to understand and absorb the new. They went to an avant-garde opera in a theater just two blocks away, but after the first act Julien shuffled away toward home and after the second act Austin, worried, followed. They would go to the Centre Georges Pompidou, which was in the neighborhood, for an opening, but each new style of painting (new to them, at least) demanded extra energy; it was a promissory note that would be redeemed only years from now, if ever. Julien just tore it up.

His doctor kept trying to stimulate his appetite with, first, an analogue to marijuana (but Julien didn't like to feel stoned), and then with the patches of estrogen, which caused the predicted loss of libido. When Julien still failed to gain weight the doctor surgically inserted a shunt in his chest through which he could be fed. Before the operation Julien had tried to be gay and courageous: "It's the twenty-first-century way to eat. *Chewing* is hopelessly twentieth century." But the day he came back from the hospital he wept in Austin's arms: "I've been disfigured. Never before was the envelope of my body broken. It's the beginning of the end." Within three days the wound was exuding pus and the shunt had to be removed. Later another doctor said almost casually, "Shunts almost always become infected. They never work."

Julien, who'd been high-spirited or stoic in the face of pain, in any event fastidious and dandified, now became querulous. He spent more and more time in bed, shouted at the Chilean cleaning woman who came once a week, grumbled at Austin. He said that Gloria hadn't dusted the living room or that Austin had disturbed his pills on the night table. He complained about Ajax jumping up on the bed and spreading infections. He complained about the raucous drunks in the street below, singing and shouting at two in the morning. He complained about Austin's carelessness in treating his sketches and paintings, which were kept in large racks in the studio where Austin slept; was Julien worried that Austin would just throw his work away once he was dead? He complained about Austin's long phone calls with Rod. He didn't know Rod, but he resented their intimacy. He complained about Austin's cooking, about Joséphine's trivial conversation ("Does she think I want to consecrate my remaining time to listening to that shit?"), about his brother's dullness ("Oh, *Petit, you're* the only one I still like").

Austin didn't let himself think about tomorrow or even really take in today. When Robert came up for a few days on All Saints Day, he was shocked by how unpleasant Julien had become and how he snapped constantly at Austin, but Austin hadn't even noticed. Julien associated an old perfume they used to cover odors in the toilet with his constant vomiting; he could no longer bear the scent and threw it out.

Austin longed to massage Robert's massive shoulders and to sleep in his arms, but he didn't dare to touch him. Robert had said something that revealed he just assumed Austin had been the one to infect Julien.

One night, when they were alone, Julien was sitting up in bed in striped pajamas. At the corner store he had bought a gauzy black scarf with a repeating white pattern of a skull and crossbones and had tacked it on the white wall above his bed, as if he were a pirate flying this grim flag; putting it up had been a provocation as well as a kind of "performance piece." Now Julien said, "You and Robert are attracted to each other, aren't you?"

Austin felt caught in Julien's headlights and froze. "Well, of course I can see he's handsome, but that would never have occurred to me, I mean—"

"It's okay, *Petit.*" Julien smiled weakly. His teeth were chipped and discolored, perhaps from all the vomiting induced by the DDI. "I can see that you two have a private little thing, a crush . . ." (*un béguin* was the French word, which made Austin think of beginning the Beguine).

"But we've never done anything, not so much as kiss—"

"I know, I know." Julien laughed, a shrunken death's head bobbing on a chain with feeble joyousness. "Don't panic. Above all, don't panic" (*Surtout ne panique pas*). "I *like* it that you're attracted to each other. Maybe you'll become lovers. Then one day when you're wading at Saint-Jean Cap Ferrat I'll float by as a jellyfish and startle you by brushing against your feet. Or I'll sting you."

Austin was tempted to say once again, "You'll outlive us all," but he didn't want to break the delicately playful mood Julien was spinning nor the almost hypnotic insistence.

One day Julien could no longer bear Ajax. He'd been out walking with the dog and had almost been knocked over when Ajax had spotted another dog's delicious-looking rump and had lunged for it.

"He's too strong for me now," Julien said. In the past he would instantly have relented, kissed Ajax on the stomach and whispered, "Poor little beast," but now he just glowered at him resentfully.

Robert flew up from Nice again for a few days and when he left he took Ajax with him.

Three days later Julien bundled up and went in a taxi with Patty to Père Lachaise. They were gone for several hours but when they came back Julien said, "*Ça y est,* it's done, I've made all the arrangements." He explained to Austin that only Parisians—official residents of the city and its twenty *arrondissements*—had the legal right to be interred at Père Lachaise. But Julien had thought of a loophole. He had bought a niche for their ashes for the next fifty years (which their heirs could renew for a further half-century), but had paid for it in Austin's name. They couldn't refuse Julien, who was a Parisian by virtue of voting here and because he was enrolled here for welfare benefits; by assigning ownership of the crematorium niche to Austin, Julien had made sure they couldn't refuse Austin either when the time came for him to be interred.

"I looked at the vases for holding the ashes; I chose something very sober. Patty was so much help. So this is the plan. When I die you'll make arrangements with one of the funeral homes up there to cremate me and you'll give them this piece of paper. I don't want any ceremony or anyone to come except my brother and Fabrice. You must write *your* plans into your will."

Austin couldn't help calculating that Julien was spending all his savings and that now he must be almost at the end of his resources.

In December Julien suffered from the cold, which ate into his bones and attached itself like leeches to his joints, attacking the marrow now that there was no more flesh to consume. He who'd been a thoroughbred had become a nag. Even his nose and ears looked longer. His beard grew in; only his dark-blue eyes suggested he wasn't what people back home in the South called "an ethnic."

He spent more and more time in bed watching television. Although he urged Austin to go out, Austin didn't want to leave him. Taking care of Julien, feeding him, enduring his complaints and insults—that was what Austin did now. Maybe because Austin had lost his mother when he was still a child, he was drawn to mothering Julien, even singing him silly little lullabies he made up as he went along. Austin would lie beside Julien in the dark transected by the splinters of light that shot through the gaps between the drawn curtains and he'd sing his silly songs and rub his back, which was in almost constant pain. Julien had rejected Ajax and refused to see his few friends. He wouldn't even take their calls. He'd say to Austin, "Tell them I'm thinking of them. They're constantly in my thoughts." But as he became more and more isolated, he wanted to be with Austin all the time; not even the dog, their child, was there to serve as a distraction now.

Because he could no longer keep food down, Julien went to restaurants armed with airplane vomit bags. Austin would sit staring at his lap while Julien threw up the entire dinner he'd just eaten. He was seated at the table, too weak to excuse himself. Austin wasn't embarrassed, or not usually. Nor did he identify with Julien's pain, or if he did it was bone to bone, nerve to nerve, not thought by thought. He couldn't see how it would be *useful* to feel Julien's pain all over again, even if it was possible, and these days he'd reduced everything to its use. They were stripped for action, the action of dying.

Julien's back ached all the time. Austin massaged him many times a day; he was shocked—and moved to tears—by the sight of his withered buttocks, which looked like the skin of stewed fruit, and by his coccyx, bright red and rubbed raw because he had no flesh to protect or cushion the bulb of bone. When their activity had finally died down like flames, then the only wakefulness that still glowed was in the studio. Austin was alone and made himself enormous bowls of cereal and plates of toasted muffins soaked in butter and freighted with marmalade. He'd sit on the floor on a thick oriental rug with his back to the single bed and leaf through his pornographic magazines; he liked only the color pictures of a young blond man with hair so straight it must have been chemically relaxed and with a downturned, thick-lipped, garnet-colored mouth as beautiful as a wound. What he liked most—what excited him—was any suggestion of a flaw, a broken and badly mended little finger, slightly rotated out of position, a mark that looked like a splash of paraffin on that deliciously taut stomach, a swollen toe or the hint of a red vein in the instep. A flaw seemed to make a boy more accessible. Austin liked the way the boy, photographed through a metal fence, clung to the wires with his hands, a dreaming expression on his features, an erection shoved through one of the openings—it was a reference to impassioned yearning and forbidden love, not to lust.

"Let's go to Morocco," Julien said. "I've always wanted to show you Morocco. And it will be warm."

Austin couldn't bring himself to say no. It had been so long since Julien had wanted to do anything. He contacted a glossy magazine and asked if he could do a story on Marrakesh. "It's the hot new place, you know," Austin said brightly to the skeptical woman in New York at the other end of the line. It seemed grotesque that he would have to sell this tragic trip to *Home and Hearth* as the latest trend.

The day before they left, Julien broke an appointment with his doctor. He called, saying he was too ill to come to see him in Villejuif, half an hour away, but asked if the doctor thought he was up to a trip to Morocco.

The night before they were to leave, Julien insisted that Austin pack his bag and bring it to his bed so that he could go over every pair of socks or underwear.

"The light has burned out, *Petit*," Austin said. "I'll do it in the morning. I've started, but I'll finish in the morning."

"There won't be any time in the morning. Do it now."

"I don't want to. I'll do it in the morning, I said. I can't *see* anything!"

"Then I won't go," Julien said. "I won't go."

"Fine," Austin said bitterly. "I'll go without you." He knew that Julien was afraid of being abandoned; Austin instantly regretted his strong-arming, but he'd made such an elaborate itinerary for Morocco that he was reluctant to undo it. And he knew that even if Julien forced them to cancel the trip, two days later he'd be craving the warmth of the south.

In the morning Austin packed in silence and they rode in the taxi to the airport without saying a word. Julien was irritated that Austin hadn't ordered a taxi to come to the door, but they found one quickly on the corner. At the airport Austin had arranged for a wheelchair. Julien made the man push him through duty free. He wanted to ogle all the gold watches and compare them with his own. He bought *Maison et Jardin* and one of his adult comic books. Once they were in the air Julien relaxed. He said, "So far so good. Better than could be expected. But ask the hostess for vomit bags. I want a good supply."

They stayed in a chic new Marrakesh hotel outside the city walls. Because it was warm, Julien wanted to go out every day, sometimes twice. They'd head in a horse-drawn carriage to the big square in the center of the old city, the Place Djema'a el Fna. Along the way teenagers with beautiful black hair and bad teeth would ride by on bicycles and hitch a ride by grabbing onto the side of the buggy. "Meester, meester! English? French? Dutch?" They'd offer their services as guides. For every one waved away by the exasperated driver, another two would sail up, either on bikes or on foot.

Out in the square, mounds of oranges were stacked high under big parasols. Women in black veils pushed brightly striped and starred and colored caps toward them. A fortune teller seated on a folding metal chair was carefully following the movements of his hen, which was strutting over a board hand-painted with numbers. Julien and Austin sat in a café and drank chewing-gum-sweet mint tea around which a few lazy bees hovered. Despite the intense noontime heat, a fire was burning somewhere, which rendered the air sweet and pungent with the odor of burning grass. They could also smell the smoke of cooking lamb.

Few of the buildings were more than two stories tall; most were a muddy brown or a salmon pink dulled by dirt. Once in a while a man would walk by wearing a sweater or sports coat, but mostly the Arabs were dressed in long robes, usually with a hood pushed back. Some of the men with black skins had immaculate cream-colored robes and close-fitting turbans to match. Children held their mother's hand or clung to the gathered folds of her caftan. A snake charmer was blowing his flute and a seedy-looking cobra responded drowsily. Next to him, a dentist was seated beside a card table covered with boxes of loose individual teeth. An ancient transvestite—dirty and mustached—was doing a comic belly dance, accompanied by an orchestra of six dignified old men seated tailor-style on mats.

They wandered through the maze of the covered market, surrounded by the boys who would be guides. Bamboo poles held up a roof of clear green plastic. The boys hovered like the bees around sugared tea; but then maybe they noticed how frail and old Julien appeared. Austin supported him by the elbow while they inched their way past stalls of jewelry and daggers, shoes and shirts, rugs and lamps, nuts and popcorn being roasted in big shallow pans. There were mounds of raisins and almonds for sale as well as stacks of graduated ceramic bowls, painted an indigo blue. There were smoked sheep's shanks.

In the spice stall a bespectacled salesman showed them a jar of Spanish fly. He said, "I'm forbidden to sell this," and from behind his glasses raised his eyebrows. "Who uses the Spanish fly—men or women?" Austin asked. The salesman said, "The man, of course. The man does all the work, *n'est-ce pas?*" He indicated to them jars of carmine for staining the lips. They bought a morsel of musk, smelling like burnt sugar and body odor, as well as a hand of Fatima for good luck.

"It's about as restful as an LSD trip," Austin murmured to Julien as a boy of nine in a white nightshirt and sequined red fez spun past rattling large tin castanets. Julien laughed faintly, as a saint might who has already moved halfway toward transcendence.

Chapter Nineteen

They rented a car and headed south through the mountains. The highway was just two lanes. What appeared on the map to be a straight line turned out to be hundreds of hairpin curves. At first the landscape was innocent enough—the melting snow in the mountains was flowing into the irrigation ditch beside the road and making it into a clear, clean stream, leaping and cascading from step to step down the slope, the flow as thick as a cable. At some points the falling water was so capacious its splashing was audible through the closed windows. The fields were just beginning to take on a bit of spring color. The two men drove through a village of charming old wood houses, neatly painted.

And then they began to climb, up and up. At a scenic spot high in the mountains they stopped for gas; they could see their breath. A little girl came toward them with something for sale, a small, stoppered vial of attar of roses. Along the roadside three men were crouching beside sections of quartz geodes. The amethyst-colored points made Austin think of sharks' teeth.

With his peripheral vision Austin was constantly monitoring Julien. He was aware of how Julien was sitting up or slouched down in the car, whether his mouth sounded dry when he spoke, whether he was in pain or developing a cramp.

Their car climbed higher and higher. They drove through clouds, which they could see from below as they approached them. No one was living up here, not even shepherds, and they encountered only one vehicle, a bus barreling down from a higher peak and pushing them perilously close to the edge of a ravine. When they got above the clouds they saw an eagle wheeling past, its wings spread, looping in slow, majestic circles.

At last they descended onto the plain beyond and by dark they were at their hotel in Taroudant, a small city east of Agadir.

Julien loved the hotel and they spent four days there. He was worried when he saw the room with its bed on a mezzanine, fifteen stairs to go up, but in fact he managed them well, if sometimes with a little push from Austin. The hotel, which occupied the former palace of a local ruler, was built against the old mud city walls. In the evening, sitting out by the modern pool in deck chairs, they watched the starlings swooping into and out of the square niches let into the thick terracotta walls. The pasha's massive wood gates were thrown open and the noisy, chaotic road was dimly visible behind an intricate metal grill. The blue pool was lit from within. Four tall, skinny palm trees in a row soared up above the walls and their parapets. Outside the walls they could hear the clip-clop of horses and the gruff voice of a driver, and even see a cart moving, dusty, behind the grill. A muezzin, his voice tinny and amplified, called the faithful to prayer, while by the pool the bartender tuned in a little radio to dance music. The bartender was wearing black knee breeches with a tiny waist, the *sarwel*.

Every meal was torture. There was a European dining room and a Moroccan. Nine times out of ten they chose a table far from the other French tourists in the formal European dining room. There they'd sit in nearly total silence. Julien would take a long, long time to eat. Usually the other guests had left and their dishes had been cleared while Julien still faced a full plate. Julien would try to eat a few things, just several sips of clear broth, or a bit of dry toast, but within a few minutes his diaphragm would start to heave, his face would lengthen and he would grab one of the sacks from the plane and throw up in it. Austin would fill the silence and try to lessen the feeling of defeat by saying something absurdly general and pleasantly genteel, what he thought of as "dowager chat," but in the midst of his babbling Julien would suddenly stand and totter out, walking with his slow, dragging tread. Often Austin was impatient with Julien for walking so slowly but revealed nothing. He remembered hearing that "toward the end" even if some nourishment got down nothing was absorbed, the digestive system could no longer extract any benefit from food—but could this be the end?

Some evenings they stood by a pond and looked down at big wet boulders that would suddenly crack apart and slide: turtles. One of the turtles was so lazy, almost inert, that they nicknamed it "Lucy." As the evening came in, the cold arrived with it. Julien was cold all the time and he bundled up in several layers of clothes; when Austin touched his hand it was always icy. Julien wore pale tan jeans that rode very low in the back; Austin turned quickly once and saw two Arab bellboys laughing and looking at Julien's skinny ass, nudging each other in the ribs.

In one of the big sitting rooms some of the local notables sat around the fireplace with their beads, eating from big plates with their right hands and watching television. On the screen, the king was participating in a religious ceremony in Casablanca, in a building that was projected to be the world's largest mosque, but was only partially finished. The king wore a white silk cloak and hood. So did the *imam*, whose big black glasses looked disconcertingly modern under his hood. Austin asked the clerk behind the desk what the holiday was. "We're toward the end of Ramadan," he said.

Ah, Austin thought, that's why the notables are eating so late and the hotel staff looks so pale by day. No food until sundown, not even any water, and of course no cigarettes. It was hardest on the smokers, people said. Usually Muslims slept as much as they could by day and then feasted till midnight. Then they set their alarms for four in the morning so they could eat breakfast before dawn and a new bout of fasting. The thought flickered through Austin's mind that the whole population must be partying now, eating and making music and talking and laughing. He could imagine slipping out of the hotel once Julien fell asleep and trailing through smoky streets past open doorways giving onto rooms lit by kerosene lamps and crowded with robed figures. . . .

The next morning a guide, who spoke fluent French, attached himself to them as soon as they came out of the hotel. He lined up a carriage (undoubtedly the driver would slip him a commission later). The carriage was painted green and was bedizened with dangling hands of Fatima cut out of black plastic and spotted with red and yellow stars. They asked to be shown the outside of the walls. The carriage rolled past low olive trees with small gray-green leaves. Children were playing with a rubber tire. In some places the walls, which were medieval, had started to crumble. The carriage lurched when it went across a deep rut and almost turned over. Austin let out a little cry ("It's going to turn over!"), and Julien laughed at him with his deep but no longer resonant laugh. The driver called out something like "Geesh" to the horses in a reproachful tone, as one might say, "Giddyap." They went past some crudely fashioned cages in which rabbits were being raised. Then they passed a tannery. An old man was washing skins in a well of foul-smelling green liquid in which he was standing waist-high in rubber hip boots. When their carriage turned in through the gate, into the winding narrow streets, few people were out; the demands of Ramadan had driven the lethargic but uncomplaining population indoors.

One day they rode out to a chic hotel compound where millionaires vacationed and played golf. The hotel itself was empty. At the end of a long walkway beside a stream was a swimming pool, surrounded by English people, bright red and fat, slathered in sun lotion. They were eating hamburgers; the smell of the cooking meat on the grill was heavy and wintry, nauseating. Five or six of the English had been talking all at once, fluty and merry, until they caught sight of Julien and Austin. The bathers were wearing swimsuits, but Julien and Austin, intimidated by the reputation of the place, had put on coats and ties. The English guests just stared at Julien with hostility. Austin became very nervous and said he wanted to go back to the main hotel dining room, which was deserted. But first Julien had to make the grand tour of the grounds—fields planted with vegetables, rose gardens, tennis courts, individual bungalows. He had the strength for all that. In the distance they saw the greens under the wide-cast arc of sprinklers. Julien hadn't noticed how his presence had reduced those English men and women to appalled silence.

At lunch they were waited on by an old, dignified Moroccan who treated them with a deference that concealed a certain tenderness. They were self-quarantined in the formal dining room, which was painted pistachio green and hung with chandeliers the shape of grape clusters. Julien started with a melon and went on to boiled fish and steamed potatoes. It turned slightly cold and they took their coffee (mint tea for Julien) in the dark, empty *salon,* looking at a television program from France.

On the drive back to town they were hailed by the guide from the day before, a skinny man in his early thirties who smelled of old tobacco. He'd overheard them saying during their tour of the city walls that they were interested in buying an old Koran. Now he showed them a well-preserved hand-written Koran with glossy illu minated letters at the beginning of each *sura.* He said a friend of his needed to sell it in order to have enough money to pass his driver's test (the *baksheesh* apparently ran very high), but Julien said to Austin, "We can't take on the world's problems," and added to the guide, "I don't like this copy, I don't think it's beautiful."

Back at the hotel they sat beside the pool and looked at the star-lings rushing out of the old wall like sparks up a chimney. Thinking of their life back in Paris, Julien began to criticize Austin's friend Rod, whom he had never even met. "You like him just because you two can gossip all night long like housewives. But he sounds to me like a ne'er-do-well and a drug addict."

Indignant, Austin said, "At least his conversation is lively and interesting."

Julien was quiet so long that Austin, against his will, looked over to verify his expression, which was stony. But when at last he spoke, his voice sounded deeper and more vulnerable: "It's too bad I didn't die six months ago when I was still interesting. Now you'll remember me only as I was at the end—boring and drugged on morphine."

Austin said, "You mean too much to me to judge you as either dull or interesting." And it was true, true that Austin was so *enthralled* by

Julien's health and survival that he never thought he was dull, even though sometimes he became irritated when Julien started nodding off. Apparently he needed the morphine to mask the pain in his back and to calm the impulse to vomit, but the drug meant that he was alert now only for a few hours each day.

On the way back to their room, Austin said, "I think you're a bit better."

"Well, I didn't vomit my meals today. It's not exactly miraculous but I can't complain."

A furniture dealer in Paris had told Austin to be sure to see the Berber Palace that was just off the road between Taroudant and Ouazarzate, before the turn-off up through the mountains back to Marrakesh. "It's completely out-of-the-way," the dealer had said, "and very beautiful. We ate lunch there."

Julien and Austin drove there with the guide. He had another Koran to show them, badly battered, perfectly square, slipped inside a leather satchel that folded shut like an envelope and could be worn on a chain around the neck. "You put a chain through this hoop," the guide said. Then he laughed, showing his stained teeth. "Not *you*, of course, but *one*." His laugh turned into a cough. Julien shifted away from him, afraid of being exposed to tuberculosis. Austin was *certain* that that fear was going through Julien's mind.

Despite his fears, Julien bought the Koran and was never seen without it afterwards. He fell asleep with it on his lap, usually still in its scuffed and water-stained leather case with the coarse stitching. Sometimes, when he was drowsy from morphine, he'd thumb through the pages with their long, cursive comet-tails and their bug-track vowel signs which looked like those radiating dots in comic strips that indicate delighted surprise or sudden enlightenment. It was the perfect book for a weary, dying man—pious, incomprehensible pages to strum, an ink cloud of unknowing.

Julien was wearing a cotton caftan with tan and white vertical stripes over a T-shirt, under a gauzy white caftan and a white wool sweater he'd draped over his shoulders. He kept the sweater close by in case he began to shiver. He'd abandoned his jeans since the seams cut into his fleshless hips and legs. Only in these robes did he feel comfortable. His black hair was thin and oily, pressed into a cap on his head; many white hairs were scattered through the black. Seen from behind his ears looked immense, especially if the sunlight was shining through them, perhaps because his neck had become so scrawny. His eyebrows had grown shaggy and his nose looked much bigger, as if old age, frustrated by his quick decline, had decided to rush ahead and hit him now.

Although he walked very slowly, he was still game. He wanted to go places and see things. If he sat tranquilly in one place the morphine would make him fall asleep. He smiled sweetly wherever he went, though he spoke so softly people couldn't hear him and Austin would have to repeat what he'd said. When he smiled his face broke into hundreds of lines that hadn't been there six months earlier.

The guide, who knew not to wear them out with his talk, kept silent in the back seat and spoke only to indicate the way to the Berber Palace. Austin appreciated his discretion; he obviously sensed that they were living through a difficult moment, but he didn't ask questions or let his curiosity show through. The day was hot except when a breeze blew; then they were reminded that winter had just ended and that the mountain peaks on the horizon were still deep in snow. They slowed down as they rolled into a village of low houses and teeming streets. The pedestrians' dull-witted stares were the look of grouchy nicotine withdrawal.

They took the road to the right. A little farther on, the macadam gave out to be replaced by gravel. Soon they came to the massive structure of the Berber Palace with its alternating square and rounded arches, its tile roofs and its pale blank walls. Sometimes a small window, barred, was pierced into a wall, always at an improbable place, as if the rooms inside were of madly varying heights. As soon as they'd gone down two steps and along a walkway redolent of thyme, they were in an immense garden planted with palms crowding up from geometric plots of clipped bushes. The walkways were lined with white and faded blue tiles. A few tiles were missing. The inner courtyard was still large enough to seat a symphony orchestra.

No one was around. Caged birds hanging in doorways were singing and flickering in the shadows, twitching shuttles of gold through the gloom. A small fountain drooled into a clear basin. Through the water green moss could be seen, waving from black boulders like hair on drowned heads. The thrown-open doors here and there were carved and painted wood decorated with abstract sunbursts. Like a bored shopper at the bazaar, the sun itself was feebly fingering the dusty lusters of a chandelier far inside a room, with no intent to buy. They went in one door and could smell stale smoke from last night's banquet. An empty plastic water bottle had been thrown on the carpet. A tile dado lined the walls all the way round at shoulder height.

Their guide, Ahmed, clapped loudly and called out something in Arabic. At last a white man in his fifties could be seen crossing the courtyard. He was wearing sunglasses and had a full head of graying hair cut short and spiky that grew low on his forehead. He had a goatee that emphasized the squareness of his jaw. His loose orange sweater was decorated with wide black bands on the sleeves, like an exaggerated sign of mourning. He seemed self-conscious walking toward them in sunlight as they watched from the shadows. At least his stride looked unnatural and he hung his head until he'd come within calling distance. He tried to speak French but with a German accent. Within a moment they'd all found their way into English.

He explained that he was German and a friend of the owner, who was Muslim and sleeping through the difficult Ramadan day.

"Do you think we can eat something?" Austin asked.

"An omelette. I'm sure they could make you a cheese omelette and a green salad. Would you like to eat outside? In the sun?"

Austin turned to Julien; would he be too cold? The German suddenly shrugged and said, "I don't work here. I'm a guest." He smiled. "I don't know why I'm interfering." He looked at Julien. "You won't be cold. It's protected from the wind." Julien asked where the toilet was and shuffled off toward it with Ahmed. The German said in a low voice, "I can see how ill your friend is—is he your son?"

"Friend."

The German, who said he was called Hermann, touched Austin's arm. They were seated at a rusting white metal table on the pale blue and white tile floor. Unseen birds were chirping from within the stand of trees toward the entrance to the grounds.

"What's that delicious smell?"

"Orange blossom," the German said, then added, confidingly, "I know what he has. My friend just died of it. Your friend is not long for this world."

"Oh?" Austin asked nervously. He felt a flutter of panic play like fire over his solar plexus. The early spring was so calm with all the daytime torpor of a small Moroccan village, and even though it was noon the sun seemed veiled and remote. Was Julien about to die? "He's come so close to dying before, but he always survives. He has miraculous powers of recuperation."

"No," the man said, shaking his head, "he's dying."

This is "German coarseness," Austin said to himself, quick to label the offending stubbornness, although he knew few Germans and usually detested the almost inevitable generalizations everyone made about national character.

Hermann added, "I'm a doctor. I watched my friend—" He interrupted himself and touched Austin's sleeve again, "It's all right, we needn't say the name of the disease, but I know what he—do you say, what he suffers *of?*"

"*From*. You say *from*." Austin put on a bright social smile. "And what brings you to Morocco?"

"I will tell you all," the man said solemnly. "I am bisexual. I have a good wife I live with since thirty years. But my real love was my friend. I am a doctor, a *Narkosearzt*."

"Anesthesiologist?"

"Yes, but a doctor of that. But my friend was a famous surgeon. You see?" He pointed to a neat scar fifteen centimeters long buried in his clipped hair. "I had a brain tumor, most unusual. That's why I have trouble speaking. I know English very good before, but now I forget and only slowly, slowly the words come."

For a moment Austin was confused. He thought the "friend," the surgeon, had been a brain surgeon and had removed the tumor, but a moment later Austin had reshuffled the kaleidoscope and saw the same elements in a new configuration. He smiled and said, "Your English is perfect. Don't worry. Did you know your friend for many years?"

"Yes, yes, all my life. He was twenty years older than me, but age means nothing to the souls—"

"Kindred spirits."

"Yes. That."

"And did your wife know him?"

"Oh, yes, we were all very close. You know, in Europe we do not go into details, no, but she knew. Ah! Here comes your friend."

Julien was slowly coming down the long *allée* of trees and box-wood hedges. He stopped to gather a mass of orange blossom in his arms and to breathe in the fragrance. He was smiling as he walked with tiny, stiff steps toward them, accompanied by the deferential guide, who was frowning. Julien's outer robe was faintly damascened, which made it shine when it caught the light.

Over lunch Hermann talked on and on. It seemed that his older lover, the "friend," had fallen for a Berber from this very village. "My friend bought this palace and installed Ali in it. His plan was to turn it into a hotel that Ali could run. But Ali, who is thirty now—ah! how time, like a bird . . ." He mimed flapping wings.

"Flies?"

"Yes, how time flies." He said that Ali had never learned how to run a hotel. He'd become obsessed with sports-car racing and had never concentrated on ordering food, supervising the staff, holding down expenses.

"When my friend was dying he asked me to look after Ali. Now I'm here, although I have had much mental loss with the tumor. Ali's family is challenging his inheritance of this palace, as is the commune, as are the pasha's original descendants."

This man with the unsmiling mouth, the big, unironic eyes and the look of confusion traceable to his scarred skull, seemed disturbingly intimate and real. For so long now Austin and Julien had been rocked in the comforting arms of French gaiety and discretion, the illusions made possible by silence or elision. Now here was a flat-footed (if unsteady) German with a metal plate in his head and a verbal problem in several languages who was, with all the misguided kindliness in the world, making them look at the inevitable, from which they'd so long averted their eyes.

"It's strange for me," Hermann said. "I'm here to recuperate but all I can do is worry and worry about Ali." With a familiar Teutonic gesture, he performed an immense shrug of his shoulders and let his lifted hands collapse rhetorically onto the slats of the chair he was sitting on. With the same gesture he propelled himself into a standing position and said, much more loudly, *"Gut!* We go?"

"Go?" Julien asked, blinking. He'd been smiling into the garden and looking at his uneaten omelette as though he were a mildmannered child to whom the gruff natives had offered an inscrutable toy. "Where are we going?"

The German said, "I don't have a car but you do. I thought we could all take the dirt road up into the mountains to Ali's village. They'll make us mint tea, which for them is a great luxury, and you can meet Ali who you'll see has lost his looks and become fat as a *younook."*

Oh, Austin thought. As a eunuch. What a drool-making temptation. . . .

They drove a few miles out of town into the foothills where the gravel road gave out and there were just two continuing ruts in the mud. After another mile Austin decided they couldn't continue because the bottom of the car was scraping against the turf.

Julien said, "Go on! Go on! I want to see the village."

"No, we can't," Austin said. "We're scraping the bottom of the car. We'll destroy the motor. We'll be stuck here. Our insurance won't cover the repairs—it will so clearly have been our fault."

Julien, who was sitting beside him, said, "Oh, I'm so disappointed, you have no sense of adventure. I wanted to go there."

Something about the way he said it made Austin think he was referring to the foothills of death. No, that was a fancy way of putting a simpler intuition, that Julien was expecting something to happen to him up there that now would never happen.

Julien left them and went walking across the valley. Somewhere, out of sight, over the next hill possibly, several men were hammering something and all talking at once. "What are they doing?" Austin asked.

"Building a house," the guide said, though how he knew exactly Austin wondered.

The sound was peculiarly close and present, irregular but frequent blows of hammers on something hollow-sounding, perhaps stakes being driven into the earth after all.

A soft breeze was blowing and tossing and gathering the folds of Julien's white robes as he walked. The ground up here was stony and barren, the color of sand though the pebbles and rocks would need another ten thousand years to be ground down to grains that fine. Green trees, wind-trained and full as giant bushes, were dotting the tan hills all the way down to the distant, verdant valley. There were no clouds in the sky except along the horizon; at first Austin wondered if they might be snow-covered mountains, but then they drifted slightly.

The guide stood apart, as if afraid of disturbing them with proximity. He suddenly hunkered down in a crouch, with his back to them, and looked off to the valley. Hermann stood near Austin, kicking a pebble with his right foot. Austin looked at Julien, whose white caftan was glowing with the suffused daylight and was floating in the shifting but constantly flowing breeze. Austin took three pictures as Julien walked back toward them. Austin thought, Julien's such a romantic boy, he's probably communing with nature in preparation for his death.

And then he thought: That's exactly what he's doing, it's not a pose, it's a reality. He's communing with nature in preparation for his death.

Chapter Twenty

The next day they left their hotel in Taroudant at ten in the morning, retraced their path in the car past the Berber Palace and drove for four hours on to the oasis town of Ouazarzate. As soon as they drove into town the streets were broader, the buildings more luxurious—this was a tourist town with a big Club Med compound somewhere, even if it was off-season and there were few Europeans to be seen.

They checked into their hotel, a brand-new collection of low pavilions, air-conditioned and smelling of just-opened packing cases and overheated electrical circuits. A series of linked inner courtyards led them to the pool and a scattering of guests at tables shaded by parasols. Julien and Austin ordered lunch by the pool.

All morning Julien had been peeved with Austin because yesterday Austin had permitted Hermann to come along to the Berber village in the mountains. "That German was so fat he weighed down the car. You and your American compulsion to be nice to every stranger. You spoiled our trip and you—well, you have plenty of time in front of you to waste but I don't."

That evening they went out as the light was dying. Storks, pure white except where their tails and bellies were black, settled on their unkempt nests wedged between two chimneys. The two men headed to the casbah, a fortress in mud tattooed with hen tracks dug into the adobe around blind windows above smooth troweled walls. The casbah was honeycombed with boutiques, all closed tight because it was the next-to-last night of Ramadan and soon the festivities would be beginning. Two shops, however, had stayed open. Julien bought a silver hash pipe, slender and incised with Tuareg spiral symbols of eternity, and a thick silver bracelet. Austin became nervous because two middle-aged Arabs in dark brown wool robes seemed to be shadowing them.

"Let's go back to the hotel," Austin whispered. "These men make me nervous and I have too much money on me."

The following day they drove south through the Valley of the Draa. After the town of Agdz they passed through the oases of Tamnougatt, Tinsouline and Tissergate. A river that sometimes was just three meters wide and at others sank into the sand and seeped its way through, only to reemerge as a trickle half a kilometer further along, irrigated the fields and a line of slender palms. Inside the fortified casbahs, villagers lived on the floors above the stables. Here the windows were slits just wide enough to poke a rifle through. In the background rose black lava mountains, the range called Jbel Sarhro, lunar and plantless. Not a single bush or blade of grass grew on the heavily fissured, rocky soil. It made a strangely out-of-scale contrast to the wood gates and mud crenelations of the casbahs and the luxurious palms lining the stream. Was this the desert?

In the strong steady sunlight women, unveiled but hooded, moved in their cobalt-blue or black robes; they were all walking somewhere. No men were to be seen, although near the town of Tissergate two little boys were selling freshly picked dates in baskets of woven palm fronds. Austin stopped to buy a basket; Julien complained about the bees it attracted and, after they'd eaten two or three, they threw it out the window. Julien said he was disappointed by the Valley, which had looked so much better in photos. "But that's probably just my mood," he said.

Zagora, an ugly modern town, was squeezed into the crook of the elbow of the Draa. The sole beauty of the oasis was in its agriculture—

the soaring date palms protecting the almond and lemon trees from the sun and they, in turn, shading the plots of wheat and barley.

They checked into their modern hotel, which seemed to have no other guests. Julien tottered around the pool, then crept to their room, supported by Austin. He fell asleep instantly. A feeling of dread came over Austin as he sat in the dark and looked at this bony shadow on the bed, breathing in a labored way but scarcely moving. Austin thought he'd been foolish to bring Julien to such a remote place. What was going to happen to them?

After an hour or two had drifted by, Julien awakened and said he was hungry, if too weak to go to the dining room. Austin ordered some chicken and cooked peas from room service, but when the waiter, looking wide-eyed and frightened, wheeled the table in, Julien was dozing again. Austin dismissed the waiter. He turned on all the lights, even those overhead, and tuned in the television, which had only one channel, showing the inevitable king sitting cross-legged in the mosque.

At last Julien sat up on the edge of the bed and looked at the food with no interest. He tried to eat a few forkfuls but kept dozing off. He crumpled back onto the bed and slept.

Austin, sitting in the blue, shifting glow of the television, thought things were getting out of hand. They were far from everyone they knew, and the steps needed to undo their trip this far into the desert would require at least two or three days. They couldn't just rush to the nearest airport and fly home to Paris. No, they'd have to drive slowly back to Ouazarzate then a whole day through the mountains to Marrakesh before they could find a plane to France. Maybe Marrakesh was even farther.

Julien acted much, much weaker, but he had no fever. What was happening to him? Driving in a sealed car down a highway in warm but not hot weather seemed a diverting but not tiring activity, but who was he, Austin, to judge, cushioned as he was with his seven hundred T-cells, fifty extra pounds and rosy cheeks, fore and aft?

Julien awoke after an hour and waved his hand impatiently at the table of cold food, which Austin pushed out into the hall. Then Julien wanted to take a bath. His body was all feet, knees and shoulders, with dry boards for bones connecting them. The skin was hanging loosely and yellow. The knees were nodes that bulked far larger than the thighs or calves. The head was huge and heavy, hard to maintain upright, like a painted papier-mâché carnival head worn by a frail child, a head with just one expression.

Austin, no longer afraid to hover, stood in the bathroom and watched Julien unbend, apparently from a great height, into the water. Immersed, he looked so frail tears came to Austin's eyes.

Julien cupped water with his translucent hands, and dribbled it over his shoulders; the scar from his shunt was still visible and the hair hadn't grown back yet where it had been shaved from his chest.

When he wanted to stand to get out he couldn't. Austin tried to pull him up with a powerful tug, but Julien said, "You're hurting me." Austin took off his own clothes, bent over the tub and lifted Julien in his arms, but at one moment he almost dropped this long, skinny thing and his own back felt as if he were about to slip a disk. He laid him, dripping and nerveless, on the bed and dried him off although even the softest strokes hurt him.

"We have to go back to Paris, Julien. You're not well enough to go on."

"But, *Petit,* don't be a coward," Julien said. "I want to go to Erfoud and then back to Fès. You've got to let me see Fès, that's where I did my student work, preparing for my thesis on the hammam. I've been waiting for five years to show you Fès. And this is my last chance."

Austin slept beside Julien in the empty, modern hotel that was peculiarly silent except for its throbbing air-conditioners. In the morning Austin asked the desk clerk if they should head back to Ouazarzate before crossing over to Erfoud, or whether there was a shorter route. The clerk explained that the direct route, describing a triangle, was far shorter though the road wasn't always in the best condition. Julien was eager to see the desert. They stocked up on several bottles of water.

The road, far from being just sketchy, simply disappeared from time to time; they thundered their way across arid, rock-strewn wastes, their wheels spinning up pebbles that clattered against the chassis and showered out behind them. They'd rise to the top of a hill, then sight a hamlet of seven houses or a lone house of just one room, built in cement, colored blue, two sheep staggering across the desolate landscape in front of it, as surprised to find themselves there as Austin was. With a frantic eye he monitored the gas and water gauge, the temperature—and the vital signs of his passenger.

After two hours they came to a village and stopped for lunch. A man with a white beard indicated a restaurant; his gesture was so negligent, even scornful, that Austin assumed he took no responsibility for the cuisine. Austin called and clapped and at last a shy man in a dirty white turban, smelling of lanolin, came sleepily blinking out into the sunlight. He was persuaded to help Austin escort Julien up the ten stairs to the open-air balcony that was above the dust level. Julien was smiling sweetly but he seemed in a daze, as if the poet had got it all wrong and flesh became wood and fingers leaves not instantaneously but slowly, very slowly, and under the stern supervision of an unblinking sun.

Julien wanted a Coke but the bubbles burned his throat. He looked benignly out over the passersby just below, stirring up clouds of dust every time they took a step. He picked up a slice of orange and sucked on it, but he whispered, "It's bitter," and put it aside.

By evening they'd crossed the desert and arrived at Erfoud, an oasis of just five thousand people but looking surprisingly modern with its electric lights, cafés and freshly painted houses and stores. Their hotel was brand new.

But when Austin went to help Julien out of the car, Julien burst into tears and pissed through his robes in a copious yellow soak. "What are you doing!" Austin exclaimed like an angry father—he could hear the harsh voice of his own father. "They'll never let us in if you're going to do that!"

Julien's voice was so feeble that Austin had to crouch down to hear him. "I can't help it. I've lost control."

Austin found one of his own dirty shirts and mopped Julien dry as best he could. "Well, let's go check in, then we'll worry about the bags."

Julien's knees were buckling as they walked the twenty feet to the lobby, which was air-conditioned and empty, lit by outsized copper lanterns made of thick gobs of colored glass—the "native" note that was played off against the freshly upholstered chairs and the glassy white and black marble floors, which a uniformed man was polishing with an electric chrome machine.

The desk clerk asked rudely, "What's wrong with him?"

Austin said, "Oh, him? He's fine. He just had some serious surgery and has decided to recuperate here in Morocco. But give us a room on the ground floor." Austin put a tone of matter-of-fact authority in his voice, because he could feel the clerk was still making up his mind whether to admit them. He probably didn't want someone to die in the hotel—maybe he was superstitious, or maybe he was afraid a death would be bad for business. Or perhaps he just feared the paperwork.

"We have our coupon for the room," Austin said and handed over a piece of paper. This hotel belonged to the same chain as their last three and Austin had paid for them all in advance. The clerk looked at the paper dubiously and at last tossed a tasseled key down on the counter and sauntered away. Perhaps he was tense because today was the last day of Ramadan.

Their room, which was at the far end of an inner courtyard, stank of backed-up sewage. As soon as they were in it and the baggage had been brought to them, Austin undressed Julien and washed him slowly, tenderly. They were both smiling. "I'm sorry I shouted at you," Austin said. "I was just afraid they might not let us into the hotel if we looked, uh, *problematic* . . . and then where would we have gone?"

"If they can throw us out then we should go back to France. I don't want to be at their mercy." Julien was speaking so softly that Austin bent over him and pressed his ear close to his mouth.

"I'm afraid that an ordinary plane won't accept us now," Austin said. "You know they won't take people who are obviously ill. But we have traveler's insurance and they guarantee they'll repatriate us, even if they have to hire a private plane. The only problem is that they mustn't suspect you were already *critically* ill when you came to Morocco. If they see all your medicines they'll be able to say that anyone traveling with so many pills had no right to leave home in the first place."

"I think I can simplify them," Julien said. "Bring me the sack."

Julien made two piles in his bed but he kept dozing off. He forced himself awake again and again; he applied himself to the problem with urgency. "You can put half of my medicines in your bag; I'll keep the rest. But I'm throwing a lot of the ballast overboard."

Austin called the insurance people in Paris and explained the situation to a sympathetic young man who kept saying, "Of course, I understand, no problem." After an hour he phoned back to say they'd need the opinion of a doctor, someone who'd sign an affidavit attesting to the gravity of Julien's condition.

Julien said, angrily, "Once you paid hundreds of dollars extra to fly back from Spain to Paris a day early because you had opera tickets that night with Henry McVay, but now you're so cheap—"

Austin nearly wept, he felt so misjudged, but then he said to himself, He can't help it. He can't help what he's saying and doing. He's very ill, he's bitter, his personality has been distorted by all he's suffered—and by the morphine.

"My back hurts so much," Julien said. He'd been looking at his Koran, but now he put it aside.

Austin rubbed him as delicately as he could but he still felt he was leaving bruises and injuring internal organs. When Julien dozed off, he perfumed the room with the attar of roses they'd bought from the little girl in the High Atlas mountains, but still the odor of backed-up sewage was omnipresent. Just outside their window was the desert— not rocks or scrub brush this time, but the real desert of windswept sand dunes, sculpted into sharply defined crests and shadowy valleys, the whole thrown into dramatic relief by the setting sun, which cast slopes on the right into tawny warmth and on the left into cold purple darkness. The curves of the crests and the long ridged wind lines traveling up to them displayed an abstract anatomical beauty, as if they were molds cast from the bodies of athletes.

The young man in Paris called back to say that if they could get to Marrakesh and find a doctor who'd certify the gravity of Julien's illness, the company would arrange for a private plane. Austin remembered that Marie-France had once offered to pay their medical bills, no matter how extraordinary, but he felt far from Paris. And he felt incapable of phoning her.

The next day they drove along the paved two-lane highway that led back to Ouazarzate and from there up through the mountains to Marrakesh. Ramadan was over at last and their road took them through one village after another where laughing men were dancing in the streets. The effect of pushing through the crowds in a car was similar to brushing through high reeds in a motor boat except Austin dared not touch these merrymakers. Women in white caftans, girdled with gold belts, were jogging past on the backs of donkeys; the men, outfitted in freshly laundered white djellabahs, looked washed and pressed themselves, joyous at the end of their onerous religious duties. People were eating, drinking and smoking with an exaggerated pleasure, as if such simple daily acts were themselves signs of daring revelry.

Outside the car were the swirling, laughing crowds and inside two somber men, one as gaunt as a saint or his relics. The big, leering faces swam up to the closed windows like those of sharks in an aquarium that swerve away only at the last minute, oblivious to the passive expressions of human visitors just on the other side of the glass—except here the Muslims were the ones who appeared animated and fully human, whereas the Christian tourists were stunned into nearly mineral torpor and indifference.

They drove past one adobe casbah after another as they skirted the foothills of the Atlas Mountains. Some of the villages appeared abandoned, others flourishing. If there were inhabitants they were dressed in all their finery, the Berber women in hoods hung with gold coins, two clown-like circles of rouge painted on their cheeks.

Hour after hour went past and still they didn't reach Ouazarzate, which was only half the distance to Marrakesh. Austin said, "We'll have to stop at our hotel in Ouazarzate for the night. It was comfortable, air-conditioned. We'll order up room service and watch CNN and make our calls to Paris. Maybe we'll even find a doctor who can fax in the necessary documents."

Julien didn't say anything. In Erfoud, Austin had washed out his robes, which had dried out quickly in the desert air and looked as fresh as those of the celebrants in the streets. When they'd stopped for lunch he'd eaten nothing but had sipped an orange soda. Austin had nearly carried him to the roadside table. Two truck drivers at the next table stared and one said, "He's very sick, you need to get him to a hospital."

Austin started to explain that he was recovering from an operation and looked worse than he was—but suddenly Julien, eyes swimming with morphine, pain and weakness, stood up and was trying to walk toward the car. Austin helped him into the car and ran back to throw some money on the table, smile at the truckers and shrug. Julien saw the smile and shrug with cold, ancient, unforgiving eyes.

Now he asked Austin to pull over so he could piss. Austin said, "Not here, wait a minute, here the roadbed is too high, there's a steep slope—"

"Here!" Julien roared.

Austin did as ordered, though when Julien opened the door he had to run down the gravel hill and lost his footing and nearly fell. The urine splashed out of him; obviously he was becoming incontinent. What did that mean? Was this the end?

He asked to sit in the back seat where he could stretch out and sleep, which sounded reasonable but Austin felt he was angry and wanted to have some separation from his tormentor, his enemy.

Julien even said, "I just figured when I must have first contracted the HIV virus. Remember that terrible flu I had?"

Austin couldn't remember it, but the implication, not wasted on him, was that Julien had been infected since knowing Austin—infected *by* Austin. Because Austin knew nothing about Julien's other dalliances with men, if any, he had to ascribe the blame to himself.

When they arrived in Ouazarzate at last, Julien said he couldn't walk into the hotel.

"You can and you will!" Austin shouted angrily. "We just need to get to the room and you'll feel better. We've got to spend one more night in a hotel—"

"No," he whispered. "I can't. Don't you see it's over?"

"It's *not* over. We're going to get that plane back to Paris—"

"I hate you!" Julien hissed. "*Je te déteste!*" was what he said in French, the exact words. "Don't you see? I'm covered in shit."

"I'll clean you up." Austin lifted him up, stood him beside the car, threw his dirty robes on the ground and helped him step into trousers.

"Now we're just going to walk normally past the desk and to the room."

"I can't," Julien wailed. "Can't you see? It's over. Why won't you let me go?"

Austin, grim and determined and cold with fury, put his arm around Julien's waist and walked him toward the entrance to the hotel, but suddenly Julien fainted and crumpled onto the grass. A Frenchman who was walking by said, "What's happened? Call an ambulance. For God's sake, I'll call an ambulance," and he ran into the hotel and insisted the clerk phone the hospital.

Austin looked down at this tiny, shit-stained effigy in the grass and he sobbed, "I can't, I don't—" but he didn't know what he was saying and his whole body was seized with a violent fit of trembling which was only more sobs and at last tears. It was as if his will, so long screwed up to its highest, tautest pitch, had at last snapped and now was hanging down as useless as a violin string. After so much tuning and sawing and plucking, after so much rapture and suffering had been wrung out of it, at last it had snapped and no one was more surprised than the instrumentalist himself.

Two bellboys and the clerk had gathered around Julien. It was they who were stroking him, giving him human comfort and holding him. They were the ones to show poor Julien some normal human sympathy rather than this cold, neurotic Austin, who despised himself. He heard those words again, "I hate you." The three Moroccans were crouching down beside Julien and looking, looking into his face, as if memorizing him, like those intense, scrutinizing figures painted by Giotto. Austin, so bizarrely dissociated from his feelings during this crisis, could not help thinking that the attitudes of these men were Biblical and that for thousands of years, until the recent past in Europe, people had had no idea of privacy, no social distance between them, and that when they looked at an afflicted man, a dying man, they drank him in with their eyes, studied him as if to memorize him, leaned in closer and closer and closer, peeling back a veil from the eyes so that they might truly see and know this suffering creature, about to disappear. Austin felt ineffectual and broken as well as devoid of normal feeling. He thought maybe he was crazy. Yes, he'd gone crazy during the long, intense vigil of these last few months, and he hadn't even noticed at what moment he'd passed over the line. He felt out of control now, slightly awed by his own jangled, broken organism; he couldn't predict its next responses.

Suddenly, out of nowhere, an ambulance, fly-blown and ancient, a big white truck hand-painted with red crescents (the Muslim equivalent of a red cross, Austin half-remembered), came rolling up, its red light revolving and its siren shrieking. Two male orderlies in white, short-sleeved, semi-transparent polyester uniforms put a stretcher on the ground beside Julien, lifted him onto it and slid him into the back of the ambulance. Austin asked if he could ride beside him and they said yes. He noticed they didn't take Julien's blood pressure or give him oxygen or glucose through an intravenous tube.

When they arrived at the hospital, an Arab hospital, Julien was shoved into a dirty room and left unattended. Austin wandered the corridors, asking questions, and soon learned that the hospital was understaffed, did not provide food, and had few nurses. The families of the patients camped outside the main door and cooked for their sick relatives and looked after most of their needs. Austin bought bottled water and a candy bar from the man in the kiosk near the main gate and took them back to Julien, who'd now reawakened. He was alone in his room, but his sheets looked as if someone else had slept on them. There were no towels in the bathroom and the shower didn't work. The toilet was a foul-smelling hole in the ground, what was called a Turkish toilet. Austin thought that the French tourist who'd insisted they call an ambulance must have imagined there was a conventional European hospital in town, not this third-world *mouroir*, the French word for a place to die in.

Austin tore one of the sheets off the bed and moistened it in the sink and used it to wash Julien's body clean. "It's not impeccable," Austin said, "but it's much, much better."

Two Arab doctors came by on their rounds, one of them young and handsome, the other corpulent and middle-aged. The older one did all the talking and meant to be cheerful and reassuring. "Well,

well, who do we have here? Was your holiday interrupted by a touch
of dysentery?"

"He has AIDS and he's dying. We must get him in an ambulance
and to a fully equipped hospital in Marrakesh," Austin said. "Our
insurance will pay for the ambulance and even a private plane back to
Paris, but we need an affidavit from you, Doctor, saying he is gravely
ill. If I pay—"

"Wait a minute, wait a minute!" the doctor exclaimed, holding
up his hands comically as if to stop an avalanche of words and looking with exaggerated incredulity at his colleague, who merely pulled
at his very black mustache trimmed with surgical precision above
his embarrassingly pink, dry lips. "Why do you say he is dying, *Monsieur?* Only God, whom we call Allah, can give or take a life, and the
most important thing for us to do is to hope. We must never lose
faith."

Austin was sure that in another mood he'd have taken an epicurean delight in this display of folkloric wisdom, but now he was
seized with rage and impatience at the old blowhard, though he was
determined to be as polite as possible. "Yes, of course, your words
remind me of our duties to God—and to ourselves! But I assume you
agree with me that this is an emergency and I am responsible for the
welfare of my friend, whom I've raised as a son. If I get the insurance
official in Paris to phone you here, Doctor, uh, Doctor—"

"Ayoub."

"Dr. Ayoub, would you explain his condition to the authorities?"

"Of course. But you can't phone out of this hospital to Paris.
We're—uh, we *can't!*" He opened his hands with comic resignation, as
if to evoke the principle of human helplessness once again.

Austin said he'd dash back to his hotel, make the necessary calls
from there to Paris and give them the hospital phone number and the
name of Dr. Ayoub, who promised he'd be on duty at least for another
half hour.

The man at the food kiosk said taxis rarely came out in this direction, but even as he was explaining the problem, Austin spotted an old
Peugeot with a green light on the roof, packed with passengers. He
squeezed into the front seat next to the driver, whose right hand was

soon traveling up Austin's left thigh. From time to time he'd take his eyes off the teeming streets and look at Austin meltingly and flash a big gold smile. Austin thought how grotesque sex could be and how inept its timing.

People got out of the car and into it every few minutes. The driver took Austin's hand and placed it on the lump under his pale blue djellabah. No one could see what he was doing. At last they arrived at the hotel. Austin rushed in and called the insurance people in Paris. With a voice boyish from hysteria he gave the number of their dossier, waited for the woman to call it up on her computer, then said, "Now we can't put this off any longer. He's dying. He's in a terrible Arab hospital where they don't even have nurses and have never treated anyone with AIDS before, or so they claim."

He gave her Dr. Ayoub's number and begged her to arrange for an ambulance to be sent to his hotel. She said she'd call their representative in Marrakesh, a Mr. Azzit. Azzit telephoned ten minutes later and they made detailed plans for the drive through the mountains to Marrakesh, a seven-hour trip.

Austin ran out to the rented car in the hotel lot with a plastic wastepaper basket full of warm water and soap. With a washcloth he scrubbed the shit stains that Julien had left in the back seat. He then dashed back to their room, washed out the cloth and basket and gathered up their luggage. He gave the desk clerk a very large tip and the car keys and the contract. "Tell them that the car is here and they must send someone to pick it up. They won't object, since we've already paid up for another week's rental."

The ambulance had pulled into the parking lot. Austin loaded it up with their baggage and instructed the driver to go over to the hospital. There he and Austin loaded Julien onto a stretcher and carried him out to the car. At least, Austin thought, the stretcher's been made up with fresh sheets. Dr. Ayoub waved goodbye, assuring them he'd given all the necessary information.

All night long they drove through the mountains, twisting and turning and ascending higher and higher. The weather turned bitterly cold and Julien began to tremble. Austin hoped he'd say something tender, but he seemed obsessed with the problem of having too many medications. "Don't let anyone see the bag of drugs in your suitcase," Julien whispered, "or we'll never get our private plane."

Austin knelt close to his knife-thin, foul-smelling body and whispered, "I love you, Julien."

But Julien wouldn't say anything affectionate. He kept obsessing about the excess drugs and where he'd concealed them. He didn't move much or even seem to be breathing, but his mind was obviously racing. At last he exhausted himself and fell asleep. Austin was perched on a hard, small jump seat beside the stretcher in the back of the ambulance, just behind the driver. He was mesmerized by the green glow of the dashboard up front and the brilliance of the headlights on banks of snow.

"It's freezing back here. Can't you turn up the heat?"

The driver didn't reply but fiddled with the dial. They went slowly past an all-night truck stop and gas station where loud men in caftans over jeans, their faces covered with red and white checked *kaffiyehs*, probably to stay warm, were shouting to one another, laughing and either clapping their hands together against the cold or sipping from steaming glasses of mint tea.

When the lights swerved away behind them and they began their ascent, Julien awakened and complained about something sharp and painful poking into him, under him. Austin was exhausted and mumbled, "It will be all right, Julien," but Julien raised his voice indignantly and said, "It's hurting me."

"What's that?" the driver asked loudly. "What's he saying?" He didn't ask Julien directly but addressed his question to Austin.

"Something hurts him. It's under him. I'll feel under him and see if there's anything wrong." Too late Austin realized he hadn't said, ". . . and see if I can fix it," but rather, ". . . and see if there's anything wrong." These two healthy men were in cahoots against this terminal patient and his absurd demands invented just to annoy them. That's how it must sound to Julien.

The driver stopped and got out, opened the side doors and shouted at Julien, "Where is it? Where's the pain? What's hurting you?" Brusquely he jabbed his hands under Julien, then announced to Austin, "There's nothing wrong," as if to say, "Just as I suspected."

After that Julien wouldn't talk to Austin at all, although Austin knew this would be their last chance in this life to say something important. Austin felt excruciatingly guilty for having sided with the driver, and now Julien was punishing him by remaining silent.

At long last they were just pulling into Marrakesh when a tire blew out and the driver was forced to bring them to a bumpy, gravel-spitting halt by the roadside. He swore and sighed and talked to himself in Arabic as he jacked the ambulance up and changed the tire. At least it was hot again. Finally they pulled into the back of the Clinique du Maroc, which was not at all the clean, modern, fully staffed hospital Austin had expected. Some time passed before the driver returned with an orderly, who helped him carry the stretcher into the lobby, where they left it on the floor. A nurse emerged and looked at Julien contemptuously: "What on earth does *he* have?" she asked, as if dying were comical, certainly a humiliation. "Is he still alive?"

"Alive and conscious," Austin said with controlled fury. "Didn't the insurance people alert you to our arrival?"

"Yes, but I had no idea the patient was in *this* condition," she said.

A young doctor in a white coat came through swinging doors and he, too, looked at Julien as if he were a bit of garbage a greengrocer had had the audacity to offer for human consumption. "Are you sure he's alive?" he asked.

"He's alive," Austin said. "He can hear everything you're saying. He has AIDS. He's very ill."

"Oh, yes, AIDS," the doctor said. "They're treating that with something now, we don't have it yet, what's it called?"

"AZT."

"Yes, AZT," the doctor said, pleased, continuing in fluent French, "But as I said—"

"*I can't stand this!*" Julien shouted in English with surprising force. The doctor understood what Julien had said and looked abashed. He no longer acted bemused and speculative but suddenly sobered up and said, "Take him in for a chest X-ray, then put him in a private room and give him a glucose transfusion."

The man from the insurance company arrived, though it was very late at night, a short, bald, bespectacled Arab in a frayed three-piece suit and food-stained tie. "Mr. Azzit," Austin said, "why are we here? I thought you were going to prepare a private plane for us."

"Tomorrow, tomorrow," he said, waving his hand as if to shake off flies. "Tonight he must rest up for the trip. A trip like that is very tiring." He began to shout in Arabic at the nurse but perhaps his words weren't as angry as they sounded, for she merely shrugged without changing expressions.

Julien and Austin had to wait for a long time before the X-ray machine was free. Again the operator, a black man with a bulbous nose and hard, disapproving eyes, shook his head in disgusted disbelief at Julien's condition.

At last Julien was wheeled into a bright, modern room with a window and a clean bathroom and a crank-up bed. The nurse said that Austin could sleep in the bed beside Julien's. The ambulance driver brought their luggage up. The nurse was incapable of finding a vein in which to insert the intravenous tube. She tied Julien's arm up with a red rubber tourniquet, she slapped the inside of his arm with the back of her hand, but nothing came up.

The ambulance driver said, "Here. Let me do it. I can always find a vein when no one else can." He huddled over Julien. A minute later Julien let out a scream and sat up, galvanized: "He's killing me!" He spoke again in English.

And then they were gone. Austin glanced at his watch, which read four a.m. The lights were dimmed. The sheets rustled with starch and cleanliness. Far away soft chimes signaled nurses to their various duties. Although his eyes were swimming with weariness, Austin sat beside Julien and said, "The glucose is going to help you, *Petit*. It will give you energy and nourishment for the trip. Tomorrow we'll be on the plane to Paris and this ordeal will be over."

Julien didn't respond, though Austin could see he was awake and could hear the intravenous feed slowly bubbling.

Austin awakened in a flood of sunlight coming through the vines and flowers crossing the window. He wasn't sure where he was, though it felt reassuringly institutional. The window was closed, the room must be air-conditioned—ah! the hospital. Too exhausted to feel anything more than mildly curious, he turned towards Julien. He looked at the glucose sack and saw it was no longer bubbling. Then he looked at Julien's face and saw his eyes were wide open and his mouth frozen in a sudden grimace. He was half-raised out of his bed, as if responding to a sudden cry or to violent pain. He was dead.

At the same moment a nurse (for it must have been her coming into the room that had awakened Austin) rushed over to the bed, took his pulse and said, "He's dead." She hurried away on crepe soles.

Austin was too stunned to say or do anything. The dead body frightened him. He didn't really like this stiff, gaping thing—it wasn't Julien. He was afraid of it. He looked at it obliquely, almost as if it brought bad luck. And it was proof that he, Austin, had done something disastrously wrong.

There was a sound of whispered consultation in the hall. Then the uniformed woman came back with another nurse. They lowered his bed, straightened his limbs, removed the drip, closed his eyes and mouth, took his pillow away, folded him inside the sheets. An orderly arrived and the whole bed was wheeled away. Later Austin realized he should have wept over the body, caressed it, at least kissed him farewell. That was the right thing to do: propriety had taken the place of emotion. Not for a moment did he imagine Julien was still *in* the body.

Austin shaved and dressed, then sat on the edge of his bed with his luggage. He had his bag and Julien's bag. A nurse brought him a cup of coffee. Mr. Azzit appeared from the insurance agency. He was extremely cold. He said, "Well, you can go now."

"And Julien?"

"You can't leave with the body," he scoffed. "You must make the funeral arrangements in France, there's a lot of paperwork on both ends, eventually the remains will be shipped."

"Where is he now?"

"Downstairs. In the morgue."

"Refrigerated?"

"In Muslim countries the dead are buried within twenty-four hours in a simple sheet. We don't practice embalming. Or cremation. The most I can do for you is to have the body sealed in a lead coffin."

He left. Austin realized that he had two tickets for a plane that would be flying out of Marrakesh for Paris in an hour, but the public taxi, the only one he could find, made so many stops that he missed the flight and had to wait four hours for the next one.

Chapter Twenty-one

B ack in Paris, Austin lived in a fog, one that softened feelings and even the features of friends and their words, although occasionally it would lift and light would pierce him to—well, not the *quick* but the *slow,* for everything in him had been tuned down to the lowest possible setting still sufficient to sustain life.

He wasn't sure he wanted to live and was relieved when he found the suicide kit in the drawer of the black desk. There they were, the bouquet of many colors in the Chinese sewing kit, all the pills he'd need to push the dial down below zero.

But first he needed to make the arrangements for Julien's cremation and the burial of his ashes in the Père Lachaise columbarium. In America they called the ashes the "cremains."

The day after Austin's return to Paris, Robert and Fabrice flew up from Nice to help him—to go with him to the funeral parlor and to fill out all the legal forms for the repatriation of the body. They'd encountered a nasty Catch-22. The Moroccans wouldn't release the body until they knew its exact destination in France, but as Muslims they did not approve of cremation and would never send it to a Paris crematorium. Austin knew someone in the French foreign service who agreed to smooth things over. Then a second problem arose: normally a body about to be cremated was placed inside a (highly flammable) pine coffin, but Julien had been sealed inside a lead coffin. After ten days in the spring heat of Marrakesh, the corpse had probably turned into a bubbling minestrone—no time to open the lead lid. Fortunately Père Lachaise had the only crematorium ovens powerful enough to blast their way even through metal.

Fabrice stayed in Paris only two days, long enough to do everything practical, including filling out the death certificate at the Town Hall and ordering a three-line bereavement announcement in *Le Monde*, to be published only after the cremation, a stipulation that followed Julien's will. The insurance company was paying for the transport of the remains, but it sent Austin several forms to fill out as well.

After Fabrice flew back to Nice, Robert and Austin were alone at last. They slept in the same bed and wore just undershorts, but they didn't make love. When he was alive Julien had teased them about being attracted to each other, perhaps because he'd wanted to plant the idea in their heads. Austin certainly was attracted to Robert with his intense stare, hairy, muscular chest, powerful biceps and low voice, the sort that could set a wine glass vibrating against the water glass.

Sleeping with Robert was cheating. He was far too handsome to be in bed with someone like Austin; it was all a dreamlike chance, like having your mother say, "Now, your cousin Chet is going to be bunking with you for a week," and Chet is a sixteen-year-old football star too shy to meet girls. Robert and Austin were like brothers. They'd been through so much, they were both in mourning for the very man who was pushing them at each other. Some divine dispensation not only allowed but also encouraged Austin to sleep within Robert's embrace, held by muscles that felt like warm basketballs sliding under cool silk.

But neither of them got erections. It wasn't sexual. It was exactly what it was supposed to be, mutual comfort in great grief. They who'd eyed each other for the last two years over the barrier of Fabrice and Julien were now enjoying their first long moments together, in bed, in each other's arms, and nothing was happening.

Julien had always said that after his death Austin would find someone else, almost instantly. "Just don't forget me completely," he'd say. "*Petit*, don't forget me." Because Julien had loved him so much, Austin had become someone as privileged, as legendary, as a member of Julien's own family; Austin had been lulled into believing he was desirable. But his hair had turned white, he noticed one day with alarm, and he'd put on thirty more pounds. His hair was shaggy and lusterless, and all his clothes (as he discovered when he looked through his closet) were dirty, wrinkled and out of fashion. Julien's long illness had made him shabby; Austin took the fewest, shortest steps necessary to correct his disgrace.

But nothing seemed real. He was packed in Styrofoam peanuts, which crunched like subzero snow whenever he attempted to move. Nothing could touch him; he was wedged tight inside a weightless void. The days were becoming longer and longer, the first tourists were arriving in Paris, the cafés were thronged until late at night, but Austin considered the good weather almost as an affront. He would have preferred a Parisian winter, which was like living inside gray sand on its way to becoming a pearl.

He thought he'd find the apartment unbearable without Julien and he was quick to offer Julien's clothes to Robert and to contribute all his boxes and tubes and vials of medicine—thousands and thousands of doses—to the corner druggist, a mustachioed gay man who collected for an AIDS charity on the Ivory Coast. Joséphine suggested he put away some of Julien's photos.

"But I couldn't!" Austin said. "The maid would be scandalized."

Joséphine smiled but was firm about it: "I think you shouldn't have a rule. Put the pictures away, take them out, light candles in front of them, exactly as you like. There's no rule, or none you must observe."

"I wish there was," Austin said, "because if I followed the rule, any rule, maybe I'd feel less guilty."

He called Julien's Paris doctor, gave the exact date and hour of the day when Julien had died, as if the doctor would need that information to close Julien's dossier.

The doctor dropped his formal manner for a moment and said, "Mr. Smith, I'm very moved. Julien was such an . . . *elegant* man, always in good humor, never complaining, always impeccably dressed, wonderfully cheerful with the nurses and the other patients. He called me, uh, two weeks ago and said he was too ill to come see me but was he well enough to go to Morocco—well, you can see he was sending me a mixed message at best."

"Do you think it was a terrible mistake to go to Morocco? The last two days, he'd become incontinent and—" Austin recounted the all-day drive from Erfoud to Ouazarzate, the collapse on the lawn in front of the hotel, the horrors of the Arab hospital, the ambulance ride all night long in an unheated vehicle through the snowy mountains, the indignities Julien had suffered at the Clinique du Maroc—

"Yes, yes," the doctor said, "but I would have done the same—X-rayed his chest to see if he had pneumocystis and given him a transfusion of glucose for energy and a few minerals to rehydrate him—"

"Is that what happened? Was he dehydrated?"

"You've heard of those anorexic girls, Mr. Smith, who die of heart attacks? Their bodies have been stripped of all the electrolytes necessary for the basic biological functions. Now Julien's pancreatitis had become so severe that he couldn't absorb any nutrition. I'm sure he died of a heart attack."

"But if we'd been in Paris perhaps he would have received better care."

"And then what?" the doctor asked in his soft, beautifully modulated voice. "Died three weeks later in total isolation in a gray little hospital room? No, Mr. Smith, with you in Morocco he could share a great adventure; that was rare, suspenseful, a challenge, something you were doing *together*."

They talked some more and before he hung up the doctor said, "Pancreatitis, you know, is terribly painful. He's well out of it. *Au revoir, Monsieur Smith, et bon courage.*"

At first Austin felt exhilarated by so much concrete information, until he began to listen to the echoes. The doctor's exoneration he was eager to embrace, but he felt he'd betrayed Julien in a dozen little ways during his last two days of life. "I hate you" (*Je te déteste*), he kept hearing over and over. Why hadn't he sided with Julien against the last ambulance driver? Why had he been so willing to make bourgeois small talk with the bizarrely optimistic and fatalistic doctor in Ouarzazate and the ignoramus in Marrakesh? Why hadn't he defended Julien against that final martyrdom when the ambulance driver had plunged the transfusion needle into his fleshless, veinless arm?

Had he brought on the whole last illness by encouraging Julien to take DDI?

If he'd had the right minerals, Austin thought, he would have lived. Julien died for want of a bottle of Gatorade.

Henry McVay invited Austin and two concerned, handsome men to dinner at the Ritz, where Austin had never been before. The others kept up a tentative, merciful conversation until Austin himself indicated he wanted to tell them his story. He started at the beginning and by the time he'd arrived at Marrakesh they were drinking their decaffeinated coffee.

"Then the ambulance pulled into the clinic," Austin said.

"The clinic at the Mamounia Hotel, I suppose," Henry said, never doubting the answer.

"No," Austin said tonelessly. "The Clinique du Maroc."

"Oh," Henry said, "the only good hospital belongs to the Mamounia. Very modern and European. French doctors. I wonder why they didn't take you there."

Austin went home, climbed his steps, opened his door, hating himself, and hated himself as he undressed and brushed his teeth. Why had he trusted the travel insurance people? Why hadn't he hired his own ambulance, his own private plane or at least phoned Henry, who was so worldly, to find out the name of the only good hospital in southern Morocco?

"I'm sorry, *Petit*," he said out loud when he was in the dark in bed. "I'm so sorry."

As he lay in bed he replayed every scene yet again—the encouraging recovery at the hotel in Taroudant, the appalled silence that Julien's skeletal thinness had created among the sunburned English bathers at the luxury resort outside the city walls, the kindness of their waiter there, the tubercular guide who'd sold them the Koran. . . . But then Austin came up against the memory of the day when he'd invited Hermann from the Berber Palace to join them and the car had been too heavy to go up the dirt road into the mountains and Julien had been so bitterly disappointed. And why hadn't Austin driven them back to Taroudant or even to Agadir and found a plane to Paris the instant Julien had given the first signs of weakening? Oh, that painful day in the empty, modern hotel in Zagora when Austin had had to strip and lift Julien up out of the bathtub in his arms, as if he had been cradling a Flemish Christ, brown and bony, wrists and ankles nerveless, his wet hair dripping into a crown of thorns.

At last the body was repatriated to Paris, ten full days after Julien's death. The coffin sat for yet another day in a warehouse at the airport. Robert and Fabrice flew back up to Paris for the cremation. Robert suddenly succumbed to an obsessional fear that Julien's corpse was not in fact inside the lead coffin. "How do we know for sure he's in there?"

"Why wouldn't he be?"

"Perhaps they switched two bodies at the clinic in Marrakesh. They wouldn't care. One Frenchman—one Christian—is worth another. You don't know them. In Nice—"

"Please, Robert. And anyway there'd be a terrible scandal if the other people opened their coffin and found the wrong body." Privately, Austin thought it made absolutely no difference if they burned one dead person rather than another. He wondered whether he felt that degree of indifference because he was rational or because he was faithless.

Robert then railed about the Arabs having stolen Julien's gold watch. Austin felt bad that he hadn't remembered the watch; he asked the maid about it and she told him where it was. "I hid it," she said over the phone. "Monsieur Julien left it behind and then, after he disappeared, I worried that someone would steal it." Austin found it exactly where she said it would be and gave it to Robert.

"Are you sure you don't want it, *Petit* Austin?" Since Julien's death Robert had taken up his way of calling Austin *Petit*, ludicrous as it was as a nickname for a snowy-haired fat American.

"No, no, it's for you," Austin said, delighted to get the gold watch out of the house. He knew that Julien had revered it, but Austin couldn't help thinking it looked terribly . . . well, Vegas and was . . . well, vulgar.

Even thinking such a thought was sacrilegious, which made Austin smile bleakly.

Julien had said he didn't want anybody at the funeral except Fabrice, Robert and Austin. Once before Austin had been to a Père Lachaise cremation, but this time they were not required (or even allowed) to watch the coffin being lowered into the flames. As the mortician explained, the "incineration" of a *lead* coffin would take three hours and they'd have access to the chapel for only half an hour. All the actual cremation, therefore, would have been done well in advance and the ashes brought out in the alabaster urn Julien had selected that day he'd gone to the cemetery with Patty. Now the three men sat in silence in the darkened, cold vault of the chapel with its cheerlessly non-denominational windows. Austin had requested that his own tape of the Fauré *Requiem* be played, but they all three got bored before the "Paradise" section began.

A guard accompanied them down into the lower level of the crypt. The urn was placed in their niche, the guard put an official seal on it and then troweled it over with plaster. He explained that the white marble stone inscribed with recessed gold letters giving Julien's name and dates would not be ready for another week or ten days, but at that time, it, too, would be fixed indelibly in place. Robert nodded solemnly and said, with even more deliberation than usual, "Gold letters on white marble: excellent."

"It's what Julien chose," Austin said briskly, though he wasn't at all sure that that was the truth.

Only after the funeral did Robert call his maternal grandmother in Nancy and tell her that Julien was dead. She wailed and wailed. Her husband had hanged himself, her daughter had committed suicide and now her grandson had died of AIDS.

Robert talked to her for a very long time and left out none of the details, the explanations, the lamentations or the words of comfort that were her due. After he hung up, he said, "The poor woman. She's such a jolly little lady, always so merry, a nice little peasant lady who's had to bear so much. . . ."

"Peasant?" Austin asked, certain he'd misheard.

"Of course," Robert said, smiling and even chuckling with the same laugh that Julien had used. "She worked the earth as a real laborer when she was a girl. Then she married and worked in a little *tabac* selling cigarettes and stamps and eventually newspapers and stationery. Her husband was a train conductor all his life, but two years after his retirement he hanged himself."

"Julien used to say it might have been an erotic strangulation, that he died at his mistress's. . . ."

"His what?" Robert's eyes widened and he laughed boisterously. "He didn't have a mistress, at least this is the first I've ever heard of it. No, he became melancholy after he retired and had to live at home all the time. Our poor mother was sad because her father had died. . . ."

"And then," Austin said, "she'd given up her career as a concert pianist—"

"As a concert pianist?" Robert asked with incredulity. "No, she was an accordionist. Our father hated the sound of the accordion and made her give it up, but I have some beautiful tinted photos of her playing the accordion when she was studying to be a beautician."

Austin realized that everything Julien had said about his family had been compounded of lies. His parents had not been aristocrats but a beautician and a shipping clerk, just as his maternal grandparents had been a railway man and a farm worker. That was why Julien hadn't let Austin meet his grandmother that time they'd gone to Nancy. That was why Julien had heaped such contempt on Joséphine's origins (which turned out to be more elevated than his) and had doted on all of Austin's rich or titled friends, such as Henry McVay, Marie-France and Vladimir. Maybe that's why Julien had dropped all of his friends—perhaps he was worried they'd make allusions to his plebeian past in front of Austin. Poor Julien, Austin thought. He felt he had to lie in order to appear worthy of me.

Robert must have notified their father that Julien was dead, for soon afterwards Austin received a letter from him, saying he would like to come to Paris to meet Austin. The letter astonished Austin since it had two spelling mistakes and two mistakes in grammar. And in it Julien's father said, "I know my sons blame me for their mother's death, but what killed her was the knowledge that both her boys were homosexual." Dutifully, Austin read the letter over the phone to

Robert, who became indignant about their father's accusation and said, "Don't answer him. He's a crook. He wants to visit the apartment so he can figure out what belongs to him as Julien's heir." Austin didn't respond to Julien's father, though he felt bad about his silence.

A month after Julien's cremation his grandmother came to Paris and stayed with Austin. Robert flew up yet again from Nice, this time using the small amount of money Julien had left him—small but all his earthly treasure. *Maman,* as they called her, was at first intimidated by someone as learned and important as Austin. He was so unused to the idea that anyone could be impressed by his status, which was both low and uncertain, that at first he couldn't understand why she stared at him as though he were a zebra who'd been trained to whinny *oui* and *non.*

She had pretty plump hands and small wrists, wide hips and a quick, agile way of moving. She was like one of those octogenarian former ballerinas who come hobbling into the room but can throw their head back at a defiant angle and still demonstrate the raised arms required for correctly performing the tarantella. She sketched in lightly the merriment a good-time gal must have known how to turn on in the 1930s—and then suddenly she was red-faced and sobbing silently against Robert's broad chest, her eyes, when she looked up, flashing forth a clear, shockingly girlish blue.

Austin had seldom met elderly ladies in Paris who weren't countesses, as exquisitely transparent as their own bone china, their bodies carefully coiffed and molded inside couture clothes constructed around darts, seams and stays. They were ladies who had opinions, mannerisms, pasts and who goaded themselves on to keep up, to read this season's novels, take in the latest movies; but here was an old lady from the provinces with a face as fresh as today's bread and who was . . . well, humble. She was afraid of Austin, this exotic son-in-law she'd met too late and whom she'd always associate with her third loss, the last act of a life that had the clean trajectory of a dynastic tragedy.

They all hugged and sniffled their way through two long evenings, recalled the adorable things Julien had said as a child, trotted out once more the story about his running away with his teddy bear and head-

ing for the airport where he hoped to be transported to Africa in order
to become a veterinarian. And then there were other stories.

Austin had almost dozed off when suddenly he realized they
were talking about Julien's lovers—the effeminate Spaniard named
Edgardo and the—"But who were these guys?" he asked. "Of course I
know who they were. . . ."

"You met Jean-François on the street one day, right here on the
rue de Rivoli," Fabrice said. "Don't you remember?"

"Oh, he was with him a long time," Granny was saying. "They
lived together next to the Cordeliers. Jean-François's family owned
that shoe store."

"And Edgardo," Fabrice said. "Don't you remember how effeminate he was? He thought he was Julien's wife. He'd cling to his arm in
public and make Julien blush."

"Yes, yes," Austin said, heartsick, with a big smile on his face, "I
can just see Julien, always so proper, so aristocratic. . . ."

"Don't you remember, *Maman*," Robert asked, "how he'd always
write the address of your apartment block as the *Palais Fitzwilliam*,
when it was just the plain old Fitzwilliam. Oh, that Julien (*sacré
Julien*), he liked to hint that everything was grander than it was. No
harm there, of course; he never used it to his advantage. It was just a
dream world he was living in."

After the grandmother had gone to bed, Austin asked Fabrice and
Robert, "When Julien would come to Nice, would he go wild with the
boys?"

Fabrice smiled. "Well, you know the mountain behind our house
where we walk Ajax? That's a famous cruising spot. Julien would
come to visit us when he was in his last year of high school and run in
and out of the bushes till four in the morning. He couldn't get
enough."

"But why did he ever get married?"

Robert said, "Why not? You don't like Christine? What's wrong
with Christine?"

"These brothers!" Fabrice exclaimed, appealing to Austin in
shared grievance. "They both claim they're bisexual. They're always
coy about which sex they prefer, even Robert talks about getting mar-

ried someday. I'll tell you, Austin, these brothers will be the death—"
And then he remembered Julien was dead. He stubbed out his cigarette and knocked a tear out of his eye with the back of his hand.

Austin liked *Maman* and loved Robert and Fabrice, but he felt that
he and Julien's family members were all a bit lackluster without
Julien, as if the only thing that had raised them all above the ordinary
was existing in Julien's consciousness, exactly as if his mind had been
a stage—small, floored with reflecting black stone, lit with inquisitor-
ial intensity—and they'd been allowed to appear on it only as figments
of Julien's imagination.

At last they all left, full of solicitude for Austin, the foreigner and
widower, doubly isolated. And Austin did feel less integrated into
French life without Julien. As long as Julien had been alive Austin
was always learning things, not necessarily reasoned or researched
information but rather all those thousands and thousands of brand
names, turns of phrase, aversions and anecdotes that make up a culture as surely as do the moves in a child's game of hopscotch. Now,
without Julien he was a tourist again.

He was too distracted to read anything but he often sat, vacantly,
with the Koran in his lap. He liked the curving, cursive strokes under
every third or fourth word and bristling vowel marks above them, as if
ferryboats loaded with standing passengers were floating on long,
swelling waves. The dots were the passengers' heads against the sky.

Austin missed Julien—not the Julien of the last months, a skeleton turned malign from suffering, a death's head shaking on a stick—
but the Julien who'd called him *Petit,* who'd first made love with him
on the lumpy bed in the Île Saint-Louis apartment under the clenched
fist of the great stone volute of the church across the street, the curled
hand thrusting up through the roof like a military salute. He remembered when Julien, that summer in America, had told Lucy he didn't
mind living a short life so long as he could live it with Austin.

Julien's death wasn't a sentimental loss, a sweet, fierce absence,
and in no way was it an aesthetic loss, if that meant his life was less
agreeable without Julien. No, it was as if they'd fused, as if Julien had
been an alien who'd snatched his body, encoded his nervous system
and changed his blood type, colonized his organs and rescripted his

memory bank. He wouldn't be able to go on living now that the alien inside him had died. The only thing that still belonged to him, that resembled his old self, was his face, his arms and legs, his body, but they, too, had been impaired by this devastating inner metamorphosis.

Once Austin had read a description of couples who were deemed "co-dependent." The description sounded like Austin's idea of love. Hadn't Romeo and Juliet been co-dependent? Tristan and Isolde?

Christine had him to dinner. Her baby, Allegra, sat and stared at him with the immobility of a doll. In fact, she resembled, with her plump, cool cheeks and long-lashed eyes, an old-fashioned doll with a porcelain head and hands. Christine said that she was glad Julien had known Austin. "With me he was never happy. We squabbled over little things. You gave him the big, glamorous life he wanted."

Christine's Italian husband had apparently moved back to America, where he and his brother were running a successful restaurant. She was living on a small stipend from the National Center for Scientific Research and was planning to move to Montpellier to be closer to her parents.

Seeing her reminded Austin that she'd remained seronegative. If Julien had become positive while jumping in and out of the bushes in Nice before his marriage, wouldn't he have infected Christine? But even up until a few weeks before he'd definitely been diagnosed as positive, he'd continued having sex with Christine, yet she'd never seroconverted. Why should that be?

He saw old friends—Gregg and Pierre-Yves—but now, for the first time, he felt the age difference as distracting and absolute. Joséphine tended to him constantly, almost as if he was one of those fussy, hypochondriacal but adorable old men in a Jane Austen novel. She was by turns tender and funny, *légère* in the best Parisian manner—but he felt even her ministrations could not reach him.

A weightlessness came to modify all his actions; he walked lightly, silently around the apartment and found, after his months of nursing, he now had big, dilute prisms of free time to swim through. He was light, hushed, insulated, and even so he'd find he was buried at unexpected moments under a falling drop curtain of sleep—yes, sleep would fall on him and engulf him in its quilted silk.

One day Austin looked at a video version of the home film that

Herb Coy had made of Julien and him behind Notre-Dame. There was Julien—fresh-faced, smiling, looking years younger—and there was a still dark-haired Austin, greeting each other with obvious love in their eyes, a secret understanding uniting them as well as a shared self-consciousness. And then the camera was opened and the screen looked as if it had caught on fire.

Austin received almost a hundred condolence letters, which he read avidly, as if they'd provide him with still more revelations about Julien, about what they'd lived through together, about what he'd confided to other people regarding him, Austin, and their relationship, but the letters seldom rose above the conventions of sympathy and when they did it was only to idealize Julien in terms that obliterated any likeness. Lucy, married and the mother of a baby girl, wrote him to say that Julien and she had shared a secret spiritual sympathy. He wanted to answer them all with a personal note; when he couldn't bring himself to write anyone, he intended to print up a response in his name and Robert's; in the end he did nothing. He asked Marie-France if it was permissible not to acknowledge condolence letters. She laughed, disconcerted, and said, "No." She said he *had* to do something, but finally he was too weary, his attention too scattered, to compose a message, print it up and address a hundred envelopes. He kept all the letters in a big folder, almost as if he was going to show them to Julien someday; Julien would be pleased that he'd brought in such a heavy load of mail.

He wrote to Sarah, Julien's English girlfriend, the older woman he'd met in Ethiopia and to whom he'd sent bits of jewelry during the year before he died. She wrote back, saying that she'd scarcely known Julien, they'd spent such a short time together, and she had no idea why he'd singled her out for special attention from among all the hundreds of women he must have known, but she was grateful—"if a bit embarrassed by"—the gifts he'd showered on her. She sent Austin photographs of a very boyish Julien in Ethiopia.

Austin felt that an enormous thing had happened to him, Julien's death, and he wanted to share it with the most important person in his life: Julien. His frustration about Julien's silence made him talk out loud to him.

The summer months at last were blown out of the skies by the big advancing clouds of autumn. Because he'd been alone he hadn't known what to do with summer and the long holidays. He'd stayed in Paris all through August.

The first cold spell excited him. Something new was about to happen, children were returning to school, the red-faced tourists in shorts to whom the city had been lent were chased away, he was about to come back—he?

Who? Julien?

He visited the church across the street several times a day, bought candles and lit them before a painting of the Virgin. In the winter the church was unheated and Austin was sometimes the only worshipper. The painting was a sentimental work of the early nineteenth century, all in tones of blue, picturing a sweetly smiling young woman who seemed almost bathed in the smell of human milk, the one odor that works on most men as an anti-aphrodisiac. As if to protect her further from human desire, she was flanked by the heads of angels supported by wings. The angels were rendered harmless not only by their lack of bodies but also by their age, for they could not have been more than two or three years old.

She, of course, noticed no peripheral danger since she was focused serenely, even smugly, on Baby Jesus, who slept in her arms, sated after a hearty feeding. Austin could almost picture a tiny lactic bubble about to pop blissfully from between his lips.

Austin hated the Catholic Church, the nineteenth-century church that smelled of washed blackboards and sauerkraut farts under soutanes, as much as the medieval church with its plagues and plainsong, its greed and self-flagellations. But he needed it, or rather he needed its altars, candles, music, holy water and poor boxes, so that he could blast it into bits in his mind and fashion out of the ruins his own infantile faith, one that required the believer (the sole member of the cult) to kiss his thumb twice, sketch in a loopy, cursive cross from forehead to waist, pocket to pocket ("Spectacles, testicles, wallet, watch," as he used to chant in a singsong when he was a child), to light a five-franc candle before the painting and then stand back and watch, almost as if he'd baited a trap for someone else. If no one was around, he'd draw closer to the altar, his hands folded in front of him in semi-respect, and he'd look at the painting for what he knew it to be: proof that Julien had been reunited with his mother, a saint whose symbols were the accordion and hot comb (not pictured).

Julien had often said he wanted to outlive Peter, and he had assumed he would since Peter had already been ill for several years when Julien had first been diagnosed. But Julien had died first. Although Julien stopped mentioning his rival, Austin suspected that he was still brooding over him. That was the unpredictable aspect about AIDS: the robust man nursing the invalid could end up being buried by the very person he'd helped.

Austin had never stopped calling Peter nor sending him little gifts, including money, but Peter only forgave him for his treachery after Julien died. In January, ten months after Julien's death, they agreed to meet in Miami. Peter would fly down from Boston, which wasn't far from his parents' house in Concord; Austin would fly there direct from Paris. From Miami they'd rent a car and drive on down through the Keys to Key West.

Austin brought along a twenty-two-year-old English gerontophile he'd met on the street in Paris. His name was George, he was six foot four and worked as a personal instructor for the gym clients at the Ritz. He'd been a successful soccer player on an amateur team back home in a London suburb—but had moved to France when he was nineteen in order to come out (that was Austin's interpretation, because George would never have tolerated any part of the subject to be mentioned in his presence, nor the word *gay* pronounced).

George wanted to be an actor and had paraded as a rabbit at EuroDisney, had toured the malls of France for Reebok in a crack gymnastics team dressed, of course, in Reebok products, and had gone to every film audition the few times a six-foot-four youth with an English accent had been required. Although he had a classical profile he wore his smudged glasses on the tip of his straight nose at a weird angle and stooped a bit when he wasn't reminding himself to stand up straight. He wore loose, baggy clothes of odd English colors (grape-purple sweatpants, celluloid-tan short-sleeve shirts with anemic blue vertical stripes). He leaned right into someone's face, as if he was slightly deaf, and laughed with more general enthusiasm than specific hilarity. He could have played a rustic in Shakespeare—or stripped of all his funny clothes and mannerisms, a god or prince, since he had a noble face and a body worthy of Praxiteles.

He'd studied acting with a woman in the seventeenth *arrondisse-ment* and Austin had attended a presentation of various scenes there, adapted from films, TV shows, novels and even plays. George had been the only actor with a grain of talent. In fact he was very good—or so Austin thought, though he admitted he was besotted with lust.

George wasn't sleeping with Austin, although they held each other for hours fully clothed on the sofa. Austin thought he had noth-ing to offer someone as young, athletic and desirable as George—until he saw the wrecks George would cruise on the street, men even older and rounder than Austin. No, George claimed he was holding Austin off because he was faithful to an obscure lover, Pierre-Henri, a florist in Coulommiers (a town near Paris famous for its cheese, as Austin loved to say in order to torment George). As George told the story: "I was living out at EuroDisney, I was determined to meet a *man,* I took the train into Paris on my one night off. I sat down on a bench in the little square next to the Bibliothèque Nationale, a toff sat next to me, a pleasant-looking chap, and I panicked and started running. I ran and ran and ended up in the park near the Tour St.-Jacques and the first person who spoke to me was Pierre-Henri—and we became friends. He was my first friend. He lives in Coulommiers with his mother but he comes to Paris one day a week. He's got a studio he bought in Paris, Place de la République, and that's where I live. The bed is kept up against the ceiling but at the push of a button it descends automati-cally and fills the entire apartment. In the morning I have to stand in the loo and wait for the bed to go back up."

Austin gloried in George's youth—his thick blond hair which he could pull in great handfuls, his sweet breath, clear eyes, coltish ways, quirky intelligence (though he wasn't at all educated). George was a creature of nothing but instincts, and he could become angry and flushed over nothing at all. Frustrated because George had decided to be faithful to poor old Pierre-Henri, Austin would tease George: "Darling, your phone message in French is rather elegant, but then when you give it the second time in English—my *dear!* Are you a cockney?"

"But I can talk posh if I want, me mum's frightfully posh," George would say, and tears would spring into his eyes. He was a very sensitive, slightly crazy boy whose father had been murdered—or had he committed suicide? George was vague about it. George could cry if a friend teased him but beat up two men who tried to rob him on the métro and forget to mention it until the cut on his cheek and his bleeding knuckles drew Austin's attention. He was quite routinely paranoid and was convinced strangers were discussing—and acquaintances plotting against—him. He hung out with macho gym instructors from around town and got drunk with them in an Irish pub and picked up girls in their presence—he probably would have beat up fags if it had come to that. He was afraid to be seen by one of these guys on the street with Austin, so Austin cooked for him at home. He always arrived with idiotic gifts for Austin—bad chocolates tasting of powdered cocoa and emulsifiers, a ceramic Loch Ness monster in three curving sections, stuffed animals with silk bows, once even a barometer set into a pressed plastic anchor. Greeting cards of hearts, flowers and Cupids arrived in the mail every day.

Austin invited George to come along with Peter and him to Key West. He explained that Peter was very ill and had some dementia and would be dead in a month or so in all probability. "I want you to help me make him happy, to cheer him up, to drive the car, to laugh a lot—but above all to help me out with the shopping. This trip must be perfect."

At the chaotic Miami airport they met a skinny, trembling Peter dressed in new clothes his mother must have bought him but which had already become two sizes too large. Retrieving everyone's luggage and finding the bus to ferry them to the car-rental agency—all that took time and effort and the responsibility fell entirely on Austin, since George had never been to America before and Peter was in a benign haze. But George drove well and the January sun wasn't too hot and the two-lane highway through the Keys never got bogged down too much in traffic.

The house they'd rented was big, cool and quiet and had been built in the middle of the last century. It had a giant tree in the back yard which was so stalwart it squeezed every last bit of sunlight out and its falling leaves had paved the garden, but the house lived under its reassuring tutelary presence. A small Abyssinian Baptist church was next door and its few members, all old, flung open the doors whenever they congregated and wailed to the accompaniment of an organ, tambourine and drums. When their preacher talked his voice was scarcely audible from their back porch, but when the little orchestra and the half-dozen quavery voices lurched into song, then their sweet, gay sounds floated around the seated, smiling, silent Peter and Austin.

Not around George. No sooner had he arrived in Key West than he began popping No-Doz and drinking vast quantities of beer. He seemed determined not to consecrate a single valuable moment to sleeping. All his fears of being considered gay had vanished the moment he'd arrived in the New World—along with his vows of fidelity to Pierre-Henri. If he'd ever made such vows in the first place.

Handsome men in their forties and fifties were casually dropping by for him; George had met them at the 801 Bar on Duval Street. George was never at home. He came stumbling in at three a.m., angry and cursing, stomping up the stairs in his boots. If Austin asked him to buy some orange juice or bread, he'd be sure to forget. Once he came back before dawn, danced alone to a very loud Phil Collins CD, then stormed out and drove away. The car was never around, so Austin either walked or called the same bicycle-powered carriage he'd hired for Julien; the cheerful cyclist with the prodigious buttocks and strong legs remembered Austin but was too discreet to ask him what had happened to Julien. Perhaps he thought Austin was someone whose profession called for him to accompany the dying.

Austin apologized to Peter for having invited George along. "You can't believe how sweet and shy he is back in France. I thought he'd be a nice addition, Peter. I had no idea there'd be this appalling transformation. He's surly, tempestuous, randy, not even grateful for the airline ticket."

Peter said, "He's certainly the belle of the ball. Anyway, it doesn't matter. Maybe he'll settle down."

Austin said, "Oh, Peter, I love you so much. But it seems like every time I try to do something for you I screw it up." Austin remembered the disastrous trip to the Yucatán. "I'm always inviting along some impossible, angry guy."

Peter smiled. He was lying in a sleigh bed under an old patchwork quilt. The dry light was filtered by heavy, brown wood blinds. Austin had put small, old-fashioned roses beside Peter's bed; their petals felt as soft as Peter's hand in his. Drowsily, Peter said, "It's not your fault, Austin, if all these guys are in love with you."

"In love—whatever—" Austin sputtered.

"No, they are. We all are. We're all jealous and possessive." Peter had trouble staying awake since the burning pain in his feet, caused by the unrelenting neuropathy, required that he take painkillers round the clock.

Just as Julien had had his Koran to hold and look through, puzzling over the different hands and styles of calligraphy as well as the passages penned in red (the Prophet's utterances, no doubt), in the same way Peter had a book of consolation and wisdom his priest had given him. His mind was too clouded to absorb much that he read, but he took comfort from the feel of the little book in his hand while he dozed.

Peter no longer drank liquor or cruised, he didn't even follow the soap operas now, though he'd sit in front of the TV as a quiet way of keeping Austin company. He'd move the food Austin would prepare around on the plate a bit, smile and say, "It's very good. I'm just not too hungry after that big lunch, Aussie."

Austin slept just across the hall from Peter and came to his side several times during the night. Sometimes he'd just stand there in the doorway and look at him.

One day an old man who'd been born on Key West invited them all out to an island he owned. He was very attentive to Peter and though he was himself more than seventy gave his sturdy arm to his guest when he got into his powerboat. They rode south over the spanking surf for nearly an hour; Peter whispered into Austin's ear, "It's great!" They sped past several deserted islands of white sand and curving palms that were rising out of a matrix of mangrove tree roots.

Big white cirrus clouds with gray bellies rolled slowly along the horizon as if they were galleons on their way out. The gray was the stone ballast that would be replaced by bullion for the trip back to Spain— golden tomorrow at dawn. A skipper and a single crew member in crisp white uniforms maneuvered the boat and served them drinks. When they pulled up to the dock, a maid and a butler were on hand to help them out and to receive the food hampers they had brought over from Key West.

The host gave Peter and Austin a tour of the island in a dune buggy; it was the only vehicle on the island and Peter was terribly pleased because everything reminded him of *Fantasy Island,* one of his favorite TV shows. The host had done all this a hundred times before and advanced and backed up his dune buggy with well-calibrated expertise. Then they returned to the house, which was built high on concrete stilts to resist powerful winds and waves. Upstairs, the rooms themselves had no glass windows, just louvers that could be opened on all sides so that a hurricane would blow right through.

Before lunch they all went swimming. George had skipped the dune-buggy ride, perhaps to avoid Peter and Austin. Several other old men in their seventies had arrived (their boat was tied to the dock) and they were all in swimsuits following George. The water stayed shallow for hundreds of yards out to sea; even after walking twenty minutes it still hadn't come above waist height. At least not above George's small, muscled waist and long legs. To the degree he looked goofy in clothes, with his broken glasses mended with plumber's tape and his crinkly black tracksuit and huge running shoes with the neon insets, to the same extent he was beautiful in a swimsuit, electric blue stretched over his small, hard buttocks, his back an inverted pyramid soaring out of his waist to shoulders that remained supple despite their breadth and musculature. He was big, yes, but he was also still a boy, turning to splash his retinue of admirers, who hadn't been so insolently treated by a kid in half a century: they were in bliss.

Every bleary, clouding eye was trained on that electric-blue suit, the massive neck and thick blond hair, the small flexible waist and, when George turned, the flash of a smile as white as edelweiss.

Later that afternoon, when they were all back in Key West, George went off with a little Englishman he'd met during the afternoon on the private island. The Englishman phoned Austin to say, "Thanks for giving me such a *big* present! My dear, I haven't had sex in ten years—well worth waiting for, I'd say."

Peter had been happy, too. Once he would have had all these men at his feet. Now he was just a fragile old man himself, tiptoeing into the warm, salty water, but he'd smiled while the others laughed and seemed to follow the conversation, though perhaps all he was doing was producing social smiles and frowns and raised eyebrows to indicate astonishment; social reflexes were all that remained.

And a great sweetness toward Austin. As they were sitting on the beach, digging their toes into the sand, Peter said, "You've gone through so much with Jules—"

"Julien."

"—Oops!—that I just didn't think you should have to be with another sick person."

"But, darling," Austin said, holding Peter's hand, "you're not just a sick person, you're my own beloved, someone I've known for fifteen years and lived with through so many things."

"Remember that perfect lunch in Paris at the Bagatelle? I was still cute and healthy and it was a perfect day—all those prize roses named after duchesses. And our lovely, complicated lunch under an umbrella."

"I have lots of pictures of that day," Austin said.

"But let's not live in the past," Peter said, "not when we're here in Paradise, it really is just like *Fantasy Island*, too bad you never saw that TV show."

As Austin thought back to that day at the Bagatelle he realized he'd already forgotten many details—had it been cool or warm? What had they eaten? Oh, he was even beginning to forget all the things he'd lived through with Julien, although he'd been dead less than a year. He could scarcely picture his face or hear the sound of his voice. Patty said she had a long recording he'd left on her answering machine, but she seemed reluctant to make a copy of it. If Austin was forgetting Julien it wasn't at the normal rate of attrition. No, healing

nature was erasing all those painful memory banks, stripping them
empty.

George remained irritating to the very end of the trip; as Austin
drove them back up the Keys, George sat in the back seat, so exhausted and grumpy from a hangover that he refused to say a word to
them. He wouldn't even look at the scenery, which in any event he'd
already taken in on the way down. He slept most of the way.

They had trouble finding the Budget car rental lot in Miami and
Austin was worried Peter would miss his plane back to Boston. At last
they figured out where they were going and Austin stuffed Peter on
the airport bus with careful instructions: "You're getting off at American. Can you remember American? And just check your bag in at the
curb side."

In the confusion Austin didn't let himself think that this would be
the last time he'd be seeing Peter. There was time only for a hasty
peck. George was sullen; he just waved vaguely in Peter's direction.

Austin was in a white fury against George. They didn't speak the
whole time they registered for their flight and ate lunch at the terminal.

At last Austin broke the silence: "I've never been so shocked by
anyone's behavior as by yours. It's not as if we're lovers. We're *friends*
and I paid for you to come over to help me out as a friend with a dying
lover, the dearest person in my life whom I'll never see again, but all
you did was whore around the island—"

"I didn't!"

"That Englishman called to thank me for such a *big* gift, as if I'd
put you up to it. No, don't lie, George, I know you were a whore, but
why not, that's none of my business, but the only reason I invited you
along, frankly, was to be a cheerful, decorative presence for Peter and
to help out with the cooking and shopping and to drive us around, but
you disappeared for days on end with the car, I didn't even have a way
to transport poor Peter, and when you did make an appearance it was
only as a pit stop to change clothes and head off to a new assignation.
Well, I don't like cruel, selfish people, and it will be a cold day in hell
before I see you again once we're back in Paris."

"Forgive me, Austin, it was the No-Doz and the beers—it was
stronger than me, I guess I was jealous."

"Jealous of a poor dying man while you hold all the cards, beauty, youth and health? That's absurd!"

They didn't speak again, but once they were seated on the plane next to each other and they'd taken off, George began to sob silently. He cried and cried and then fell asleep on Austin's shoulder. Here was this big blond giant, his face blotched and red, spreading the splendor of his hair across Austin's shoulder, his huge hand with its sportsman's calluses pressed to Austin's chest in the dark as the other passengers watched the movie or slept.

THE FAREWELL SYMPHONY

This final volume of White's groundbreaking autobiographical trilogy is the story of a man who has outlived most of his friends. As he marks the six-month anniversary of his lover's death, the narrator leads the reader back on a thirty-year journey of reminiscence and desire. As the flow of memory carries us across time, space, and society, one man's magnificently realized story grows to encompass an entire generation.

Fiction/Literature/0-679-75476-8

FORGETTING ELENA

White's first novel suggests a hilarious apotheosis of the comedy of manners—for, in the privileged island community in which *Forgetting Elena* is set, manners are *everything*. Or so it seems to White's excruciatingly self-conscious young narrator, who desperately wants to be accepted in this world in which everything from bathroom habits to the composition of "spontaneous" poetry is subject to rigid conventions.

Fiction/Literature/0-679-75573-X

GENET
A Biography

Bastard, thief, prostitute, and jailbird, Jean Genet was one of French literature's sacred monsters. His career was a series of calculated shocks marked by feuds, rootlessness, and the embrace of unpopular causes and outcast peoples. This most enigmatic of writers has found his ideal biographer in White, whose eloquent chronicle does justice to the unruly narrative of Genet's life.

Winner of the National Book Critics Circle Award
Biography/0-679-75479-2

SKINNED ALIVE

Here, White measures the distance between an expatriate American and the Frenchman who tutors him in table manners and "hard" sex, the gulf that separates a young man dying of AIDS from his uncomprehending Texas relatives. In this collection of nine stories, our most influential chronicler of gay life invents a new vocabulary of difference.

Fiction/Literature/0-679-75475-X

VINTAGE INTERNATIONAL
Available at your local bookstore, or call toll-free to order:
1-800-793-2665 (credit cards only).